GHOST OF A CHANCE

ALSO BY CHRIS TULLBANE

<u>The Murder of Crows</u>

See These Bones
Red Right Hand
One Tin Soldier *

<u>Stories from a Post-Break World</u>

The Stars That Sing
The Storm in Her Smile
A Sure Thing
Fire of Unknown Origin *

<u>The Many Travails of John Smith</u>

Investigation, Mediation, Vindication
Blood is Thicker Than Lots of Stuff
Ghost of a Chance
The Italian Screwjob *
A Dead Man's Favor *
Godswar *
John Smith Doesn't Work Here Anymore *

*Forthcoming

GHOST OF A CHANCE

CHRIS TULLBANE

NEVADA

First published by Ghost Falls Press 2021
Ghost of a Chance. Copyright © 2021 by Chris Tullbane.

GHOST FALLS PRESS

Publisher's Cataloging-in-Publication Data
provided by Five Rainbows Cataloging Services

Names: Tullbane, Chris, author.
Title: Ghost of a chance / Chris Tullbane.
Description: Henderson, NV : Ghost Falls Press, 2021. | Series: The many travails of John Smith, bk. 3.
Identifiers: ISBN 978-1-955081-02-3 (paperback) | ISBN 978-1-955081-01-6 (ebook)
Subjects: LCSH: Vampires--Fiction. | Ghosts--Fiction. | Mediators (Persons)--Fiction. | San Diego (Calif.)--Fiction. | Humorous stories. | Paranormal fiction. | Fantasy fiction. | BISAC: FICTION / Fantasy / Urban. | FICTION / Fantasy / Humorous. | FICTION / Occult & Supernatural. | GSAFD: Fantasy fiction. | Humorous fiction.
Classification: LCC PS3620.U45 G56 2021 (print) | LCC PS3620.U45 (ebook) | DDC 813/.6--dc23.

Book cover design by Jake @ jcalebdesign.com

This novel is entirely a work of fiction. The names, characters, places, and incidents portrayed in it are either the product of the author's imagination or are used fictitiously, and any resemblance to actual persons, living or dead, events or locales is entirely coincidental.

FIRST EDITION

For Nami,

the reason for everything

ACKNOWLEDGMENTS

Thank you to all the usual suspects:

Nami, my angel-wife.

Johanna, who knew this series was a romance.

Jamie, protector of the free world, who has yet to relinquish his crown as the best and only brother I've ever had.

Keith and Shawn, who *still* don't get paid to beta read my nonsense.

Simon, poet and friend.

Kerri, Sam, and Mark, who keep me laughing, even if at least two of them are on the wrong side of the pancake vs. waffle debate.

And last but never least, my mom and dad.

CHAPTER 1

The world is a funny place. Sometimes, it's *haha* funny, but mostly it's *swift kick to the groin* funny. You can spend your whole life preparing for the worst without having it happen, but the moment those concerns leave your mind…

Bam! Frying pan to the face.

Growing up in the ever-sunny city of San Diego, I'd never been too worried about my future, which was probably why the world took such delight in treating me like a human-sized soccer ball. After two kidnappings and even more attempts on my life, I should have learned to keep an eye open for potentially fatal situations, but Friday found me once again far from alert. Maybe the past half-year of peace had lulled me into complacency. Maybe the approaching summer had my guard down. Or maybe it was all the beer I'd had.

Yeah, it was probably the beer.

I was seated on the patio bench in front of my house, letting the cool night air soften the four-beer buzz I'd brought home from the bars. As usual, said buzz was the *only* thing that had come home with me. *The old Smith charm*, as my dad liked to call it, was on a losing streak for the ages.

Kind of like our hometown Padres. The season had barely started, but 2014 was already looking an awful lot like 2013. And that wasn't good if you were a baseball fan in San Diego.

I was wiping at what appeared to be a stain on the left leg of my jeans—where had *that* come from?—when I felt a cold breeze on the back of my neck and a trembling in my bones. It was a sensation I'd grown accustomed to over the past months.

I looked to the right and found a ghost staring back at me.

Once, that would have sent me screaming through the streets of Chula Vista, masculine pride forgotten in the interest of self-preservation, but a lot had happened in the past year. I liked to at least pretend I was now made of sterner stuff.

Besides, this particular ghost was a friend of mine. Back in November, she and several of her spectral sisters had been hired to keep my home and my parents safe. While that danger had since passed, she'd elected to stick around.

As always, she was clothed in a heavy white nightgown—the sort of thing I imagined people had worn in the '50s—her dark, curly hair bedraggled and hanging in front of her face. As I watched, a black stain appeared in the middle of that nightgown, darkening as it spread until the material was drenched with blood.

That was another thing I'd grown accustomed to. The White Ladies were ghosts of women who had been killed, and the wounds that had killed them replayed on a never-ending loop. This ghost had died of a gunshot to the chest, although the identity of the killer and the reason for her death remained shrouded in mystery.

I'd been working up to asking her about her past, a process made more difficult by both the seriousness of the subject and the fact that she didn't speak. After six months, I still didn't know her name.

Tonight, her spectral face was even more grave than usual. Dark eyes intent, she refused her usual seat next to me on the bench.

"What is it?" The last time I'd seen her so solemn was when she had shown me the corpses of the three rather nasty people who'd tried to get at my parents—a mistake they had barely begun to appreciate before their deaths.

If she had fresh corpses to show me…

I was starting to regret that last beer.

In response, the ghost offered me her spectral hand. I could see the balustrade of the porch through both hand and body, but only dimly. Like so much else, a spirit's visibility appeared to be under their own control.

"You want me to come with you?" I interpreted. Our conversations were always like this: a weird blend of charades and monologue.

She nodded.

"Okay."

I'd seen the ghost phase through solid objects, so I was surprised to find resistance when our hands made contact. Her grip was cold—bone chillingly cold—but solid. She cocked her head at me for a moment, lips pursed.

Then we began to move.

More accurately, the world began to move around us. One glance down was enough to verify that my own legs were still, but we were flowing through the world, first at a walking pace, and then at an outright sprint. There wasn't time to wince before we reached the porch railing, and I breathed a quick sigh of relief as we passed right through it like it wasn't there.

What followed next was a straight-line journey into and through the neighboring houses. As we phased through Ms. Givens' home, I caught a glimpse of the smoking hot divorcee, curled up on a loveseat with a grey-haired man, a bowl of popcorn, and a half-finished bottle of wine.

They weren't just holding hands.

Thankfully, neither one saw us, but as we blurred past, the final remnants of my long-running crush faded away. I couldn't count the number of times over the years that I'd mowed Ms. Givens' lawn for free as a feeble excuse to spend time with her. Clearly, I'd have been better served collecting my usual fee, buying a gym membership, and pining for someone a little closer to my own age. But I'd never been all that smart about money. Or women. Or a bunch of other things, really.

We continued to accelerate until the world we were traveling through devolved into a blur of light and color. It might have been pretty if I weren't on a four-beer buzz… and badly susceptible to motion sickness. I squeezed my eyes shut and held on tightly.

After an indeterminate span of time lost in the battle against my own queasy stomach, I felt the ghost's cold fingers squeeze my hand. I cracked one eye open and found that we had come to a halt… and were no longer in Chula Vista. We stood atop a low hill overlooking the ocean.

Having lived in San Diego all my life, I knew most of the city's coastline, but this place was unfamiliar. The lack of construction around us was inexplicable; given the spectacular view, some developer should have started cranking out luxury condominiums decades earlier.

In fact…

I looked up the coastline. Wherever we were, there should have been *some* lights visible. Pacific Beach, La Jolla, Coronado, or even Del Mar. Instead, there was nothing, dark shores merging seamlessly into black waters.

Had the ghost taken me into Mexico?

More importantly, were the local police still pissed off about that one weekend in Tijuana?

As I pondered the mystery of our location, I became aware of another oddity; my companion—usually a pale presence in the night—was glowing, providing an illumination that outshined the stars and moon in the cloudless sky above us. And she wasn't the only one.

At least a dozen other White Ladies had appeared around us in a circle that slowly contracted, like a noose being tightened.

They came in all shapes and sizes, from tall and fleshy to small and thin to mid-sized and boulder-shaped. Like my own ghost, they each bore evidence of their death, from the foam that bubbled between one woman's blue lips to the extended and visibly twisted neck of another.

I wasn't sure which of them was Graciela, the White Ladies' leader, but it was the ghost with the broken neck who ended the silence. Her pale mouth opened and she began to speak.

Finally, a ghost that could answer my questions!

Too bad I couldn't understand a word she was saying.

○○○

I met the strange ghost's black eyes with a smile and a shrug. "I'm sorry. I don't speak Spanish."

Broken-Neck's countenance darkened, but she gestured to one of her companions, a woman built like a tree stump and barely clad in a tattered pink bathrobe.

"You live twenty minutes north of the border and don't speak the language?" The robed ghost's voice was deep and surprisingly melodic, more suited for radio than for a dead woman who looked like she'd seen decades of hard road before her untimely demise.

"I took French in high school." Not that I spoke *that* either. This probably wasn't the time or place to explain my high-school crush on Aurélie, the Canadian exchange student. "What can I do for San Diego's White Ladies?"

Tree Stump looked to Broken Neck and received a stiff nod in reply. As the older woman turned back to me, her fuzzy pink bathrobe gaped open to expose a long, jagged tear in the naked meat of her stomach, a wound that vanished even as I became aware of it.

"We would like to hire you, boy." With a black-eyed scowl, she cinched her robe shut.

Which suited me fine, really. There are things a man shouldn't have to see.

"Call me John," I said, feeling more secure now that a job offer was on the table. "What's the nature of the conflict you need mediated?"

One of the other spirits, a tiny slip of a girl who couldn't have been more than fifteen when she died, threw back her head and laughed. There was something deeply disturbing about that high-pitched sound, and not just because of the bruises that appeared and vanished all over the teenager's ghostly skin.

When the merriment had died down, the squat woman met my gaze. "We have no interest in hiring you as a mediator," she explained. "We've seen what happens to those you mediate for."

That was kind of unfair. I had a grand total of three mediations under my belt, and all of them had been successful. Granted, the first had indirectly resulted in a vampire coup, the second had almost led to a pixie blood feud, and the last had nearly ended the local werewolf pack, but still…

"None of that was my fault," I told the gathered ghosts, who seemed disinclined to believe me. "And if you don't need a mediator, then why am I here?"

"You're also a detective, yes?"

"Oh. Right." The paranormal community had only hired me as a P.I. once before, but I wasn't going to complain. Especially with how slow business had been lately.

"What can I do for you?" I asked yet again. The bulk of my investigations involved cheating spouses or basic background checks, neither of which would be of any interest to the deceased. Unless adultery was a problem in the afterlife too? "And which of you is Graciela?"

That question touched a nerve. One spirit tore ineffectually at the tattered remnants of her dress. Another wailed piteously through the mouthful of curly red hair she'd been chewing on. Even the two ghosts who had spoken so far seemed upset.

"Graciela está desaparecida," the broken-neck ghost told me. "She's missing. We need you to find her."

CHAPTER 2

IN WHICH A HILL IS NOT A HILL AND ALL THINGS FLEE THE DAWN

According to my research, ghosts had been around at least as long as humanity itself. San Diego had seen its share of spectral encounters dating back to the eighteenth century, when the local mission was first established by Spanish monks. Even so, ghosts were little more than footnotes in the few marginally reliable supernatural histories I'd managed to acquire. The occasional haunting or exorcism made its appearance, but San Diego's ghosts had never been a force to be reckoned with on more than an individual basis.

Graciela had changed all of that. I didn't know anything about the ghost's mortal life, but in death she had proven an active and able administrator. She'd organized the city's White Ladies into a coalition to be feared. They, the vampire House, and the ocean-dwelling Mer formed the triumvirate that ruled San Diego.

In short, if the local spirits had a queen, it was Graciela. Which made the agitation over her disappearance easy to understand, even if that disappearance itself was not.

○○○

"When you say she's missing—" At my words, the redhead wailed again, the shrill sound piercing the night. That was going to get old rather quickly. "—what *exactly* do you mean?"

Broken-Neck spat forth a stream of Spanish which no doubt contained disparaging comments about my intelligence. Or my appearance. Or my fashion sense. The only Spanish words I knew were the expletives my friend Mike had taught me. Even so, I recognized insults when I heard them.

The sneer on her translucent, glowing face was kind of a dead giveaway too.

"Okay," I admitted, "that could have been phrased better. What I meant to ask was: when did you become aware that she was missing and what makes you think that something happened to her?"

"It's been more than a month since anyone saw Graciela, boy, and she's missed Assembly twice," said the ghost in the bathrobe, gesturing to her Spanish-speaking companion. "Begoña traveled to her haunting and found the building empty and deserted."

"Is it possible that she just moved on?" I asked carefully.

"She saw the light!" squealed the teenage ghost, in a broken voice every bit as disturbing as her laughter. The woman closest to her, a gray-haired matriarch wearing a tie-dye poncho, turned and shushed her ineffectually.

"Graciela would never abandon us," growled yet another ghost, this one middle-aged with a prominent nose, "and I'll have the tongue of any lying, no-good bastard who says otherwise." She began to float through the tall grass toward me, as if to make good on that threat.

I took a careful step backward and found myself shoulder-to-shoulder with my house's ghost. She bared her black-gummed teeth at the aggressor in an unmistakable challenge.

"Peace, Ruth," said the ghost in the pink bathrobe. "This boy is a guest. We will not harm him for asking the questions of his profession."

"Yes," giggled the broken-voiced teenager, who had somehow crossed the space between us to whisper directly into my ear, "Instead, we should welcome him with open arms!"

Thin, spectral arms wrapped around my body in a hug that shook my bones. Lips branded my neck with white-hot fire. I tried to shake free, but my body was suddenly heavy and sluggish.

My eyes drooped shut.

A flash of light blinded me even through my closed eyelids. When sight returned, I was flat on my back in the grass, warmth slowly returning to frost-coated limbs. Standing above me like an angel of vengeance was my ghost, her dark hair and blood-soaked nightgown fluttering in a wind that had arisen from nowhere. She threw back her head and let loose a wordless scream of rage that echoed and rumbled like it was emerging from the depths of the earth itself.

The teenage ghost who had attacked me huddled where she'd been tossed aside, sobbing inaudibly in a broken little voice.

"Valentina!" Begoña's sharp voice cracked like a whip, slicing through the wall of sound.

My ghost didn't acknowledge the broken-necked woman, but her dreadful wail cut off. Silence descended upon the hilltop, broken by my own labored breaths, the whimpers of the teenage spirit, and the quiet murmuring of the ghostly circle that had tightened even further around us.

"Nobody begrudges you the right to protect your human," the bathrobe-wearing ghost said soothingly, the metaphorical good cop to

Begoña's bad, "but your point has been made. I'm sure Jennifer has seen the error of her ways, yes?"

My ghost—Valentina?—seemed unmoved by the other's words. I wasn't sure if she had even heard them. Under her pitiless gaze, the teenage Jennifer was squeezing herself into an increasingly tiny ball, the way only someone who was mostly ephemeral could do.

The deep bruises that had killed her again flickered across translucent skin.

I was up before I even knew my legs could support me, stepping between the two ghosts in what my biographer would no doubt call *the damn fool move that got John Smith killed.*

"Valentina?"

She turned her head to regard me, hair falling back in front of her face as the wind went still. Behind that veil, her black eyes were angry. I had a small glimmer of what my would-be killers had felt before their deaths the previous winter, and almost felt bad for them.

Except that they'd been assholes intent on murdering my parents.

"It's okay," I said. "I'm fine. Thanks to you. Again." I offered a smile, trying not to let my teeth chatter.

Valentina held my gaze for a long moment, and then returned a black-gummed smile of her own, stepping away from Jennifer like the other ghost no longer existed.

Begoña rattled off another stream of incomprehensible Spanish, and the bathrobe-wearing ghost nodded in agreement. Around me, the illumination began to dim as ghosts flickered out like candles. In a single breath, I was alone on the hilltop with Valentina and the two women who had seemingly inherited the mantle of leadership in Graciela's absence.

"You were right," the squat ghost told Begoña grudgingly. "It was a mistake for us all to be here."

Begoña's reply, even in Spanish, had the recognizable tones of a satisfied *I told you so.*

"The girls have as much invested in Graciela's fate as any of us," the other ghost continued, now facing me, "and they wanted to be here for your hiring. I apologize if you came to any harm."

"You can make it up to me," I said, "by introducing yourself. And by calling me John, like I asked. I stopped being a boy more than a decade ago."

"Ha!" She barked a laugh. "Fair enough. I am Margaret. Call me Marge and not even Valentina will be able to protect you. My companion, as you have no doubt gathered, is Begoña. And you are John Smith, and not a boy, even though I have great grandchildren older than you."

"Uhm, right." Great grandchildren? The only math I did these days was on my wonderphone's calculator app but given that Marge looked to have been in her forties when she died, that meant she'd been a ghost since long before I was born. I had nothing against the elderly—some of my best friends counted their lives in centuries, after all—but the whole thing still made my head spin.

"So then, *John*," continued Marge, "will you take the case?"

A smart man would have said no and found himself abandoned on this unlikely hill in the middle of what couldn't possibly be San Diego, never to be seen again.

A wise man would have sought assurance of safe passage and then made the same choice as the smart man.

Sadly, nobody had ever accused me of being smart or wise. I liked to think of myself as a *good* person though, and this was a chance to help the ghost at my side. Valentina had now saved my life twice and continued to protect my parents and keep me company.

I owed her, and Smith men paid their debts.

Moral debts, anyway.

"I'll take the case."

"Excellent," said Marge. "Ask your questions, and we will do our best to answer."

○○○

After all the drama leading up to that point, the actual briefing was anti-climactic. And short. Part of that was because we no longer had a dozen other ghosts hanging on—and reacting to—every spoken word. But mostly, it was because I'd spent the night drinking at a bar and was having trouble figuring out what I needed to ask.

As Marge had already told me, Graciela hadn't been seen for a month, and the location she'd been haunting for the past twenty years was free of her presence.

Whatever *that* meant. I was guessing the phrasing held more significance for the ladies than it did for me.

Because ghosts didn't own or use cell phones, neither Margaret nor Begoña had been able to leave their absent leader a voicemail, check her Twitter status, or even review her Foursquare check-ins. That was why they'd finally decided to hire me, on the off chance that a mediocre private investigator would make an exceptional ghost finder.

It was one more skill I'd have to add to my business cards and LinkedIn profile. If I ever bought business cards. Or signed up for LinkedIn.

"How do you know," I asked, aware that I was repeating myself, "that she's still alive? Or, well, I mean, you know." Flustered, I fumbled for the right words. "Couldn't she have passed? Again?"

Marge and Begoña—who clearly understood English, even if she refused to speak it—gave me matching looks of condescension and pity.

"Ghosts go *somewhere* eventually," I pointed out, "or the world would be drowning in them. And I think humanity might have noticed that."

"You'd be surprised what mortals fail to notice," Marge murmured, shrugging heavy shoulders and tightening the pink bathrobe about her for at least the fifth time. I was starting to think that was a nervous tic from her mortal life. Certainly, the action served little purpose when both that robe and the woman beneath were translucent. "It's true that we eventually fade, but only when we are ready to do so. Graciela is young and driven. She has centuries left to her. She would never have abandoned us. We're more than just a group to her; we're a—"

"Vocación," supplied the other ghost, and even my non-existent Spanish was sufficient to make the necessary translation.

"So, you suspect foul play?" It was the sort of line I'd always wanted to say on a case, but now that the opportunity had finally arrived, there was no joy in it. Go figure.

"Maybe," Marge admitted. "I can't think of anything else it might be, but I also don't know who or what would have the power to keep her imprisoned or to…"

Do away with her entirely, I finished silently. If that was even possible. How do you kill a ghost? I shook my head. I was woefully uninformed. Worse, my buzz was starting to fade, leaving only exhaustion behind.

"Dawn approaches," said Marge, "and its arrival will bring an end to our meeting spot. We must go."

I guess that answered my question about why there weren't any lights on the coastline. Sort of, anyway. A place that existed only at night? That was… Actually, it was pretty damn cool. Although it was hard to believe it was already almost dawn.

"How do I contact you if I find something? Or if I have more questions?"

Like, for example, who was going to pay my fee? Or why Begoña's neck remained perpetually broken, when all the other ghosts I'd seen cycled between full health and the wounds that killed them?

Marge was already floating away but she paused long enough to toss a reply back up the hill to me. "We will meet here again next week. Tell Valentina if you must speak with us sooner." With those words, she and her companion disappeared.

"Tell Valentina," I said. "Well, that's straightforward enough, I guess. Shall we go home now then?"

Silence. I was alone on ghost hill.

"Uhm." Somewhere to the east, the first rays of the sun began to light the real world's sky, and I could feel the ghost hill shiver in reaction.

"Valentina? Hello?" I didn't want to see what happened if I was still here when the sun fully rose. Well, to be totally honest, *part of me* did, but that was the part that invariably got me into trouble. I was learning to ignore it.

I was spinning about in increasing desperation, when the dark-haired ghost appeared directly before me, her mouth wide in a silent giggle.

"Yes," I said, "you're very funny."

She nodded, eyes sparkling, and took my hand in her cold grip. Once again, we began to move.

CHAPTER 3

IN WHICH ALL WORK AND NO PLAY IS
TOO MUCH TO HOPE FOR

I was in the office by noon on Saturday, which practically qualified me for sainthood. Dale, the homeless guy who'd taken up residence on the curb outside, seemed unimpressed, but I didn't take it personally. He was still holding a grudge over the time I'd asked him to move so I could open the door.

I let myself into the building, checked the mailbox for any items of note among the stack of fresh bills, and climbed the stairs to my second-floor office.

It was time to do some work.

The well-to-do private investigator no doubt had a surplus of contacts to draw upon, whether it was his inside man at the police department, or the politician whose dirty secret he'd helped bury back in the day. Maybe he even had access to a dedicated research department. That seemed dangerously close to bourgeois excess, but who was I to judge?

As one of the have-nots, my primary source of information remained the internet. Unfortunately, its track record was spotty when it came to the paranormal world. A search on vampires, for example, might return fan fic for that one CW show with the super-hot brunette, or a high school book review of Bram Stoker's (almost entirely inaccurate) opus, or even paintings by someone with a serious BDSM fetish and an equally serious lack of talent.

I liked women in skintight leather as much as the next guy—probably more—but a basic grasp of anatomy didn't seem like too much to ask for.

My search on ghosts proved similarly frustrating. On the bright side, ghosts' relative lack of popularity compared to vampires, werewolves, and zombies meant that a healthy portion of the sites I found were focused on the actual subject. (The other results? Split between ghost movies and fan sites for one of the Call of Duty games.)

On the less-bright side, few of the relevant sites had any real information beyond blurry photos of random white lights or the static-laden audio file of something that *might* have been a ghost speaking, but was more likely the wind outside a window, or even the hushed breaths of the person making the recording.

Having spent my night on a hill that didn't exist, conversing with a small army of female spirits, I was less than impressed by the so-called evidence our country's ghost hunters had amassed.

Marge was right; we humans really *were* clueless.

Once I narrowed my search to San Diego, the quality of information improved, but none of it seemed applicable to my case. The city had its fair share of haunted locations, from the Whaley House in Old Town to the William Heath Davis home and the Hotel del Coronado, but none of those hauntings seemed to point to the White Ladies.

I found even less on Graciela herself. A forum post from several years earlier mentioned the sighting of a dark-haired woman in white along the pier at Garnet in Pacific Beach… which could have been any number of the White Ladies, including Valentina herself. It could also have been a mortal human woman out for a walk. I was starting to realize the internet wasn't the most trustworthy of resources.

Regardless, old ghost stories weren't going to be useful in my search. What I needed was something recent that could point me to where Graciela had gone. But when I narrowed my search even further, to focus only on results from the past few months, Google failed to return any results at all.

Which almost *never* happened.

I held back a sigh as the anticipated headache finally made its presence felt. Truthfully, while a full-length biography of the missing ghost, accompanied by turn-by-turn directions to where she was currently residing, would have been convenient, I hadn't been expecting this case to be that easy. As fascinated as my fellow humans were with things that went bump in the night, they remained remarkably blind to those creatures' very real existence.

I'd been every bit as blind until the day crab men tried to kill me on the streets of San Diego, but that had been almost a year ago. These days, I considered myself a veteran of the supernatural.

More or less.

Mostly less, to be honest.

With the internet a bust—yet again—it was time to leverage some of my *other* sources. In their own way, those sources were even more useful than the police informants or government stooges my high-priced competition had access to. Unfortunately, they were also very frequently giant pains in the ass.

And not *just* the ass.

As my skull continued to throb, I finally realized that my headache wasn't just the result of a few beers and several hours of dead-end research. The greatest of those pains in my ass was contacting me telepathically.

Over the past half-year, I'd gotten used to tuning Queen Lucia out, especially after January's heated argument regarding my so-called duties as her thrall, but the ice-cold voice in my head was far stronger than it had once been. By now, Lucia's insistent call was like an endless banging of pots and pans in the back of my brain. Even with the volume turned all the way down, it was damn difficult to ignore.

I mentally checked the femmepire's location and was relieved to find that she was still far to the north of me. Probably at the House she ruled with an iron, if well-manicured, fist. I didn't know what she wanted, but it could wait.

As they too often did, my thoughts turned from the irritating queen to a very different vampire, one I'd gone on a date with almost exactly six months prior. If you'd asked me back in November to describe that date, I'd have told you my dinner out with Lady Anastasia Dumenyova was a first ballot, no-brainer inductee into the Dating Hall of Fame.

In the months that followed, I had come to realize that Ana might not have shared my enthusiasm. The fact that she'd yet to return even one of my phone calls was a pretty big clue, as was her continued absence from San Diego.

As an investigator, I was trained to recognize such things.

Apparently, the elegant femmepire had decided to move on with her glamorous vampire life, and I was trying to do the same. I'd grown a beard, just to show that I could. Another month or two of continued personal development, and I might even find myself trading in my gently used (and thoroughly defaced) Toyota Corolla for a Harley.

Really, I was a whole new person.

Which made my mind's tendency to dwell on the absent Anastasia all the more annoying. She wasn't the first woman I'd fallen for—not even close—but she was proving to be the most difficult to forget.

With an effort, I pushed those thoughts to the back of my mind, where they could keep the persistent echoes of Queen Lucia's summons company. I finally had a case, and a case meant I might be able to pay my bills. This was neither the time nor the place for sentimentality.

For the next few hours, I decided, *I'm going to focus on the White Ladies' case, make some calls to my contacts in the paranormal community, and do my best to forget that vampires exist at all.*

A knock sounded at my office door before I could even finish the thought. In theory, any visitor should have had to call from the building's front entrance to be buzzed inside, but I'd gotten used to people finding their way inside. I took a careful glance out through my door's peephole.

In the hallway, a slender woman with spiky dark hair glared back at me, her distinctive yellow eyes glowing with irritation.

"Open up, little bird," she said, tipped off to my presence by the shadow behind the peephole, or the sound of my breathing, or even the smell of my (delicately applied) aftershave. "We need to talk."

It was clearly going to be one of *those* days.

ooo

Juliette Middleton, femmepire, Council member, and the woman I called the Duchess of Snark, swept into my office. She was wearing her standard uniform: a pair of jeans so tight they looked like they'd been painted on, and a loose-fitting, well-worn t-shirt trumpeting the name of one of the many punk rock bands she'd loved in the 60s and 70s. I had it on reasonably good authority—hers—that she'd spent the better part of a decade following those bands on their tours across the continental United States.

She'd also developed a habit of snacking on the roadies, but that was neither here nor there.

Juliette was stunning, like all vampires, but she had an edge to her that only an idiot would ignore. Tigers were beautiful too, after all, but if you decided to stick your arm in the cage… Well. *Maybe* that great big cat would let you pet it, or maybe you'd end up eating breakfast burritos with one hand for the rest of your life.

The tiger analogy was particularly apt, given that Juliette had fed on me twice. Both times, she'd taken blood from the wrist, and only enough to heal her own wounds, but that knowledge did little to blunt the memory of how much it had hurt. Or the fact that I'd had to punch her the first time to make her stop.

"Take a picture, moron. It'll last longer."

"I was just checking which band you're promoting today."

"Sure you were. The Sex Pistols," she added, as if I had been unable to read her cropped tee. "1978. Sid was out of his mind on heroin almost the whole tour, and Johnny Rotten left the band after the San Francisco show. It was like watching the sun implode over the course of two glorious weeks." She dropped into one of the two client chairs on the other side of my desk. "I'll always have a soft spot for those boys."

"Good to know." I liked the band's music well enough—Anarchy in the UK, and all that—but their heyday had been way, way before my time. "So, what did you want to talk about? And what's with the bag?"

The bag in question was a black canvas duffel, straining at the seams, and almost as big as the femmepire herself.

She shifted about in the chair for a moment. "I quit."

"Cool." I nodded and waited for her to elaborate. A long moment of silence ensued. "Quit what, exactly?"

"The House. Lucia. The dumbass freaking Council." Juliette leaped to her feet and began stalking about my office. "Do you have any alcohol in this dump?"

"Second drawer on the left," I said, still fixated on her confession. She'd quit the House? Was that even possible?

"Of course it's possible," the femmepire growled, when I voiced the question. "We're not slaves, whatever the elders believe." She pulled out a slim golden bottle. "Tequila Joe's? You have better taste than I thought, little bird."

"It was a gift from Mike," I said, watching tequila disappear from the bottle as if by magic. "And what do you mean *you quit?* How can you quit? You helped found the House in the first place!"

"Oh please." She rolled her eyes. "The only reason I was on the Council is because my flock and I had a prior claim to the city before Lucia and her—" She made air quotes with both hands. "—*noble subjects* arrived."

This wasn't actually news. Juliette was still a few decades shy of her first century, which made her impossibly young to have a spot on the Council of any House, even one as dysfunctional as San Diego's. "Still, I thought being part of a House was every vampire's dream. And weren't you *proud* of being on the Council?"

She polished off my eighty-dollar bottle of tequila with a shrug and tossed it across the room and into the trash can by the door. "It's not all it's cracked up to be, really. I'm ready for something new."

"But… where are you going to live?"

"I own other properties in the city, John. I'm not an idiot."

"I wasn't saying you—" My voice trailed off. "Wait… how many properties? And why is this the first time I've heard of them? You remember that I'm still living with my parents, don't you?"

I knew I wasn't the only twenty-six-year-old living at home, but it didn't make the situation any less frustrating. The recent dearth of mediations meant office rent was back to being a month-to-month thing, and I'd had to table the idea of moving out yet again.

"Trust me," Juliette said, with a roll of her eyes, "even my smallest home is way outside your price range."

"And the idea of letting me live in one of them rent-free is…"

"Ludicrous," she confirmed. "You'd piss off a dragon and get the whole damn block burned to the ground. I can't afford insurance premiums like that."

"Dragons aren't real… are they?" Before she could reply, I waved off the question. "Never mind. It doesn't matter. So, you quit the House. But why are you *here?*"

"Well…" Juliette looked uncharacteristically nervous again, but that could have been the bottle of tequila she'd just guzzled. "Now that I've left the House—"

A knock at the door interrupted our conversation. I eyed the offending slab of wood with annoyance. "Maybe I'll get a dragon to burn *this* place down," I muttered, "since the landlord can't be bothered to install a real security system."

I stalked over to the door and yanked it open.

In the hallway stood an auburn-haired woman with sparkling jade eyes.

"Mr. Smith," said Anastasia, "may I come in?"

Well, shit.

ooo

Wordlessly, I returned to my desk, allowing the elegant femmepire entry. She nodded to Juliette, her long hair swaying gently with the motion.

"Lady Middleton," she offered in cool, cultured tones.

"Just Juliette is fine," said the other woman. "When did you get back, Anastasia?"

"I flew in this morning." Despite the warm May weather, Anastasia had on a long black coat over a deep blue silk blouse and tailored black slacks, the very image of a sophisticated woman of means. Over one shoulder hung a designer bag that was probably worth more than my Corolla. When we had first met, I'd assumed she was a supermodel assassin, or a billionaire, or a billionaire supermodel assassin… and I still wasn't sure I'd been wrong.

All vampires were gorgeous, regardless of gender, but Ana was something special. I drank in the sight of her from across the room.

"I did not expect to encounter you here," she was saying to Juliette. "I thought you were still working long hours to adjust to your new duties on the Council."

Juliette shrugged. "You can't believe everything you hear."

"Might I have a moment to converse with Mr. Smith?"

"*Now* you want to talk to him?" Juliette rolled her eyes but headed for the hall. There was a fine line between disrespect and insanity, and actively pissing off a femmepire three centuries her elder—let alone one who had killed a Battle Lord with her bare hands—strayed rather definitively into the realm of the latter.

I was trying to think of something to say when a phone rang. Anastasia fished a wafer-thin device out of her bag and raised it to one ear.

"Greetings, my queen."

Juliette froze in mid-step, three feet from the door, and did a slow fade into the woodwork, as if the stained beige walls could mask her presence.

"Yes. I landed less than an hour ago." Anastasia's eyes met mine. "I was dealing with a personal—" She paused, her classically beautiful face slowly emptying of emotion, as Lucia continued speaking. "Of course. I will be there shortly." She tapped the phone and slid it back into her bag. "I apologize, Mr. Smith. It seems that Queen Lucia has urgent need of me. Might we continue this discussion another time?"

"Maybe six months from now?" suggested Juliette helpfully.

I gave the spiky-haired femmepire a subtle shake of my head. As nice as it was to have someone on my side for once, this probably wasn't the time.

"As you wish, Lady Dumenyova," I replied formally. "You have my number… at least I think so."

Okay, maybe it was *kind of* the time.

"I do." Another enigmatic look flashed across her face, her lovely lips parted, as if to say something, and then she was gone.

"Well, *that* went well."

"Did it?" I sank back into my chair, rubbing my eyes. "I have no idea what that was about."

"From where I was standing—"

"More like *skulking.*"

"—it sounded like the worst, most awkward foreplay ever."

"Foreplay?"

Juliette smirked. "She's ancient and you're human. Pardon me if I have no idea what sort of weird sexual practices either of you might be into these days."

"Your guess is as good as mine at this point." I sighed, ignoring the pitying look coming my direction. "Anyway, thanks for sticking up for me."

"Is that what you thought I was doing?" The femmepire chewed it over, yellow eyes glowing slightly. Finally, she gave a sharp shake of the head. "Sorry, little bird. Just because we're partners now doesn't mean I'll be taking an active role in your dating life. If I wanted to die of boredom, I would have stayed with the Council!"

She wandered back out the door, duffel bag in hand, leaving me alone in my office with a raging headache and an empty bottle of what had once been expensive tequila.

A long moment passed before her words sank in.

"What do you mean *partners?*"

Unfortunately, she too was already gone.

As I sat back down behind my desk, Queen Lucia resumed her mental summons, sounding for all the world like a marching band in my brain. It was all I could do not to scream at the ceiling.

And that's when someone decided to steal my car.

CHAPTER 4

It was Dale who tipped me off. Like most people who spent significant time in the city, I'd learned to tune out its ambient noise; the cars, the sirens, even the planes flying in and out of Lindbergh just to our northwest. But when Dale started cursing up a storm, I couldn't help but check on him from my office window. He'd been staking out our street corner for months now, and I sort of felt responsible for the guy.

Even after the spitting incident.

Down on the street, our unpaid doorman had risen to his feet, tattered sleeves flapping like the wings of a deranged bird. He was stalking towards a heavyset man in a baseball cap.

The other man was keeping a wary eye on Dale, but remained primarily focused on whatever he was doing, crouching down at the front bumper of my Corolla, and extending one arm under its body. My first—admittedly silly—thought was that the man was planting a car bomb in broad daylight. Then, I noticed the vehicle parked in front of my car, a logo-emblazoned truck whose flatbed had been replaced with a sort of crane-like contraption, the far extremity of which was extended under my own…

"Oh, hell no!" It was a fancier type than I was used to, but I still knew a tow truck when I saw one. My shouts joined Dale's, but the driver ignored us both, straightening up from where he had finished inserting the pins that secured my Corolla's front tires.

If I'd ever achieved my adolescent dreams of parkour mastery, I could have hurled myself out the second-floor office window, clung to the drainpipe, and descended to the street in a dizzying series of acrobatic flips and somersaults. But parkour was a lot harder than it looked, and athleticism had never been my strong suit.

I turned and ran for the door.

I took the stairs at a sprint, promptly missed a step, and barely caught myself from tumbling the rest of the way down, after which I adopted a slower, less suicidal pace. My beloved late-90s Corolla had never been worth killing myself over… even *before* the local gang had decorated it with colorful slogans and anatomically incorrect penises.

At least, I *hoped* they were anatomically incorrect. My ego didn't need another hit.

I was sucking wind by the time I reached the lobby. My friends Kayla and Darlene had been gently encouraging me to exercise, but I remained a long way from peak physical condition. This time, it cost me. It had taken less than forty seconds to reach the first floor, but when I made it out onto the street, the tow truck was already disappearing into the distance, dragging my Corolla behind, broken taillight, graffiti penises and all.

"Son of a bitch!"

"Rock-eating commies," agreed Dale, who was at most fifteen years older than me, and had likely never seen a Communist in his life.

"Why did they tow my car? I've been parking here for years."

"Plus it's a piece of shit." The excitement over, Dale wandered back to his pile of possessions, casting suspicious glares in my direction as he performed a quick and careful inventory.

"I didn't take any of your stuff, dude."

"Like I'd believe *that*," the other man muttered, carefully placing what appeared to be a wad of tinfoil next to a half-decayed candy necklace. "You just let them take my car!"

"It's not—"

The polished hum of a powerful engine cut off my reply. A gleaming black Mercedes E-Class pulled up to the curb, filling the space that my own car had so recently vacated. The man who emerged had skin the color of dark coffee and a mohawk dyed bright red.

"Steve?"

"John." Wraparound shades hid his eyes but a wide smile gleamed white against the darkness of his skin. "Her Majesty requires your presence."

Running was out of the question; even if my brief trip downstairs *hadn't* already sapped my wind, Steve probably sprinted marathons before breakfast. And then ate marathon runners *for* breakfast. Plus, as a vampire, he had the sort of speed to make an Olympian weep. And it wasn't like I had a car to escape in...

Wait a minute.

"Tell me Lucia didn't just have my freaking car towed!"

"Goddamn commies," muttered Dale.

○○○

The interior of the Mercedes was every bit as plush as I remembered, if more cramped than the House Escalade the manpire normally drove. I closed the front passenger door, buckled myself in, and turned to give Steve what I hoped was a baleful look. The fact that he was both a friend and physically capable of twisting me into a pretzel may have lessened the impact.

"Seriously, man… did Lucia have my car towed?" I asked again, as we pulled away from the curb and made the series of turns that would take us onto the 5.

"No clue. Maybe your neighbors just got tired of the penis-mobile." Steve grinned again. "Were you *ever* going to get that thing a new paint job?"

"Eventually. Maybe. I don't know." I stared out the window as we drove. It was another beautiful day in San Diego. Our usual *May Gray* had taken the day off, and the sky was a crystalline blue, unblemished by clouds. "Why did she send you to pick me up, anyway?"

"Other than the fact that you've been ignoring her summons, you mean?" Steve seemed amused by that little detail. The burly vampire had a laidback outlook on life, completely at odds with both his position as second-in-command of the House Watch and his talents as a badass-ninja-death-machine-on-steroids.

"Yeah, other than that. Besides, Ana was *just* here."

"Lady Dumenyova? She's back?"

"As of today, apparently," I confirmed. "Why didn't Lucia just have her bring me in?"

"Did the queen know Lady Dumenyova was with you?"

"I don't think so."

"Well, there you go." Steve shrugged broad, muscular shoulders. "Anyway, I'm just a worker bee. I stay the hell out of Council business."

"Wish I could be so lucky." I felt at the part of my brain that represented my bond with the vampire queen and got a distinct sense of the femmepire's smug satisfaction. Since the moment Lucia had made me her thrall, we'd been able to sense each other's location, but this business of emotions leaking across the bond was new… and worrisome.

"I hear you. You swim in deep waters, my friend."

"It's that or drown." I sighed. "Oh well. I guess I might as well see what Queen Crazy Pants wants."

Steve's reply was a thinly concealed laugh. When I'd first been introduced to the vampire House, my relative lack of respect for the exiled queen had been considered scandalous. Now, most of the vampires—the ones who saw me regularly, at least—simply accepted it as a matter of course.

We drove in silence for another few minutes, north up the 5 and then east onto the 8. We were almost to the 163 when I finally remembered my case for the White Ladies. With Google a bust, I'd drawn up a list of people who might be able to help track down the missing Graciela. Steve wasn't on that list, but he was my best shot at contacting one of the beings who was.

"So," I said, breaking the comfortable silence, "how's Barry?"

Barry was a wereboar. More significantly, he was Steve's wereboar boyfriend, an inter-species relationship that still had me scratching my head. Steve and I got along famously, but Barry always seemed to be one bad day away from tearing my arms off.

"He's doing okay," Steve said, the hint of a question in his tone. "Sick of being cooped up, as always, but I'm trying to find a solution to that problem."

"Really?" Barry was more than a century old, ancient for humans, and beyond impossible for weres, whose average life span was roughly forty years. He'd spent the last eight decades as the bouncer for—and permanent resident of—San Diego's only paranormal watering hole, the Bitter End. "Does Kala think it's possible?"

"*Lord* Kala," Steve corrected me sternly. "And I'm… still working my way up to asking him." He shivered, hands tightening momentarily on the steering wheel.

I could understand Steve's apprehension. In addition to being Barry's employer and an ambulatory skeleton in a heavy black robe, Lord Kala was an immortal—a demigod of death and time, to be precise. Within the confines of his domain, he was pretty much all-powerful.

It was that power which had enabled Barry's continued existence; if the grey-haired wereboar remained within the bar's pocket dimension, time didn't pass for him. But if he were to ever step outside… well, nobody was sure if he would go insane the way all weres eventually did, or if he would simply crumble to dust. Neither fate seemed worth risking to me, but having their relationship confined to the bar's small interior was starting to wear on the long-time couple.

"Let me know if I can do anything to help," I said, knowing that it was unlikely he'd take me up on that offer. Steve was a big believer in self-reliance. And there wasn't much I could do, regardless. Beyond a genetic condition that made me mostly immune to glamour, illusion, and compulsion, I was as human as they came. Which was to say, damn near useless by most supernatural creature's reckoning.

Still, it didn't hurt to offer.

"Thanks, man. I know you and Barry don't always get along, so I appreciate it."

"I do have an ulterior motive," I admitted. "If he can swing it, I'd love a face-to-skull with his boss."

The Bitter End was not—officially—off limits to humans, but the portal to access it couldn't be activated by my species, and Barry himself only allowed humans into the bar if they were chaperoned by someone of the supernatural persuasion. I'd been inside a number of times, usually with the vampires, but an audience with Lord Kala required something a bit more. Like having the one and only bouncer make a request on my behalf.

"Are you sure that's a good idea?" I couldn't see Steve's eyes, but his voice was skeptical. "I know you're starting to figure your way out around the community, but Lord Kala is not someone to screw with."

"You're not telling me anything I don't know, dude. But it's for a case and it's important." Who better than a demigod of death to help me track down my missing ghost? It was one of the few good ideas I'd had all day.

Given that it was already mid-afternoon… well, it hadn't been a very good day, even by my intentionally low standards.

Steve shrugged, cutting across three lanes of traffic with the casual aplomb of someone with nothing to fear from car accidents. "I'll talk to Barry tonight, and see what can be done. But if Lord Kala doesn't want to meet…"

"…then I'll drop the matter," I agreed. "I'm not looking for trouble."

"You never are," he said darkly, before spoiling it with a grin. "And yet, it somehow always finds you."

Since the vampire at my side had nearly died saving me from some of that trouble, I wasn't going to argue.

CHAPTER 5

In vampire society, the House was, first and foremost, a political entity, like a werewolf pack, a pixie congregation, or a shambling of anemones. It also served as a sanctuary for its members. From all accounts, unaffiliated vampires didn't survive long on their own; it was a big, scary world out there, and vampires weren't nearly as far up the food chain as they wanted to believe.

But the San Diego House was also an actual house. A mansion, to be honest. I assumed European Houses were all situated in castles or underground labyrinths or secret evil genius island lairs, but Lucia and her minions lived in a massive but otherwise ordinary estate deep in the well-to-do community of Scripps Ranch. Its sheer size was impressive enough, but I had always found myself a little bit disappointed in the plainness of its exterior, not to mention the absence of fundamental security features like a moat and drawbridge, active hell portals, or cybernetic guard dogs.

The manpire at the iron gate waved us in with barely a glance, apparently unconcerned by the fact that the House had suffered not one, but *two*, assaults in the past decade alone. I waited for Steve to say something, but he gave no sign that he had noticed his underling's lackadaisical attitude. Given that the manpire standing guard had always been a huge dick to me, I decided it was my *obligation* as a friend and ally of the House to inform Kayla—my very good friend, and the reigning Captain of the Watch—that one of her men was shirking his duties.

Revenge was petty, but it was also glorious.

We drove up the long curving driveway, past the orchard and the small pond that remained sadly empty of man-eating piranhas or miniaturized sharks, and parked at the base of a short flight of stairs. At the top of those stairs was the House's front entrance, a pair of massive wooden doors, elaborately carved and older than America itself.

A year ago, the doors had been flanked by human security guards, but that arrangement had ended when those same guards were used in a failed but bloody coup by the previous Captain of the Watch. Now, the vampires were intent on handling their own security.

Steve pushed open one of the doors and I followed him past the banquet hall and the living quarters for the on-site human staff and blood donors. Tucked in one corner, beyond the sweeping staircase that led up to the second floor, was a small bay of elevators.

The House consisted of six stories—four above ground, and two below—each roughly the size of an aircraft carrier. As Lucia's nominal human servant, I'd been granted my own palatial suite on the second floor, but I had so far resisted the blonde queen's relentless suggestions that I relocate there permanently. Like all of her gifts, the suite came with far too many conditions attached.

Which was a bummer, because the rooms were a hell of a lot nicer than my small bedroom in my parents' basement. And the food was both plentiful and free.

Steve and I took the elevator up to the fourth floor, which consisted primarily of conference rooms and offices. The People, as they liked to call themselves, owned space in several gleaming high-rises sprinkled throughout downtown and La Jolla, but most of the distinctly vampire-centric business was handled here.

We picked up a few additional guards as we left the elevator, a sure sign that Council members were present. Black-clad vampires trailed us down the long hallway to a conference room I'd been to before. I looked at Steve.

"Do we knock or—"

"Enter," came a command from inside the room, the word delicate and sharp, like barbed wire fashioned from fine crystal.

That someone could have heard us from inside, despite the closed door, and my own hushed voice, would have blown my mind once. These days, it didn't even give me pause. With a shrug, I did as the voice commanded.

Steve stayed behind in the hall… which just went to show that even badass mohawked manpires knew when discretion was the better part of valor.

A room that might have comfortably held thirty had even fewer occupants than usual, each seated a careful distance from one another around the polished wooden table.

There was Marcus, of course, darkly handsome and wearing a multi-thousand-dollar suit and the kind of pompous sneer that only a vampire accountant could adequately achieve.

There was Zorana, seated in an island of silence at the foot of the table, toying with a strand of her hair, and regarding me like a bug she couldn't wait to dissect. The perpetually preteen Blood Witch wore a purple and yellow polka-dotted halter dress that in no way detracted from her homicidal aura.

Next to Marcus was a manpire I didn't recognize, dark haired, olive-skinned, and disgustingly handsome in a suit that rivaled Marcus' for cost, but which was somehow just a little bit more stylish. I made a mental note to point out that very fact to Marcus at my earliest opportunity.

Standing behind him was yet another stranger, close enough in appearance to be the seated vampire's twin, wearing the all-black of the House Watch.

Even given Juliette's recent defection, we were short a few Council members. Andrés was absent, of course, given the slight case of death he'd caught during my very first mediation, but Anastasia and Kayla both should have been there.

Seeing as how those women had historically been my strongest supporters in the House, my already low expectations for the meeting drooped even further.

My gaze turned to the one other individual in the room, currently simmering like a malevolent crockpot at the head of the table. Queen Lucia Borghesi remained the most beautiful woman I had ever seen, the sexual equivalent of chocolate crack; a platinum blonde whose golden tan and lush curves were unfailingly highlighted by her all-white wardrobe.

As it so often did, the sight of her struck me like a fist to the diaphragm, taking my breath away. It was almost enough to make me forget our mutual antipathy.

Almost.

As attractive as the exiled queen was, her beauty was offset by an overbearing, selfish, and downright manipulative personality. Lucia had sufficient arrogance for ten normal people (or four vampires), paired with a self-confidence that bordered on reckless delusion. Any accord we'd found in dealing with the wolves had vanished over the course of Anastasia's months-long absence. Recently, the queen had grown even more aggressive and derisive.

Normally, that sort of thing would have been right up my alley—contempt was basically my sexual Kryptonite—but the femmepire's focus had been on reshaping me into a properly subservient thrall. Given my own fixation on personal freedom, our few conversations had ended as arguments.

Judging by her expression, this was going to be another one. "What have you done to your face?"

I ran a hand through my beard. "It was time for a change."

"It looks like a virulent breed of fungus," she informed me. Marcus snickered.

I shrugged. Some people had no appreciation for rugged masculinity. Or… whatever it was I was trying for. "Did you kidnap me—again—just to discuss my facial hair?"

The queen's gaze darted briefly toward the two strange manpires, and then back to me, full lips thinning with irritation. "Is this how you would greet your queen, my thrall?"

I met her hard gaze with one of my own. As hard a gaze as I could manage, anyway; I wasn't sure the gaze of a twenty-six-year-old carried the same weight as that of a four-hundred-year-old monarch. Even a monarch who had managed to get her ass exiled.

"For the last time, I'm *not* your thrall, Lucia. Now, can we skip all the posturing and discuss why I'm here? I have a case—"

The black-clad manpire across the table blurred into motion, somersaulting neatly over both furniture and private investigator. My brain was in the process of drafting a letter of recommendation that the rest of my body do something to defend itself when I found myself face-planting into the table's heavy wooden surface.

"Manners, monkey," the strange manpire whispered in my ear, voice thick with an accent I vaguely recognized as Spanish, or Mexican, or… well… not American. "Speak in such a manner to Her Majesty again, and I will remove one of your hands."

"Make it the left one," I managed, cheek squashed against the wooden surface by a vise-like grip that I had no chance in hell of breaking. "I need the right to drive stick."

If I ever got my car back.

Zorana giggled, the sound of her magic-infused voice doing its usual number on my intestines. To the best of my knowledge, the Blood Witch didn't have a sense of humor, so her laughter was almost certainly delight at my pain.

She was a charmer, that one.

"Thank you for explaining the situation to Mr. Smith, Thales," Lucia told the vampire behind me smoothly. "Your attitude does this House credit, but *I* will decide when and how my thrall is to be disciplined."

"Of course, your Majesty." The force pressing me down against the table vanished.

By the time I was upright once again, the manpire was back on the other side of the table, standing behind and to the left of the other stranger. *Thales, eh?* I mentally added his name to the shit list I'd been keeping since elementary school. One day, when they least expected it… I'd egg every last one of their houses.

"Now then, my thrall," said Lucia, as if nothing had happened, "I believe you were saying something about a case? Someone has finally enlisted your skills as a mediator?"

"Well… no." I flushed as I remembered the White Ladies' comments on my professional reputation. I was so *not* going to pass that little snippet of dialogue on. "It's a missing persons case."

"Ah." The single syllable was sufficient to convey the many flavors of disinterest Lucia had in my primary occupation. "Pity. It is your role as a mediator that I have summoned you here to discuss."

"Not a problem," I said with forced cheer. "After all, you're paying me for the privilege." In fact, that not-inconsiderable monthly stipend had been one of the few things allowing me to make rent. And the *only* reason Lucia and I had maintained any relationship at all in Ana's still-unexplained absence.

"What I am paying you for is performance. And your performance to this point has been far from satisfactory."

Even Marcus had to suppress a snicker at the unintentional double *entendre*. Whether twenty-six or three-hundred, men were idiots.

"I perform just fine," I answered under my breath. Not that anyone had borne witness to that fact for a far longer time span than I was interested in sharing.

"Do you? How long has it been since you mediated the settlement between San Diego's wolf cubs?"

"Six months, give or take." Carolyn and Jason had been the married alphas of the local Pack and were now—thanks to my efforts and an unfortunate incident of interstate war—much happier as the divorced leaders of the world's first werewolf democracy.

"Indeed." Her sneer was far lovelier than it had any right to be. "So, what exactly has the stipend I am paying you gained me in the ensuing months?"

"My continued good will and the right to summon me to your House of Doom for lovely gatherings like this one?"

"Your value hinges upon your position as mediator." The queen bit off each word, less than happy—as usual—with my attempts at humor. "And recently, that value has been negligible."

As much as I hated to admit it, she kind of had a point. Part of the reason Lucia had formalized my relationship with the House was because my role as San Diego's mediator added to her prestige. However...

"What am I supposed to do about that?" I shook my head. "Believe me, I'd love to have more mediation cases. They pay a hell of a lot better than staking out cheap motels. But it's not like I've been turning down offers or anything. I can't just *invent* situations that require my services."

I stopped short of calling them skills, not wanting to suffer through even more laughter from Zorana.

"It is your position then that there have been no conflicts in the greater San Diego area that required mediation?"

"Uhm... yes?" Hadn't I just said that? "Maybe I've just been *too* good at my job?"

Lucia glanced down the table at Marcus, who rose to his feet, hands clasped behind his back like a schoolboy prepared to deliver his first book report.

"In January, the Clippers tribe nearly went to war with a visiting band of chupacabra. In late March, the Mer excommunicated ten of their own over a quarrel that could not be resolved. And last month, a skinwalker sued our local zombie prince over access rights to an object he claimed had been stolen from ancestral lands." With a smug smile, the manpire unbuttoned his suit coat, and returned to his seat.

"Jesus. You people are worse than humans," I grumbled. Three inter-species conflicts in six months? The supernatural world didn't need mediators… it needed an army of shrinks and remedial lessons in conflict resolution.

Even the long-sought confirmation of zombies' existence failed to cheer me up.

"It sounds like they all worked out fine. Except for the ex-communicated Mer, I guess." I glanced at Lucia as I said the last bit; she was touchy about references to banishment or exile for some reason.

Nobody seemed inclined to respond.

"Fine. I'll bite. If they were having issues, why *didn't* they hire me? I'm the city mediator. And it's not like I'm hard to find. I even have my own website now."

"One that looks like it was crafted by a child," said Zorana.

You would know, I very carefully did not reply. The Blood Witch was damn near a thousand years old, insanely powerful, and not at all amused to be trapped forever in the body of a twelve-year-old girl.

Again, Lucia glanced to Marcus. This time, the bean-counter flipped open a manila folder on the table in front of him. He held up a color photograph and slid it down the table to me.

A middle-aged man, moderately handsome and exceedingly well-groomed, had been caught exiting a building downtown, his long coat swinging open to reveal a three-piece suit and what looked suspiciously like a Roman gladius at his waist. In the picture, he was gazing past the photographer, pale eyes sparkling. There was something inherently likable about the man, even in two-dimensional form.

"Marcus, is this really the best time to announce you've found a new boyfriend?" I gave the manpire a sad shake of my head. "Can't you just use social media like the rest of the world?"

"That *man* is not my boyfriend, you uneducated, mewling pile of human excrement."

"This is Caleb Van Stahl," added Lucia, in a sweet tone I immediately distrusted. "Formerly of Los Angeles, and recently moved to San Diego."

"Cool. Who's Caleb Van Stahl?"

"A mediator for the supernatural world."

Well, shit.

CHAPTER 6

"Wait a second," I said, struggling to process the revelation that I was no longer the only active mediator in San Diego, "That's cheating! Why was he allowed to move in and set up shop when I'm already here? One town, one mediator. Isn't that the rule?"

"It's more of a guideline, really," said Marcus.

"It is the custom, yes." Lucia's crystal blue eyes never left my face. "However, in any city, if the current mediator is thought to be unsuitable for the position, another may offer his services instead."

"That's bullshit!"

"That's capitalism," Marcus countered.

"From all accounts," said Lucia, her lovely face marred with a scowl, "Mr. Van Stahl's clients are satisfied with his efforts thus far. I am starting to believe I backed the wrong horse in this race."

"Wait… what?" That got my attention. My basic lack of professionalism in no way prevented me from having at least a modicum of job-related pride. "I have yet to fail a single mediation!"

"Yet things have a habit of exploding in your vicinity, monkey," Zorana said with a small smile. "While *I* consider it to be your one redeeming characteristic, it's not the sort of detail to excite potential customers. Unless they're fire imps, I suppose."

"Additionally," said the vampire queen, interrupting my attempts to ask what a fire imp was, "there is the matter of how you present yourself."

"Is this still about the website? I admit I got it done on the cheap. Mike knew a guy who knew a guy who took a web-design course once… It's not Amazon or anything, but you have to agree that it's still way better than my old Yellow Pages ad!"

The unnamed manpire seated across from me leaned back and said something to his subordinate in a stream of foreign-sounding syllables. When Thales laughed in reply, I snapped.

"Look dude. I have no idea who you are, or why you're here, but if you have something to say about me, you can damn well use English, and not…" I trailed off, as I realized once again that I had no idea what language they were speaking. "…Spanish?"

The manpire turned back to regard me, holding up one hand to prevent Thales from hurtling the table to remove one or more of my limbs. "It is Portuguese," he told me, his accent heavy, "and I was telling Thales that our new House would be better off simply killing you and replacing you with someone even halfway competent." He nodded to the photo still in front of me. "Perhaps this gentleman, yes?"

I made an executive decision to stop asking for translations.

The manpire turned to Lucia. "If you wish to leave this minor matter in my hands, your Majesty, I will find a mediator who does you proud. You can simply toss this human in with the other blood donors, where he belongs."

"Whatever his current struggles, Lord Barros, I can assure you that Mr. Smith has served this House well and ably in the past." Anastasia's voice preceded her into the conference room.

"Lady Dumenyova." If Barros was as surprised by Anastasia's sudden appearance as I was, he hid it well. "It is an honor to again make your acquaintance. But it is Duke Barros now." He smiled expansively. "We are each of us moving up in the world, no?"

"Thank you, Duke Barros." Lucia's voice was cold and sharp enough to shave with. "I will take your suggestion under advisement." She rose from her seat in a soft rustle of fabric. "We will reconvene later tonight. I would speak with my Secundus alone."

The other vampires filed out of the room. I rose to join them but a sharp "Not you, Mr. Smith" from the queen sent me back to my chair. Honestly, I hadn't wanted to share a hallway with Duke Barros, Thales, Marcus, and Zorana anyway. For once, Lucia seemed like the lesser evil.

As the door shut, Anastasia stepped past me to stand before her queen. Her coat was missing, but she otherwise looked the same as when I'd seen her an hour prior, which was to say unspeakably lovely and devastatingly competent. She bowed to the other woman.

I expected something high-handed from the queen—maybe a carefully arched eyebrow and professionally cultivated look of cool disinterest—but instead she pulled Anastasia into a brief embrace, trading cheek-to-cheek kisses with the taller femmepire. Her smile was open and genuine and all the more disconcerting for that fact. "Welcome back. I was surprised to hear from our contact in Romania that you would be returning so soon."

"I was forced to cut my business short," Anastasia admitted, her words cool and precise. I might as well not have been in the room. "News of my presence reached the Courts."

"But you were still able to...?"

"Yes." Anastasia bowed her head again, unbound auburn hair sliding forward in a rush of silken waves to obscure her features. "I said my farewells and performed my duty."

There was a moment of silence, which I had no prayer of deciphering. Farewells? Duty? Why had Ana been in Romania? And... where exactly was Romania anyway?

"We will speak more of this, at a time and place of your choosing," Lucia told Anastasia, squeezing her hand briefly in another mystifying show of affection. She turned to me, eyes hardening like pale blue icicles. "As for you, my thrall... if you wish to remain employed by this House, you will start taking your role as mediator seriously."

"Do you think I'm not?" I asked, fighting to keep my gaze from straying to the tall femmepire at her side. "Has it ever occurred to you that it might be my association with your House that's keeping people from hiring me? It's no secret that two of my mediations ended up benefiting you directly."

Lucia waved a golden hand dismissively. "I do not care about your excuses. Devise a strategy for how you will win back your clients and drive out this interloper. Deliver that plan to me by tomorrow or face punishment. As of this moment, my patience has officially reached its limit."

"I'll alert the media," I muttered under my breath.

On another day, that sort of off-hand comment might have gotten me killed. Today, I simply found myself out in the hall, sitting on my ass and rubbing my head from where it had impacted the far wall. The conference room door swung shut again with a bang.

"I see you're making friends, as usual," Steve said with a grin, casually pulling me to my feet with one hand.

"It's why I'm a mediator," I said. "People just can't help but like me."

○○○

After my dismissal, I did what any mid-twenties fratman would do; I rode the elevator down to the second floor, wandered over to the kitchen, and took advantage of the plentiful food within. One sandwich and half a Tupperware of grilled steak later, I left my plate in the sink, polished off my soda—Diet Coke, in deference to the battle I continued to wage with my slowly expanding midsection— and headed down the hall to the suite that belonged to my two best friends in the House.

I'd met Darlene and Kayla the first time I was a prisoner of the House and over the past year, the three of us had remained close. D was human like me, barely five feet tall, and Kayla's blood donor and girlfriend. She also had one of the filthiest minds it had ever been my pleasure to encounter. Kayla was an Aussie transplant, as tall as D was small, with long ash-blonde hair, and a slender frame that disguised the fact that she could bench press a car and fight off a minotaur or three while doing so.

A knock on the door gained me entrance to their infamous den of sin—cunningly disguised as a bedroom suite—and I passed out the cookies I'd liberated from the kitchen. We shared several quiet minutes of chocolate chip nirvana as I gave them the cliff notes for the Council meeting.

"Wait... Lucia wants *you* to figure out what to do about the other mediator?" Darlene shared a look with Kayla.

"Well... yeah." Their concern intensified to the point where I could no longer pretend not to see it. "What's wrong?"

"Plans aren't really your strong suit," Kayla explained.

"That's why I have minions," I said airily.

"Minions?"

"You two! So, plan away! I'll supervise… with my eyes closed." Thanks to the White Ladies, I hadn't gotten nearly enough sleep. "Maybe you could wake me up when everything is done?"

"You do remember that K can shove that cookie so deep up your ass that an entire team of doctors would be needed to retrieve it, don't you?"

The ass in question clenched reflexively, and I discovered I wasn't quite as tired as I'd previously thought.

"On second thought, maybe we should figure this out together." I polished off the last cookie—an act of anal preservation as much as it was gluttony—before another thought occurred. I glanced over at Kayla, who was sprawled out on the acre-wide bed. "Why weren't *you* there, anyway? At the meeting, I mean."

The silence that fell in response to my question was weirdly uncomfortable. Darlene sat stiffly in her overstuffed easy chair, a small frown on her equally small face. And Kayla…

"It was a Council meeting," the femmepire finally said, her brown eyes as distant as her tone.

"But you're the Captain of the Watch. That makes you an honorary Council member, doesn't it?" I was pretty sure it did. In fact, she'd even been given the option of moving up to the third floor with the other Council members.

"I'm not Captain anymore," she informed me. Off to the side, Darlene's frown transformed into a full-blown scowl. "That position has been granted to one of our new recruits from Brazil."

"Wait… you don't mean that *Thales* asshole, do you? Screw that! That pajama-clad moron is—"

"At least a hundred years older than me. And a Battle Lord."

Both points were telling. As vampires aged, they grew stronger. Occasionally, they also gained Talents. One of the rarer ones was that of the Battle Lord, a vampire whose skills at combat made normal vampires seem… well, ordinary.

"I don't care if he's a *Sith lord*," I said. "This is total bullshit."

Darlene nodded in agreement, but Kayla just shrugged, her face uncharacteristically solemn and tired.

"When I gained the position, I knew it might be a short-term appointment. I'm too young to have achieved the rank in any House but this one. Besides, we gain prestige by having someone like Thales as our Captain."

"You stood by Lucia when the House's *last* Battle Lord staged his bloody coup. Shouldn't loyalty count for *something* around here?" You couldn't take a step in the House without tripping over a potential traitor or a spy for the Italian Courts, and Lucia was treating one of her few trustworthy subjects like this? It was ridiculous.

"What do you want me to say, John? I have my duty. And speaking of duty… it's time for my guard shift." Kayla rose to her feet in a smooth motion that outed her as something more than human every bit as effectively as a mouthful of fangs. "If nothing else, the hours of boredom should give me time to ponder your mediator problem."

The door closed quietly behind her, and I gave Darlene an apologetic shake of my head. "Sorry, D. I didn't mean to stick my foot in it."

"It's not your fault." She rolled her eyes in the direction of the departed femmepire. "You just wandered into the middle of the shit storm I've been dealing with for the past few weeks."

"Is that why you guys have been incommunicado?"

"Yeah. Ever since Duke Barros arrived from Brazil with Captain Asshole in tow, things have sucked giant donkey dong around here." She moved from the chair to sit on the carpet next to me. "Is there anything you can do?"

"Well," I said after a moment's consideration, "I *could* invite Thales out to my secret, underground lair, and feed him to one of my trained crocodiles."

"If only."

I blinked. I'd meant that as a joke. And normally, Darlene would have laughed.

"It's that bad? Kayla seems mostly okay with the change…"

"Sure she is." Darlene snorted. "A hundred years older yadda yadda, Battle Lord blah blah. Kayla might not have grown into her first Talent yet, but she's a hundred times the person that Brazilian asshole is!"

"You're preaching to the choir on that front, D."

"So, you'll help?"

"I'll try," I found myself saying, even though I hadn't a clue what I could possibly do, given that Lucia was pissed at me, Anastasia and I were… well, whatever we were… and Juliette had defected from the House, something which nobody but me seemed aware of yet. "You two have been there for me again and again this past year. It's past time I returned the favor."

"Thank you, John." Her voice was almost a whisper, and for the first time, I found myself seriously considering schemes that might rid the House of Thales. I didn't have any trained crocodiles handy, but I *did* have a friend with access to a hell dimension and its multiple fields of eternally burning human candelabras. And all it would cost me was a pint of ice cream and maybe a Winnie the Pooh DVD…

I took hold of those runaway homicidal impulses. This sort of situation called for restraint and diplomacy. After all, the vampire hadn't done anything wrong other than displacing Kayla.

And shoving my face into a table.

And threatening to remove one of my hands.

Come to think of it, restraint was overrated.

I gave Darlene a hug. "You know I'll help however I can. Maybe something will come to me tonight. In the meantime, I also need to figure out what to do about this other mediator. And I need to make some progress on my new case too."

"You have a new case?"

"Yeah." I nodded, rising to my feet with a sigh. "I'll tell you guys about it tomorrow… assuming we're still on for brunch, that is?"

"We'll be there," said Darlene.

"Noon?"

"As always." She stood up to see me out.

I stopped as a thought struck me. "Damn it!"

"What's up?"

"I don't have a car," I told her. "The Corolla got towed."

"Seriously? Someone towed the dick-mobile?" She looked confused, and far less distressed than I had been. "But why? And why now?"

"I don't know," I said, scowling up at the ceiling. "I'm pretty sure Lucia had something to do with it, but I forgot to ask during the Council inquisition. And I have no idea how I'm going to get home. Steve picked me up, but…"

"It's okay, John." She patted me on the arm. "I'll give you a ride in our Jeep. Maybe we can swing by a store and pick you up a bicycle or something."

"That sounds depressingly like exercise."

CHAPTER 7

Darlene never got a chance to sell me on the wonders of cycling. As we reached the ground floor, my phone rang. I didn't recognize the number, so I muted it, and tucked it back into a pocket. Less than ten seconds later, it began to buzz, but this time, I very clearly felt an accompanying push from Lucia in the back of my brain. It wasn't like we could communicate telepathically or anything, but the message was still obvious: answer the damn phone.

With a sigh, I did just that.

"Thrall." Lucia sounded every bit as imperious over the phone as she did in real life. "It occurs to me that you may presently be lacking in transportation."

"Yeah, I don't suppose you have any idea how *that* happened?"

"I had your monstrosity of an automobile taken to the junkyard where it belongs," she acknowledged, sounding not the least bit sorry. "While the onus is on you to rehabilitate your flagging reputation as a mediator, I recognize that there are some small actions I will be forced to take on your behalf. Ridding you of that metal deathtrap and its genitalia-obsessed décor was one such step."

"You *junked* my Corolla?!?" Next to me, Darlene's mouth formed a silent *O* of surprise, and—I had to assume—horror. "You have no right—"

"I have *every* right," snapped Lucia. "When you finally accept that fact, your life as my thrall will be far less aggravating. For both of us."

"I. Am. Not. Your. Thrall." I said through gritted teeth, ignoring the permanent presence in the back of my mind that indicated otherwise. "And while the Corolla may not have won any beauty awards, it got me where I needed to go. Most of the time." Except when it was cold out—anything below mid-fifties—but I didn't want to talk about that. "I'm sure your peers will just be *delighted* to hire a mediator who arrives by skateboard!"

"Speaking to you on the phone is every bit as tiresome as dealing with you in person. Cease your ignorant prattling and go to the front of my House."

With a sigh, I did just that, Darlene trailing behind me. As I stepped into the sunlight, my mouth fell open in shock.

At the top of the circular driveway, someone had parked a shining automobile, so new that even its tires gleamed in the afternoon sun. In the back of my mind, I felt Lucia taste my shock and surprise with something approaching contentment, the way a cat might sip from a saucer of milk.

"It's... another Corolla," said Darlene.

"Yes," I breathed. "It really is." A shiny new 2014 Toyota Corolla, with half again the horsepower my older model had offered, an engine that presumably started without the need for divine intervention, and a suspension that might be a match for the pothole-ridden streets by my office.

"You will find the deed in the glove box." Lucia's voice in my ear reminded me that I still had the queen on the line. "The car is yours."

"Are you serious? I don't know what to say," I told her, taking the stone steps two at a time. "Only… did it have to be white?"

Because it was. White, that is. Glistening, gleaming, pure-as-driven-snow white. Even the *interior* was white leather, which I was pretty sure had to be a custom job.

"Yes," she said flatly, "and a scant modicum of research will tell you that white is the most popular color of choice for new automobiles."

It also just happened to be the color of everything the femmepire owned. In fact, outside of the obvious difference in sticker price, my new Corolla would have fit right in with her own fleet of Ferraris, Jaguars, and Bentleys. What was next, *an all-white wardrobe for that thrall in your life who has almost nothing?* Even as I excitedly peered through the brilliantly clean windshield, some part of me recognized that this was just one more way for the queen to mark me as hers.

On the other hand, it was a *car*. A *free* car, and brand new. I'd never owned a new car before, and I was quite frankly looking forward to the experience. If Lucia's strategy was to ply me with expensive gifts… well, the Smith men weren't above a little bit of bribery, and it beat the hell out of the *harass, irritate, and bite* approach she'd been employing so far.

"Thank you. She's beautiful." I thumbed off the phone, ignoring whatever it was Lucia had started to say.

"Did you just call the car a *she? And* hang up on Queen Lucia?"

"Shhhh," I said, one hand stroking the Corolla's hood, "We're having a moment here."

"You *so* need to get laid."

I was too busy admiring my new ride to reply.

○○○

The Corolla handled like a dream. Or like a more powerful and less broken version of my old car, which was the same thing, really. I hummed down the 163 at an effortless seventy-seven mph, windows open, and FM 94.9 blasting through the car's surprisingly bass-heavy speakers. I drummed my fingers on the leather-wrapped steering wheel and debated what to do next.

As much stuff as had just been dumped onto my plate—this other mediator, Kayla's job, and whatever was going on with both Juliette and Anastasia, my first priority had to be finding Graciela. Thankfully, I'd already made a small bit of progress. If Steve's bouncer boyfriend was able to arrange an audience with Lord Kala, I might even have the case closed in time for Taco Tuesday. In the meantime, it wouldn't be a bad idea to put the word out to some of my other contacts, like I'd intended to do before the whole Juliette/Anastasia/Corolla fiasco.

I eased my wonderphone out of my pocket, scrolled through the contact list, and held the device up to one ear, turning down the radio with my other hand. This was the second phone I'd bought in the past year, replacing the one I'd lost when I was kidnapped by a senile werewolf who believed I was the genetic key to werewolf super-babies.

God, my life was ridiculous.

The phone rang half a dozen times on the other end before someone finally picked up. "Wassup?"

"Uhm." I'd been trying to reach Carolyn, the co-leader of the local Pack, but this was a guy. In fact, it sounded almost like… "Jason?"

"Duh," he replied. "Marco?"

"It's John," I said, manfully resisting the urge to say 'Polo' instead. "Sorry. I didn't expect *you* to be answering Carolyn's phone." An awful thought suddenly occurred to me. "Wait, you and she aren't…"

"Really, bro? Been there, done that, barely escaped with my fur intact."

"Well… good." Jason and Carolyn had been the married leaders of the Pack until last year, when their divorce had very nearly gotten me killed. "So… why *are* you over there?"

"Pack movie night," he told me cheerily, "but it was a romcom so I went for a smoke. You called as I was coming back in through the kitchen. Anyway," he continued, voice suddenly lowering to a deep, suspicious growl, "what are *you* calling Cara for? Is there something going on between you and my ex that I should know about?"

"Oh, *hell* no," I said quickly. Carolyn was a nice enough girl, but… yeah… no.

"Smart man. Just remember… bros before hos, or you gots to goes."

"Uhm… okay?" Jason was one of the few people in the world who made *me* feel old and mature. It was hard to believe he was twenty. Even harder to believe that it made him middle-aged for a werewolf. "Do you mind getting her?"

"No prob." I heard him promptly bellow Carolyn's name at a volume that, in and of itself, did a lot to explain why he was now single. Mission accomplished, he returned to our conversation. "A few of us are gonna hit PB tonight. You in? Wanna invite some of the fang babes?"

"Thanks, but I think I'll—" I cut off as flashing lights appeared in my rear-view mirror. I slowed down and waited for the police car to blow by me in pursuit of an escaped murderer or deranged celebrity, but it followed me into the slow lane, and then again over onto the shoulder.

With a sigh of disgust, I parked and killed the engine.

"You'll what?" Jason asked for at least the second time, but I ended the call and dropped my phone into the seat next to me, hoping the cop hadn't seen me using it. Technically, talking on a phone while driving was illegal without a headset, but it was one of California's many laws that pretty much everyone ignored. Had I been speeding? More than everyone else on the road, anyway? Was one of my taillights already cracked?

Or—I felt my spirits sink even further—had Lucia given me a stolen car? I fumbled in the glove compartment for what I really hoped was a deed in my name.

Considering the increasingly terrifying situations my mind managed to conjure as the highway patrol officer approached my vehicle—including one that involved me fighting off my hairy cellmate Bubba using a sharpened toothbrush—escaping with only a citation for speeding and a second one for driving while using a cell phone *should* had been a relief. But it was a ludicrously large ticket, and I had no idea how I was going to pay it. To say nothing of what it might do to my insurance premiums.

Part of me rolled over and died at the realization that I was thinking about things like insurance premiums. *When had I gotten old and lame?* The rest of me remained focused on the matter at hand. I really, really needed to start making some money again. As much as it pained me to admit it, maybe Lucia was right. Caleb and I needed to chat.

For the remainder of the drive home, I stayed carefully within a few miles of the posted speed limit, used my blinkers to change lanes, and generally acted like a high school kid taking his driving test for the fifth time. When my phone buzzed insistently from the passenger seat, I ignored the instinctive urge to pick it up and answer.

I had learned my lesson.

Safety first, San Diego.

CHAPTER 8

For the first time in years, I parked my car at the curb in front of my parents' house, in plain view of Mr. Brown. Whereas the crotchety old man's many, many complaints to the homeowners' association about my old car had been vaguely understandable, even he would have difficulty finding fault in my new ride. I patted the car and started up the driveway. And then, once there was absolutely no chance of another ticket, I checked my phone.

I had four missed calls, three voicemails, and one text in all caps, all of which seemed a bit ridiculous considering it had only been fifteen minutes. Then I realized they were all from the same person; Carolyn Hawthorne, co-leader of the local Pack, aka the person I'd called and then hung up on. Oops.

Rather than reading her text or listening to her voicemails, I took a seat on our porch bench, and re-dialed the werewolf's number. This time, she answered almost immediately.

"John?"

"Hi, Carolyn. Sorry abou—"

"I know that humans have a different concept of courtesy than the Pack—" Her tone suggested *lesser* was a more suitable adjective. "—but I'm pretty sure even your species thinks it's rude to call someone and then hang up."

"I'm sorry. I ran into a bit of trouble and didn't have time for proper goodbyes."

"Trouble?" Her voice softened minutely. "Who's trying to kill you now? Mold demons? Possessed mosquitoes? The zombie prince?"

"Does *everyone* know about that guy? How is it that the city mediator is the absolute last person to learn that zombies are a thing?!?"

"Natural talent, I guess. So, what did you do to piss him off?" Carolyn's voice was merry. Death threats against one bumbling detective and—apparently undesirable—mediator were a source of entertainment to everyone who wasn't me.

"Nothing. I've never even met the dude. Nobody is trying to kill me. That I know of. So far, anyway," I qualified. "I got pulled over by the cops."

"Oh." She pondered that for a moment. "That's it? So why didn't you return any of my calls? Or my text?"

"I was driving," I reminded her.

"Annnnnnnnd...?"

"It's illegal to talk on the phone while driving."

"Yeah, right!"

"Seriously, it is."

"That's the dumbest thing I've ever heard," she snickered. "What else are we supposed to do to pass the time on the road?" Carolyn drove a cute little Prius, part of her one-werewolf environmental crusade.

"I don't have a clue," I said, "but I hope you'll start taking traffic safety as seriously as I do."

"Yeah, because driving around in a prehistoric, gas-belching scrapheap held together by bubblegum and duct tape is the height of safety," she muttered, just loud enough to make sure I heard it. "Anyway, what did you want to talk about? My moron of an ex didn't know."

"Uhm…" It took an embarrassingly long moment to remember why I'd called her, but I filled her in on the disappearance of Graciela. The retelling took all of thirty seconds, given how little I actually knew.

"Sounds like a funky case. Where does the Pack fit in?"

"I was hoping you could keep your eyes and ears open… you know, let me know if any of you see or hear anything about our missing spirit."

"You do remember that we're wolves, right? Ghost hunting isn't our thing," she pointed out in the sort of mildly condescending tone that did a lot to explain why *she* was now single.

"Join the club. But you guys have members all over the county. And Tijuana. That's a lot more ground than I can cover."

"Especially in that car of yours," she muttered again.

"*Anyway.*" The fact that my penis-bedecked Corolla had gone to the great automobile graveyard in the sky didn't mean people could speak ill of it. "I'm just looking for some basic recon."

"Have you asked the vampires?"

"Lucia is already questioning my competence. I'm trying to prove myself without their help."

"By asking us for our help instead?"

When she put it like that, it didn't sound great. But my options were limited. "You guys already know I'm awesome. So how about it? Can you do it?"

"Okay—" said Carolyn.

"Great! I really appreciate—"

"—as long as it passes a Pack vote."

I tried not to sigh. Was there some sort of mystic law that *everything* I did would come back to bite me in the ass? Oh… that's right, there was, and it was called karma. And in this particular instance, my karma was to be at the mercy of the very first werewolf democracy, a democracy I had helped encourage.

"Don't worry," she said, when the silence had lasted long enough to convey my dismay, "we'll be gathering out on the grounds this week. I'll call for a vote then."

"I'd really appreciate it. I owe you one." We spoke for a few more minutes, and then said our goodbyes. I was just about to end the call when something else occurred to me.

"You still there, Carolyn?"

"Yeah, but make it quick. It's movie night, and the popcorn is getting cold."

"I just wanted to pass on word from Lucia. Apparently, there's a rival mediator in town. Caleb Van… something or other."

"Really? Another mediator? Hmm."

"What?"

"I wonder if he's any good. The Pack's current guy is a bit of a basket case."

"Not funny."

The riotous laughter on the other end told me I was mistaken. As Rodney Dangerfield used to say, many years before I was born, *I don't get no respect.*

ooo

After Carolyn, I reached out to my few other sources in the paranormal community. Sadly, the supernatural species of our world loved to play phone tag every bit as much as the average human. I ended up leaving brief and vague messages on a number of answering machines. At least one of those machines had been endowed with a rudimentary form of intelligence, along with an explicit vocabulary that wouldn't be earning its owner any friends.

I called that number twice, just to listen to the increasingly inventive insults.

The few times I did reach someone, I kept my questions general, giving a summary of the particulars of my case without any mention of specific names or dates. The White Ladies probably wanted to keep the news of their leader's disappearance as quiet as possible. Graciela's absence might be all that was needed to convince some other group, tribe, species, or conglomeration to make a power play in the city. And that would be bad for all of us.

Granted, I'd spilled the beans to Carolyn *before* having that epiphany, but I didn't think the Pack would be a problem. The wolves had barely survived an incursion by a rival pack from New Mexico and weren't in any position to make a move. Plus, their fledgling democracy would require half a dozen meetings and at least one specially formed committee to even *consider* voting on the idea. I was sure telling Carolyn wouldn't come back to haunt me.

Reasonably sure.

More or less.

Well, shit.

For the third time, I interrupted the werewolf's movie night.

ooo

By the time I finished, I was no longer alone on the porch. At some point during my one-man telethon, the sun had set, and Valentina was seated next to me, hands folded primly in her lap, bare legs swinging gently back and forth.

I wasn't sure why the ghost only showed up at night. Maybe she was always present, but invisible during the day? Or maybe she wandered the country like a spectral Bruce Banner, righting wrongs and killing evildoers? Whatever the truth was, I was happy to see her.

I tucked my wonderphone back into a pocket—noting that the battery was already almost depleted—and offered her a smile. "Hello, Valentina."

She gave a black-gummed grin in response, dark eyes hidden behind the ever-present curtain of hair. As usual, she said nothing.

"I hope you had a better day than I did?"

Valentina gave it a moment of thought, shrugged, and grinned again. Right on cue, blood began to soak through the front of her nightgown in the now-familiar pattern. By this point in our relationship, I didn't pay it much attention.

"I've started looking into Graciela's disappearance," I said, noting that her legs had stopped in mid-swing at the other ghost's name, "but it's tough going so far. One of the problems I'm running into is that I just don't know enough… about her specifically, or you Ladies in general. If you could answer some of my questions, it would really help."

She didn't say anything, but I could feel her gaze intensify, and decided to take that—and the fact that she hadn't just ghosted away—as a positive sign.

"For starters," I began, "Marge said last night that Graciela's haunting is empty of her presence? What does that mean? And how can you tell? Do you have some sort of innate spirit-radar or something?" I shook my head before she could reply. "Of course you don't. If you did, you wouldn't need my help to find her."

"Do you maybe know anything about Graciela's life when she was… you know, alive? Could someone from her past be after her again? Maybe her murderer became a ghost themselves?" I'd seen a movie like that, although its name escaped me. "Does she have any other enemies that you know of? Like a renegade exorcist?"

A palpable sensation of frustration arose from my companion, and I cut the questions short. "Sorry, V; I didn't mean to bombard you. And some of that info is probably confidential, huh? Whatever you're allowed to tell me would be more than sufficient. I don't want to get you in trouble with the man. Or the woman."

If anything, Valentina's aura of frustration only grew. Without standing or turning or… well, changing position at all… she floated down the bench until she and I were hip to hip. I could feel a chill through my jeans, but it was far from the life-sapping cold I'd experienced in the arms of the crazy little teenager ghost less than twenty-four hours earlier.

(What had been that other ghost's name? Rachel? Sarah? Harriet? Not remembering was going to bug me all night.)

I shoved those thoughts aside when Valentina turned to me, and brushed away dark hair, exposing her face. She leaned in slowly toward me and opened her mouth.

"Hey!" I didn't jump back, but it was close. "I'm flattered. Really, I am, but I already have a girlfriend. Or someone I thought might one day be… although I'm fairly sure she doesn't feel the same way… and it's not like…"

I paused at the look of confusion on Valentina's face.

"But you already knew all that from having listened to me babble for the past half-year." I swallowed. "You weren't trying to kiss me at all, were you?"

She shook her head, dark curls flying everywhere with the motion. I noticed a few strands pass right through the aluminum siding of our house. *So* cool. Less cool was the way she was wrinkling her nose in apparent disgust. I hadn't *wanted* her to kiss me, but even community college dropouts have feelings.

"I'm sorry," I offered. "What *were* you doing then?"

In reply, she opened her mouth again, like a child might do when their mother needs to stick a thermometer under their tongue. Which is when I realized that my friend had been silent all these months for a reason.

That hypothetical mother wouldn't have had anything to place her equally hypothetical thermometer beneath. Valentina was missing her tongue.

One glance down told me that her nightgown was back to being pristine and pure… which meant the organ had been removed sometime *before* the death that made Valentina a ghost.

"*Oh my God!* I'm *so* sorry," I said in a shocked whisper. "I didn't know. I'm such a moron… and you must be sick of hearing me talk!"

She floated slowly back out of my personal space, the warm San Diego night air immediately rushing in to replace her ghostly chill, but when she had arrived at the far side of the bench, she shook her head, and offered another black-gummed smile.

"I'm not an idiot?"

She waggled her hand and grinned again.

"Sometimes I am?" Well, it was hard to argue with that. "But you don't mind me talking?"

This time, she nodded her head and made a gesture that even I could recognize as an invitation to continue.

"Well, if you *do* ever want me to shut up, just let me know, okay? This is your house too, and you have as much right to peace and quiet as any of us." I looked at her sternly until she nodded in acceptance.

"As far as the case is concerned, do you think you could arrange an earlier meeting with Margaret so I can ask her some questions? Maybe *without* all the other Ladies this time?"

Valentina nodded, hair once again falling in front of her face like a curtain.

My next words were drowned out by a car tearing down the street past our house, its windows rolled down to better share the music being blasted at full volume. Next to me, Valentina's skinny legs swung back and forth in rhythm with the car's music.

"Really?" I asked with a grin. "You like death metal?" It was almost *too* on-the-nose.

She waggled her hand again, even as her legs continued to dance.

"Only kind of? Are you just a fan of music in general?" At her nod, a thought occurred to me. "You know, my bedroom window is just over here." I stood and paced to the far side of the porch, peering around the corner of our house. While my room was in the basement, it had a row of high windows that were located just above ground.

I pointed it out to Valentina. The windows were too narrow for anything but light to enter—and the screen kept out the insects— but if I opened them just a crack… well, there was no reason sound couldn't *exit*.

"If you want," I told her, "I'll leave my stereo on while I'm sleeping. I can't turn it up too loud, or it'll wake my parents, but a few thousand mp3s on shuffle should give you all the music you could possibly want."

She clapped her hands excitedly, literally dancing through the air as we returned to the bench. I could have kicked myself for not making the offer sooner. All those weeks of offering her food and drink, despite knowing that she didn't consume either, when I could have made her haunting that much nicer with the flip of a switch on my ancient mp3 player.

At least I'd thought of it now.

Next to me, Valentina was pointing to the curb where my shiny new Corolla was parked, a confused expression on her face.

"You noticed my new car?"

She nodded and pulled her feet up under her—through the bench—to sit cross-legged next to me.

"Well, you'll never guess who gave it to me."

As I'd done almost every night since finding her on our porch, I regaled Valentina with the story of my day. As always, she was an exceptional audience.

ooo

I had a late dinner with my parents when they got home from the movies and promised to show them my new car in the morning. Before going to sleep, I turned on my mp3 player and its speakers, cranking up the volume enough so that it would carry outside. I stood on my bed to crack the small window open, then dropped back down with a contented sigh.

I was out as soon as my head hit the pillow.

Much later, I woke up again, pillow clutched tightly to me as a stand-in for the cartoon animal I'd been spooning in my dreams.

Jennifer, my 3AM mind informed me. *That* was the name of the teenage ghost who'd attempted to hug me to death.

Those YouTube videos on associative memory were finally starting to pay off.

The mp3 player was still going, of course, playing something light and bouncy, although I couldn't remember that song's name either. I cracked one eye open, and then paused, all thoughts of music forgotten.

Dim light streamed in through the outside window to spotlight Valentina, in my basement bedroom, twirling about in a soundless swirl of nightgown and hair. I watched silently as she danced around and through the furniture.

This wasn't quite what I'd had in mind.

But if it made her happy…?

I was cool with it.

Besides, what could it hurt?

CHAPTER 9

South Park had a vibe that set it apart from the rest of San Diego. Coffee houses next to art galleries next to food stands offering cheap Mexican food. Unwashed space cadets sharing the sidewalk with perky joggers in head-to-toe Lululemon. Two-story-high murals bordering squat rowhouses whose cracked and peeling paint jobs belied their historical significance. Basically, hipster central.

Very Portland-esque.

Or Austin-esque, maybe. I'd never been to either city, but they both seemed to take pride in staying weird.

A chocolate bar and bistro fit into that neighborhood so well that it was hard to imagine Eclipse being located anywhere else. Their food was even better than their service was bad—and their service was legendarily bad—and it had become our default choice for Sunday brunch.

Kayla and Darlene were already inside and seated. I made my way to their table, past the unmanned register and the line of customers waiting for an employee to take notice of their existence.

"Ladies." I sat down next to Darlene. Kayla was sipping delicately from a tall glass of orange juice across the table, looking lean, attractive, and dangerous in a pale grey tank top and khaki shorts. "Thanks for leaving me the window seat."

"We know how much you like to people-watch," D teased. Like Kayla, she had a glass of orange juice in front of her. Unlike Kayla, she was about as dangerous as a fluffy-haired kitten. Maybe even less so. Today's faded t-shirt had a stylized spider on it and the words "I've got red in my ledger", dripping down across the chest. "After all, the future Mrs. John Smith could walk right by at any moment!"

I glanced out the window—just to be sure—but saw only an unshaven man whose potbelly peeked out from under his dirty white tank top. A small hat perched precariously atop what looked like the faded remnants of a Brady Bunch perm.

"Maybe not this very second," Darlene conceded.

"Thank God. I'm not ready to give up on women just yet." I waited patiently for a member of the staff to display a modicum of interest in taking my order. "Besides, who's to say I haven't *already* found Mrs. Right?"

"The fact that you're having brunch with us is a pretty good indicator," suggested Kayla with a smile.

"Nonsense," I told her. "Everyone knows, it's bros before…" I stopped myself before I could get into trouble. "I mean friends before…"

Shit. What rhymed with friends?

"Trends?"

"That doesn't make any sense, but I'm going with it." I thanked Darlene with a smile and a fist bump. "Any girlfriend of mine has to accept that I have certain pre-existing obligations."

"Obligations?!" Darlene snorted.

"Like driving into South Park every month to entertain my friends with the new and ever-exciting tales of my daring forays into the San Diego night life."

"Struck out again, did you?" Kayla asked, dry humor mixed in with a faint dose of sympathy. "Have you thought it might have something to do with that thing you're calling a beard?"

ooo

I'd fought vampires and hiked through hell dimensions. I'd escaped from a burning house surrounded by werewolves and argued policy with a congregation of pixies. But none of that held a candle to the challenge of getting one of Eclipse's many—seemingly idle—employees to come take my order.

I started with direct eye contact. When that strategy failed, I added in a subtle head nod. Then a slight wave of one hand. Then a big wave. Finally, I stood up and walked over to the register, but even though the cashier had finally made an appearance, she was too busy checking someone out—and bagging up the half pound of unbelievably tasty gourmet chocolate they'd bought—to even glance my way. I returned to the table in defeat, convinced that our assigned server had been kidnapped by aliens.

Which sucked, because I was hungry.

And also because alien abduction was probably less fun than Hollywood made it seem.

But mostly because I was hungry.

It was only after I'd exhausted every option short of setting our table on fire that our waitress finally came by, laden down with platefuls of delicious-looking food for my friends. She was short and heavy, with a skullcap of closely cropped hair, but her smile was dazzling. Its wattage trebled as she brought it to bear on Kayla.

"Is there anything else I can get you, honey?" The words positively dripped with innuendo. Out of the corner of my eye, I watched Darlene grip the fork in her hand like it was a dagger. All comparisons to a fluffy kitten immediately vanished.

As a supposed mediator, I probably should have said something to soothe D, but I thought her stabbing the waitress might improve my chances of getting something to eat. At this point, a little bit of bloodshed couldn't hurt, could it?

"We're good, but thank you," Kayla told the waitress, her lovely features expressionless.

I cleared my throat noisily, and both waitress and femmepire glanced in my direction.

"Actually," Kayla amended, "I think my friend here is ready to order."

There was a reason I liked her.

ooo

Say what you might about the service at Eclipse, the food made it all worthwhile. Less than fifteen minutes later, our waitress returned with my order; parmesan biscuits smothered in a sausage gravy with rosemary sea salt. She slid the plate in front of me, flashed another brilliant smile towards our femmepire friend, and then retreated to the kitchen.

Conversation slowed dramatically as we all gave our food the attention it deserved. After inhaling the first biscuit, I gave the two a brief rundown of my case, and what little progress I'd made. Neither Kayla nor Darlene had any advice on how to find an absent ghost, but they were sympathetic listeners, which was almost as good. I even found myself telling them about Valentina's late-night dance session, which elicited an *awww* from Darlene and a concerned look from her femmepire lover.

Throughout my tale, we were regularly interrupted by various members of the staff, all of whom seemed suddenly enthralled with the ash-blonde vampire in their midst.

"Do you ever feel like you're dating a rock star?" I asked Darlene under my breath, after the fifth such interruption. I mean, Kayla was gorgeous and all, but this was borderline ridiculous.

"You have no idea," D responded through gritted teeth. "I mean, who can blame them? K is sex on a stick. But still…"

"Yeah. There are limits." I glanced across the table at Kayla. "K? Would you mind?"

"What's that?" She glanced from me to her girlfriend, and her face softened. "Oh. Sorry, love." Tucking a strand of hair behind one ear, she glanced around the room. Her eyes glittered momentarily, like copper pennies catching the sun.

The effect was immediate, as if a curtain had been lowered about us. The staff suddenly seemed to remember that their jobs involved serving more than just the leggy goddess in their midst. It wasn't like they'd forgotten Kayla entirely—she continued to attract quite a few lingering glances—but their attention faded to a more reasonable level, and the interruptions stopped entirely.

I wasn't always wild about vampire compulsion, but it was hard to deny how useful it could be.

"Sorry," the femmepire said again, polishing off her plate of spiced-pumpkin French toast. "Sometimes I forget the effect we can have on humans."

I shared a concerned look with Darlene. Kayla never forgot anything. It was one of the things that made her so good at her job.

"You affect some of us more than others, sweetie," Darlene said brightly, reaching across the table to clasp her girlfriend's hand, "and not just because you're freaking gorgeous."

The two shared one of those smiles where it was clear the world around them had gone fuzzy and indistinct.

"Yeah," I agreed, "it's also because of your infamous tendency to sunbathe nude in the House gardens."

Kayla snickered, and their tender moment passed by. "It was only the few times, John. And well before I made *your* acquaintance."

I sighed dramatically. "Even so, you know *the effect your kind can have on us humans…*"

"That sounded a bit conceited, huh?"

"Not when it's true."

"Speaking of *femmepires*," Darlene jumped back in, her mouth twitching with delight at the word I'd coined the previous year, "you'll never guess who's back in San Diego, John!"

"Anastasia." The look of surprise on D's face almost made up for the mixed jumble of emotions that swelled within me at Lady Dumenyova's mention.

"How did…?"

"I saw her yesterday." I shrugged, still confused by the whole encounter. "And then again at the tail end of Lucia's meeting. Didn't I tell you?"

"You most certainly did not." Darlene's eyes danced, even as her lips tried mightily to curve downward into a frown. "Which means you're in big trouble. Huge!"

"I'm sure he had a perfectly good reason for sneakily hiding things from us like some sort of traitor," Kayla offered, in an underwhelming show of support. "Isn't that right, John?"

"Uhm." Between the meeting with Lucia, and the news of Kayla's demotion, I'd just forgotten. Or I'd been trying to avoid thinking about an uncomfortable and unhappy issue. One of those.

"Well. It's a good thing we're all here together, with full glasses of orange juice, and nowhere to go then, isn't it?" Darlene smiled sweetly in my direction. "So, spill! Where are you going for your next date?"

"It's been six months, D. I don't think there'll *be* a next date."

"Maybe that's for the best," said Kayla.

"Excuse me?" Darlene stole the words right out of my mouth.

"I know it's not my place to say anything," said the femmepire doing just that, "but you're our friend, John, and I don't want to see you hurt."

"And?"

"Anastasia is old. Her alliance with Queen Lucia began before this country of yours had even been born. In all that time, Xavier is the only man I've heard of who was more than a dalliance and she executed *him* with her bare hands."

"To save my life." Xavier, traitorous Battle Lord and Kayla's predecessor, had been moments away from introducing me to the business-end of his sword.

"Or to protect her Queen," she countered.

"Tomato, tomahto. What's your point?"

"It's a mistake to think of Lady Dumenyova as a person."

"That's unkind. And not at all like you," I murmured. By my side, Darlene had gone quiet, watching her girlfriend with a confused look that I was sure mirrored my own. "If she's not a person, then what is she?"

"Lucia's weapon."

"I've spent enough time with Ana to know she's more than that." I took a deep breath, drawing upon my mediation experience to keep my voice level. "Yeah, she's loyal to Lucia, and a stone cold badass, but she's also smart, and thoughtful, and—" I paused to study the femmepire's face. "What is it that you're not saying?"

"And why is *this* the first time any of us are hearing about it?" agreed Darlene.

Kayla looked uncomfortable. "How much do you know about Lady Dumenyova?"

Hadn't we *just* covered this? I answered anyway. "She's around four hundred years old, has exquisite taste in cars, kicks ungodly amounts of ass, and smiles far too rarely."

"What of her position in the House?"

"She's Lucia's Secundus, or second-in-command. She became the queen's vassal at a young age and followed her into exile here at some point in the past century or so. And between your demotion and Juliette's departure, she's pretty much my only ally on the Council."

"Secundus doesn't mean second-in-command, John."

"Are you sure? I looked it up. It's Latin for second."

"To the People, it has a deeper meaning. Anastasia held that rank long before she joined the Council. In fact, she was groomed for the role since childhood."

"What *is* a Secundus then?" I could already tell I wasn't going to like the answer. One of the things I liked most about Kayla was her blunt honesty. For her to be taking so long to get to the point… well, to quote a certain space smuggler, I had a bad feeling about this.

"The Secundus is a lord or lady's shadow, the echo of their voice, and the extension of their eyes. But most of all," she continued, "they are their blade in the darkness. A Secundus may act without the political repercussions of those actions falling upon their liege."

"K, sweetie," said Darlene, "that just sounded like gobbledygook."

"Totally," I agreed. "What are you saying, Kayla? That Ana is some sort of—"

"Killer." Kayla's voice was cool and brisk, the emotionless tone she employed when combat was unavoidable. "The House assassin and one of the most famous of her kind in centuries. I grew up hearing legends of the Italian Court's Stone Lady."

I tossed the idea about in my head. It made sense. Certainly, Anastasia was as deadly an individual as I'd ever encountered… which was saying a lot, given that the weakest of vampires could squash me like a bug. "Okay. And?"

"I beg your pardon?"

"So what?" I clarified. "When I'm not chasing down missing ghosts or helping werewolves get divorced, I take lousy pictures for a living. I'm in no position to judge. And who among your species *hasn't* killed someone?"

"It's really a question of volume," she began.

"Screw volume! Ana's had every opportunity to hurt me, yet she's gone out of her way to keep me safe. In fact…" I paused, as another new thought worked its way through my biscuit-filled brain. "Wait, she's an assassin?"

"That *is* what I just said…" Kayla gave me a searching look.

"And she left the House in late November." The day after our one and only date, but I wasn't going to dwell on that small fact. Any more than I already had, anyway.

"And returned yesterday… so what?"

"He's got that look on his face again," Darlene murmured, "like he's constipated or just thinking really, really hard. Use your words, sweetie."

"Well, what happened in December, Kayla?"

There was a moment of silence as the femmepire thought it over. I saw the moment the realization hit.

"The scion to the New Mexico Pack and several of his lieutenants disappeared under mysterious circumstances. Their bodies were found weeks later."

"Exactly." Given that Georgie had been behind a plot to kill me—and his younger brother, Jason—I hadn't shed any tears over his demise.

"So, Anastasia was sent to deliver a message to the Pack after their attempted invasion," mused Darlene, effortlessly picking up the thread. "I guess that explains where she disappeared to and why. But that was months ago. What has she been doing since?"

"I don't know," I admitted, the smile sliding from my face, "although supposedly it has something to do with Romania. But you know what? I'm going to find out."

"How?"

"By asking her," I decided. "I left high school behind a long time ago; maybe it's time I started acting like it."

CHAPTER 10

My newfound maturity was a heady thing, empowering and energizing. It also only lasted long enough to get me to my Corolla. With the door closed and my friends gone, I felt that resolve start to slip away. Maybe it would be better to think things through before I tried to speak with Anastasia? I could wear something that was clean and wrinkle-free. Brush my teeth. *Try* to comb my hair. Being presentable *and* prepared couldn't hurt, could it?

I hit speed dial number one on my wonderphone before I could talk myself out of the whole thing. If I truly did want to keep seeing Anastasia, I needed to tell her so.

The phone rang a half dozen times before it clicked over to voicemail. As I'd learned repeatedly over the past six months, Ana didn't even have a message. Instead, a robotic voice informed me of the number I had dialed and offered to take my message.

"Ana, this is John. I'm looking forward to catching up, now that you're back in town. Give me a call whenever you have the time."

Mission accomplished. Sort of.

On the drive home, I received a text and a phone call. Through considerable effort, I resisted my desperate urge to dig out the wonderphone and respond. One ticket might have been a simple mistake, but two tickets would be a pattern of behavior. And I couldn't afford that kind of behavior.

I started to park in front of Ms. Givens' house, stopping only when I remembered that I was no longer driving the neighborhood eyesore. As soon as I was safely parked in front of my house, I grabbed the phone, heart pounding. After six long months, this was the moment of truth.

Or not. There were actually several texts, all of them from Darlene. They read:

> 1:44PM – Sry about brunch. K stressed.
> 1:45PM – Did u figure out a plan for that yet?
> 1:45PM – And what do u mean, J's departure?!?
> 1:46 PM – Dont reply til u get home. $$!!!!

I laboriously translated the texts into something approaching English. It was nice to see that even my friends were trying to help me avoid future tickets. It was less nice to realize that I'd accidentally spilled the beans on Juliette leaving the House.

Oh well. Maybe Juliette should have told Lucia that she was leaving the House. Or told me that it was supposed to be a secret. Or fled the country before the inevitable—and inevitably messy—fallout. Really, considering the handicap I'd been working with, I had done an awesome job of keeping her secret.

For a whole day.

Almost a whole day.

First the ghosts' secret. Now Juliette's. This was *not* my weekend.

I decided not to text Darlene back, in the optimistic—but likely futile—belief that she would just let the whole Juliette thing go. Instead, I checked my missed calls, feeling that same internal cocktail of nerves and excitement. It made more sense that Anastasia would have called me, really. I wasn't sure if she even knew how to text.

Unfortunately, the call wasn't from Ana either. Instead, it was from Kristin, the diminutive head of the local congregation of pixies, and one of the people I'd been unable to reach on Saturday night. I hadn't expected a reply at all—pixies weren't known for their reliability—but it seemed my luck was finally turning. When I called back, she picked up on the first ring.

"Hey Kristin, this is John Smith."

"John! There you are!" I couldn't decide if her voice was truly bubbly and adorable, or if my brain just perceived it that way because it knew she was a foot tall and as cute as a button, with prismatic wings that shimmered like a dragonfly's.

"Sorry I missed you. I was driving when the phone rang."

"And?"

"I called back as soon as I could," I assured her, sidestepping the question. Apparently, I was the only person in all of California who cared about safe driving.

"I got your message last night. You're looking for a ghost?"

"Sort of," I told her, wrestling with exactly how much I should divulge. "I have a client who's interested in the migratory patterns of local spirits." I mentally patted myself on the back. *Migratory patterns? Brilliant!* "I figured if anyone knew what was going on in our town, it would be you and yours."

It was blatant flattery, but it was also kind of true. The pixies were marketing geniuses by trade, and snooping busybodies by nature. They were way, way down the city's unofficial power rankings—while still far above humans—but very little happened within the county that they were unaware of.

"Hmm!" She pondered the subject, humming something that sounded suspiciously like the jingle for our local bail bondsman's commercials. "You know, I think I can put something together for you that might help. And maybe there's even a way we can monetize the effort. I mean, people buy Star Maps, right?" Another few bars of the King Stahlman's Bail Bonds jingle. "If I put my best people on it, we could have it done by dinner. How does eight o'clock sound? Bencotto?"

"Uhm." I hadn't really been looking for a dinner date but wasn't sure how to tell her that.

"Great," she said cheerily. "I'll see you then. Bring your appetite!"

I looked at my cell phone and shook my head. Talking to a pixie was like staring down a hurricane. Sooner or later, you wound up flat on your back, with no memory at all of what had just happened. I was almost glad that Anastasia hadn't called since I suddenly had plans for the evening.

At least Kristin had good taste in Italian.

○○○

I lasted almost an hour before guilt convinced me to give Kayla and Darlene a call. Darlene's first two texts had reminded me that I was supposed to be figuring out a way to get Kayla her job back. In fact, I'd meant to discuss the matter with both women at brunch… until the ever-depressing topic of my non-existent love life had taken center stage.

I was a really crappy friend sometimes.

And if the duo asked me about Juliette? Well, given that the spiky-haired femmepire hadn't been particularly forthcoming about the situation, there wasn't much else I could tell them.

"John," Kayla answered, a bemused tone in her rich voice, "didn't we *just* see you?"

"Yeah, I know. I hope I'm not cutting into your Sunday afternoon or anything?"

"Not at all." In the background, I could hear something that sounded like explosions. "D's just watching superhero movies again."

"She's a keeper."

"Yes, she is." I could visualize Kayla looking over at her tiny girlfriend with a fond smile.

"So anyway, in the middle of all the Ana stuff—"

"I hope I didn't come on too strong," Kayla interrupted. "Maybe I'm wrong about everything. But most of the House is terrified of your would-be girlfriend. Myself included. The stories we've heard… Anyway, I don't want to see you get hurt."

"I know and I appreciate it. Anyway, that's not what I'm calling about. I really didn't mean to spend all of brunch talking about me and my problems."

"It was your turn, I think," she teased.

"Somehow, it's *always* my turn. But I really wanted to talk about you."

"About me?"

"Yeah. I've been thinking a lot about the whole Watch situation, and I thi—"

"John." Kayla's voice was stern. "Didn't I tell you yesterday not to worry about it?"

"Well sure," I admitted, "but when has that stopped me in the past? And D asked me to look into—" There was a loud thump in my ear, like the phone had just been tossed aside. "Uhm, hello?" I heard a door slam, and then the sounds of the television faded away.

"John?" Darlene's voice was hushed when she came on the line a moment later.

"D? What happened to Kayla?"

"She stormed out of here. What did you say?"

"Nothing! I just said we were trying to figure out how to fix her job situation."

"Oh my God! Why would you *tell her that?*"

"Because it's true?" I was starting to get a headache. Another one.

"Of course it's true," she agreed loudly, "but we were supposed to be fixing it without her knowing! Why do you think I texted you instead of calling?"

"I'd have a much easier time keeping secrets," I told her acidly, "if people would just *tell* me when something was supposed to be secret!" I stared up at my bedroom ceiling and counted to ten. "Look, I'm sorry, D…"

"It's fine," she told me, though the tension in her voice suggested just the opposite. "You didn't know. Besides, Kayla doesn't stay mad for very long."

I hoped that was true. Other than my parents, D and K were the only truly happy couple I knew. Plus, they were kind of the poster children for cross-species relationships, a subject near and dear to my own heart.

"Anyway," she continued, "have you made any progress? What did Lucia say?"

"I haven't spoken to her yet," I admitted, "but I did come up with an idea." It only took a few seconds to fill her in on the basics, mainly because it wasn't much of a plan. My bigger concern was…

"Should we keep pushing on this? Kayla's stance on the whole thing seems pretty clear."

"K's happiness is *my* responsibility, whatever she thinks," retorted Darlene, "and I take that responsibility very god damn seriously."

"So, full speed ahead on Operation Get Kayla Her Job Back?"

"Ramming speed, Mr. Smith. Thrusters on full."

"Aye, aye, Captain."

In Star Trek, ramming another ship was usually the last act of a captain with no other options. I really hoped that analogy didn't hold true here.

At least neither of them had asked me about Juliette.

CHAPTER 11
IN WHICH SMALL IS ANOTHER WORD FOR SNEAKY

I arrived at Bencotto at twenty past eight, which either made me fashionably late or unspeakably rude. I'd spent three hours trying to dig up more information on Graciela and the White Ladies, an hour ironing out the details of my Kayla plan… and more time than I was willing to admit watching cat videos on YouTube.

Those suckers were just too darn cute.

I'd have been even later if I hadn't lucked into an empty parking spot on Fir Street. Someone was clearly looking out for me. I offered a small prayer of gratitude to whoever our local demigod of parking might be.

The entire street-facing side of Bencotto was glass, offering a great view of passers-by to the diners inside, and a great view of the diners to those of us in the street. I scanned for Kristin as I walked to the host's desk but didn't see her. Given her size, that was not altogether unexpected.

"Welcome to Bencotto, sir," the elderly man at the host's desk told me, carefully ignoring my disheveled state. At least my jacket was nice: a hip-length leather coat I'd inherited from my mediator predecessor. And by *inherited*, I mean *stolen from his closet* a week or so after his untimely, violent, and very messy death. Lucia's people had burned the whole place down soon after, so I saw myself as more savior than thief. Thanks to me, that leather coat could continue to fulfill its destiny of looking completely badass.

"Hi there," I said with a winning smile. "I'm running a bit late, but I believe my companion might already be here? Kristin? We had an eight o'clock reservation."

He scanned the list in front of him and nodded. "Yes, sir. She and her guests have already been seated. Eduardo will show you to your table."

Guests? Nobody had said anything about guests. Was this going to be a multi-pixie presentation, or had Kristin dug up a ghost expert to help with the map?

At least it meant our dinner *wasn't* a date. I had nothing against pixies, but a five-foot height difference seemed to be an insurmountable obstacle for any relationship. Plus, rumor had it that Kristin had traded her last boyfriend *and* his pet mouse for a prime commercial spot on the Super Bowl pre-game show. As I'd learned while mediating for the pixies, small was just another word for sneaky.

At the host's direction, Eduardo led me into the restaurant and up the stairs. Tucked away in the corner was Kristin, all eleven inches of her. And as the host had told me, she was not alone; she had a man and a woman seated with her.

"John!" bubbled Kristin as I neared the group. The pixie soared across the table in a shower of iridescent dust that was only half as colorful as the bits of scarves she had sewn together into a small but fashionable dress. That dress had me momentarily revisiting the whole *date-a-pixie* topic.

Darlene was right. It really had been way too long since I'd gotten laid.

"I was beginning to think you weren't coming," she scolded, wings beating furiously to keep her stable in mid-air, "and why is your face so hairy?"

I took a peek at the tables around us, but nobody had noticed the live-action Disney character in their midst, which meant Kristin's glamour was in full effect. The other diners would see whatever she wanted; presumably someone tall, elegant and mysterious. Or fabulously rich, which was just as good.

That was just me guessing though. For all I knew, she could have disguised herself as a seventy-five-year-old truck driver. Or she might have been straight-up invisible, causing me to look like a nutcase who enjoyed talking to himself in the middle of crowded restaurants. Being immune to mind control in all its many facets had been—quite literally—a life saver in the past, but it kind of sucked that I didn't at least have the *option* to see whatever illusions were being cast.

"Sorry to be late," I said, ignoring her unsolicited criticism of my beard. "Parking was a huge pain."

"Don't spend another thought on it." She took me by the arm, her small hand making my bicep look enormous by contrast, and dragged me to the table. "There are some people I'd like you to meet!"

"You know," I told her, just loud enough so the others could hear, "if this is about a timeshare or some sort of multi-level marketing opportunity, I've already been to plenty of those meetings." Four of them, to be precise. They'd all ended right around the time the presenter realized I could barely afford my electricity bill, let alone the *limited time, bargain-priced, pseudo-franchise buy-in opportunity* they were pitching.

The woman waiting for us laughed softly and rose to shake my hand. "Nothing so crass, thankfully." As far as I could tell, she was as human as I was, in her mid-to-late thirties, with golden skin and glossy black hair that fell well past her shoulders. Her grip was firm without being flirty. "I asked Kristin if she might arrange our introduction while I was in town. I'm delighted to have the opportunity to meet San Diego's mediator at last. I am Nepenthe."

"I feel happier already," I quipped, winning a smile.

A *very* small smile.

"You get that sort of joke a lot?" In Greek literature, nepenthe had been one of the first anti-depressants; a drug of forgetfulness. Basically, Eternal Sunshine of the Spotless Mind without Jim Carrey, a computer, or two hours of deeply felt angst.

"Yours was one of the more charming renditions," Nepenthe assured me, turning to introduce her companion. "And this is Tom."

"Thomas," corrected the man, in a whiney tone that suited his appearance perfectly. He was small and dressed in black: shirt, vest, pants, shoes, socks, goatee… even his fingernails had been painted to match. His grip was warm and a little bit moist, and he did his best to crush my hand as if he were a middle linebacker for the Chargers, and not the world's oldest goth.

I disliked him on sight. And not because he had just slimed my hand. I had a great radar for dicks and Tommy-boy was showing up on that radar like a dick of epic proportions.

Not *that* kind of dick radar.

And by epic proportions, I really meant…

Oh, hell.

I decided to scrub *dick radar* from my mental vocabulary.

John Smith, creature of the night, would have introduced Tommy to the business-end of a katana, unwilling to dirty his fangs with such a meal when he had gorgeous blood donors awaiting him at home. That guy was all kinds of awesome.

John Smith, furry Alpha of the Pack, would have simply torn the little man's head clean off. He was… well, considerably less awesome, but still kind of cool in his own fuzzy way.

But John Smith, private eye and out-of-work mediator…?

I gritted my teeth, offered a smile, and took my seat.

Where I wiped my hand on the tablecloth.

As soon as I was settled, the waiter arrived to take our orders. The others already had their drinks, and I fumbled my way through the menu as quickly as possible, settling on a sausage fettuccine which looked awesome and would only add three inches to my waistline.

When the waiter had departed, I looked at Kristin—who was sitting *on* the table next to her plate—and Nepenthe.

"I'm always happy to make new friends, especially over good food, but I'm guessing there's something you two wanted to talk about? Or is Nepenthe an expert on the migratory patterns we spoke about earlier, Kristin?"

"Migratory patterns?" Nepenthe quirked one eyebrow, which pretty much answered that question.

"I have my best people working on that, John," Kristin assured me, "but it's taking longer than expected. Anyway, this seemed like too rich an opportunity for us to pass up."

Now *that* sounded like the sort of line I'd been fed in the time-share meetings. If the pixie started throwing in phrases like *synergistic relationship*, I was going home.

Rich, on the other hand, was a word I liked very much. As much as I needed to make some actual progress on Graciela's disappearance, it wouldn't hurt to hear what Kristin's friend had to say. "Well, it's a pleasure to meet you, Nepenthe."

"I'm here too," interjected the small man at her side.

"Sure thing, dude." I went back to addressing Nepenthe. "What is it that I can do for you? I *am* currently available for mediations."

"What a shock," scoffed Thomas. "Don't worry; if we need to have a minor internal dispute escalate into a full-fledged war, we know just who to call."

That... well, actually that kind of stung.

"Shouldn't you be off somewhere writing bad poetry?"

"You want bad poetry?" His voice lowered ominously, and he waved a hand in my direction while muttering under his breath. A moment passed, and then he stood. "Now then, look upon me and despair!"

"Uhm." I looked to Kristin for aid, but the pixie just shrugged. "How about... no?"

"Thomas." Nepenthe's voice was mild, but the other man wilted almost immediately. As he sank back into his chair, she turned an appraising eye on me.

"It's true then."

"What's true?"

"That you are a unique individual," she said simply. Which was kind of a flattering way to phrase it, really. "If I hadn't just witnessed it, I would never have believed someone without any training could be so utterly immune to illusion."

"I did take taekwondo for a few months," I offered inanely. "Wait... is that what that was? An illusion?" I smirked in Thomas' direction. "Weak sauce, dude."

Look upon me and despair? Talk about embarrassing.

"My deepest apologies." Nepenthe offered a small bow without leaving her seat. "My adjutant has been under a great deal of stress these past few months, to the detriment of his otherwise considerable social graces."

She was nice, and pretty, if that mattered—and it does to most people—but it was impossible not to treat that last point with considerable skepticism. As for the apology itself… well, if I was any judge of character—and I assumed I had to be, after several years as a private eye—she was sincere. Which was a rarer thing than you might expect.

I decided to meet her halfway. A courteous individual was a well-paid individual. And I really did want to try the fettuccine.

"Don't mention it. We can't always be at our best, especially in difficult situations. And did you say *adjutant?* Are you both in the army then?"

Nepenthe's laugh was as pleasant as the rest of her. "We couldn't be less of an army if we tried. I represent the Children of the Sun, which is the admittedly grandiose name we chose for our coven." She leaned across the table, and stage whispered. "It was an open vote. What can you do, right?"

Having witnessed democracy in action with our local werewolf pack, I couldn't help but grin. "Coven? You're witches?" Was that the polite term? For the sake of my bank account, I dearly hoped so.

"Minus the pointy hats!" chirped Kristin, who was busy drinking her cocktail through a straw almost half her size.

"Why didn't anyone tell me there were witches in San Diego? That is so cool! Can you turn someone into a frog?"

"Transformation spells are a bit of a myth, I'm afraid," she told me with a twinkle in her eye, "and they would be illegal, if they existed. Our coven is based up in Temecula, but there are a few solitary practitioners down here in the city. I'd be happy to introduce you. Many of them are… well, a little bit eccentric, but charming once you get to know them."

"That would be fantastic," I told her enthusiastically. The key to running a successful business was networking. Or so I'd read. As marketing strategies went, it seemed more productive than taking out yet another Yellow Pages ad, even if "Got Mediation?" *was* an amazing tag line. "But if you aren't looking for a mediator, what do you need me for? Surveillance? Background checks? Security audits?"

"I beg your pardon?"

"Mr. Smith also does investigative work on the side," Kristin explained. "He handled a job for the Superchargers tribe last year."

"Ah." Nepenthe took a sip from her wine glass. "Actually, I wasn't looking to hire you at all."

My visions of dollar signs faded away.

"Instead," the witch continued, unaware that she'd just dealt a death blow to my dreams of financial solvency, "I was hoping to speak with you about a project that is both near and dear to my own heart."

"I think you'll like this, John," Kristin chimed in confidently. "You and the coven have a lot of things in common. There's potential here for a truly synergistic relationship."

And *there* was the magic phrase.

Luckily for Nepenthe, our waiter returned just then with several trays of food. My fettuccine looked phenomenal and smelled even better. *And* there was fresh garlic bread. I picked up my fork and waved it magnanimously at the witch and the pixie.

"I'm all ears."

Some people say that the way to a man's heart is through his stomach. I'd love to tell those people all the reasons that adage is both ridiculous and borderline insulting to my gender… but I'm usually too busy eating to bother.

CHAPTER 12

IN WHICH THE QUEEN IS A SUBJECT
AND THE SUBJECT IS A QUEEN

The food was awesome, and the company was too. Kristin was a great dinner companion once you accepted that every third or fourth sentence out of her mouth would be an attempt to sell you something. Nepenthe, meanwhile, had the unruffled calm of a life-long yogi, and a collection of entertaining stories about life as a witch.

And Thomas? Well, not even San Diego's skyline was perpetually free of clouds. He remained a dick, but at least he was being quiet. That was a win in my book.

When we'd all made sufficient headway in our respective entrees, Nepenthe took up the conversation again. "Part of the reason I wanted to meet you was because of your success with San Diego's Pack last year."

"Success?" I flashed back to my multiple days of captivity, the aborted attempts to infect me with lycanthropy, and the fact that I'd almost gotten the entire Pack wiped out. "I mean… of course! Success!"

"I know you've only recently been introduced to the realities of our world, John, but I suspect you can still appreciate how rare a thing it is to see democracy take root in the traditionally feudal domains of the supernatural."

"Well, a lot of the credit goes to Carolyn Hawthorne," I admitted. "All I did was make the suggestion… and resolve her marital dispute… and stave off an invasion that might have left her Pack dead and eastern San Diego a bloody wasteland."

Come to think of it, it really *had* been a success. I sent Thomas a superior smile, but he was too busy cutting his ravioli into long thin strands to acknowledge my awesomeness.

"I plan to speak with Mrs. Hawthorne about my proposal but wanted to meet with you first. As San Diego's mediator, you occupy a position of great significance. Your support for our cause could potentially sway much of the city."

"Really?" I looked to Kristin for confirmation, and the pixie nodded her tiny head gracefully while chewing on an olive the size of her fist. "You do know there's another mediator in town now, right?" said the part of my brain that clearly wanted my business to crash and fail.

"We've heard as much," Nepenthe admitted, "but he is new to the city, and has yet to prove himself here."

"I don't know," I found myself saying, "he seemed pretty trustworthy to me. Not to mention capable."

Seriously, I asked my brain; *what are you doing?!*

"You've spoken with him then?" For the first time, Nepenthe seemed surprised.

"Well, no. But I saw a picture." I shrugged. "Seems like a good guy, really. I'm looking forward to meeting him."

"That is *precisely* the sort of attitude that makes me think we could be friends and allies," the witch told me, her lips curving into a smile that warmed me considerably.

"Allies in what, exactly?" I pressed. Beneath the pleasant blissfulness that a good meal and ample flattery had provided, a small part of me remained alert and even suspicious. Multiple near-death experiences had that effect on a guy.

"In establishing a council for the various species of San Diego, one with equal representation for all, where even the smallest disputes could be settled through democracy and debate, rather than bloody conflict."

That sounded pretty good. And potentially lucrative for yours truly. The problem was that San Diego already had an established power structure, and the people at the top weren't going to want to relinquish their authority. Especially since one of them was…

"Yes," she continued, reading my face like it was a book. "Queen Lucia Borghesi must be dealt with first."

ooo

There were two reasons I never played poker. The first, obviously, was that I didn't have money to waste on anything but beer and dead-end first dates. The second was that I possessed quite possibly the worst poker face in the history of poker faces.

I'd been working on both of those issues for years without any success, and I was sure Nepenthe saw every emotion I experienced in response to her declaration. Hell, she probably knew what I was feeling better than I did, because I was… conflicted.

And a little bit shocked at how easily a nice dinner had turned into a conspiracy to commit murder.

"Uhm…" I began uncertainly, half waiting for armed police officers to leap out from behind the nearest potted plant, "I'm sorry.

I've never been Lucia's biggest fan, but I'm not going to help plot her death."

I whispered the last part as quietly as possible, aware from a lifetime of television procedurals that listening devices might be trained upon us at that very moment.

"Her… death?" The fine lines that appeared like magic around Nepenthe's eyes were the first sign that she might be closer to forty than I had previously guessed. She peered at me quizzically for a moment, and then began to laugh.

Kristin quickly joined in—whether out of solidarity or because it seemed the political thing to do—leaving only Thomas and me as reluctant comrades in solemnity. Although I think he was mostly just sulking.

"Mr. Smith…" Nepenthe finally managed, when her laugh petered out into surprisingly girlish giggles, "I didn't say we should kill her!"

"Queen Lucia Borghesi must be dealt with," I quoted, adding an even more ominous tone to the pronouncement.

"Meaning *talked to!* Convinced that a city-wide Council is in her best interests." She pulled a compact out of her purse and checked to make sure the tears of laughter hadn't caused her mascara to run. They hadn't… which was more proof of witchcraft, from what little I knew about makeup. "We're not monsters, Mr. Smith. Really, that's what this whole initiative is about."

"The world has changed in the last few centuries," she continued. "Regardless of species or talent, we need to change with it. The old ways are wasteful, ego-driven, and destructive. If we humans have managed to evolve beyond cave-dwelling Neanderthals, the rest of the world's species should be able to do the same."

I glanced over at Kristin. There weren't a lot of supernatural individuals who would be thrilled to be compared to my own kind, and Nepenthe was busy holding humanity up as a *positive* role model.

"Don't expect an argument from me, John. When's the last time my congregation had a say in what happened around this city?"

I acknowledged the point and turned back to Nepenthe. "Let's say I agree with you that the current system *is* archaic. Why San Diego? Why not someplace more important... New York? San Francisco? Rome?"

"Why San Diego? Maybe because there've been a half-dozen armed conflicts here in the last decade?"

"The last decade? Try the last year," I muttered.

"Or even the last year. Which tells me that our city's power structure is flawed at its core." She shrugged, her voice matter of fact. "I'm an idealist, Mr. Smith, not an idiot. What I'm proposing is a radical shift. The best chance of implementing it lies in finding a place—"

"Where the ruling species are in disarray and vulnerable?"

"Where the population has already been exposed to the flaws in the current system," she corrected.

I thought of Lucia, vaguely conscious that her presence in the back of my mind seemed more muted than usual. Flawed was *one* way to describe her rule. But tyrannical seemed a lot closer to the truth.

"And it doesn't hurt that you and your coven live just an hour north of here, I'm sure." I shook my head slowly. "I still don't see Lucia agreeing to the idea, no matter how persuasive your argument."

"Of course not." Nepenthe took a slow sip of wine. "That is where you come in. As someone who has a formal relationship with the House and is the mediator of this city, I believe she will listen to you."

She really didn't know Lucia at all.

"Not to mention the matter of your… special bond with the queen," the witch continued. "You are the next best thing to a Council member in that House."

"Uhm, yeah. Not so much." I fumbled a bit for how to best explain the situation without making myself look bad in front of two potential clients. "Look, I won't deny that Queen Lucia has listened to my advice occasionally—very occasionally—but our relationship is less amicable than you think."

Amicable. Nice. That was a *very* professional sounding word!

"It was my understanding that there are few relationships closer than that between a vampire and her blood-bond." Nepenthe looked concerned.

Blood-bond sounded way more polite than *thrall*.

"I suppose that might be true," I hedged, "assuming both people had agreed to that bond."

Her mouth opened in a small, surprised O. "Now, *this* I hadn't heard. What happened?"

"Long story," I told her, "and probably not one suited for dinner conversation. Things happened, words were said, and now we're stuck in a relationship neither of us is particularly thrilled with."

"I don't mean to disagree with you, John, but if the queen was unhappy with your relationship, she would have broken the bond."

"Apparently, it's not possible." I pointed at my temple. "One of the downsides of my so-called gift."

"Is that what they told you?" Nepenthe met my eyes from across the table. "John, *any* bond can be severed. My coven could do it easily enough."

"Seriously?" I didn't want to get my hopes up, but the idea of not having Queen Crazy Pants in my head was irresistible.

"A vampire's bond is just energy, woven to connect two psyches. Admittedly, it is weakest at its inception, and it does strengthen over time, but…" She paused. "Has the queen started seeing through your eyes yet, or speaking with your voice?"

"What? No!" I'd been informed of that possibility once before, but the idea remained freaking terrifying. "But… I *have* been feeling her more strongly. You know, in my head. Are you saying that it will keep getting worse?"

"For someone who volunteers for the position, I'm told it's amazing. We have bonded life-partners in my own coven, and they seem blissfully happy with the arrangement."

"Witches bond too…?"

"Not by blood," she assured me, "but energy is energy. The only real distinction is in our chosen vehicle for interacting with it."

"That makes sense," I admitted. "Anyway, *this* relationship wasn't by choice."

"Then we will endeavor to end it for you. Slavery is one of the many abominable institutions I would see abolished."

"That would be awesome. If you really think you can…?"

"Witches specialize in energy, John. Tell me," she asked, "can you feel your queen, even now?"

Having just recently felt at the bond in my head, I didn't have to pause to consider. "Yes, but she's a little bit… fuzzy?"

As fuzzy as my skills at self-diagnosis, anyway.

"Precisely." Nepenthe sat back with a satisfied air.

"Wait… that's you?"

"Indeed. A general spell to interfere with scrying and other magical forms of observation. Ending your bond will require far more energy and a spell attuned to you specifically, but I have no doubt as to the end result."

I decided then and there that witches might very well be my favorite people ever. If I'd had even a shred of magical talent in me… well, John Smith, Warlock of the Ninth Realm, sounded pretty badass, didn't it? I also decided to forgive Kristin for luring me to Bencotto under false pretenses. I *still* needed that ghost map, but a plate of fettucine and the possible end to my bond were phenomenal consolation prizes.

"Assuming you're right and Lucia has been lying to me about not being able to sever the bond—" And that sounded like *just* the sort of thing the femmepire would do. "—she's not going to be happy with you for interfering. Or with me for that matter."

"He's right," agreed Thomas, piping up for the first time in a long while. "This gains us nothing. We should just let the mediator wallow in his misery."

"Not *at all* my point, but it would lessen my odds of convincing Lucia to… you know, give peace a chance."

Such odds were already infinitesimally low, but I wasn't going to point that out a second time. Especially not to the people who might finally give me freedom.

"It will take some time to fashion the spell, Mr. Smith," said Nepenthe, "and we would need to cast it on the next full moon, which is still several weeks away. So, if you wished to speak with Lucia in the meantime…?"

"I can do that. But again, I can't promise anything. Lucia is always focused on what's best for her."

"With luck, you'll be able to show her that a strong and unified San Diego will reflect well upon her House. She can only profit from a prolonged time of peace."

"I'll do my best," I told her. I meant it too. I'd already had enough near-death experiences to last me a lifetime… and lost too many friends or potential friends in the process. If a new approach could keep people like Kayla, Juliette, Carolyn, or even Anastasia alive… "But what if she says no?"

"Then she says no." The witch shrugged her slender shoulders. "And we will continue to speak with the other races of San Diego. The vampires may be a power, but they're not the *only* power. If the rest of the city buys into our movement, the queen will have no choice but to accede, or risk being isolated entirely."

"And my…" I pointed again to my temple.

"We will get started on the spell immediately," Nepenthe assured me. "You will be freed, regardless of Lucia's decision. Do you have any vials on you, Tommy dear?"

The smaller man reached into a pocket of the jacket that hung on his chair, and extracted a glass tube, kind of like the chemistry beakers I'd played with in high school. He handed it to Nepenthe.

"We will need something to bind our spell to, John." She motioned with the vial. "A few drops of blood should suffice."

"I thought witches didn't use blood," I told her. After the past year, the idea of giving blood was not an attractive one.

"It serves as a marker," said Thomas stiffly. "Or haven't you ever heard of DNA?"

"In a city of more than one million people," Nepenthe explained, "it is necessary to have some way to direct the spell. You will still need to be present for the final casting, of course, but this would allow us to work on the preliminaries in your absence. Unless you're okay spending the next three weeks with us in Temecula?"

I gave the idea serious consideration. Temecula was wine country, and while I was more of a beer guy, I didn't mind the occasional glass. But Graciela was missing. There was no way I could just leave town.

I shook my head reluctantly.

"Very well then." She reached across the table and took my hand in hers. Her fingers were calloused, the hands of someone who worked for a living. It was an obvious and immediate contrast to the silky-smooth skin of Lucia herself. "You may feel a slight sting."

Thomas handed Nepenthe what appeared to be an acupuncture needle, and she pricked the tip of one of my fingers. I'd always hated having my blood drawn, but after Juliette's feeding, Xavier's car bomb, and my—thankfully interrupted—werewolf infection, the needle's prick barely registered. Nepenthe squeezed a few drops of blood into the small vial.

"And that should do it." She stoppered up the vial and tucked it away into her purse with a smile. "Now then, who feels like tiramisu?"

CHAPTER 13

To nobody's shock, *I* felt like tiramisu. And a cappuccino. In fact, if I hadn't had plans to meet up with my best friend Mike afterward, I would have tried an after-dinner drink as well. Especially once I found out that Nepenthe was paying.

Witches really *were* all kinds of awesome.

However, all that food and drink had an effect. After saying goodbye to Kristin and the witches, I took a slight detour to the restroom. I was washing my hands when Thomas sauntered in. He skirted the stalls and took the sink next to me.

"You know," he said, "I told Nepenthe from the beginning that this whole dinner was a waste of our time and money."

"You're not a fan of Italian?" I grabbed a paper towel from the dispenser and began drying my hands. "I thought it was pretty good."

"I suspect you'd eat dog food if it were free. You may have a few people fooled with this show of respectability, but I know better. You're a rinky-dink little private dick with one not-so-useful ability to your name. If the vampire queen hadn't bonded you, nobody would even know who you are."

"Well, you'd be the expert on that subject."

"Excuse me?"

"Being unknown, little, and a dick. Although you do a poor job of keeping that last fact private." I flashed a victorious smile. "In fact, after your behavior tonight, I'm guessing Nepenthe regrets bringing you along. If you don't watch out, she might banish you back to whatever coffee shop she found you lurking in."

"Only a fool would speak so to a witch," he hissed.

"Hold on." I held out a hand to stop him in mid-speech. *"You're* a witch?"

"You just might be even more stupid—"

"Seriously, shouldn't you be a warlock, or a sorcerer, or..."

"Witch is a gender-neutral term," Thomas barked angrily.

I tossed the paper towel and regarded him with a pitying eye. "Are you sure they didn't just tell you that?"

He puffed up like a rooster and took the half step necessary to bring him into my personal space. It was... well, kind of uncomfortable. Starting a conversation in a restroom was already a little bit out-of-bounds, but this sort of behavior was entirely against the bro code.

Plus, his cologne was overpowering in close quarters.

"Look," I said, putting on my mediator hat, "I don't like you, and that feeling is clearly mutual, but I *am* on board with Nepenthe's plan. That means we may end up working together. So, let's just bury the hatchet and call it a night. After all, you already took your best shot, magically-speaking, and I'm too full of fettuccine to dropkick you into next week."

"That was nowhere near my best shot."

"Thank goodness, because it was just embarrassing," I said sweetly. "Regardless, your magic doesn't work on me, which means you're just a middle-aged goth with an overdeveloped sense of self-importance."

Instead of snarling another angry reply, Thomas smiled. "Your trick may protect you from illusion, but magic is an art of many tools—"

"I know. I'm looking at one of them right now."

"—and you doubt it at your own peril," he finished, spitting on the floor at my feet and departing.

"Well, that was gross and not particularly terrifying." I checked my appearance in the mirror one last time—hair still a mess, physique still inadequate—and turned to leave.

As I reached for the door, its tarnished brass handle transformed into the oversized, scaled head of some sort of monster rattlesnake. I stumbled backwards, falling onto my ass with a yell.

What the hell?

The snake was missing most of its body and was attached to the door just like the handle it had replaced, but that minor fact didn't seem to inconvenience it… or keep it from whipping its diamond-shaped head at me whenever I tried to get close.

Nor did it interfere with its ability to bite; something the demon snake demonstrated with horrific swiftness when I threw a handful of paper towels in its direction. Venom dripped from large fangs and splattered onto the tile floor with a hiss. Whatever Thomas had done, that snake was real, and it was dangerous.

I reviewed—and discarded—a half dozen plans for exiting the bathroom. Unlike my vampire allies, I wasn't fast enough to just dodge the snake's strike and rip it apart. Unlike my werewolf compadres, I didn't have any supernatural regeneration to keep the venom from swiftly killing me. And unlike my ghost employers…

well, if I could have phased through walls, the demon-snake-knob wouldn't have posed any challenge at all.

A small voice in my brain loudly insisted that Thomas would never risk Nepenthe's ire with a potentially fatal spell… but I wasn't prepared to put that to the test. If I was wrong… well, even if Tommy-boy earned three witch demerits *and* had his cookie rations cut for a month, I'd be too dead to enjoy it.

I was stuck there in the bathroom for another twenty minutes. After fifteen, the snake turned back into a handle. After eighteen, I was convinced that the reversal wasn't part of some fiendish plan to get me to lower my guard. Even then, it took me an extra two minutes to work up the nerve to grab the handle, jerk open the door, and flee the premises.

By the time I made it to the street, I was late for meeting Mike… and witches were no longer my favorite people ever.

ooo

I was rattled enough by the near-fatal encounter—snakes and bathrooms were a terrible enough mix already without throwing a little black magic into the mix—that I promptly took a wrong turn as I left Bencotto. I found myself heading north on India Street. It wasn't the end of the world, obviously, even if I was supposed to be heading downtown, in the exact opposite direction. Little Italy (and the rest of the city for that matter) had its share of one-way roads, but all I had to do was take a left, and then another onto Kettner to remedy the situation. That ranked low on the difficulty scale, even for a Sunday night.

What I'd forgotten—somehow—was how long the light at the intersection of India and Hawthorn could be. I watched cars blitz down the hill in front of me for a good minute, while my own stoplight continued to shine a dull—possibly malevolent—red. After two minutes, I gave up and pulled out my wonderphone.

"I know I *just* got a ticket for doing this," I told myself while glancing in the rearview mirror to make sure there weren't any cops around, "but those laws only apply while driving. Which I won't be doing until this light turns green sometime in 2015."

That settled, I placed two calls. The first was to one of the three local ghost tour groups I'd identified in my online research the day before. This company was notable both for covering a wide range of local haunted properties and for being much, much cheaper than their competition. Unfortunately, they were fully booked. Their earliest opening wasn't until Wednesday.

Who would have thought ghost tours would be so popular?

I mean… San Diego had *beaches*.

And bars.

And a professional baseball team. Sort of.

I shook my head at both the delay and the cost, and reserved a spot on the Wednesday tour, adding a reminder to my phone using the sweet new app I'd just purchased the week prior. I wasn't expecting any real breaks in my case from the tour, but a little bit of local knowledge couldn't hurt.

As for the second call? Well, let's just say that Thomas' little bathroom performance—another phrase I swore to never think again—had done its part to dim my rosy feelings towards the Temecula coven. Even if the dude was just a major dick—and God knew our city was full of them—and not representative of the whole coven, his spell had convinced me not to take any more chances.

I was going to keep an eye on my new witch acquaintances.

That said, I'd promised Mike I'd meet him for a beer. And that sounded way more entertaining than unpaid late-night detective work. So, I did what any clever-minded entrepreneur would do; I subcontracted the work to someone who preferred being paid in tequila shots rather than hard currency.

I was just ending that call when a loud honk alerted me to the fact that the light had finally turned green. I tossed my wonderphone into the passenger seat and headed downtown.

Full of fettucine as I was, I only lasted an hour at the bar. Mike's taunts followed me into the night as I made my way back to my Corolla. Between the ghosts and the vampires, the pixies and the witches, it had been a long weekend, and my feet dragged with every step.

My parents' house was dark, and there was no sign of Valentina when I arrived. I shuffled downstairs to my bedroom, splashed some water on my face, tossed my clothes into the pile near the hamper, turned on my mp3 player, and passed out on the bed.

If there was a second night of dancing, I wasn't awake to see it.

CHAPTER 14

I don't know whether it was the day of phenomenal (and free) food—first at Eclipse and then at Bencotto—or the marginal amount of light exercise I'd been adding to my daily routine, but I slept like a log and woke up on Monday feeling fantastic. A glance at my alarm clock told me it was only seven, but I felt like I'd gotten a full nine or ten hours of sleep. I rolled out of bed with a minimum of grumbling, determined to make the day a productive one.

After a quick shower, I strolled back into my bedroom and saw that someone had stacked several sheets of yellowing newspaper atop my dresser, shifting aside the pile of clothing that had been slowly growing there for the past month. The newspapers were older than I was and deeply stained. They appeared to be a collection of articles from the 1962 and 1963 print editions of the San Diego Union… a paper which I could only assume had been a predecessor of the modern Union Tribune (or, as it had been recently renamed—in a desperate attempt to be cool—the UT-San Diego).

The clippings centered on the killing of several immigrant women in San Ysidro, a neighborhood just to the south of my own hometown of Chula Vista and—more importantly—just north of the Mexican border. I scanned through the articles as I pulled on a t-shirt and shorts. There wasn't a ton of information, but it was all ugly.

In marked contrast to the televised images of hippies, peace, and harmony—the sixties and seventies had been a bloody time, even by San Diego's surprisingly terrible standards. Amid nation-wide public unrest, an unknown number of undocumented immigrants had been killed over the span of a few months. What made the incident in these newspaper clippings different—and sufficiently noteworthy to merit four separate articles—was that the bodies found had all been young women. Four of the five victims had never been identified and would likely remain anonymous forever, but the fifth...

Ah ha.

The fifth had worn a woven belt with the name Graciela stitched into the leather near the buckle.

I read carefully through each article, doing my best to ignore the ugly details as I sifted for clues that might help me find the missing ghost. Instead, I only ended up with a slightly better understanding of the woman's history. That and a serious case of nausea and the heartfelt need to travel back in time to hunt down a serial killer. If anyone deserved to burn for all eternity in Gehenna...

As I put the clippings back into a pile and moved them to one corner of the dresser, a small note fell to the carpet. An address and the words *Monday, Midnight* had been written in dark blue ink. Below that was an illegible signature, but the M told me the note had been written by Marge, the robed ghost I'd spoken with on Ghost Hill.

Valentina had come through yet again.

Next, I grabbed my wonderphone. It still wasn't even eight yet, but I had fourteen unread emails—all spam—and two new voicemails. Apparently, I wasn't the only early riser in San Diego.

The first message was from Steve. The burly manpire had gotten me an appointment with Lord Kala at the Bitter End and had promised to meet me on Fifth to escort me through the portal. An escort was a necessity, given the portal's anti-human bias, but Steve was also clearly looking for an excuse to spend more time with his wereboar boy toy.

At least someone's love life was working out.

The second voicemail was from the ghost tour I'd signed up for. Apparently, there had been a cancellation for today's tour, and there was now a spot available if I wanted to switch. I'd have to skip dinner to squeeze the tour in after work and before my meeting with Kala and subsequent appointment with Marge, but time was money.

In a matter of days, I'd gone from being the city's laziest private investigator to one of its busiest. It was nice to feel like I was making progress, both on Graciela's case, and in what my dad often described as my *glacially slow professional development*, but it was going to make for a hectic Monday.

Hopefully, the demigod would have some food at his bar.

I grabbed breakfast on the drive to my Logan Heights office. With the sort of fortification that only an Egg McMuffin could provide, I planned to spend my morning cross-referencing the articles Valentina had provided me. And I could see if there were any known hauntings near San Ysidro, where Graciela's body had been discovered.

And yeah… at some point, I'd also have to track down my rival mediator for a friendly chat. And figure out how best to broach the subject of Nepenthe's democratic dream with Queen Lucia Crazy

Pants. And have another—hopefully less confusing—talk with Juliette. And get in touch with Anastasia. And check back in with Darlene on her portion of my Kayla plan. And…

On any other Monday, I might have found myself crumbling under the weight of so many people's needs and expectations, but today I felt a renewed sense of energy and optimism. First, I'd find Graciela. Then, I'd deal with everything else.

As the world-renowned poets at Nike once said: just do it.

ooo

It was outside my office in Logan Heights where I faced the first conundrum of the day. As I pulled to a stop, it occurred to me that I was parking my shiny new Corolla on the very same street where its storied predecessor had gained a delightful penis-graffiti decor. My beautiful car's brilliant white paint job was the next best thing to a sign saying *Please! Paint genitalia here in varying sizes and colors! Anatomical exactness preferred but not required!*

I won't lie; part of me wanted to just turn around and drive back home. I'd had the car all of two days and was feeling damn protective of it.

One glance at the faded newspaper clippings ended that debate. There were more important things at stake. *Besides,* I reminded myself, *the only reason they tagged the old Corolla was because you left it parked for almost a week. A single day will be fine.*

Right?

God, I hoped so. Or Gods. In this and many other matters, I was willing to offer up libations to any deity with the power and inclination to hear my prayers.

Dale, my homeless, commie-hating doorman, was huddled in a carefully constructed nest of his possessions. The most prized items were tucked between his legs, while an outer wall of newspaper and empty bottles offered some form of metaphorical protection. He watched me intently from under bushy eyebrows and a faded and stained Padres cap.

"Good morning, Dale," I offered. "Weather report says it's going to rain on Thursday. You might want to find some place out of the wet by then."

My good deed for the day was met by a thick-knuckled middle finger, slowly extended skyward. I magnanimously decided the gesture had been directed at the incoming weather and not the helpful, friendly, and much-loved neighborhood detective.

The front door was locked—not that it had ever stopped anyone but Dale—and I dug my key out and let myself into the lobby. Really, *lobby* was too strong a word for what was essentially an entryway with mailboxes on one side and a hall and stairwell directly ahead. The mailboxes I ignored entirely; there wasn't any point in retrieving a new stack of bills when I was still trying to figure out how to pay the previous week's assortment.

Besides, my gaze had been pulled inexorably to the opposite wall, where someone had parked one of the sweetest motorcycles in the world, an honest-to-god Ducati in blood red and chrome. It was the sort of bike that might even make *me* irresistible, and I spent an inordinate amount of time drooling over it before it occurred to me to wonder why the hell a motorcycle was parked in our lobby.

On the one hand, it *would* keep it from getting stolen… something the chain lock that snaked through the frame and wrapped around the three bottom rungs of the stairwell's banister would also help with. On the other hand, who in this rat trap of building could afford a twenty-thousand-dollar racing bike? My neighbors and I rented office space in Logan Heights out of financial necessity, not because we *enjoyed* the crime-ridden ambiance.

I shrugged, gave the Ducati a few more admiring pats—guilty about already cheating on my brand-new Corolla—and headed up the stairs to my office.

CHAPTER 15
IN WHICH MONEY MATTERS

I'd taken four steps when I noticed the throbbing bass. A few more steps added strains of electric guitar to the mix, but it wasn't until I reached the second floor that I could finally hear the vocals of Alice in Chains, playing at an absurdly high volume. And the noise seemed to be coming from…

"You've got to be kidding me!" The door to my office was ajar, and the music was coming from inside. I peeked around the frame, trying to make myself as small a target as possible.

Juliette offered a desultory wave. She was sprawled in my executive chair, booted feet up on the desk in a pose that showed her legs off to their best advantage while also managing to communicate her complete and total dismissal of the person whose name was on the door. *My* feet were supposed to go up on that desk, damn it!

I reduced the stereo's volume from bowel-moving to merely unprofessionally loud and fixed the femmepire with my best glare.

She seemed unimpressed.

"Juliette… what are you doing here?"

"Keeping our business afloat, obviously." She pulled her feet off the desk and leaned forward, yellow eyes sharp. "Seriously… it's ten past eight. Where have you been, little bird?"

"Wait… what?"

"And what are you wearing?" she continued, without waiting for a reply. "It's bad enough that you're still trying to grow that pathetic excuse for a beard… are those the kind of clothes that are going to inspire confidence in our clients?"

I looked down at my t-shirt and jeans, and then at the femmepire… also dressed in a t-shirt and jeans. "Aren't you wearing pretty much the same thing?"

"These are vintage," she huffed. "And did you know you left the door open on Saturday? Not just unlocked, mind you," she growled, "but actually open?! Anyone could have just wandered in here this weekend—"

"Like the lock has ever stopped anyone," I muttered.

"—and taken our case files! Our contracts! That other stack of paper that…" She slowly trailed off. "Actually, I have no idea what those are." The femmepire gave me a look of narrow-eyed displeasure. "This place is a dump!"

"Juliette," I tried again, already regretting my decision to come into work. "What the hell are you talking about? *Our* business? *Our* case files?"

"Wow," she marveled, "these must be the astonishing powers of recall that made you into the most highly touted private dick in San Diego." Another withering look. "I'm talking about our conversation on Saturday. The one where you invited me on as a partner?"

"That absolutely didn't happen."

"It would have, if you didn't have the manners and thoughtfulness of a goat."

I let that slide. My mom had said the same thing about me, on more than one occasion. People really didn't give goats enough credit.

"This business is barely scraping by," I said patiently, still waiting for her to get out of *my* chair. "I can't afford another employee. And you don't know the first thing about the job."

"Tell that to…" She plucked a case file off the desk and scanned the header. "Harvey Dellisun."

"Who?"

"The guy whose case I just solved." She blew a self-congratulatory bubble. "And whose check I'm holding in my hand."

"Let me see that." She dodged my grab for the check like I was moving in slow motion. Stymied, I picked up the case file instead.

"Oh…" I announced, as I scanned the file. "Yeah, I remember this one. Potential client. He called last week but wasn't ready to commit yet."

"Well, he committed." She tossed the check down on the desk. I eyeballed the figure, trying not to be impressed. It was nothing like what a mediation would bring me, but it was a lot larger than a typical down payment.

"How did you get him to pay in full?" I asked the femmepire, my irritation momentarily forgotten. "Normally, we just get a partial fee to cover a set number of days in advance."

"Really? That seems inefficient." She shrugged again. "He paid in full because I solved the case last night."

"We don't say *solved* when talking about—" I scanned further down the case file. "—background checks and surveillance." I flipped to the next page. "And how could you have finished it already when the contract calls for a week of watching the perp?"

The *perp*—and yes, I had incorporated that word into my professional vernacular thanks to a steady diet of prime-time cop shows—was Mr. Dellisun's potential son-in-law, Jeremy. Harvey wasn't super rich, or he'd have found a more respectable firm for his snooping, but he'd been concerned about the character of the man who would be marrying into his family. It seemed a little closed-minded to me, but maybe I just identified with… I re-read the description I'd taken down verbatim… *twenty-eight-year-old slackers with bad attitudes, possible marijuana habits, and no career prospects whatsoever.*

Nah. Guy sounded like a loser.

"It didn't take a week," Juliette explained smugly. "It didn't even take an hour. I had a nice little conversation with young Jeremy, where he told me every bad thing he'd ever done *and* the fact that he was seeing two other women on the side. I even collected his homemade porn as proof. Took a grand total of ten minutes. Well, fifteen if you include the sad attempts at flirting. Boy really needs to work on his game."

"Fifteen minutes? And he just—oh." I shook my head as the obvious explanation presented itself. "You *compelled* him? Seriously? That's… that's…"

"An effective use of my time and talents?"

"Cheating!"

"Sounds like someone has forgotten one of the lessons from Rising Sun," she responded, smirking.

"I have no idea what that is."

"The movie? Connery? Snipes? A murder in the Nakamoto headquarters?"

"It was probably before my time." Like *most* Connery movies.

"Don't be ridiculous! It came out in the…" she tapped one long finger against her lips in thought. "…the early '90s, I think."

"Meaning I was somewhere between two and five."

"Oh." She blew a bubble. Watermelon flavor, according to my helpful nose. "Sometimes, I forget you're a freaking baby."

"We don't all get to live into our hundreds. So, what did you want to say about the movie?"

"No clue. This whole conversation is boring."

A bored Juliette was a dangerous Juliette. "I won't deny that you being, you know—" I hissed and used my index fingers to pantomime fangs.

"A deranged cat?"

"—a vampire could be invaluable in this line of work. But you can't work as a P.I. unless you have a license—"

She slapped down a sheet of paper.

"—which you somehow already have, in defiance of the mandatory three years of paid experience thing." I let out a sigh that felt like it had started all the way in my toes. "Alright. I'm willing to consider this, on two conditions."

"Which are?"

I pointed at the femmepire. "First, get out of my chair. I own this company, so I get to sit behind the desk."

"Fair enough, but you have to admit, the chair looks a lot better when I'm sitting in it."

We swapped seats and I sank into luxurious faux leather. "And second…"

"Yes?"

"If that sweet Ducati is yours, I get to take it for a ride."

"Little bird, she's way too much bike for you to handle."

It hurt because it was true.

"Why do you even want to be a private investigator, Duchess?" I waved my hand at the shabby office. "This isn't exactly the sort of lifestyle you're accustomed to."

"Clearly, you've never witnessed the aftermath of a Grateful Dead concert."

"Still. You're rich, you're practically immortal, and you can wrap any person in this city around your pinkie finger… figuratively *and* literally. Why aren't you sunning yourself by the pool at one of your luxurious estates?" I was still kind of annoyed to be stuck in my parents' basement when Juliette had bachelor pads to spare.

Something in the femmepire's lack of response tipped me off. Some sort of micro-expression, maybe. I hadn't been able to afford the absurd fee for an online training course in expression analysis, but I *had* watched half a season of Lie to Me on Netflix, which was almost as good.

"That's it, isn't it? Something's wrong with your properties. Mold demon infestation? Annual termite exorcism? The lingering smell of burned popcorn?" I wasn't a fan of any of those things, myself, but being a private eye wasn't a thrill a minute either.

"Not even mold demons would be that stupid," she said, "and I've never burned popcorn in my life. Buildings, yes. But popcorn?"

"Then why would… wait, are you *hiding*?" The thought hadn't occurred to me before that moment. Juliette was far from the strongest of vampires, but I'd never seen her back down from a fight. Usually, it was just the opposite. "Who on earth are you hiding from?"

"You know," she mused, yellow eyes glittering dangerously, "if I were to toss you out the window right now, I could become the sole owner of this firm."

"Be my guest. At least then, the bills would get paid." And I'd be dead, but that was kind of beside the point.

Juliette's wince told me all I needed to know.

"You're *broke?*"

"Temporarily," she snarled. "My assets are tied up in the House funds, and it's possible they've been frozen."

"And your houses?"

"Undergoing foreclosure. Every damn one of them. Lucia isn't taking my departure well."

"The ice queen screwing over a subordinate? What a shock."

She gazed off into the distance for a moment, frowning. "When I first proposed the idea, I thought working with you would just be a fun way to pass the time. I didn't think I'd actually need the money."

"I'm still hazy on why you quit, given how big a deal getting a spot on the Council was. I know Lucia is… well, Lucia… and Marcus is obviously no prize either, but—"

"What Marcus lacks in grace, manners, and charm, he makes up for in other areas, if you know what I mean." Juliette flashed me one of her trademark smirks.

I wasn't going to dignify *that* with a reply. Juliette had terrible taste in men.

"As for my *position?* Pardon me if I don't see the allure of working like a slave for the *exalted* former queen of the People, in the hopes that some of her magnificence might rub off on me like staph. I've spent half my life as an independent. I *enjoy* my freedom, and I'm done putting up with a bunch of centuries-old foreigners!"

"It was the paperwork, wasn't it?"

"You have *no* idea." She sighed. "Even a gnome would have lost his damn mind. I was withering away in my prime. I hadn't even made it out of the House for a little light grazing in three days! That's ridiculous!"

By *light grazing,* I assumed she meant drinking blood from random people in the city, rather than the donors kept in the House for just such a purpose. I had mixed feeling about that. My species' secondary role as vampire food was gross, but most humans seemed to get oodles of joy out of the experience.

When Lucia had fed from me, I'd gotten a taste of that pleasure, and it had been all I could do to keep standing. Our unfortunate bond played havoc with my otherwise rock-solid… protection. So, I understood why most donors were content with their status as walking blood banks.

Even so, it seemed… undignified.

"You're telling me you left behind an enormous suite in the mansion, all the free food—liquid or otherwise—that you could want, *and* risked pissing off every elder vampire in San Diego because you were *bored?*" I tried to keep the incredulity out of my tone. I failed.

"As I recall," she retorted, "you have a suite at the mansion, but choose to continue living in your parents' basement."

"That's—" *Different*, I was going to say. But I suddenly wasn't certain it was. If I wasn't eager to live under the queen's thumb, why should Juliette be?

"Besides," the femmepire continued, reluctantly, "I got drunk with some of the girls last week and may have let a few things slip."

"Things?"

"Yes, things." She began to pace, stalking back and forth across the cheap carpet. "Like—"

Whatever else she said was voiced in a mumble that my purely human ears would never have been able to decipher, even if an ambulance hadn't picked that precise moment to drive down our street, sirens blaring.

"I didn't catch that," I told her, a little gleefully. Whatever this secret was, it sounded juicy. And it was kind of nice to *not* be the one sticking his foot in his mouth for once.

"I said *like the fact that I fed from you when we were being held prisoner.*"

That wasn't nearly as salacious a secret as I'd been hoping for. "Why would that matter?"

"Lucia forgave me the one time, but she made it painfully clear that she only did so because of the mitigating circumstances involved. And because we ended up saving the House."

The mitigating circumstances she was referring to had included a car bomb and inadvertent trip to the hell dimension of Gehenna, and… it was a long story, really.

"But the second time, we'd been kidnapped by werewolves, were trapped in the basement of a burning house, and you hadn't fed for days!" I'd even volunteered my blood—again—which made me some kind of hero. Assuming *heroes* were the ones who let far more capable people use their blood as fuel.

Somehow, it didn't mesh with the fairy tales my mother had read me as a child.

"*A one-time allowance is a one-time allowance, Mr. Smith,*" Juliette told me in an eerie facsimile of Lucia's icy tone. "I wasn't going to stick around in that House for the inevitable shit storm. It may have escaped your completely undeveloped powers of observation, little bird, but your mistress is possessive as all hell when it comes to her things."

"She's not my mistress any more than I'm one of her things!" No matter how often everyone told me otherwise. If Nepenthe and her witchy sisters (and brother) came through for me, the rest of the world might finally see things my way.

"Sure." Juliette lowered herself into the chair again with a sigh. "My advice? Enjoy your status as prized possession while it lasts. Maybe Lucia will start buying you things. I hear she had a thrall back in Italy that she would dress in custom-made suits." Another casual perusal of my current clothing followed. "Obviously, she hasn't gotten that far with you yet. Maybe she'll give you a fashion sense. Or a car."

I very carefully did not glance out the window at the gleaming white Corolla.

"As for me? I'm lying low until this blows over. It'll be a while before I can extricate my assets from the House's accounts. Pissing off the Council further would just make that harder. So, no unsanctioned power use that might be interpreted as me flaunting my independence. That means I need an income. And look! Here you are!"

"For someone who apparently *needs* this job—" Mainly because her inability to plan ahead was every bit as bad as mine. "—you're not working very hard to ingratiate yourself with your potential employer."

"Oh please, John!" she batted her eyelashes at me, "Please, could I have a job? And before you answer, you should know that I will quite literally *not* take no for an answer. And Harvey's check is made out to me."

"In that case, you're hired."

"Sweet." Juliette's feet joined mine on the desk, and she flashed a fang-filled grin in my direction. "So, when's lunch?"

CHAPTER 16

As workdays went, this one was more pleasant than most. Juliette could be a pain in the ass, but she was also a lot of fun, and our relationship had, over time, settled into a fusion of good-natured bickering and harmless flirtation. I didn't get nearly as much research done as I'd been hoping for, but that was an unavoidable consequence of the two of us being squeezed into a tiny office with only one computer.

There may have been a fair amount of YouTube watching too.

Through it all, I kept one eye on my car, relieved to find it attracting no more than the usual attention such a sweet ride deserved. If anyone did show up with a spray can… well, I had an eighty-year-old femmepire in my employ, and I wasn't afraid to use her.

"Is this what you do all day, little bird?"

"Nope. Some days it's *really* slow."

"Gods. After I save this firm from bankruptcy, I want my name on the door under yours."

"Smith and Middleton?" It had a nice ring to it. "Deal. Anyway, things are busier when I'm juggling a few cases. Stakeouts are boring but time consuming. Hopefully, you can handle any clients that come in over the next few weeks though. I'm not sure how long this Graciela business will take."

"I still can't believe you're working for the White Ladies." With Juliette now my partner, I'd filled her in on the particulars of my current investigation. She had been equal parts impressed, concerned, and dismissive of the whole affair. Which was about what I'd expected from the Duchess of Snark. "Outside of your so-called internet research and the small bits of moldy newspaper your house ghost found you, what are you doing to track her down?"

After several years working alone, it was weird having to explain my actions. But I hadn't exactly been kicking ass so far on my own. Another perspective couldn't hurt.

"I'm trying to develop a picture of who Graciela is."

"Scary Mexican leader of a spirit sorority doesn't suffice?"

"Places she haunted, people she might have contacted, that sort of thing," I clarified. "If I know who she is and can put together a timeline of where she's been, it might help me figure out where she went... or at least where she was when or if something happened to her."

"And you're doing that how?" Juliette had plucked the heavy, brass, baseball-shaped paperweight off my desk, and was tossing it up in the air while she interrogated me, yellow eyes never leaving mine even when the paperweight slapped into her hand with an impact that made me wince.

"Well, the Pack will hopefully have their ears—and noses— out for anything unusual. I'm meeting with Lord Kala tonight, and

Marge after that. Plus, I have this ghost tour in…" I checked the time on my phone. "Shit. Twenty minutes. I've got to go."

"Ghost tour." The femmepire snickered and tossed the paper weight into the air again. "Stupidest idea ever… and trust me, I've known you long enough to realize what saying that means." She hopped out of her chair. "Count me in."

"I'm sorry?"

"For the tour," she clarified, heading for the door. Behind her, the paperweight she'd tossed into the air finally came back down, striking the floor like a miniaturized version of the meteor that wiped out the dinosaurs. I was lucky it hadn't gone straight through and killed one of my downstairs neighbors.

I shot my new—and junior—partner a look. "Given that I'm almost broke and you're the next best thing, could we try *not* to destroy the office? Besides, I don't think the tour has any spots left. I only got in because of a last-minute cancellation."

"Little bird," she reminded me, "they won't even know I'm there."

Oh. Right.

ooo

"Biggest. Waste of time. Ever."

"Really? I thought it was kind of fun."

For almost three hours, Juliette and I had tagged along with the tour group to a variety of San Diego's most haunted locations. In all that time, I'd only seen a single ghost: an elderly man who seemed to delight in sticking his crotch directly in the face of our oblivious tour guide. It was funny to hear the well-rehearsed speeches about white lights and paranormal phenomenon when an actual ghost was present but unseen. I'd have loved to chat with Ghost Dude, but he walked into and through a wall halfway through the lengthy monologue, and even I hadn't been able to see him after that.

"Well, some of it *was* entertaining, I guess," Juliette conceded, as we rounded the corner and the Corolla came back into view, "but did it get us any closer to finding Graciela?"

"Not really."

She gave me a serious look, yellow eyes glowing slightly in the dim light. "You know that disappointing the White Ladies is a fantastic way to end up a ghost yourself, right?"

"John Smith the ghost? Please. When I die, I'm going to ascend straight to heaven on the back of a winged unicorn."

"Is that true for *all* virgins, or just you?"

"Anyway, while it would have been awesome if we'd stumbled across our missing ghost on the tour, I wasn't expecting to."

"So why bother? Surely, even your sad excuse for a social life presents better alternatives?"

I took the high road and avoided pointing out that she had joined me on said waste of time. Those with lousy social lives shouldn't throw stones. Or whatever the old saying was. "Very funny, my soon-to-be ex-employee. This is Private Investigation 101. We're heeding one of the profession's oldest maxims."

"Which is?"

"Leave no stone unturned." If it was good enough for Sherlock Holmes, it was good enough for me. "It didn't pan out this time, but there was a chance we would find something of use. If nothing else, now we know she *isn't* at any of those places."

"I suppose that's true. So… early afternoon trip to Sea World tomorrow? I want to verify she's not there either."

"Funny. But why *Sea World?*"

She bristled at my expression. "I like marine life. Sue me. Why do you think I came to San Diego in the first place?"

"I thought it was because you'd been kicked out of New York." By her own parents, no less. I spared a moment to send grateful thoughts in the direction of my own, much more forgiving, mom and dad.

"Besides that. There are a lot of towns between Manhattan and the Pacific, you know."

"If you say so." I'd never been east of Vegas, myself. "Although I doubt any of them have our weather. Anyway, it's almost time for my meeting with Kala. Do you want to come along?"

She shivered. "I'll pass. Places to go, people to bite. That sort of thing. Just drop me off at the office."

"Got it. Where are you staying anyway? You're not sneaking into one of your foreclosed homes, are you?"

"Sneaking? You've clearly never heard a Ducati roar." Juliette grinned. "I'm crashing at one of Brenna's pads."

"I didn't know you two were that close."

"She was part of my original flock. Long before Lucia came to town, when the People did more than push paper for a living. The good old days."

"Yeah, I read about those times in History class," I said with a grin as we pulled away from the curb. "They called it the Mesozoic Era."

"Mesozoic?" I had my eyes fixed on the road, as befit a safety-conscious San Diego driver, but Juliette sounded genuinely pleased. "You do say the nicest things."

Vampires were just plain weird.

CHAPTER 17

Some years back, there had been a bar downtown on the corner of 5th and F called the Bitter End. While the name had since been changed, the bar itself stayed pretty much the same; three floors filled to the brim with people. It was a little bit fancy for my tastes—fancy being code for expensive—but still a great place to spend an hour or three.

I'd been seeing a lot of it over the past year, if only in passing.

Just outside that bar, a short stairwell led down below street level, the entrance flimsily blocked by a thin chain that I stepped over. The dim light provided by a nearby streetlamp and the establishment's own yellow sign allowed me to carefully pick my way down the dilapidated stone steps. Those stairs provided an emergency exit from the bar's basement dance floor, although I'd never seen the door actually open.

Which was just as well, as I wasn't there for dancing.

The *real* Bitter End, the one I was headed to, had existed long before the human establishment's founding, before San Diego was even a glimmer in the Spanish missionaries' eyes. It too was a bar, but that was where the similarities ended. The private domain of Lord Kala, demigod of death and time, the true Bitter End existed nowhere and everywhere, accessible from various locations across this and other worlds through portals like the one I'd soon be traveling through.

That was the plan anyway. After dropping off Juliette, I'd gotten a text from Steve, telling me something had come up at the House, and he wouldn't be able to make our appointment. Steve's message suggested he had arranged for someone else to meet me, but I wasn't sure who…

"Hey!" I recognized the little fellow waiting at the base of the stairs, large ears, bald head, and all. "It's good to see you again."

He peered at me inquisitively, and I obligingly stepped forward so that he could get a better look. With all the squinting that was going on, it appeared my brownie acquaintance was at least a little bit nearsighted.

"I'm sorry," he finally said, words slow and carefully enunciated, "but have we met?"

How quickly they forgot.

"Last November. You, me, a bunch of werewolves?"

His expression cleared. "Ah. You were the human chew toy. Your face was not so hairy then. Are you an Infected now?"

"It's a beard," I grumbled. "Did Steve ask you to meet me?"

"I do not know this *Steve*, but the door man indicated that someone would be along shortly, and I offered to open the door, as it were." He grinned, revealing a double row of needle-sharp teeth. "It is never a bad thing to have the bouncer on your side, yes?"

Now *that* was something I could agree with. The brownie turned to the far wall, where someone had spray-painted a list of impossible sex acts and what I could only assume was the phone number of their worst enemy. As my companion approached, that wall began to glow, light seeping through the mortar around individual bricks.

I waited for the little man to step through and then hurried in after him. Rumor had it that the portals to the Bitter End were at least partially sentient, and they had demonstrated a propensity for eating the occasional human. I'd never actually seen any evidence to support that claim, but still… the rumors persisted.

As quickly as I entered the portal, I was exiting it, my extended foot coming to rest on a black and gold floor that bore no resemblance to the city streets… or any stone I'd even heard of. The brownie was already scampering down the polished steps. Below us, the door to the Bitter End was every bit as open and inviting as the bouncer standing next to it was not.

That was Barry, Steve's boyfriend. I squared my shoulders and headed his way, passing between the magical tiki torches and gold-laced cavern walls. Barry looked like the illegitimate love child of Bigfoot and a Hell's Angel, squeezed into a suit that was nicer than anything in my wardrobe. His skin was an odd shade of grey, and if it weren't for the tusks and copious amounts of equally grey hair, he could very well have been a crudely shaped, boulder-sized statue come to life.

I had no idea what Steve saw in him.

"Hi, Barry," I said, working hard not to be my usual irritating self. "I believe I'm expected?"

"You are." His voice was a low growl that I could feel in my bones. Despite those words, he remained interposed between me and the door. "It's been quiet tonight, human. See that it remains so."

"Quiet is my middle name," I lied.

"Sure it is." With a grunt, Barry stepped to the side, giving me just enough room to squeeze by him. Swell guy, for an impossibly ancient wereboar.

Then again, I'd be grumpy too if I were confined to a single bar for the remainder of my existence. I reminded myself to broach the subject of Barry possibly taking field trips to our world when I spoke with Lord Kala.

As always, I found myself nearly blind on entering, peering through a haze that swallowed up the room around me after just a few feet. It was a human thing, supposedly; our eyes took a while to adjust to the slightly different spectrum of light in the Bitter End.

Minor conditions like space and size didn't apply to Kala's domain. The place could comfortably seat twenty or three hundred, from the numerous round tables that dotted the main floor, to the booths along the left wall, to the private rooms that bordered the dance floor. The right wall was dominated by the bar itself, where employees mixed drinks for the waiters and waitresses who wandered the establishment.

I glanced about me in the hopes of spotting the demigod himself, but if he was waiting for me, he was doing so out of sight. Even given my vision problems, a skeleton in a robe blacker than anything Crayola had to offer would have been obvious. I shrugged and took a seat at the nearest empty table.

I had two rules about demigods, the first and most important being *don't piss them off.* The second rule? *If you're dumb enough to ignore the first rule, don't do it in their home dimension.* Lord Kala was quite literally judge, jury, and executioner here. I was going to keep my head down, stay out of trouble, and wait for him to send for me.

That said, a beer would make the waiting easier. I glanced up as a waiter—waitress?—glided over to my table. *Literally* glided; the powder-blue tentacles it had instead of legs were hovering several inches above the floor. I had no idea what it was using for propulsion.

"Is the human claimed?" The voice was recognizably female, although the words came out garbled, like she was speaking underwater or through a Taco Bell drive thru speaker.

"Claimed?" That was a new one. "Not yet, but—" I offered what I hoped was a conspiratorial wink. "—maybe tonight will be the night."

Several tentacles waved in agitation, which I took to be a rejection of either my peculiar brand of humor or the idea that anyone of the opposing gender would be interested in me. Six of one, half dozen of the other, really.

"Unclaimed humans must wait outside," she burbled again, two crimson eyes fixed on my face, while the third glanced over to the door.

"Oh. *That* sort of claimed. Actually, I'm here because Lord Kala agreed to meet with me." I offered the waitress my best smile, the one I'd been practicing in my bathroom mirror for months now. I called it the *Dealmaker*™ and had been waiting for another mediation to finally unleash it.

She gazed at me in silence. It was possible that the *Dealmaker*™ wasn't quite ready for prime time yet. Finally, she shrugged what I assumed were shoulders. "We see. Does the human wish to partake in refreshment?"

"I'd love a Guinness, actually. And would you inform your boss that I've arrived?"

"The human is in Lord Kala's domain," the waitress told me. "Lord Kala already knows."

ooo

If it was true that Kala already knew I was there, it was equally apparent that the demigod was in no hurry to speak to me. I nursed my beer for as long as was humanly possible, but after almost an hour, I was down to just a few sips, and my host had yet to make an appearance. Luckily, there was ample opportunity for people watching, from the Will-o-wisp-esque Mistborn, drifting about the interior like floating neon snow globes, to the tuxedo-clad elephant who was the source of the music that helped drown out the conversations of those around me.

As for the other patrons? I mostly kept my eyes to myself. At the end of the day, I was only human, which made me both weaker than everyone else in the bar *and* pretty much universally reviled. I had no idea what sort of gesture or action might infuriate my neighbors, and little hope of surviving the resulting fight.

Still, the Bitter End was the closest I'd ever come to a real-world version of Star Wars' Mos Eisley cantina, and my self-restraint only went so far. I snuck a few glances at the varied beings drinking around me, but they were small glances, and subtle.

In fact, I was so busy *not* ogling a tree-person-thingy who had dipped its leafy fronds into a bucket of alcohol that I didn't realize someone had come up behind me until they spoke. Several someones, by the sound of their loud voices. And they were talking about me.

"—is a *human* doing here? And who gets to eat it?"

"Careful, Yrrm." I think that was supposed to be a name, although it was halfway between a cough and a clearing of the throat. "That's the San Diego mediator."

I puffed up just a bit. I'd only had the position for a year, and it had to mean something that the denizens of the city were starting to recognize me.

"That is Caleb Van Stahl?"

"No, the other one. Jack Black or something."

"I don't think that's it," put in a third, oddly squeaky voice, making the Vaudeville routine complete.

"Whatever," replied the second voice dismissively. "I don't care what its name is."

"And why should I care what its job is," asked the first, "as long as it crunches when chewed?"

I gripped my empty glass tightly in one hand. It wouldn't make much of a weapon, but it was all I had.

That and my suspiciously ineffective smile.

"Word is—" the second voice was low and considering, as if mulling over the idea of my becoming bar food. "—it was involved in the death of a vampire Battle Lord."

Mostly, I'd almost died at the hands of Xavier. Or, if you wanted to put it in the best light possible… I'd distracted him just long enough for Anastasia to quite literally swoop through the window and save the day.

"It was part of that wolf purge before Thanksgiving too," said the third voice. "Supposedly, it killed old Davis Hawthorne with its bare hands."

Again, not technically correct. In fact, Davis had been killed by other wolves, and only after kidnapping me for several days. I *had* killed a wolf all by myself, thanks to a one-shot hell gun I'd liberated from my slightly insane demigod friend Bill, but I'd never have made it out alive if Anastasia hadn't—once again—come to my rescue.

She did that a lot, really. It was the sort of thing that bruised egos were made of. Or love stories.

"Are you saying," asked the first voice, his words accompanied by the sound of gnashing teeth, like rocks being ground against one another, "that I *shouldn't* eat it?"

"Nah," said the second. "I'm just saying Gus and I want a piece too."

Well, shit.

CHAPTER 18

The hand that dropped onto my shoulder was roughly the size of my head. It spun me about until I was face-to-face with my would-be eaters.

Or face-to-belly, anyway. I tilted my head back and followed the line of the arm that gripped me up and up and up to a scowling, heavily scarred face. Yrrm was a giant or an ogre or… some other big, ugly thing. It wasn't like I had the time to flip through my almanac of fairy tales to be sure.

Next to him was a slightly smaller member of the same species, but the third individual was a minotaur, bull's head, cloven hoofs, and bare chest. I aimed my words at him, trying to ignore the fact that the hand on my shoulder was almost definitely causing bruises.

"Gus, right?" I offered a confident smile, which the minotaur seemed disinterested in returning. I *really* needed to up my smile game. "I've seen you around here once or twice. I don't have a beef with you, dude."

"Mmm. Beef." Yrrm smacked his lips.

Damn it. Poor choice of words.

Gus shrugged, and spoke again in that squeaky voice. It would have been hilarious, on any other day, like listening to a supernatural Mike Tyson. "This isn't personal, Jack. But my friends and I are hungry and the calamari…" He spoke the latter word with utter disdain. "…just isn't cutting it."

"Wait, *you* eat calamari? And meat?"

"What did you *think* I ate, human?" It was difficult to read expression on the minotaur's inhuman face, but the scorn in his voice came through just fine. "Tofu?"

Now *there* was an image. One I'd have to giggle hysterically over, assuming I managed to survive the encounter. Out of the corner of my eye, I glanced toward the door. What the hell was taking Barry so long? I was running out of ways to stall.

"I just assumed you were an herbivore, given your parentage."

There was a moment of dead silence, and it occurred to me— too late, as usual—that minotaurs might not appreciate being compared to cows. Then my bovine acquaintance was roaring in anger. At the same time, Yrrm plucked me out of the chair. I found myself hoisted a good ten feet in the air, dangling like a helpless kitten.

I smashed my empty glass into Yrrm's face, hoping against hope that ogre-giant-things had a special vulnerability to commercial grade glassware, but I don't think he even noticed. He pulled me closer and opened a mouth which, from my perspective, looked to be twice as big as the trunk of my new Corolla.

I had a nauseating view of what was probably a century or two of severely lacking dental work as the jaws began to close about my head.

Five seconds passed, then ten, and the terrible rending I was dreading still hadn't occurred. In fact, I was starting to wonder if ogre-giant-things preferred suffocating their food before eating it.

Was that a better or worse fate than being chewed to death?

And why hadn't I ordered a second Guinness? This was definitely a two-beer sort of moment.

I was still gagging when my trajectory into Yrrm's maw reversed. It was only when my feet were back on the bar room's floor that I realized I wasn't getting eaten after all. My three would-be cannibals were fixated on something behind me, their faces suddenly ashen grey.

"Howdy-doo everybody," announced a deep voice with a slight but noticeable Southern twang. A shadow loomed large and terrible—and in precisely the wrong direction, given the position of the retreating Mistborn—to cast a good half of the bar's interior into darkness. "Shall we wiggle our faces like proper enchiladas or IS THIS A TIME FOR FIRE?"

I breathed out a long sigh of relief.

"Hi, Bill."

ooo

It was said that Lord Beel-Kasan, Demigod of Nightmares, Terror, and Vindication, appeared to each viewer as something different, the embodiment of their greatest fear. I saw him as a seven-foot-tall asparagus, with a carrot nose, two pieces of coal for eyes, and a mouth that had been drawn on his stalk with a magic marker, which meant I was either secretly terrified of vegetables—and doing a remarkable job of repressing that fact—or my own gift protected me from the effect.

Lord Beel-Kasan, Bill to his friends, figured I was just broken. Given that Bill was himself at least a dozen cards short of a full deck, that label wasn't something I'd lost sleep over.

In addition to his duties—nebulous as they were—Bill was the guardian of a young human girl by the name of Jee Sun. The three of us had met in my initial mediation, and Bill had even entrusted his ward to me for a brief time while he dealt with some—still unexplained—disturbances in his home dimension of Gehenna. Bill had been back for months now, but I was surprised to see that Jee Sun had let him out of her sight. The little girl had a will of iron and a pout that could bring a grown man to his knees. Somehow, Bill had convinced her to stay home on their houseboat, moored in the marina downtown.

"Hi, Mr. John!"

Or maybe he'd brought her with him. To a bar. Full of monsters. I spotted Jee Sun on the bar counter, clad in her usual Catholic schoolgirl uniform. A red Supergirl cape was loosely tied about her neck, the ends of it waving gently in a non-existent breeze. After a year of knowing her, I still had no idea how old she was. Five? Eight? Eight and a half? She waved happily from across the room. Bemused, I returned the wave.

When I turned back to my attackers, nothing had changed. Bill loomed over them—a neat trick since the ogre-giant-things were taller than the demigod—his coal eyes rotating, and his magic marker mouth flattened into a single horizontal line.

"I think they'd rather talk than burn, Bill," I decided. I wasn't all that invested in saving the lives of three monsters who had been planning to eat me... but I *had* seen the fields of human-shaped candelabras in Gehenna. In Bill's home dimension, people burned, and they burned forever. A minor threat of cannibalism didn't warrant that sort of punishment.

Also? I had a sudden vision of Yrrm saving my ass in repayment someday. It was time to make karma work *for* me.

The ogre and his two friends fell over themselves agreeing with my statement. Bill's eyes rotated horizontally around his stalk until they fixated on me, even as his carrot nose and mouth continued to face straight ahead.

"Johnny-come-marching-home!" The mouth reshaped itself into a happy smile. "Have you come to drink with TINY FLOWER and I?" In a stage whisper, he added, "She orders TEQUILA, but they give her MILK with HONEY in it instead. It is VERY TASTY!"

The two ogres and their minotaur friend started to back away, but an arm extended from Bill's otherwise limbless stalk to point like a rail spike directly at Yrrm's forehead.

"We will wiggle our faces before we waggle our feet," Bill said severely.

In Bill-speak, that at least *suggested* violence might be avoidable. But even as he said the words, I realized it might be too late for that. The cannibalistic trio was no longer alone. Behind them stood a tall figure, shrouded in deepest black.

"Yrrm," said that figure in conversational tones. At the sound of the hollow voice, Yrrm's ashen face somehow went even paler. "I believe we have spoken about how you are to treat the other guests in my place of business."

The ogre-giant-thing was now visibly trembling as he turned to regard the newcomer. "Lord Kala, that was years ago!"

"Twenty-seven years, four months, nine days, sixty-three minutes, and twelve seconds, to be precise," came the reply, unleavened by even a hint of humor. "And here we are again."

"But he's just a human!"

"John Smith could be an anteater, for the difference it makes," stated Kala simply. "The devil is not at all in the details."

I was still trying to figure out whether or not I should be insulted by the anteater comparison—not that I was going to do or say a damn thing about it, regardless—when Yrrm spun with lightning speed and sprinted for the door.

Or started to sprint, anyway. As he took that first step, his grey hide darkened, and the thick hair on his head withered and fell away. By the second step, he was quite literally falling apart; his extended foot transformed into dust as it contacted the floor. Unbalanced, the ogre tumbled to the ground, but the rest of his body disintegrated as it fell. In an eye blink, the only thing left of Yrrm was a pile of fine white dust. A heartbeat later, even that dust was gone.

Kala turned to the other two, the bare skull of his face lost within the cavernous confines of a night-black cowl. "Gentlemen," he said calmly, as if he hadn't just aged their companion out of existence, "house policy is that everyone gets a single warning. Consider this to be yours." He extended a fleshless arm and pointed to the door Yrrm had been trying to reach. "You are banned from these premises for one year. After that time, return as you wish, but be mindful of my rules, and of the penalty for transgression."

If Yrrm's speed had been blinding—albeit ultimately futile— Gus and the other ogre were only slightly less swift in thanking Lord Kala for his mercy and getting the ever-living hell out of Dodge.

The demigod turned to Bill and me.

"Lord Beel-Kasan, now that our business has concluded, shall I have Tabitha show you and your ward to your usual room? And yes," he answered, before Bill could open his mouth to ask, "there will be beer."

"And maybe some HONEY MILK too?" asked Bill hopefully.

"I will make certain of it. In the meantime," Kala continued, turning his eyeless gaze on me, "Mr. Smith and I have an appointment."

"Cheerio, Johnorama," Bill told me happily, growing another arm to wave with, even as his first one stretched across the room to scoop Jee Sun off the bar. "If the Mickey hands ALLOW IT, we will wiggle our faces at each other!"

"Sounds good, amigo." I watched the demigod and his human walk into the haze that still obscured the deeper recesses of the bar. Theirs was one of the oddest relationships I'd ever heard of; an insane immortal of nightmares who had rescued a little girl from the nightmare that was her own life. Somehow, they made it work.

"I apologize for the delay, Mr. Smith," Kala said humbly. Upon Bill's departure, the Mistborn had come back out of hiding, and their dim, multi-colored light was sufficient to illuminate the depths of Kala's cowl. "My conversation with Lord Beel-Kasan and his child went unexpectedly long."

My lips twitched, as I tried to repress a smile. Bill wouldn't have caught the expression or would have immediately forgotten it. Lord Kala was another matter entirely.

"Something amuses you?"

I felt like a kid who'd been caught sneaking notes in high school. "It just struck me as funny that even a god of time could be late."

"A fair observation." He nodded his head, and I breathed a little bit easier. With only two rules about demigods, you'd think I'd have an easier time sticking to them. But I'd always sucked at following rules, even mine. Just ask the California Highway Patrol. Or my parents. "In point of fact," he continued, "I could have insured that we met on time—"

I blinked. Lord Kala was no longer in front of me. In fact, one of the tables beyond where he had been standing was now empty of people. I spun about, and found the demigod next to his bar, a half-finished carafe of some opaque alcohol on the counter beside him.

"—but members of your species sometimes have difficulty with the effects of time dilation."

Time di-what? Oh shit. If Kala had just Rip Van Winkled me, my parents were going to be pissed. Assuming they were still alive in whatever far future timeline I'd just found myself in. I hurriedly dug my phone out of one pocket, and tapped the screen…

According to my wonderphone, which thought we were still in California, no more than ten minutes had passed in the eyeblink of Kala's little demonstration. I exhaled slowly, acknowledging the demigod's point. A short wait with a glass of Guinness had definitely been the more enjoyable option, near-death notwithstanding.

"So then, Mr. Smith," continued Kala, steering me past the bar, "what is it you wished to discuss?"

CHAPTER 19

Picture an enormous office, dominated by a baroque desk crafted from the trunk of a mahogany tree older than the universe. Behind that desk are endless shelves, presumably also mahogany, filled with books or souvenirs or nothing at all, depending on when and how you look at them. The room is empty of Mistborn, lit by a single flame suspended in mid-air: the first electric spark of a conflagration that could have grown to destroy the world if it hadn't been trapped in this endless, singular moment.

That wasn't the office Lord Kala took me to, but it *could* have been. In fact, by the night's end, I'd be hard-pressed to remember anything about his office at all, including how we'd reached it after rounding the bar. It was possible that we hadn't even gone into an office. Had the entire conversation occurred in a bubble outside of time?

It was the kind of question that made my head hurt.

At the time, however, I was busy explaining the full details of my case to Lord Kala. Given the dearth of clues or information, it should have been a quick briefing, but I found myself getting hung up yet again on the whole "missing ghost" impossibility… especially the part where I was expected to somehow find that ghost.

Also? Talking to someone who could age me to death before I even twitched didn't do great things for my presentation skills.

"It sounds like an unusual situation," said Lord Kala. "Why come to me for assistance in the matter?"

"I guess I was hoping you wouldn't have anything better to do." Which seemed kind of stupid now. Borderline suicidal, in fact.

Kala shook his head with a creaking of vertebrae. "I am not asking why I would choose to assist you. I am asking why you think I could."

I gave him my patented look of abject confusion. "Because you're… you know… a dark lord of the Sith and all that. A demigod of death and time. Isn't Graciela one of your… subjects?"

"I do not have subjects," he explained, almost gently, "and spirits are not dead."

"Wait… what?"

"To be more precise, they are no longer dead. They exist in an intermediary state, neither dead nor alive. I have no dominion over such as they. Unless they enter this establishment, of course."

"Of course." It had never even occurred to me that Kala wouldn't be able to help. Did I need to track down a Demigod of the Mostly Dead instead? Because with all due respect to *The Princess Bride*, that seemed kind of ridiculous. "Could you maybe determine if something *has* happened to her? Something of a permanent nature? If she's moved on or someone managed to—you know—then wouldn't she be—?"

"Truly dead." Kala drummed his bony fingers on one robed, but equally bony leg. "That I can help you with. However, if you value what few years you have left, I will need you to be silent until I say otherwise."

Naturally, that raised all sorts of questions. *Why* did I need to be silent? And what had Kala meant by *few years*, anyway? Ten? Fifty? These were questions that I suddenly really, really needed answered, preferably before my untimely passing.

I managed not to ask any of them, but it was difficult.

And then it wasn't.

What began as simple silence mutated into… well a deeper silence. Thick, like shag carpet for the brain, the sort of silence that suggested noise at a level beyond what my ears could perceive. I felt that quietness in my bones and the palpitations of my own muted heartbeat.

I became dimly aware that I was holding my breath, as if even exhalation might prove disastrous.

The tiny flames in Kala's vacant sockets guttered out, leaving only darkness, and then that darkness, just like the silence, changed into something new. A part of me felt like I was looking through the demigod into something emptier than simple emptiness. I was peering into a bottomless well that had twisted in upon itself to tunnel into infinity.

The silence continued. The emptiness continued. Eventually, it occurred to me that I should have run out of breath weeks earlier.

Then the demigod finally spoke.

"The Lady Graciela is not a citizen of our nation. Nor has she visited those lands since the time of her first death."

Whatever the hell the demigod had done, it vanished as soon as he spoke. I couldn't tell if my sigh of relief was because of that fact, or because of the confirmation that Graciela was still alive.

Or un-live. Or… floating.

Not for the first time, I wished the supernatural world had come with an instruction manual. And a glossary.

Unfortunately, Kala's revelation didn't do much to resolve the mystery of the ghost's disappearance. Marge had been adamant that Graciela wouldn't abandon them, but the only other possibility was that someone or something was keeping the spirit imprisoned.

Which was impossible. Wasn't it?

Lord Kala looked impassively at me, tiny flames dancing once more in his otherwise empty sockets. I met that gaze and waited. And then waited some more. Finally, more than a little frustrated, I used one hand to pantomime a flapping mouth, and then pointed at myself with a questioning look upon my face.

"Ah. You may speak now, Mr. Smith. Your silence was only necessary while I communed with the lands of the dead. It would be inadvisable for you to draw death's notice at this time."

"You make it sound like death is a living thing," I said. "Well, not living, I guess, but… you know… a creature."

"Indeed. One of the great and amorphous creatures at the heart of every universe, the void into which all things are inevitably pulled. Neither I nor those of my ilk rule death, Mr. Smith. We shepherd it. We guide it. Most of all, we ensure that it remains satiated and quiescent."

And just like that, we were back to being super creepy. And confusing.

"I didn't understand a word of that," I admitted. "Death is…?"

"One of the primal forces of existence. Life and death are separate shores on an infinite plane and time is the river that separates and yet binds them both."

That was both poetic and unintelligible. If death was a creature, how could it also be a shore? And hadn't he also said it was a realm? I hadn't been this confused since my one and only philosophy class in community college, where a man named Hegel had used thousands of words to say nothing at all.

I definitely should have had another beer.

Luckily, Lord Kala wasn't *just* a demigod of death.

"If time is a river, couldn't we… paddle upstream?" I swung my arms in the vague approximation of a canoer paddling. *Vague* and *approximation* because I'd never actually been in a canoe. Even rivers made me seasick. "It would be a huge help if you could rewind the past month or so and see what happened to her."

I didn't even bother suggesting we try and *stop* whatever had happened. A lifetime of science fiction had taught me that changing the time stream was a terrible idea. That way lay madness. And an ever-increasing multitude of not-very-good killer robot movies.

Lord Kala shook his head, vertebrae again grinding unpleasantly with the motion. "I am a minor deity in my pantheon, Mr. Smith. Within the dimension you know as the Bitter End, time truly is a river. With the right ship, it may be sailed. But in the world beyond? Time is a tsunami. Only one of the true gods would dare to stir those waters."

"Is that why Barry is stuck here?"

"Indeed. The ward I have wrought for him would require an anchor in your world for it to survive the transition."

"An anchor?"

"A second dimensional locus, to provide the ward stability and sufficient energy while he was away from the Bitter End." Kala shook his head. "Given the number of the years that particular ward is suppressing, you would need someone greater than I to hold it stable outside of these walls."

Steve wasn't going to love hearing that.

"At least you've given him time." I stood up from whatever I'd been sitting on. "Anyway, I really appreciate the help."

"I regret that my assistance amounted to so little, Mr. Smith."

"No worries, dude." I was already racking my brain for ideas on where I might find a demigod of undeath. Or demigoddess; I didn't want to be sexist about these things.

"Would you be open to a word of advice on your search?"

"I'll take whatever help I can get."

"In your city, there is a singular being who might be able to help you. Like the White Ladies, he is neither dead nor alive, but he possesses certain abilities those good women lack."

"You're talking about the zombie prince?"

"I am. He has had many names, few of them lasting for more than a year at a time, but he has currently chosen to call himself Simon." As ever, Lord Kala's expression remained expressionless, but I got the sense he was laughing at me. Or maybe it was just a side effect of all those exposed teeth. "If you seek him out, I suggest you bring compensation. He has long considered himself a businessman."

I didn't want to even think about what a zombie might demand as compensation—I'd almost rather it be brains than cash—but nodded anyway. Nothing in life was free. I'd learned that lesson long before Ana and the vampires had opened my eyes to how weird the world could really get. Even advice usually came with a price.

"Speaking of compensation…" I met the demigod's fiery orbs. "Is there anything I can do for you?"

"You already have, Mr. Smith."

"I have?" At the last moment, I kept myself from checking my wallet. It wasn't like I had any cash in it anyway.

"Eternity is a long time and entertainment difficult to find, even in a place such as this. You are… interesting to me."

"Interesting? Me?" Kala clearly needed to get out more. I was one of the most boring people I knew.

"Yes. There is the gift that shields your mind. And your position as city mediator, a position that you have held through dangers that would give far more powerful creatures pause. As a human, your ability to survive is unprecedented."

When a demigod tells you that you're a badass, I'd found it best to smile and agree.

"Then there is the manner in which you allow your tongue to wag freely, despite the trouble it has and will cause you."

Okay, that was slightly less flattering.

"But the thing I find most interesting of all," Kala continued, his voice as dry as the grave, "is that wherever you go, people inevitably die."

It was hard to take that one as a compliment.

I shook my head, more in dismay than disagreement, and we were back in the main dining hall of the Bitter End. Most of the tables were empty and even the crowd of Mistborn had diminished. A fair chunk of time had evidently passed while we were conversing.

"I'm glad I could entertain you," I started to say, but Kala was nowhere to be found. A few feet away, a bartender paused in the midst of mixing a blood orange martini to give me a questioning look. I waved him off. "Not a fan of goodbyes? That's okay; I'll see you again."

Beneath the noise of the few remaining customers, the chattering bartenders, and the strings of the purple elephant jukebox, I heard a reply:

"Only time will tell."

Funny guys, demigods.

CHAPTER 20

I transitioned back to San Diego and climbed the stairs to 5th Street, leaving the human-eating portal and the secretly terrifying bar dimension behind. Given how long the meeting with Kala had seemed to last, I was surprised to find I'd only been inside the Bitter End for a few hours. It was still a few minutes before midnight, which meant I had practically the entire night ahead of me.

I was just about to speed dial Mike when I stopped and frowned. Something about *midnight* was setting off alarm bells in my head. But what…?

Shit. I was supposed to be meeting Marge at midnight. In Pacific Beach, which was at least fifteen minutes away. I hurried to my car, praying that, for once, PB would be free of traffic.

ooo

If there really was a demigod of traffic, they had apparently tired of doing me favors.

ooo

I reached the end of Garnet a quarter past the hour, and for the second time in two days, lucked into a parking spot, as a light-colored Vanagon overstuffed with drunk college students pulled away.

The address Marge had given was a circular plaza a block or so north along the beach, close enough that I could manage a vague sort of jog without having a heart attack. I arrived huffing and puffing like an asthmatic octogenarian.

The bathrobe-clad ghost was nowhere to be found.

I frowned, waited another minute to catch my breath, and then wandered around the circle. Would Marge really have brought me all the way out here just to mess with me? No, I decided. Either she had left in a fit of pique because I was late, or the heavyset spirit was running even later than I had been.

How did a ghost tell time anyway?

I took a seat on one of the nearby benches, pulled out my wonderphone, and settled in to wait.

By one o'clock, my ass was cold, my legs had fallen asleep, and Marge was still nowhere to be found. I'd made another brief sojourn around the circle, looking for a message from the ghost or a handy stack of clues as to where she had gone, finding only a couple of teenagers making out in the grass. Even that duo had since given up and gone elsewhere. Outside of the occasional people wandering across to the dark beach to stare at the even darker ocean, I was completely alone.

And tired. Meeting with Lord Kala had taken a lot out of me, and my bed was calling my name all the way from Chula Vista.

I gave Marge another ten minutes, then climbed to my feet and made my way back to my beautiful new car.

CHAPTER 21

For the second day in a row, I woke up feeling fantastic. Considering I'd gotten home after two, my lack of exhaustion was as surprising as it was welcome.

I snuggled my pillow while thinking about the day ahead of me. Juliette had taken care of Harvey Dellisun's case in her unique yet effective fashion, but a metric shit ton of stuff remained on my plate. Like finding the zombie prince, having a friendly sit-down with Caleb Van Stahl, and letting Marge know how I felt about ghosts who no-showed their own meetings.

What was I missing?

"John?" My mom's voice echoed down the stairwell and into the basement, my first indication that she'd opened the hallway door. "You have a visitor."

"I do?" I called back. For a fleeting, irrational moment, I thought it might be Graciela, and that at least one of my problems would have neatly resolved itself.

"Yes, dear. Come on up when you're decent. Anastasia and I will have a nice chat while we wait."

ooo

So, yeah. Anastasia was another of those open issues on my plate. It had been three days since our aborted reunion. Two since I'd called and left my message. Monday had been freakishly busy, but I'd still checked my phone a dozen times, waiting for a reply that never came.

And now the femmepire was talking to my mother. Again.

Kayla's warnings from brunch came back to me in a rush, but I dismissed them with a shrug. Anastasia's occupation didn't concern me. Hell, what comic-loving geek *didn't* grow up wanting to date a superhero assassin?

I ducked into the bathroom, splashed water on my face, and did my best to make myself presentable. In lieu of a crash diet and professional makeover, it would have to do.

Upstairs, Anastasia was sitting with my mother on the couch in our living room, matching cups of tea in their hands. For the second time in a year, my mother had used the good china. It was a none-too-subtle declaration of approval.

My dad's declarations were generally *less* subtle. Thankfully, he had already left for work, rescuing us from a steady stream of waggled eyebrows, sly grins, and open-mouthed stares. Dad was awesome—as only a Star-Wars-watching father could be—but I was pretty sure I'd inherited my difficulties with women from him.

We Smith men were many things, but smooth wasn't one of them.

"It is a delight to see you again, dear," said my mother to the four-hundred-year-old woman seated next to her. "I was starting to worry that you and John might have had a falling out."

"Sadly, I was away on business, Mrs. Smith."

"Please, call me Maria!"

Good luck with that, Mom. I'd been trying to get Ana to call me John since the day we'd met, and even now, it was a fifty-fifty proposition at best.

"What is it that you do," my mother continued, "if you don't think it rude of me to ask?"

Maria Smith, known around these parts as Mom, was an acknowledged master of the small-talk interrogation, her skills sharpened by decades of dealing with my dad and I, but Anastasia was a long-time veteran of vampire politics and battlefield tactics. After considerable thought, I decided that gave the femmepire an edge in this conversation.

A very slight edge.

"Not at all," Anastasia answered smoothly, glancing past my mother to where I stood in the hall. "As a problem solver for Borghesi International, I help to identify workplace concerns and resolve them before they can impact employee morale. I spent the last several months touring the facilities in Europe."

Borghesi International was a real company, owned by and named after Lucia herself, but I wasn't clear on exactly what their business was. Most likely, it involved transforming massive quantities of money into even larger quantities of the same. Given Lucia's exile, I highly doubted the company had any branches left in Europe, and I knew for a fact that the fair-haired queen didn't give a damn about employee morale.

My mom, lacking that crucial bit of context, took Ana's words at face value. "Europe! That *is* exciting." She patted Anastasia's pants-clad knee supportively. "And with you being so young!"

If I'd been drinking tea, that would have been the point I accidentally spat it across the room. It was past time I made my entrance.

"Mom." I looked at my mother, a petite, dark-haired woman who didn't look a day over forty, and then at the four-hundred-year-old next to her who didn't look a day over twenty-five. "Anastasia." My smile flickered into existence all on its own. Whatever was going on between us, whatever she'd been doing for the past half-year, it was impossible to deny how happy I was to see her.

"John." Anastasia rose from the chair in a single, graceful maneuver, clad in a pair of loose, black slacks, and a jade green blouse the exact color of her eyes.

"I'll leave you two kids to chat," said my mother, as she climbed to her feet in a considerably less graceful fashion. She turned to hug the taller woman. "It truly was wonderful to see you again, dear. Don't be a stranger. And if *this one* gives you any trouble, let me know! Like his father, John sometimes requires a firm hand."

She headed for the kitchen, leaving the two of us standing alone in the living room.

The moment stretched well past the point of becoming uncomfortable, as I watched Anastasia and she watched me. Finally, we both spoke.

"Maybe we shou—"

"I was hoping—"

"I'm sorry," I said with a self-conscious grin. "You first."

She nodded, still standing, and ensnared my gaze with her own. Even from a few feet away, I could pick out the flecks of gold in her luminous eyes. Her voice was calm, rich, and cool, like cheesecake drizzled in dark chocolate.

"I apologize for the unannounced visit. But we need to talk."

○○○

We need to talk. It had been a long while since I'd been in a relationship, but I remembered enough to dread those four words combined into that specific order. I was pretty sure my gender had been genetically hardwired to fear the phrase, just as women had been hardwired to employ it.

The terrible truth, as I had eventually realized, was that *we need to talk* usually meant *there is something badly wrong with our relationship, and I'm going to tell you what it is in excruciating detail despite the fact that you probably won't be able to do anything about it.* And that was a conversation that never ended well.

So yeah. That positive attitude I'd rolled out of bed with? That burst of semi-youthful energy and optimism? Gone in a flash, replaced with the sinking certainty that my morning was about to go to hell.

I didn't *say* any of that, of course. Especially with my mother eavesdropping on us from the kitchen. If we were going to have *the talk*, I preferred to not have my mother as a witness.

"You got my message then? I'm glad I had the right number," I said instead. "Have you eaten? There's a decent breakfast place just up the road."

"Would this place, by any chance, be an In-n-Out?" Anastasia's smile lit up the room. In-n-Out had been the first place we'd eaten together. It was a stretch to consider that outing a date, given there'd been six of us, but I still had good memories associated with it. Between that reference and her smile, I was getting some seriously mixed signals.

"Sadly, In-n-Out doesn't open until 10:30," I told her, having long ago memorized their schedule, "and it's only—" I glanced at my phone. "—holy crap, it's still super early, isn't it? Anyway, this is a pancake shop, but their omelets are good too. And it's quiet."

A small frown marred her porcelain features. "Unfortunately, I am needed at the House as soon as our business is complete. Might we speak on the porch instead?"

No pancakes. A conversation defined as *business*.

We need to talk.

I was back to being worried.

ooo

It was eerily reminiscent of the last time Ana and I had sat on the porch bench together; the sun bright in the sky, the neighborhood just beginning to wake up as the stay-at-home husbands or wives started their days. A kettle whistled through the Davidsons' open window. The femmepire next to me smelled fantastic.

Naturally, I had to open my mouth and ruin it.

"It's great to see you again, Ana. Even though Lucia told me—two months later—that you were out of the country, I was worried."

"Mr. Smith—"

"Which is dumb, I know. You're the most capable person I know, but still." I shook my head. "I think the House has missed you too. Lucia seems off her game lately. And those new manpires? Can't say I'm much of a fan of either of them. But now that—"

"John." Her voice cut through my babble like a surgeon's scalpel. It helped that she used my first name. "Time is short, and I am not here to speak about the House."

"You're here to talk about us."

"Yes."

"I kind of figured." I turned on the bench to give her my full attention. She looked… well, like a dream, as usual. But also pensive. Quiet in a way that differed from her usual stillness. Remote and unreachable, like a distant mountain I'd never even drive to, let alone climb.

"Last year, you sought leave to begin courting me."

Which… wasn't quite how I remembered it, especially since *courting* was a phrase my grandparents would have used. But I nodded anyway. I'd asked her out on a date. If that was the modern equivalent of courting, then I was okay with it.

"As much as I enjoyed that night," she continued, "the past six months have given me reason to reconsider my acceptance."

I hadn't seen or spoken to her in those six months, so I was sure I wasn't responsible for that shift.

Pretty sure.

"What changed?"

"I was reminded of my responsibilities."

"If freaking Lucia said something…"

"*Queen* Lucia, John. And she did not."

"She sent you to New Mexico. Literally the day after our date. That was just a coincidence?"

"I believe so, yes."

If she was surprised that my elite detective skills and/or close personal friendship with other vampires in the House had allowed me to discover her mission to assassinate werewolves in New Mexico, she was hiding it well.

"And sending you to Romania? For six months? That had nothing to do with our date either?" That *was* the country Lucia had mentioned, wasn't it? My grasp of geography was terrible outside of the continental United States. Or California, really.

"I went to Romania for personal reasons," said the femmepire. "My queen was gracious enough to give me leave to perform my duty."

I waited for an elaboration that never came.

"It's none of my business," I correctly decided, "but I hope that your task in Romania, whatever it was, ended well?"

She chewed momentarily on her lower lip, the equivalent of hair-pulling histrionics from anyone else, and finally shrugged. "It ended."

Which told me nothing at all.

"Regardless," she continued, "we have strayed from my original point. While I was abroad, I had a great quantity of time to think."

"About us."

"Among other things, yes." Jade eyes met mine. "You are a singular individual, Mr. Smith, and I am flattered by your attentions, but my life is not my own. I have duties that existed long before we met. To pretend otherwise would be a disservice to us both."

As far as I understood her history, she'd sworn allegiance to Lucia as a girl. Which once again made the queen the root cause of the world's most expected but also formal breakup.

Except… I'd known Anastasia for almost a year now, and she'd given me enough peeks behind her poker face that I felt like I knew the *real* her. And something more seemed like it was at play here.

What, exactly? Hell if I knew. I was a P.I., not a psychic.

"I knew from the start that you were Lucia's Secundus." If not exactly what that meant. "And that the House and the queen would always come first. I'm okay with that. Really. You're worth sharing."

"Be that as it may, I must decline your advances."

"Oh." There wasn't much else to say to that.

"John—"

"It's okay. I get it."

It was not okay, and I didn't get it. But I'd had months to accept that our date hadn't gone as well as I'd thought. Seeing Ana three times in the past week might have stirred things up, but at the end of the day, our so-called courtship had clearly been destined for failure.

That's what I told myself, anyway.

"I wanted you to hear this in person. You deserve that much from me. Perhaps if things were different or if we were…" She trailed off, uncharacteristically pensive. "The world is what it is, Mr. Smith. I am sorry."

I'd been through my fair share of *it's not you, it's me* declarations, but this was the first time anyone had gone with *it's not you, it's the world being what it is*. I can't say that mild permutation made it any more enjoyable, but I wasn't an eighteen-year-old kid anymore. I pulled on my big boy pants and tried to handle it like an adult.

"You don't owe me a thing, Anastasia. And if you had, saving my life *three times* more than paid that debt." I dredged up a smile, one that felt almost natural. "As long as you're happy, I will be too."

Her eyes met mine again.

She didn't *seem* happy.

CHAPTER 22

IN WHICH THERE AIN'T NO SUNSHINE WHEN SHE'S
GONE

"You look like shit," Juliette told me as I slumped through the door, "and I think that beard is slowly eating your face."

"Funny." I dropped into my chair and thumbed through the stack of papers on my desk. I'd headed for the office to delay the inevitable questions from my mother. Especially since she would take one look at me and know my talk with Anastasia hadn't gone well.

My poker face is just that bad.

"You really *do* look like shit. What happened?"

"Nothing," I lied, pasting on another smile. I met her disbelieving gaze. "I think this case is getting to me."

"Don't stress over it, little bird. Graciela's just one ghost in a world full of them."

"Maybe, but I promised the other Ladies I'd find her. I just don't have a clue how." The case was the other reason I'd gone straight to the office. If nothing else, maybe I could make progress on finding our missing White Lady.

"Lord Kala wasn't any help?"

"He says she's alive… or whatever you call a ghost who hasn't moved on. Again. Suggested I seek out the zombie prince for more info."

"Really?" Juliette sounded skeptical. "Are you sure talking to *him* is smart?"

"How would I know?" I shook my head irritably. "Until Saturday, I didn't even know zombies were a thing. A year ago, I was just the guy poor people hired to spy on their spouses. Then, I was juggling that with being a mediator in this crazy world you all live in. And now, nobody wants to hire me as a mediator anymore, and when someone finally *does* offer me a case, it involves tracking down a ghost in a city of two million people! A ghost! What do I know about ghost hunting?"

"Well, at the very least, you *should* know that if there's something strange in the neighborhood—"

I pinched the bridge of my nose, feeling another monster headache coming my way.

"—who you gonna call?" She snickered, but another glance my way wiped the merriment from her face. "Nope. That's not it."

"I'm sorry?"

"I get that it sucks being in over your head. I've never experienced it myself, but it must be terrible—" She flashed her trademark smirk again. "—but all of that was true yesterday when you were as happy as a toddler with ice cream to go tour San Diego's haunted houses. So, what changed?"

"Can we just drop it? I'm fine."

"Not by *either* definition of the word." When I didn't rise to the insult, she frowned again, and leaned closer, nostrils flaring.

"Gods damn it! What happened between you and Anastasia-freaking-Dumenyova?"

I wasn't at all surprised that Juliette had recognized the other femmepire's scent. "We ironed out some of the details in our relationship."

"Meaning?"

"We don't have one." I shrugged. "It's not a big deal."

"Sure it isn't." She yanked away the piece of paper I'd been pretending to stare at for the last five minutes, wadded it up into a small ball, and tossed it back onto the desk. "They don't call her the Stone Lady just because of her Talent, John. I told you that from the beginning."

"The world is what it is," I said.

"That's the dumbest thing I've ever heard."

"It really is." I shrugged again. "Anyway, I don't want to wallow. So, let's talk about this zombie prince. Or baseball. Or anything but my non-existent love life."

Juliette wasn't having it.

"I know you liked her, little bird. The *why* of it is what's been eluding most of us, but I figured it was just one more piece of evidence that you're cracked in the head."

"This is a fantastic pep talk, Duchess."

She smacked me in the back of my head, not helping my headache in the slightest.

"I wasn't finished! I know you liked her, and it's okay to be upset. But you know what's even better than that?"

"What?"

"Moving the hell on."

And then she leaned in and kissed me.

○○○

Juliette's lips were cool and soft and tasted of strawberries. She knew how to kiss too, thanks to what must have been decades of practice. And yet...

"Huh," she said, after disengaging.

"Well," I agreed.

"That wasn't..."

"I don't think..."

"Maybe if we..."

Again, she leaned into me, and again I didn't do anything to stop her. This kiss was less gentle than the first, more demanding. Her tongue darted out and across my lips and when I unconsciously opened them in reply, she took my bottom lip between her teeth.

And yet, it still wasn't really...

She bit me. Hard.

"Ow! What the hell, Juliette?" I pushed her away and ran a finger across my lip. It came away bloody.

"I was hungry," she replied with a lazy shrug, one finger making a slow circuit around her own mouth to collect any blood she might have missed. "And thought maybe *that's* what was missing. But while your *blood* is as tasty as ever, that kiss..."

"No spark whatsoever," I agreed. "It was like kissing my sister. If I had a sister. Not that I would kiss my sister if I did."

My brain informed me that it was time to stop talking.

Juliette looked uncharacteristically pensive.

"It's not you," I told her. "I'm just not—"

"Of course it's not me!" She rolled her eyes. "I was propositioned three times on my way to Starbucks this morning, *without* sending out even the tiniest of signals. I *know* I'm hot."

"You just seemed... unhappy."

"I'm not unhappy," she growled. "I'm irritated, I'm tired of your stupid drama, and I'm *hungry!*"

"Didn't you eat—well, drink—this morning?"

"Oh sure. A few sips from a random San Diegan with a BMW." She waved one hand dismissively. "And what a prized bouquet *that* was, let me tell you!"

"You didn't take your donors with you when you left the House?"

"I haven't had dedicated donors for years. I always just sampled the House larder; they're all clean, attractive, and willing. Keeping donors is a huge pain in the ass. Worse than pets, really."

"But now that you don't have access to the House's…" I damn well wasn't going to refer to it as a larder.

"Yeah. Suddenly, having my own donor seems like a much better idea."

"Was this about getting my mind off of Anastasia or getting your blood fix?"

"Maybe a little bit of both? We already work together; how perfect would it be if you were my donor too? You'd never have to worry that I was going to disappear during the day to go feed. And I'd get to drink on the job! It would be like bringing a bottomless thermos to work!"

"That sounds perfect for one—and only one—of us. And the kiss?" I could still feel her lips against my own, a sensation that was mildly disturbing for the lack of carnal thoughts it inspired.

I was clearly even more depressed than I'd realized.

"I've never minded a little bit of play with my meals. Although, I underestimated the rug burn factor," she admitted, running two fingertips over her own mouth. "Anyway, given how disastrously bad those kisses were, sex is clearly off the table. But maybe we could still—"

"Juliette, I'm not going to be your donor. Ever. I'm the one human in this city who *can't* be your donor. In case you've forgotten, I'm immune to whatever it is the People do to make biting *not* hurt."

"Except for freaking Lucia, whose bite makes you swoon like a dime novel heroine," she muttered irritably.

"Not to mention," I continued, manfully ignoring the slight to my masculinity, "that feeding on Queen Crazy Pants' thrall seems like it would be a really crappy way to convince her to forget or forgive you."

"That…" Wonder of wonders, Juliette paused to consider my comment. "That's actually a good point. Damn it."

"And *you* were a Council member?"

"Get stuffed, little bird." She smirked in response, but that expression faded quickly. "It just would have been so *convenient!*"

"Right." I checked again to make sure my lip had stopped bleeding—vampire saliva was a hell of a coagulant—and shooed her back to her side of the desk. I hated to admit it, but the dreadful kiss and even worse bite had me focused for the first time all morning. "So, let's talk about the zombie prince."

Unfortunately, finding a zombie was a lot harder than Hollywood would have you believe. In movies, they roamed the world like land-borne piranhas, but in the real world, there was never a zombie apocalypse when you needed one. Without a clumsily hacked-together script pushing us all in the proper direction of the next major plot point, we were going to have to find the zombie prince ourselves. Which meant more research and an annoying amount of legwork.

Juliette knew of one cemetery the zombie had frequented—the burial grounds in eastern San Diego that had been at the center of that dispute with the skinwalker that Lucia had mentioned—but the prince was something of a rolling stone, and rarely spent more than a few days in any one location.

Still, how many cemeteries could San Diego have?

As usual, Google maps provided the answer.

Sadly, that answer told me I'd be old before I visited them all. Or at least thirty. Damn it.

"Maybe we should break into the UCSD med school," I decided. "Don't they have cadavers there? How much brain matter do you think we'd need to lure the prince out of hiding?"

"Clearly, more than you've got in your pretty little head," Juliette replied with a roll of her yellow eyes.

"You think my head is pretty?"

"No. It's not particularly little either. And turning to crime after getting dumped is too cliché even for you."

Apparently, vampires had their own unique set of clichés.

"Fine. There's always Plan B."

"I can't wait to hear this one," muttered Juliette.

I gave her my best stern senior-partner look.

"Fine. What's Plan B?"

"Plan B is where I delegate the task of finding this dude to my firm's most junior employee." I flashed a wide smile at Juliette. It served her right for having shot down my first plan.

"I'm not your gofer, you obnoxious twerp," she exploded. "If you want someone to run around doing your job for you while wearing tiny skirts that show off every inch of her fabulous legs, you picked the wrong partner!"

I took a peek and verified that the femmepire was not, in fact, wearing a tiny skirt, but instead jeans and a t-shirt, and if the jeans were painted on… well, that was Juliette's standard wardrobe.

"I was speaking figuratively."

I shook my head. "I'm not saying you're a gofer. I just—"

"Fine."

"Fine?"

"That's what I said."

"Uhm… fine what?" I finally asked, having thoroughly lost the thread of the conversation.

"I'll find the zombie prince for you," Juliette grumbled. "But only because you're having a lousy day, and it would be inconvenient to have the White Ladies kill you for screwing up this case."

I couldn't dispute the inconvenience.

"But if that asshole gives me any grief, I'm going to pay it forward on your lazy fratboy hide," she declared.

I was just about to remind her, for at least the fiftieth time, that I was old enough to be considered a frat*man*, when my phone buzzed.

CHAPTER 23
IN WHICH YOU GET WHAT YOU PAY FOR

"You owe me big time." The voice was male, barely audible over the throbbing bass in his background.

"Mike?" I ventured. "I can't hear you."

The music on the other end of the line cut off. "It's Jason. Who the hell is *Mike?*"

"My best friend," I told the werewolf with a sigh.

"Then why haven't I met him? Does he live in Anchorage or something? Timbuktu?"

"Do you even know where Timbuktu is?"

"Do you?"

"Well… no," I admitted. "Anyway, Mike and his girlfriend live in Ocean Beach."

As far as I knew, anyway; I was still waiting for the official housewarming invitation. Sara was, to put it bluntly, not my biggest fan. As if it was my fault that Mike went out every weekend and got drunk with me.

"Sweet. I love OB!" Jason was a relative newcomer to San Diego but had spent the past year or two seeking out every bar and strip club in the county. "We should all totally hang out."

"Not going to happen, hombre. Mike has no idea the Dark World even exists. I'd prefer to keep it that way." The last thing I needed was to get my best friend—my *only* friend, for a lot of my childhood—killed.

"The Dark World?"

"Yeah. You know… weres and vamps and demons and stuff."

"Sweet name, bro."

I was pretty proud of it, myself, but had never been the sort of person to bask in other's compliments.

"You really like it?"

Ok… maybe a little basking was in order. I'd had a rough day.

"Definitely. Makes me feel like even more of a badass. I'm Batman, right?"

And that killed any chance of me ever using the term again.

"Anyway, what's up? How did it go?"

"Like I said, bro, you totally owe me. It took a bit to pick up the target's trail, but I've been following them all over town."

"Since *Sunday?*" Jason had been the other person I phoned after my meeting with Nepenthe and Thomas. My ace in the hole, so to speak, if such a description could be safely applied to a twenty-year-old werewolf dudebro.

"I did trade off with Emilio a few times," he admitted, "but just so I could get my drink on." Emilio, like Jason, was a werewolf. Unlike Jason, he was an actual functioning adult. He also possessed the sweetest mustache the world had ever seen.

"I see." Apparently, I'd neglected to inform Jason that his job tailing the witches was a Sunday-night-only sort of thing. "I mean, that's great! Anything of interest to report?"

"Not even one ritual murder," he said glumly. "The little dude went back north on Sunday, but I've stuck with the woman. She's not bad looking for an old chick."

"Are we talking about the same person? Nepenthe is… like mid-thirties, tops." And if I looked that good in another decade, I'd be ecstatic. Hell, I didn't even look that good *now*.

"Like I said, total fogey. Anyway, she's spent the last few days traveling about the city, meeting with different people, some of them norms, some of them not."

"Makes sense. I assume she's giving everyone the same pitch she gave me."

"If you say so. It's been super boring. I thought stakeouts were supposed to be awesome?"

"It's a closely kept secret of the profession," I told him, "that being a detective *is* super boring." Considering that the exceptions to that rule had involved attempts on my life, I preferred the tedium. Most of the time.

"Figures. Nothing's ever as cool as it is on television. So, how much longer do you need me to keep watching her?"

"Just a little bit," I assured him. "I don't suppose you've taken any surveillance footage?"

"Some. I got a bunch of pics with my phone Sunday night and yesterday morning before the battery ran out of juice."

I suspected Jason's battery issues had as much to do with playing Clash of Clans or one of the other half dozen mobile games he loved as it did with taking pictures, but I couldn't blame him for that.

I'd run out of charge on more than a few stakeouts myself. "Can you upload them for me?"

"Don't expect anything too juicy, man. And if this whole stakeout thing starts cutting into my weekend, we're going to have to renegotiate my fee."

"You never told me exactly what it was you wanted," I reminded him, hoping once again that it wouldn't involve actual cash. "Am I buying rounds at the Bitter End this weekend?"

"Nah." He was weirdly serious for a moment. "Nothing like that, bro. You're the poorest dude I know."

"What can I do for you then?" He was silent for so long that I thought our connection might have dropped. "Jason?"

"I was hoping," he said, voice still quiet, "that you could help me get back together with Carolyn."

It was my turn to let the silence lengthen. In one of my two guest chairs, Juliette was shaking her head.

"Carolyn?" I finally asked. "As in Carolyn Hawthorne? Your ex?"

"She's the only Carolyn I know, dude. In San Diego, anyway. There was a total smokeshow back in Taos, but she preferred Carol over Carolyn. And Georgie over me, for that matter."

"Jason, I just mediated your *divorce* last year. And last week, you were telling me how glad you were to be single. Why on earth would you want to get back together with Carolyn?"

"Would you believe she's my one true love?" he asked hopefully.

"Not even a little bit."

"That's fair," he admitted, "but our separation has given me time to think."

"And?" A thinking Jason was a terrifying concept. The laws of nature were being shattered.

"And I kind of miss her, bro. Being with her, I mean. We had our bad times, but there was some good stuff too."

"When I first met you two, there was a real chance that your separation was going to tear the Pack apart, leaving one or both of you dead."

"I already said there were some bad times. No need to bust my balls over it. Still, everything that happened—the divorce, Travis' betrayal, your kidnapping, Georgie's death—has made me realize there might be more to life than alcohol and anonymous sex."

"Didn't you spend the last six months drinking and sleeping around?" To my shock and horror, I'd discovered that the guy was practically catnip for the women of San Diego. It was like the whole gender was programmed for self-destruction.

"For sure! Guess I had to get some of that out of my system. But I think I'm ready now."

"Ready to...?"

"Ready to settle down. Shack back up with Carolyn. Start a family. You know, adult shit."

"You're twenty!"

"Twenty-one, as of last month, and thanks for not getting me a birthday present, you dick. But if I want to see my children grow into adulthood, I need to start as soon as possible."

"But you've got... oh." Given that I was only twenty-six, children were still the furthest thing from my mind. But the wolves, like all weres, tended to go insane and die in their early forties. Which meant that even though Jason was several years my junior, and as emotionally mature as a four-legged starfish, he was already middle-aged.

"Yeah. Awesomeness like mine has a short shelf-life."

"Maybe Lord Kala…"

"Hell no. Dude's not running a halfway house for aging weres. And I'd rather die than be stuck underground for the rest of my life. Even though it *is* a sweet bar."

"I understand. But… Carolyn? Really?"

"I hope you're not about to say something negative about my former wife, and the potential mother of my cubs," he growled.

"Not at all. She's a nice girl." With three-inch claws, an obsession with going green, and the jaded soul of a mercenary. "But are you sure she's the one? I mean, there *are* other women in the Pack, right?"

"If you don't want to help—"

"I didn't say that. I'll do what I can. Relationships just aren't really my forte."

"I don't know, bro." Jason had returned to his usual chipper self. "You somehow managed to hook that smoking-hot, if insanely scary, vamp chick."

I winced.

"*And* you've got Juliette as your extra bit on the side too," he continued. "She's pretty damn fine in her own right."

"Anastasia and I are through," I said, "and Juliette is not my *bit on the side*. She's also here, listening to every word you say."

"No shit?" He raised his voice, although it was totally unnecessary. "Hey fang-babe! Hope you're not too sad that I'll be off the market soon."

"Somehow, I'll survive." Juliette's voice was bone dry. The two species' supernatural hearing allowed them to converse as easily as if they were on speaker phone.

"Oops. Got to go," said the werewolf. "Fogey One has left the building!"

"She's really not—" The connection died as Jason hung up without another word. "—that old."

∘∘∘

"Bit on the side?" Juliette seemed unamused.

"Hey, I'm not responsible for what—"

"And who is this Nepenthe?"

"She's the leader of a small coven in Temecula. I had dinner with her on Sunday. A *business* dinner. I'm just making sure she's on the level."

"That's almost smart of you," said Juliette. "You *do* have a history of being kidnapped by potential clients."

"As you well know."

"And you have *Jason* following her around." She smiled. "Forget smart. That's brilliant. He's the very definition of an expendable asset."

"You're sounding a bit like Lucia there, Duchess."

That won me a hard glare from the femmepire.

"Anyway, talking to Carolyn on Jason's behalf is a small enough thing and should be perfectly safe. I mean, she only tried to kill me the one time." I booted up my aging laptop so I could download Jason's pictures. "It doesn't sound like Nepenthe is up to anything nefarious, but he's uploaded his photos anyway."

"Are you sure you have the time to take on another case, with Graciela still missing?"

"It'll be fine. I'm just consulting with the coven."

"That sounds like code for *unpaid.*"

"I got a free dinner out of it. Sometimes, you have to schmooze at the beginning of business relationships. It's called entrepreneurship."

"I don't think that word means what you think it means."

"*Anyway*, we should be done with the White Ladies before the coven requires my services. And speaking of the Ladies—" I gave my partner what I hoped was an authoritative look. "—shouldn't you be searching for the zombie prince?"

"That sounds like a task for tomorrow." Juliette yawned, exposing suspiciously lengthened canines. "I'm bored and famished."

"I'm still not on the menu."

"One of these days, you'll cowboy up."

"Juliette…"

"Fine. I'll make some calls. You look at your wolf's pictures. But you owe me lunch."

"What? Why?"

"We're partners! That means half of your free dinner with Nepenthe should have been mine." She shook her head. "Two days into our new business arrangement and you're already embezzling. Humans."

I rolled my eyes. "That was *mediator* business. And we're definitely not partners in that."

"Nor would I want to be." She chewed on her bottom lip for a second and then sent me a smirk. "You owe me lunch anyway."

"I just told you—"

"Yeah, yeah, I heard you. I'm not talking about the witch. I'm talking about the kiss."

"You bit my lip and *I* owe *you* lunch?"

"Better believe it."

"Why?"

"When's the last time you thought about *her?*" She read the answer on my face and nodded. "There you go. My distraction services don't come cheap, little bird."

I honestly had no idea what to say to that. Thankfully, a glance at my screen showed that the first batch of pictures from Jason's surveillance had loaded. "Give me an hour or so to review these photos, and then we can head out. My treat, but we're not going anywhere that requires shoes for service."

"Deal." Juliette already had her phone out, although she seemed to be browsing rather than texting.

Less than a minute later, I sighed.

"Actually, let's just go."

"Not that I'm complaining, but why?"

"Judging by the first dozen pics, this is going to be a waste of time." I gestured to my laptop and scooted out of the way as Juliette came around the desk to look for herself.

"Is that… an ass?" she finally asked.

"Nothing but butt," I confirmed, flipping to another picture. "And this one appears to be a bird on a telephone wire. And that," I clicked to another shot, "is a bachelorette party from Sunday night."

"*Why* did you hire wolfboy again?"

"Because I'm an idiot," I muttered. "I should know better than to rely on amateurs."

"Or twenty-one-year-old boys."

"Yeah. Them too."

CHAPTER 24

After a huge lunch, an unproductive afternoon, and a full night of alcohol-fueled, Anastasia-related commiseration with Juliette, Kayla, and Darlene, I expected to sleep past noon on Wednesday. Instead, I was awake by nine and full of energy. Even my hangover was a distant echo of what it should have been, a headache so faint that it barely deserved mention.

My recent transformation into a morning person was bewildering. I needed to ask my mom if she'd been sneaking supplements into my morning cereal… and if so, where I could get more of them. Maybe an extra handful a day would give me abs?

Still, while I might not have *felt* like I'd spent the night drinking, I definitely *smelled* like it. I went straight to the shower. The stench of tobacco and alcohol was gradually replaced by that of peppermint scented soap. The tiny bathroom was a far cry from the vampire House's techno-marvel facilities, but at least I didn't have to worry about people walking in on me mid-shower.

My to-do list hadn't diminished in the slightest. I needed to go through the rest of Jason's spy pics, on the off chance that his camerawork and attention span had improved as the week progressed. I also needed to touch base with Kristin, whose promised pixie-sourced ghost map had yet to materialize. And with Juliette now actively hunting for the zombie prince, I was free to present Lucia with Nepenthe's proposition. And to put Operation Get Kayla Her Job Back into motion.

Just thinking about my workload should have made me tired. The lack of progress I'd seen on multiple fronts should have added to that ennui. Instead, I was energized.

Energized and *hungry*. It was feeling like a three Egg McMuffin morning.

I pulled on a fresh pair of jeans and a t-shirt from the carefully folded stack of clean clothes my mom had left atop the dresser and turned off my mp3 player. If Valentina had staged a repeat of her one-woman dance routine, I hadn't been awake to see it. Nor had she left anything to mark her presence.

In fact, I realized, it had been a few days since I'd seen the White Lady at all.

There was nothing all that unusual about that—Valentina had a life... or unlife... of her own, after all—but given Graciela's disappearance, it was a little bit worrisome. I decided I'd wait out for her on the porch bench that night, just to make *absolutely* sure she was okay. And maybe to ask why Margaret had stood me up on Monday.

Of all the tasks on my plate, the least appealing by far was my talk with Lucia, owner of my bond and general pain in the ass While I had high hopes that she'd listen to my idea for Kayla, there was almost no chance the femmepire would agree to Nepenthe's idealized form of popular democracy. In fact, just being the messenger of said proposal was going to earn me one of the monarch's withering diatribes.

Regardless, it was only nine in the morning, and a quick mental check told me the queen was far to the north, presumably at her House. I had plenty of time to devise a clever plan to get into her domain, deliver my message, and get back out with my skin, ego, and patience all intact. In fact, I could even—

"Sweetie?" My mom's voice echoed down the stairwell. "You have a visitor."

Hadn't we just done this yesterday? My stupid heart did a tiny somersault at the faint possibility that Ana had changed her mind. Because that was something centuries-old vampires did so easily. My far more sensible head was examining the short list of who else might have come to my home. Juliette? Kristin? Mike?

I took the stairs two at a time and followed my mother's voice around the corner and down the hall. She was seated in the living room yet again, holding another cup of tea. *Not* our good china this time.

Next to her sat Lucia's new Captain of the Watch, Thales. Well, shit.

○○○

The Brazilian was wearing the uniform of the House Watch, an all-black ensemble that made me look like an out-of-shape undertaker yet imbued him with the mystique of a foreign rock star. His dark hair was slicked back, and his cheekbones were sharp enough to draw blood. He took a sip of tea, smiling faintly at the emotions that were no doubt painted across my face.

"Thales," I began, conscious of the fact that my mom was both present and within the manpire's reach, "what are you doing here?"

"John Smith!" My mom's voice cracked like a whip. "Is that how we've raised you to behave with guests?"

"It's quite alright, Maria," Thales said, patting her shoulder in a soothing gesture that made my blood boil *and* run cold at the same time. "John's poor manners are in no way a reflection on your parenting, I am sure."

"My poor manners?"

I paused. My mom was beaming at the manpire. Considering her usual response to a comment like that would have been to throw the offending party out on his overmuscled ass, that smile was way out of character. And that meant… "You asshole! Lucia made my parents off limits for compulsion!"

"No harm has been done," replied the bloodsucker with a shrug. "I was curious if this woman shared your unnatural talent, but it appears she is every bit the average monkey."

My mom sat by his side, smiling slightly and blissfully unaware. I stepped past her to loom over our visitor.

"You have five seconds to release my mom, and get out of our—"

I found myself sprawled on the carpet of our living room, one side of my face aching in pain. Thales was standing, his expression condescending. On Juliette, a smirk was almost endearing. On the manpire, it was nothing short of infuriating.

"Four seconds," I told him stubbornly, after finally regaining my feet.

He moved again, but this time I found myself awkwardly stumbling to the side, the rush of air past my face the only sign that the vampire's strike had missed.

Thales paused, surprise flickering across his face. "So. You do possess *some* skill."

"You have no idea," I told him, trying to hide my own surprise. I hadn't expected a confrontation with Lucia's new Captain, especially not on a Wednesday, in my living room, and in front of my mother, but I was gratified to realize that I was coming off like a badass. "Now, are you going to leave or am I going to get to kick your ass?"

ooo

It was the steady purr of the car's engine that finally lured me out of unconsciousness. I woke to find myself bound and sprawled across the leather-clad backseat of a House Mercedes. The passing scenery out the near window was the only indication that we were in motion. Even in my current state, I had to admit the car had an amazingly smooth ride.

At the wheel, Thales spared me a brief glance in the rear-view mirror. I had no memory of getting into the car, and that, plus the fact that *both* sides of my face were now hurting equally, told me that my skills in kung fu had been found wanting.

"Where are you taking me?" What did it say about my life that being kidnapped was starting to feel commonplace? At least this time, I had my clothes on.

"The Queen demands your presence."

"And she couldn't have just *called* me?"

He shrugged and said nothing.

"Why send *you*, for that matter?" I persisted. "Lucia never sent the *old* Captain on menial errands…"

"She did not send me. I volunteered for the mission. And now," he said, with a fang-filled smile into the mirror, "I know where you live."

That was just scary enough to shut me up.

Which may have been his intent all along.

For once, I didn't look at the mansion as we followed the long driveway through the estate grounds. Instead, I was furiously putting together a plan for my meeting with Lucia. On top of everything else I had to say, I was going to make damn sure that her new vampires learned my parents were untouchable. The idea that Thales, of all people, had been mucking with my mother's brain… well, that sort of shit was unforgivable.

Thales removed my handcuffs, tucking them away as I flexed and extended my wrists to restore the blood flow. "You must know, monkey, that if you try to run…"

"Yeah, yeah. You'll chase me down. Because you apparently have nothing better to do." I waved away his words and started through the foyer toward the elevator. "What you need is a hobby."

We went to the third floor, where the Council had their private residences, and down the hall to Lucia's palatial suite. After receiving permission to enter, Thales shoved me through the door. We passed through a waiting area larger than my entire living space at home, then around the corner into the main sitting room, whose far wall was dominated by an enormous bay window overlooking the estate grounds.

Lucia stood with her back to us, the sunlight streaming through that window to silhouette her exquisite form.

"Your Majesty," Thales said at last, when it became clear the femmepire wasn't going to greet us. "I have brought the mediator, as requested."

"I am aware, Thales. You may return to your duties." Her voice was hard. She continued looking out the window, as if we were both beneath her notice.

It was gratifying to discover that I wasn't the only person Lucia treated like garbage.

"Yes, my queen." A dark look passed across Thales' face, but his voice remained smooth and unaffected. He bowed in the direction of the uncaring monarch and left. The door was too well-crafted to slam shut behind him, which probably irritated the asshole even more.

I waited for the queen to do... well, anything... but she seemed content to keep looking out the window. Which she could have done *without* sending one of her thugs to brainwash my mother and kidnap me.

"What did—"

Lucia gave a sharp wave of her hand, and I stopped talking immediately. Then, annoyed at myself for having done so, I decided to keep going.

"What did you want to talk to me about, Lucia? And why couldn't it have waited until *after* breakfast?" My stomach was moodily reminding me that the three Egg McMuffins I'd promised it had yet to materialize.

"What did I say, thrall, when last we met?" Her tone was icy, even more so than usual.

"That the Corolla was registered in my name." I was suddenly struck by a horrible thought. "You're not taking it back, are you?"

"I said," she growled, spinning on one skyscraper-like heel to look at me for the first time, "that you needed to take care of the rival mediator!"

"It's been *four* days. These things take time."

She stepped out of the sunlight, blue eyes blazing so brightly I could barely see her. "One." She extended an index finger. "You identify his weaknesses. Two." Her middle finger joined the index. "You locate his place of rest. And three." Her ring finger joined the other two. "You put a bullet in his brain. Why would this take longer than the day I already gave you?"

"I'm not going to *kill* him!" I protested. "That's absurd. I'm going to talk with him. We'll hash things out. It'll be fine. You'll see."

"What I *see* is that you persist on treating my commands as mere suggestions." She stalked past me in a flurry of silk, circling me like a lion might circle its prey. "What I *see* is a boy unwilling to get his hands dirty."

"Then look closer!" I shot back. "One of the reasons you wanted this relationship was because my methods work. Foiling the coup. Creating an alliance between you and the Pack. Maybe I don't do things your way, but you can't argue with the results! And that'll be true with Caleb Van Stahl too. You just need to get off my back and give me some time." I turned to look her in the face as she continued her slow circling. "Trust me on… uhm, are you okay?"

With the sunlight now on her face rather than obscuring it, I was seeing something I'd never noticed before on a vampire's face. Lines. The queen remained as lovely as ever but looked… unwell. Pale and tired. A far cry from the woman who had brought all of Mister A's to silence just six months earlier.

Did vampires get the flu?

"I am under the weather," Lucia growled, "and it is none of your concern."

"Fair enough." I was already wondering how I was going to rid myself of what had to be superhuman germs. A bug that would bother a vampire would straight up kill someone like me. How many pieces of furniture had I touched on my way in here? How many times had I rubbed my eyes after Thales released me from the handcuffs?

"We could have discussed this over the phone like civilized people," I said, "or this afternoon, when I'd planned to swing by anyway. You didn't have to send Thales to kidnap me."

"He was told simply to fetch you."

"And brainwash my mother?" My anger came roaring back at the thought.

"Of course not." The queen's voice was iron. "Your parents are off limits to the members of my House. That was my promise to you, and a Borghesi does not break her word."

"Then your employee orientation sucks, because that's exactly what Thales did."

"I will speak to him. It will *not* happen again."

"Thank you." I found myself slightly mollified, which was pretty much the exact opposite of how our conversations usually went. "Anyway, I can handle Caleb. And I will. In my own way. With enough time."

"You have one month."

"That's not what—" I stopped as her eyes drilled into me like icicles. Tired and sick, Lucia was in a mood. "Fine. One month."

"So be it. You may leave now."

"Actually, as long as I'm here, there are a couple of things I was hoping to discuss with you anyway."

ooo

"If I understand you correctly," said the queen, after listening to me ramble on for almost twenty minutes, "it is your recommendation that I set aside my authority and join the other species of this city in some manner of democratic government?"

"Kind of? Yeah." And that was a much more succinct way of putting it than I had managed. I shifted uneasily in my extremely expensive and uncomfortable chair. "I'm just passing the idea along for a friend."

"And this *friend* would be… what? A pixie? A goblin? Perhaps a gnome?" Lucia's voice was taking on the caustic edge that I was all too familiar with, but she otherwise seemed relaxed, seated in the twin to my own chair, her unbuttoned suit jacket revealing an acre of golden cleavage.

"A witch."

"Of course. That would fit."

"I'm not following." What did pixies, goblins, gnomes, and witches have in common? Besides being the start of a joke whose punchline I really wanted to hear.

"Should you live long enough to attain a small measure of wisdom, you will find that the ideal of democracy *always* takes seed amongst those furthest from power. Witches," she added dismissively, "rank even lower than pixies. Monkeys with magic? It's an abomination."

"You don't say."

"Indeed. Those without power always desire it, my thrall. If they are unable to seize it on their own, they attempt to legislate for it. It's appalling, really."

"Even if that were true," I began carefully, thinking of how little Nepenthe had seemed interested in power for its own sake, "does it invalidate the idea itself?"

Lucia narrowed her eyes, but the fact that she wasn't tossing me around her suite like a man-sized rag doll suggested she was at least willing to listen. Or too tired and sick to end me just yet. "Explain yourself."

"How many times in the past half-century have you or the other ruling species had to get things done on your own? If the races of the city could work together…"

"That is an idiot's fantasy," she informed me icily. "I have devoted too much of my life to protecting my birthright to simply relinquish such authority upon request."

I decided not to point out that, as an exile, she'd pretty much already lost her birthright. "Nobody's saying you would have to stop being a queen."

"Nor would I allow such a suggestion to go unpunished."

"But I don't see what's so terrible about a city council. Hell, the People are clearly okay with the concept already, considering each House has a Council of its own."

"The House Council exists to serve its ruler. I might be amenable to the idea of adding your so-called city council to my rule—"

"That's really not the way democracy works."

"—but I have no desire to waste time and energy on the affairs of other, inherently lesser beings."

"But what if—"

"I have given you my answer." Her voice crackled with suppressed power. "Take it to your witch and tell them that my House will treat any attempt to diminish our standing as an act of war. And you, my thrall," she added in a dangerous tone, "would be wise to exercise better judgment in your choice of allies."

Swallowing my own angry retort was difficult. I don't think I'd have managed it at all if I hadn't expected Lucia to react exactly as she had… and if I hadn't had another, equally important, proposition to discuss with her.

"I'll pass the word," I finally said, "but you don't get to tell me who my friends are."

"As you wish," she allowed regally, as if I had been seeking her permission. "Is that all?"

"Not quite," I said. "We need to talk about Kayla."

CHAPTER 25
IN WHICH NO GOOD PLAN GOES UNPUNISHED

"My former Captain? What of her?" Lucia had seemingly put aside her anger, but I wasn't fooled. With the vampire queen, more rage was always on its way.

"Exactly that. Your *former* Captain. A woman who put her life on the line for this House on multiple occasions. Who survived the massacre of the Watch at the hands of her superior, Xavier, and kept the peace through your quarrel with the gnomes and the near war with the New Mexico Pack."

"Does this history recital serve a purpose? I not only lived through the events in question but possess a far greater understanding and appreciation for the factors involved than you do."

"My point," I grated, "is that she's displayed the kind of loyalty a queen should be grateful for."

"Gratitude is not the province of royalty, Mr. Smith," Lucia told me. "I honor her allegiance."

"Then why did you kick her to the curb as soon as Duke Whatshisname showed up on your doorstep with Thales?"

The queen frowned at my choice of words. "I have not *kicked her to the curb*. Is she not a member of my House?"

"Sure. A member whose loyalty you rewarded with a prompt and public demotion as soon as another alternative presented itself."

"Thales is a Battle Lord." Lucia's voice was a mixture of anger and the weariness that looked so unnatural on her features. "Do you have any idea what that means?"

"That there's every chance he'll turn traitor and try to depose you, just like the last one did?" I shot back. "Yeah, I understand."

She pinched the bridge of her nose in a distinctly human gesture and waved the other hand at me. "From the moment I took power, my Captain of the Watch has always been the greatest warrior of the House, excepting those upon the Council itself. Before Thales' arrival, that was your friend Kayla. But she is young still, and the newcomer is better suited to the role."

"Which I'm sure is a comfort to Kayla."

"As a member of the People, she understands. And if she does not, then she should accept the lesson I am providing her, rather than suborning my thrall into speaking on her behalf. This will serve her well in the future."

"I'm sure it's been instructive for the entire House—"

"I do hope so."

"—to see that power matters more than loyalty with you. That blood spent in your service weighs less than the potential of relative strangers."

Lucia's expression hardened and the temperature in the room plummeted. "Your ignorance becomes more apparent with every word you speak!"

"Why don't you enlighten me then? Tell me why it's okay to treat your subjects so poorly!"

"My first priority is my House, Mr. Smith. For this House to survive, it needs allies."

"As long as those allies aren't pixies, goblins, gnomes, or witches," I muttered.

"Allies among the People, you inbred fool. My brother's court wields immense power. Brazil gives me a foothold in the South American empire. Duke Barros' decision to join my House has already shown dividends in the politics of his homeland. And that," she continued dangerously, "is worth more than a single individual's wounded pride. Regardless of her past service or her relationship with my thrall."

"What is the point of safeguarding your House," I asked quietly, "if you lose the subjects who matter most along the way?"

"Thales deserves a place of honor, and I have given it to him. I will not controvert that decision. Nor will I have my actions dictated by the bleeding heart of the city's lame-duck mediator."

"I'm not suggesting you strip Thales of his place of honor," I said, trying not to show how much her words had hurt. *Lame-duck mediator? Really?* "Just the opposite, in fact."

"Explain."

"Create a new position for him. Knight of the Council or something stupidly grandiose. Task him with the security of the Council. Restore Kayla to her role as Captain of the Watch, with duties encompassing everything but those given to Thales. The Watch will be happy to have one of their own back in charge. Thales will be happy to move up in the world. And everyone, vampire and otherwise, will see that you're able to balance the needs of your people with the needs of your House."

Somehow, I'd managed all of that in one breath. Now, I found myself holding the next one in nervous anticipation. It was a good plan. Frankly, it was the best plan I'd been able to think of, and Darlene's own careful inquiries had told me the rest of the Watch would support it. All we needed was Lucia's approval.

"There is some merit to your proposal," the queen mused, "but my answer is no."

For a moment, I was so shocked that I couldn't speak.

"Why not?" I finally asked. Good plan? No, it had been a *great* plan. It had been the closest thing to a win/win any of us could ask for.

"Because I am the queen of this House," she told me, her voice low and dangerous, "and as my thrall, it is past time that you learn your place."

"Even queens can take advice…"

"You are *not* my advisor. You are not a member of my Council. You are an employee, Mr. Smith."

I took another deep breath. How did one convince a megalomaniac of *anything*? I'd come with arguments founded in logic, offering solutions with a high probability of success, but Lucia simply wasn't interested.

"If the advice is good, who cares what the source—"

"Enough!" she cut in ruthlessly, flowing to her feet to somehow tower over me despite her relatively short stature. *"I will not relinquish my power.* Not to your witches, not to their council, and not to you! I am the ruler of this House. I make the decisions!"

"Which explains why this place is fifty percent traitors and thirty percent spies," I growled, rising to my own feet.

"We are done here, Mr. Smith," she said icily. "When next we meet, you will have regained primacy as San Diego's *only* mediator or you *will* be replaced."

"Assuming your House still exists in a month. Given its sterling leadership, that doesn't seem likely." I turned to leave.

"Scurry back to your mother's basement." Lucia's angry voice followed me into the foyer. "Small wonder that Lady Dumenyova wants nothing more to do with you."

I froze in mid-stride, one hand on the doorknob.

"I was gratified to hear that she had finally expressed the futility of your infatuation," Lucia continued sweetly. "In fact, she would make an excellent match for Thales, cementing our alliance with Brazil even more. Gods know a useless blood bag like you could never hope to deserve her."

ooo

Multiple thoughts warred in my head. Anger swept through me like a Santa Ana wind, but a loud voice in my mind urged caution, urged restraint. *You've done what you could*, it told me. *It's time to get out.*

It made sense, that voice. It spoke for the prudent side of me, the side that was slowly maturing, that understood responsibility and the value of a cautious approach. But if I'd listened to that voice, I would have ended up in a cubicle and a tie, filling out spreadsheets while daydreaming about being a private investigator. I would never have learned the truth about the world we lived in.

I would never have met Anastasia.

I turned back to face the queen.

Lucia was just a few feet away, a satisfied expression on the face that I suddenly couldn't remember ever having found lovely. She was a four-hundred-year-old vampire, she could deadlift a bus, and she was an ice queen in both the literal and figurative sense.

And I really didn't give a damn.

"You're right," I said, anger making my voice go thick. "I don't deserve her. She's an amazing person, and I am who I am."

"On that, we are in agreement—"

"But what about you?" I asked. "The great Queen Lucia Borghesi, whose so-called authority was granted simply because she was born to the right two people? How long did you manage to hold on to that authority? Was it one century before you got yourself exiled? Or two?"

"I know," I continued, "your brother had you banished so he could claim the throne. But you know what I can't figure out? If you were the queen of all of Europe… if you had all that power at your beck and call, why did *nobody* take your side? Why is it that every country but America closed its doors to you?"

"Mind your words, thrall—"

"Because they were all happier with your brother in charge. That's why. Because they realized you are a spoiled brat who believes other people exist merely to serve her dysfunctional whims."

Lucia made a low noise in the back of her throat, halfway between a snarl and shout, but I kept speaking, the words rushing out of me in a torrent. All the frustration of the past year was swelling up to combine with the many indignities I'd suffered at her hands, from having my mind cracked like an eggshell, to the multitude of threats on my life.

What formed was a truth bomb of epic proportions.

I smiled as I let it fly.

"And what do you have for it? A tiny little House on the Pacific, unclaimed by any empire, full of vampires who are either actively conspiring against you or just content to loathe you passively. You have a city that goes through some sort of crisis on an annual basis despite your so-called leadership. Your exalted Council included a traitor, an accountant, an insane Blood Witch, and a Human Resources stooge whose own hirelings were used against him."

"And then you have Ana. Lady Anastasia Dumenyova. Well regarded, *despite* your association. The Stone Lady, who even Kayla's people have heard of in Australia. Brilliant. Deadly. Loyal enough to follow you into exile despite your many, many faults."

"Do you see what piece *doesn't* fit in this broken puzzle, your Majesty? The one part of your kingdom that actually functions correctly?" I asked mockingly. "I don't deserve Anastasia? Maybe you're right. Maybe I don't. But neither do you. I'm only human. What's *your* excuse?"

There was a pregnant pause, during which it occurred to me that I needed to get the hell out of Dodge. And that my fit of temper might have just gotten me killed. Then, frost literally exploded out of the femmepire queen, coating the nearby furniture in a thin layer of ice. The queen shook with a fury she was no longer even bothering to repress, eyes glowing blue and gold, hands clawing the air at her sides.

"You pathetic, mewling little monkey," she spat out, her breath forming little plumes of vapor that hardened and fell to the floor in a musical wreckage of ice. And then she was in front of me, though I hadn't seen her move, hoisting me into the air with one hand. "You have outlived your usefulness to me and to my House."

I felt her mind invading mine through the cracks she'd made when taking me as her thrall. I couldn't tell if her next words were spoken aloud or planted directly into my brain, where they rattled about like bone dice.

"But I will now rectify that matter."

And then?

Pain. And more pain. Explosions of brilliant color behind my eyes. A white light that eclipsed even those fireworks.

I struggled for the blessed oblivion of unconsciousness, but it eluded my grasp, and the pain went on and on and on. It was only when I stopped reaching for it that the darkness finally rose and swallowed me whole.

CHAPTER 26

I woke into darkness and pain, flat on my back, a stone floor cold against my… bare skin? For an awful moment, I was back in Davis Hawthorne's basement. Naked, chained, and slowly being infected.

No, wait; I was wearing pants. That realization was enough to make my panic subside. No matter how bad things might be, pants had to be a good thing, right?

There was some sort of weight on my bare chest, pinning me to the floor. My arms were stretched out to the side and shackled, making me basically Jesus of the dungeon. But where was I? How was I still alive? And why couldn't I see?

Oh. Once I filtered out the aches and bruises that made me feel like I'd been tackled by the entire roster of the San Diego Chargers, the answer to that last question became apparent.

I couldn't see… because my eyes weren't open.

I decided to change that immediately, but the signal seemed to take forever to get from my brain to… whatever biological receptor was responsible for opening eyes. Science had never been my strong suit. While I waited, I focused my other senses around me.

The stone was cold beneath my bare torso, arms, and feet, which told me virtually nothing. My still-shaky breathing was the only sound I could hear, which at least suggested I was alone. Hopefully, *alone* didn't also mean *buried alive a quarter mile beneath Scripps Ranch.* As for smells… my nose appeared to have been clogged entirely with dried blood and snot, leaving me every bit the mouth breather former classmates had once accused me of being.

So, that was touch, smell, and sound, with sight hopefully still on the way. But what about the fifth sense? I couldn't seem to remember what it was, which scared me every bit as much as my current predicament. My body felt like it had been fed into a blender… but what had Lucia's attack done to my *mind?*

Thoughts of the vampire queen activated that space in the back of my head where she remained in permanent residence. The femmepire was above me, somewhere, but her presence was muted. Either she was shielding again, or she was a very, very long way away.

Which gave unfortunate credence to that whole *buried alive a quarter mile beneath Scripps Ranch* possibility.

Then, my eyes finally opened, and I had a whole new reason to worry.

"Hello, monkey," purred Zorana, her small face inches away from my own.

○○○

I tried to shrink away from the tiny vampire before remembering that I was shackled to the floor. The source of the weight on my chest and abdomen was clear now; the Blood Witch was seated on my abdomen, both palms flat against my bare chest.

What had been a dark and empty pit with my eyes closed now resolved itself into a dimly lit cell, either the exact same one the vampires had held me in a year ago or its identical dungeon twin. Light leaked in through the partially opened door, a convenient escape path rendered irrelevant by my wrist and ankle cuffs.

"Zorana?" I coughed as I spoke past the pain in my chest and head. "What are you—"

"Shhhh." She laid one finger against my lips, and icy chills swept through me at the contact, counterpoint to the stomach cramps her soprano voice always provoked. "I will ask the questions."

"But Lucia—"

Zorana's other hand, which to this point had been flat against my chest, suddenly clenched, four fingers and a thumb digging in.

"You will speak when spoken to," she said, giving one last spiteful twist to my savaged pectoral. "As for Lucia? She is indisposed. Which is what," she added, with a wink that looked particularly ghoulish on her childlike face, "this is all about."

The Blood Witch waited for a response, but for once, I was smart enough not to say anything. Or still too busy gasping in pain to speak. Either way, she nodded in sickening approval.

"It seems you *can* learn, with the proper instruction. As I told Lucia once, it's like training a puppy. A firm hand is required."

"You... train puppies?" I asked before remembering that I wasn't supposed to be speaking.

"One or two over the centuries. One cannot always rely on poultry for blood sacrifices."

And that was just awful. And unbelievably uncool.

"Now," she told me, removing her chilling finger from my lips to run it around one of my exposed nipples, "I have some questions of my own for you. Like how it is that you are still alive, let alone conscious."

"I'm happy to help," I told her, trying not to show how badly the Blood Witch was scaring me, "but I honestly don't know what the hell you're—"

She pinched my nipple, and it was like being stabbed with an icicle. My words died unspoken.

"Your claim of ignorance is as predictable as it is irrelevant." She threw her head back and giggled like the child she really, really wasn't. When she looked back down, her overly large grey eyes were rapidly filling with crimson. "Because blood *always* knows."

And then she splayed both hands across my chest, fingers writhing like a clutch of snakes, and began to speak in the alien tongue I'd heard only twice before.

The pain that followed made my prior aches seem inconsequential.

○○○

I woke to find Zorana still atop me, this time in a new dress. My chest was on fire, but my limbs were numb and unresponsive. Before passing out, I had watched the femmepire command my blood to drip *upwards* out of the wounds she had casually incised in my flesh with a thumb. In the dim light of the cell, that blood was black and thick as molasses, ignoring gravity's pull to circle Zorana's outstretched hand.

Other than her clothing, very little had changed. How much blood did one human have in him anyway?

I was painfully certain I was going to find out.

"Zorana," I wheezed, flinching as wet, crimson eyes darted to my face, "maybe my blood *doesn't* know anything after all?"

"I think you're right," she confided, waving her hand, and watching the floating pool of blood follow it like a dog on a leash.

"Then why—"

"Lucia has yet to wake, monkey," the femmepire told me sweetly, a small pink tongue darting out to sample the passing ribbon of crimson. "And when the cat is away…"

ooo

I don't know how many times I lapsed in and out of consciousness, or how long the agony continued. I just know that every time I opened my eyes, Zorana was there, ignoring my pleas, my cries, and my threats. The light coming into the cell never changed, but time was passing. And the cloud of blood that floated in the air above me slowly thinned, slowly lightened, even as my own vision faded.

ooo

The next time I woke, things were different. The now-familiar weight upon my chest was absent. Something scraped loudly against the concrete floor, and it was only the location of that sound that made me think it might be my manacled wrist. I couldn't feel the arm at all. Nor could I see anything… and this time, I was pretty sure my eyes were open.

"It's even worse than I thought," whispered a voice.

I flinched away from those words and from the cool hand that touched my shoulder and sparked a torrent of fire. I twitched like a limp rag, pulling myself into a small ball, dimly aware that the arms I still couldn't feel were no longer confined.

"Rest easy, John," murmured a second voice at my ear. I felt like I should know that voice, but the face and name associated with it refused to come.

"You are safe," the voice continued, and though I didn't know who was saying those words, I knew, deep down, where some part of me remained whole, that I could trust them.

As I was lifted from the concrete, it was that realization that sent me slipping into darkness.

○○○

Confusion.

Murmured voices.

I woke once when a cold spoon filled with something warm was lifted to my lips, woke again when something soft brushed my face. All the while, there was a steady current of black-watered pain.

The cycle repeated.

Voices murmured. Warm liquid dribbled into my mouth. Pain overshadowed everything.

I struggled, not to wake, but to sleep, to drift back into peaceful oblivion.

Then, a new pain as something was inserted into my arm. Cold ice leaked into my body, and I was floating above that dark river, rising into the clouds, flying toward a sun that spoke my name.

○○○

I woke slowly, troubled by a dream I couldn't recall, luxuriating in the softness of the bed beneath me.

Then, I remembered everything.

I bolted upright.

Or tried to, anyway. My body wasn't responding like it should have, even though I could feel my limbs for the first time in possibly months.

Following on the heels of *that* realization was surprise at the absence of agony. No, not absence, precisely; I could still sense the pain, but it was distant and unreachable.

A cool hand cupped my cheek, so different from Zorana's own punishing touch that I didn't even think to be terrified. I opened my eyes, squinting against the light, and looked up into a face I recognized.

"Ana?" I croaked.

"I am here." Jade eyes shimmered as she looked down at me, her soft hand slowly stroking the one part of my face that did not hurt. "I am here, and you are safe."

I meant to say something, but I don't know what it was, and the words never made it to my tongue.

I drifted away.

ooo

When I woke again, Anastasia was still there, in exactly the same position, as if she had used her Talent to become a living statue. But her eyes were dark and wet and so sad that it hurt something deep inside of me, far beneath the pain I had already suffered.

"Am I dead?" I asked, in a voice that sounded nothing like my own.

"No." Her words were quiet and resolute. "You are alive and will stay that way."

Once again, I trusted her instinctively. Relief swept through me, even more powerful than the drugs that kept me floating above the pain.

I tried to smile and couldn't.

I tried to speak but couldn't do that either.

My body trembled, but it wasn't until hot liquid dripped down my face that I realized I was crying.

I didn't want *her* to see me cry. I rolled away, toward my far arm and the IV that jutted from it like a plastic antenna.

"Zorana…" I tried to say, tucking my head down against my chest, as tears trickled down my face to wet the sheet beneath my cheek. "She…"

"I know," she said quietly, one hand running through the tangles of my hair. "But I will not let her hurt you again."

And then that hand left my hair, the bed shifted, and Anastasia's strong arm wrapped around me from behind. I sank into her embrace, and my quiet tears became great, body-wracking sobs.

ooo

Eventually, the tears stopped. I rolled over to apologize, my needled arm left behind like an anchor, and found myself face to face with the femmepire. Strands of auburn hair had escaped a utilitarian bun, and thanks to the pillow beneath her head, those strands were now sticking out in every direction. Her eyes were enormous, large enough to swallow planets, and full of emotion.

"I'm sorry," I started to say, but was silenced by the soft press of her lips against my own. It was a chaste kiss, and I was riding high on unknown pain medications, and in no position whatsoever to take it further. And yet…

If the kisses I'd shared with Juliette had lacked a spark, that one kiss from Anastasia was enough to burn down a city. A country, even. I leaned into her mouth, felt her body lightly pressed against my own, and gloried in that shiver of energy. Her lips were sweet, like sugar water, and her breath smelled like the roses of her perfume.

Which was when I realized how bad my own breath must be.

I pulled away, my free hand moving to shield my mouth. "I'm sorry," I began again.

This time, I was apologizing for my breath instead of the emotional breakdown, but Anastasia didn't seem to care. She pulled my hand away and slipped past it to kiss me again.

Whatever I'd been planning to say was forgotten, along with any thoughts of halitosis or of having wept like a baby in her arms. Instead, I returned her kiss, and let myself disappear into the moment, into the electricity that arced and sizzled between us.

All too soon, it ended. Our kiss had deepened slightly, the play of her slowly spreading lips against my own, when I unthinkingly tried to hold her. The needle in my right forearm remained inserted thanks to the clear tape securing it to my arm, but the IV stand fell onto the bed, where it hit the mattress and my leg, bounced, and began to topple in the opposite direction.

There was a blur, and Anastasia was there to catch the stand. Her hair was even more of a mess, her lips slightly swollen, her eyes open and vulnerable. She was wearing a simple tunic-length shirt in rich blue and it had an unmistakable wet patch just below one shoulder, from what was probably the puddle of my tears.

I had never, ever, seen anything more beautiful.

"I love you," I said softly, as reality slowly began to reassert itself, "but I am very, very confused." My free hand came up to trace my lips, where I could still feel the echoes of her kisses.

"I know," she said, stepping around the IV to take a seat on the bed near my head, "but for now, you must rest and recover."

And because she was Anastasia, I knew she was right.

And because she was right, I closed my eyes, and drifted away.

INTERLUDE

I sit in the high-backed chair that Papa had specially crafted for me and do my best to ignore the comments of my younger brother's friends, parading by on their way to market. I know their names, their parentage, and their houses, and when I am of age, they will learn to regret those words.

But for now, I can do nothing more than ignore their quietly whispered spite, as I sit stiff-backed, uncomfortable in my seat. The chair is both too large and of a style that would never be comfortable without a cushion or several blankets, but Papa had shrugged off my complaints, telling me—in that quiet voice that made even other adults tremble—that I would grow to suit it… and that discomfort was the price we paid for primacy.

I wasn't sure what primacy meant, and didn't dare to ask, but I have never again complained about the chair when he, or one of our many servants, was present to hear. And now, I sit like my spine is a sword, as the room bustles around me, as the household makes itself ready for guests.

CHAPTER 27

IN WHICH TIME (OR LYCANTHROPY) HEALS ALL WOUNDS

The next time I woke up, I was alone. Which was for the best, I guess, because I really, really had to pee.

I wiggled my arms and legs experimentally, relieved both at the general absence of pain and the fact that those limbs obeyed my commands. I swung my feet over the side of the bed where my IV stand still stood, and then, with one hand gripping the stand's metal post, levered myself to my feet.

And then sat right back down, as the rush of blood informed me that even my current glacial pace was far too ambitious for the rest of my body.

Eventually, I made it to my feet. I was even able to walk without leaning too heavily on the IV stand that was part walking stick and part ball and chain. The bedroom I was in was one I'd never seen before, but a door in the near wall looked like it might lead to a bathroom, and that was all I cared about.

Somewhere between thirty seconds and two hours later, I felt better. I was washing my hands in the gleaming white sink when three thoughts occurred to me.

First, I was almost naked, wearing only a pair of boxers I'd also never seen before.

Second, someone had shaved off the month's growth of facial hair I'd been desperately trying to pass off as a beard.

And third, Zorana's handiwork had left my body even less attractive than usual. *Frankenstein* ugly.

I tried for a dispassionate review of my wounds—really, I did—but every mark sparked memories of what the Blood Witch had done to inflict it upon me… and there were a lot of marks. If there was a bright spot, it was that her perch atop my diaphragm had left her unable to reach beyond my chest, shoulders, and arm. The rest of me seemed untouched beyond the bumps and bruises from Lucia's attack and whatever parts of me had been scraped raw against the concrete floor of my cell.

Also, the wounds really drew the eye away from my still-too-pudgy midsection. So, the news wasn't *all* bad.

My laugh threatened to turn right back into a cry.

Deep bruising covered my torso, a mix of blacks, purples, and yellows. More worrying were the many spots on my chest that had been covered by gauze and bandages. Given how bad my *exposed* skin looked, I didn't want to see what those bandages were hiding.

But I kind of had to. Especially since one of them covered the nipple Zorana had been brutalizing. Wincing, I slowly peeled the bandage back.

The good news was that I still had two nipples. The bad news… actually, the bad news was less dire than I'd been expecting. While there were places where my skin had apparently been torn and then stitched back together, the result wasn't so much worse than the rest of me. I'd been expecting blackened flesh or mutant growths or a silly-putty simulacrum of my unimpressive pectoral, but this was just a continuation of the bruising and tenderness that covered the rest of my chest, along with a few scabs that seemed almost ready to fall away.

It didn't even hurt *that* much.

I peeled the other bandages from my torso, revealing more of the same. I'd need to avoid flexing in the mirror for possibly the rest of my life, but nothing seemed permanently damaged. Only one bandage remained, a long swath of fabric wrapped around my left collarbone and one side of my neck. For the life of me, I couldn't remember what Zorana had done there. With a half-shrug, I pulled it free.

"Holy shit, little bird."

I hadn't even heard Juliette approach, my attention fixed upon the row of neat, child-size toothmarks that dotted my shoulder and neck. This wasn't just the four holes of a vampire's canines—though the deeper divots left from those canines were clear—but an entire set of teeth. Like my other wounds, these had scabbed over and were well on the way to being healed, but the bite marks were unmistakable.

I felt my gorge rising but fought it down. I'd already wept like a baby in front of Anastasia; I wasn't going to blow chunks in front of my partner. Not again anyway.

"It looks like you were gnawed on by a tribe of baby cannibals," she decided.

I dove for the toilet bowl, miraculously managing not to bring my IV stand down with me.

Afterward, I rinsed my mouth out, and splashed cold water onto my face, before turning to give Juliette an unfriendly glare.

"Don't look at me like that," she said. "I forgot about your weak stomach."

"What are you doing here?"

"She was *supposed* to be watching over you." Anastasia stood in the bedroom's other doorway, a frown marring the calm beauty of her face. "And preventing you from doing something that might cause further injury… like standing up and walking about."

"I *was* watching over him," retorted Juliette.

"And then?"

"I got bored," the femmepire admitted. "It's less fun watching him drool than I thought it would be. And while I got some quality pictures, I realized he doesn't even have any friends for me to send them to."

I shook my head. I had so many questions I didn't even know where to start. Like *where were we?* And *why were Juliette and Anastasia hanging out together?* And *whose boxers was I wearing and who had dressed me in them?*

Before I could ask any of those questions or respond to Juliette's own comments, Anastasia stepped past the other femmepire.

"You shouldn't be out of bed yet, John. Or removing bandages without assistance."

"He seems fine to me," said Juliette.

"I know I look like crap, but I actually do feel okay. Mostly okay. And," I added, pointing to one of the now-exposed wounds on my chest, "everything seems to be healing up just fine."

Anastasia ran cool fingers across my chest.

I manfully caught my squeak before it could be verbalized, uncertain if that squeak had been because she was touching my battered flesh, or… because she was touching my bare and naked chest. After a moment, I decided it was the latter, and that I was very much okay with her doing a lot more of it in the future. I leaned slightly into her hand.

"Keep it in your boxers, little bird. Or *I'll* be puking next."

"Lady Middleton?" Ana's voice was as soft as her touch.

"Yeah?" Juliette's was… well, less soft.

"Could you give John and me a moment, please?"

"I thought you'd never ask." The femmepire stalked to the door with one last smirk and a roll of the eyes in my direction. In the hallway, she paused. "Do you have any food in this place?"

"Speak with Gustavo," Anastasia replied, her eyes never leaving my own. "He will cook whatever you request."

"Hot damn. That almost makes the last forty minutes worth it." And then Juliette was gone.

I turned to Anastasia. "Don't be pissed at Juliette, please. I really am okay."

"You do seem to be healing well." Her face gave away nothing, as she examined my wounds again. She guided me back to the bed and took a seat next to me, drawing one leg up under her with the sort of flexibility I'd never had even as a child. "Which raises some questions."

"Like what? I know we're not weres or even vampires, but humans *do* heal. More or less. I'm just sorry you've been stuck as my nursemaid this whole time. How long have I been recovering for? And where are we? And…" A thought occurred to me. The fact that it had taken so long for me to even think of it made me a horrible son. "Shit. My parents!"

"They are fine—" Anastasia began.

"No, I mean, has anyone spoken to them? They're used to me pulling the occasional all-nighter, but there's no way they'll accept an absence of multiple weeks!"

"John—"

"I don't want anyone brainwashing them, but I'd be shocked if my mom hasn't already filed a missing person report. And—"

"John." This time, Anastasia laid a finger against my lips, silencing me instantaneously. "Your parents are unconcerned. I told them that you were with me."

There was no question I loved the way *that* little phrase sounded.

"Nor has it been weeks since they saw you."

"It hasn't?"

"No." Her tone was cool and calm, giving away nothing, but the hand that had touched my lips was now stroking my unblemished forearm.

"How long then?"

"Today is Sunday. We rescued you from the House on Friday night. As far as I know, Zorana had you for two days."

I tried to grapple with that idea… something that was made more difficult by my conviction that the Blood Witch had tortured me for weeks on end. Then, what Ana was saying sank in. I took another look at the fading evidence of my imprisonment.

"So, why am I almost healed?"

"Exactly my question," agreed Anastasia. "I had expected you to be bedridden for quite some time."

"Huh." I rolled the IV stand back and forth between my legs and looked for something to say. "Well, I healed pretty quickly after the fire at Davis Hawthorne's too."

"I remember. However, your system was full of the werewolf virus at the time, which is no longer the case."

"Are we sure?" It had been months and I had yet to turn furry, but that wasn't necessarily definitive, was it?

"It takes three bites to infect someone, Mr. Smith, and those bites must be administered on a strict timeline. Failure to do so results in either the death of the target or a failure to infect them. With only two bites ever given, your immune system must have driven out the virus months ago."

"Huh." I drummed the fingers of my free hand on the mattress, seeking for an alternate explanation even halfway as cool as *regenerative abilities brought on by latent werewolf virus.* "What about the bond? With Lucia?"

"What of it?"

"Is it possible that it's helping me heal?" Supposedly, Lucia would one day be able to pull sustenance from me using the bond. Could I be doing the same?

"If humans could draw upon the bond, the People would never willingly create it." The femmepire shook her head decisively, the motion sending ripples through the silk curtain of her hair.

God, I loved that hair. My hands twitched, imagining what it would be like to run fingers through it. Maybe the next time we kissed? If there was a next time; I was still a little hazy on why and how it had happened in the first place. Especially given that Anastasia had ended things not even a week earlier.

A small smile touched the femmepire's lips, and for a moment I was certain she had divined my thoughts. Instead, she spoke. "On the other hand, *nothing* about your bond has behaved as expected. Perhaps this is simply one more oddity resulting from your own gift."

"Whatever's causing it, I'm good," I decided. "Especially if it means I can get this thing out of my arm sooner rather than later."

"I believe we should be able to manage that."

CHAPTER 28

IN WHICH NINJAS ARE ITALIAN

I'm not sure exactly why I decided to watch as Anastasia drew the IV needle out of my arm. Maybe I wanted to prove to the lovely femmepire that there was more to me than just a randomly vomiting, often-injured human male.

Or maybe I wanted to prove it to myself instead.

Either way, it was a decision I regretted immediately. I redirected my gaze to the far wall, where a wooden dresser had been polished until it glowed. Other than the nightstand and bed, that dresser was the only piece of furniture in the room, and its countertop was empty. There was no indication that anyone had ever lived here. Which really made me wonder about the history of—

"All done," said Anastasia.

Thank God; I'd had serious doubts regarding my ability to rhapsodize much longer about what was, in the end, just a bedroom. I glanced down at my arm, but other than the small red mark on my forearm, there was little evidence of the IV that had been pumping drugs into me for days.

"I imagine you must be hungry?"

My stomach chose that moment to growl loudly, making a reply almost superfluous. "Yeah, I guess I am. But could we talk first? I'm glad to be here, obviously, and equally glad to not be dead, but I need to know what's going on."

Ana already had her cellphone out and to her ear, but she nodded silently at my request, holding one finger out in a request for time.

"Gustavo," she said into the phone, "please prepare several plates of food for Mr. Smith, and bring them to the upstairs dining room." She ended the call, and rose to her feet, offering me her hand. "Why not do both? It will take a few minutes for food to arrive, and I will endeavor to answer your questions in the meantime."

I placed my hand in hers, and she pulled me to my feet like I weighed almost nothing. Which, for someone with her strength, was pretty much the case.

"So then," she continued, once we were both certain I wasn't going to fall over without the IV stand as a makeshift crutch, "where would you like to begin?"

I had so many questions I didn't even know where to start. Until I looked down. "Maybe with some pants?"

ooo

I'd known from Ana's brief conversation with the mysterious Gustavo that the house was big; in *most* homes, there is no need to specify *which* dining room food should be delivered to. But beyond that, I wasn't sure what to expect.

By the time we reached that dining room, I had decided the place fit comfortably in the sizable gap between my parent's own house and the vampires' sprawling mansion. Which meant it was *at least* a million-dollar home, assuming we were still in Scripps Ranch.

The décor was expensive but subdued, the hallway immaculate but empty.

The dining room itself was cozy, with a table that could seat six, comfortable chairs that ringed it, and a glass-enclosed china cabinet along one wall. All of that was just background detail though, my eyes drawn to the far wall, where a sliding door led out onto a balcony of clean white stone. And past that balcony…

"Is that the ocean?"

"It is."

Ana followed me to the door. All I could see was rolling blue water beneath a light cloud cover. A cool breeze slipped in through the open door, and I was grateful for the ridiculously plush bathrobe Ana had given me. It wasn't as modest as the pants I'd been hoping for—especially considering I was still half-naked, scarred, and pudgy underneath—but the thought of pulling on a pair of jeans had filled me with a sense of dread. I was just as happy to avoid *that* trial until my werewolf-infused blood had taken me a little bit further down the path of a full and unnatural recovery.

We stood in silence for a time, gazing at the Pacific. I was notorious among my friends, family, and the father of at least one ex-girlfriend for getting violently nauseous within moments of setting foot on a boat, but from this distance, I felt nothing but my usual awe for the vast expanse of water before me.

"Unless Scripps Ranch moved fifteen or so miles west while I was unconscious, I'm guessing we're in your Cardiff house?"

"Indeed." Ana stood by my side, unmindful of the cold, despite her clothing. Today's outfit was a twin to yesterday's; a long, sleeveless tunic in rich blue, and deep grey leggings. I was in a slightly better frame of mind to admire the way those clothes exhibited her long and exquisitely toned legs and took a moment to do exactly that.

Respectfully, of course. She looked every bit as spectacular in casual clothes as she did in business attire. Or her battle leathers, for that matter.

I dragged my eyes back up to her face to find a small smile curving those lovely lips, eyes sparkling in amusement.

Busted. Again.

"I own a number of properties throughout the county, but this is my favorite, and it is where Gustavo, Teresa, and I spend the majority of our time."

"I forgot you don't actually live at the House." It had taken me a while to remember where I'd heard Gustavo's name, but he and his wife were Anastasia's blood donors, an elderly pair of Italians. Thank God for that too; the very thought of Ana with a harem of young, handsome, CrossFit-loving surfer dudes as her donors was enough to give me heartburn.

"I do spend the occasional night at my suite there, but a Secundus must be able to come and go as they please. Even in a healthy House, there are too many eyes and ears to make that possible."

"Plus, you won't get a view like this in Scripps Ranch."

"Indeed." The smile was evident in her voice.

My questions from the past few days clamored to be voiced, but I held them at bay for a few moments longer, entranced by both the view and the way the breeze toyed with stray strands of Anastasia's silken hair.

Unfortunately, I really did need answers.

"How did I get here? I vaguely remember what must have been you finding me, but how did you know I needed rescuing? Or where I was? And why bring me to your home?"

"Following our breakfast this week," Ana explained, her voice suddenly flat, "I was again sent out of town on business."

"And by business, you mean…?"

"House business." Her tone gave away nothing.

"So…" I made a throat-slashing motion with one hand, prompting a surprised chuckle from the lovely femmepire. "…Secundus stuff?"

"Secundus stuff, yes, but nothing quite so… overt as you are thinking. I don't know what you have uncovered about my role, John, but I am not merely an assassin."

"I would never call you *merely* anything."

"You truly are feeling better." Anastasia shook her head with a smile. "There are many who would disagree. Regardless, my position in the House is to serve as a…" She paused, mulling over the proper word choice.

"Problem solver?" It was the line she'd sold my mother. Even if her real job had nothing to do with Borghesi International, the description still seemed appropriate.

"Precisely. All too often, that involves sending a message of the kind you have alluded to. In this instance, however, I spent several days up in Irvine, speaking with factors there on an intelligence gathering expedition."

"Should I even ask?"

"Would you truly stop if I said no?" She gave me an honest-to-god grin, the expression so open and disarming that I found myself grinning back like a loon.

"I'm pretty sure I'd do *anything* you asked me to." Especially if she kept smiling at me like that. Or smiling at all. Or standing in my general vicinity.

"We may soon put that to the test. As it turns out, my mission concerned you, at least indirectly. Queen Lucia tasked me with the investigation of Mr. Van Stahl."

"The mediator?" I felt an irrational surge of jealousy. As far as I knew, Anastasia had never been ordered to investigate *me*. Granted, there wasn't much *to* investigate, outside of the churro incident back in seventh grade, and that one weekend in Tijuana. But still...

"Indeed. She failed to inform me that she intended to meet with you on that very matter in my absence. It was within her rights to do so, but..."

"The timing seems suspicious. Kind of like she wanted you out of the picture. Again."

"Yes. Either that," she decided in a thoughtful tone, "or she was concerned that it would be difficult for the two of us to meet again so soon after Tuesday's discussion."

Tuesday's... discussion. Even the euphemism sounded horrible. It was the perfect opportunity for me to give voice to all the relationship-related questions bubbling up inside of me, starting with *those kisses*, but...

I chickened out.

Honestly, I was terrified that pressing the issue would somehow blow up in my face. After all, I had barely said a word in two days, and Anastasia had gone from deciding that we couldn't be together to offering me kisses (two) and cuddles (one... sort of).

So far, silence seemed like a winning strategy.

"I haven't been particularly impressed by Lucia's compassion for others," I said instead, "so I'm betting she just wanted you elsewhere. But I guess that's kind of irrelevant now."

A small cough from about five feet behind us was my first clue that someone else was in the room. I tried to hide my surprise—with limited success, considering I had jumped at least an inch in the air—and turned to see a little old man, dressed in a dapper three-piece suit. He was entirely bald, his tan head dappled with liver spots, but the eyes underneath his bushy grey eyebrows were a warm brown, lively and mischievous.

"Gustavo." Ana's voice was welcoming.

Gustavo offered a slight bow, first to her, and then to me, and cheerfully addressed me in a language I didn't understand. Between Begoña the White Lady, the two Brazilian manpire assholes, and now Ana's blood donor, I was starting to regret being monolingual. Not to mention perpetually under-dressed.

Over his shoulder, I saw that the dining table had magically gained full settings for two, along with several dishes of steaming hot food. Seriously… the dude was a ninja. It was the only possible explanation.

Anastasia traded sentences with her donor in the same language and then turned to me. "I explained to Gustavo that you do not speak Italian. He wishes to convey his happiness that you are feeling better and would like you to know that, if he or his wife Teresa can provide you with anything, it will be their honor to serve."

As she spoke, Gustavo was examining me from head to toe. I reflexively started to suck in my gut before remembering that the fluffy robe hid that sort of thing anyway. The old man offered another stream of gibberish to my companion.

"He also says," Ana translated, "that while the clothing you arrived in was beyond repair, he will see to it that you have something to wear beyond just a bathrobe."

I matched eyes with the wizened old ninja butler/blood donor and offered a smile and a bow of my own. "Please tell him thank you. I don't want to be any trouble."

What I had intended to be a dignified reply was undermined slightly by my stomach yet again making itself heard. That food smelled *amazing*.

Gustavo clapped his hands together delightedly and came over to me. Before I could react, he had given me a warm hug, one dry-lipped kiss on the cheek, and was scurrying back out into the hallway.

"He likes you," Anastasia told me, still smiling, "but then, Gustavo likes almost everyone. Teresa will be a tougher sell."

"He seems like a good dude. But he's not going to go out and get me a suit, is he? Part of the reason I became a private investigator was to *avoid* ties."

Anastasia's laugh was a musical sounding of bells that never failed to send my pulse into overdrive. "Don't let the dear man fool you. He and Teresa have both gone thoroughly native here in Southern California. This is the first time he's worn that suit in months."

"I'm honored," I told her. And I was. But again, my stomach decided to verbalize its own feelings on the matter. "And really hungry, apparently."

"Then by all means, let us eat."

CHAPTER 29

"So, you were in Irvine investigating Caleb?" I asked, having shoved enough delightfully seasoned and thankfully abundant lasagna into my mouth to silence even my stomach.

"Yes. Mr. Van Stahl has a track record as a very successful mediator for the greater Los Angeles area—"

"Yeah, he seemed like he'd be good at his job." Based on the one and only picture I'd seen anyway.

"—yet there are rumors about his practice that necessitate further research."

"Like what?" Judging by how quickly every species in San Diego had dropped me for my competitor, it couldn't have been anything too terrible. Unless the city really *was* holding me responsible for the House coup and Pack invasion, in which case any alternative might be preferred.

"I have nothing definite yet," Anastasia admitted. "Not all of his mediations have been successful, which is only to be expected. Yet even in the case of his failures, Mr. Van Stahl emerged from the ensuing melee untarnished." She shook her head and took another sip of water from her own glass. "As I said, it bears further investigation. But I believe we have gone off on quite a tangent from your original query, yes?"

"Uhm…" I honestly couldn't remember what that question had been. "Maybe?"

"You no longer remember your own question?"

I gestured at the platefuls of food I had demolished. "It's hard to remember anything after consuming my body weight in home-cooked meals."

"I will keep that in mind for the future." Anastasia's eyes sparkled.

"Oh!" The thought finally made its way back through my carbs-based mental block. "Right; I was asking how I got here."

"Yes. While I was in Irvine, you were meeting with my queen. From the scattered accounts I have managed to put together, you and she were both found unconscious, shortly afterwards." She gave me an assessing look from across the table. "Would you care to provide the missing details?"

I wasn't thrilled to relive the experience, but I also wasn't going to say no to Anastasia. So, I shrugged, and walked her through the details of my incredibly lousy Wednesday morning. Which had, of course, been preceded by an incredibly lousy *Tuesday* morning… and followed by two days of torture.

In retrospect, it had been a shitty week.

It's possible that my retelling left out some of the words Lucia and I had hurled at each other. Including the fact that Anastasia herself had ultimately been the spark that burned the whole place down.

"Anyway, after summarily dismissing both the witches' proposal, and my idea for how to soothe hurt feelings among the Watch—"

"Your idea for Kayla and Thales had merit," murmured Anastasia, which was pretty much an outright condemnation of her Queen's decision.

"—then Lucia tossed some insults my way, and I…"

"Responded in kind."

"Right. And said some things I probably shouldn't have. At which point, she tried to kill me. And the next thing I knew, I woke up with Zorana in… well, wherever you found me."

"One of the cells on sub-level two. Not far from where you were originally incarcerated last year."

"I'm not a big fan of that sub-level," I said, in the understatement of the century. "So that's the part you missed. Meanwhile, you got back from Irvine on… Thursday?"

"Actually, I was still in Irvine on Friday when I received a call from Duke Barros," she clarified, "informing me that Lucia had been stricken by some manner of malady."

"He waited until *Friday?*"

"Perhaps he believed she would recover on her own. Shortly after, I received a second call, from one of the House operators."

"Celeste or Akiko?"

"I forgot you had befriended them both."

"*Befriended* might be overstating things a bit. I've never met either one face-to-face. But they're good people. Or People."

"They are. In this case, it was Celeste. The operators work out of the same sub-level, and she had heard the… noises. When Zorana left to meet with others on the Council, Celeste located the cell, and was startled to find you imprisoned within. She called me immediately."

"Why? I mean… I'm glad she did, obviously. And if I never, ever see Zorana again, it would still be too soon. But why didn't Celeste just bust me out of there herself?"

Especially if it could have saved me from an hour or two of additional torture.

There was no missing the compassion in Anastasia's voice. "Zorana is Council, John. Celeste, for all her admirable qualities, is not. Attempting to free you could very well have cost Celeste her place in the House, if not her life. Even contacting me was a breach in protocol."

"Oh." I chewed on that. "Vampire politics suck."

For once, the pun was both unintentional and not particularly funny.

"As do politics in general," she agreed. "I returned to the House with all possible haste and enlisted Celeste's help in retrieving you from your cell."

The mystery of who the other person in the cell had been during my rescue was finally solved. "And Zorana?"

"I have not yet spoken to her, but from all accounts, she was attempting to discover what you had done to Lucia, only to, in her words, *get carried* away."

I tried to hide my reaction by taking a bite of still-warm biscuit. The light, fluffy bread tasted like ash in my mouth.

"I will not let her harm you again, John," Anastasia promised, eyes intent upon my face, "but I lack the authority to do more than that. And if it should come to battle between us, the advantage will be hers."

"Seriously?" Given what I'd seen Anastasia do, it was hard to imagine that anyone could be a match for her. Then again, I'd seen the child-sized Blood Witch decapitate a werewolf with her bare hands...

"She is a thousand years old, and terribly strong in body and magic. I once saw her destroy an entire noble House in Rome, room by room, person by person. Nobody could stand against her. Yet if she ever touches you again," she continued, her voice growing cold, "we *will* see whether that power can protect her."

I'm pretty sure I swooned, just like the dime store novel heroine Juliette had accused me of being. God loves a strong woman.

"After Celeste and I released you from your cell, I smuggled you out of the House," Anastasia continued, "and brought you here, far from any member of the People who might hold you responsible for Queen Lucia's current state. I contacted Lady Middleton and asked her to come as well, to watch over you on those occasions when I would be unavailable. I had expected," she admitted, "that such a vigil would span several weeks, at a minimum."

"Me too," I muttered, my words lost within an enormous yawn that felt like it had come all the way from my toes. With food heavy in my belly, I was suddenly struggling to keep my eyes open. There was still so much to ask about, but...

"Come, John." I didn't even see Anastasia move, but I felt her hand at my elbow, again easily hoisting me to my feet. "Whatever power is healing you, its work is not yet done. Let us return you to bed, so that you may continue your recovery."

"Will you stay?" I asked, struggling to get the words out as my entire body decided that sleep sounded like the best idea ever. "With me, I mean?"

"For as long as I can," came the soft reply.

INTERLUDE

Papa walks through the far door, as large and angry as a mountain. His crystal blue eyes meet mine in silent warning, and then he turns to the open entryway and ushers in a man and woman.

They are of the People but dressed like servants. The man, grey-skinned and stooped, does not even have a proper vest on beneath his overcoat, and his boots show the dust of a long and difficult journey. The woman is equally shabby, legs bare beneath a mud-stained overdress, though she at least has the decency to wear a proper cloak over it all.

I wonder why they haven't changed into more appropriate attire before their audience, and if Papa and I are meant to take offense at this breach of etiquette, but before I can ask him, both adults step forward and drop to their knees. That show of respect almost makes up for the dust they have tracked in with them.

Almost.

Under Papa's hard gaze, I rise from my chair, and offer a greeting.

CHAPTER 30

I slowly shook myself awake, troubled by the odd dream. Whatever pain medication Ana had me on had apparently left its mark on my subconscious mind. I mean… when the hell had I *ever* concerned myself about a dude's vest… and for that matter, what exactly made a vest proper? And had I…

I fumbled for further details, but the dream was like smoke in my hands, slipping away no matter how tightly I tried to hold on. Finally, I gave up, and opened my eyes instead.

I was in the now-familiar bedroom, sprawled out on a bed that, with the IV removed, had proven to be extremely comfortable. The room had no windows, and there was nothing to indicate the time of day, but I had to go to the bathroom again, so at least some time had passed.

I felt rested. And not at all like a guy who'd been tortured by a demented preteen just a few days earlier. So that was good.

I sat up and stretched, feeling the new skin across my chest pull with the motion, and swung my feet over to the edge of the bed. Only then did I realize that I was, once again, not alone.

As promised.

Anastasia looked over from her seat by the hallway door. The chair must have been brought in from the dining room, and she was curled up on it, with a tablet in her hands. Her hair was pinned back in an elaborate-looking bun, and the comfortable clothing of the past two days had been replaced with a knee-length black pencil skirt and a crisp button-up dress-shirt of immaculate white. Simple pumps lay on the hard wood floor beneath her chair. Simple but *expensive*, the part of my brain devoted to shoe-related trivia informed me.

On most women, the outfit would have looked good, if a little plain. On Anastasia, it was transformed into something spectacular. All the femmepire needed was a pair of glasses, and she would have been the embodiment of every sexy librarian fantasy I'd ever had.

Except way, way hotter.

"How are you feeling?"

"Better," I decided. "Much better."

"Excellent." Even from ten feet away, her eyes were intent. If she had been anyone other than Anastasia, I would have thought her worried. "Because we need to talk."

For once, those four little words didn't trouble me.

"We really do. Only..." I tucked my dude parts more securely away in the boxers that remained my only clothing—seriously, Gustavo; what the hell?—and rose to my feet. "I need to use the restroom first. And take a shower."

ooo

When I emerged, Anastasia was absent, but a stack of clean clothes on the nightstand had me taking back my harsh thoughts toward Gustavo. They weren't mine, but the dark blue t-shirt and equally dark jeans fit every bit as well as if they had been.

I was beyond glad to not be mostly naked anymore. I was starting to develop a complex.

I verified that my hair remained a soggy, if clean, mess of tangles and curls, ran the provided comb through it in the futile hope that that would somehow help, and set out in search of Ana.

In the hallway, I screeched to a halt to avoid running over Gustavo. The elderly man had, yet again, appeared out of nowhere. He beamed up at me, clapped me on one shoulder—a shoulder now apparently healed enough for that contact *not* to hurt—and babbled something in what I had decided must be Italian.

I still didn't understand anything he was saying, but the dude seemed pretty cheery, so I offered a smile back.

One hand still on my shoulder, he turned and pointed down the hallway to the dining room I'd eaten in previously.

"Anastasia is in the dining room?"

A series of head nods, gestures, and pantomimes followed. I was pretty sure we were starting to get the hang of this whole non-verbal communication thing. Either that, or I'd just agreed to marry his granddaughter. Assuming he had one.

I hoped she was cute. And cool with me being in love with a woman four centuries her senior.

Gustavo stopped at the dining room door and patted me on the back as I walked past him. Italian men were kind of awesome.

Once again, my eyes went to the balcony and its glorious view. The sun was hanging low over the water, which made it evening. That meant I'd only slept a few hours; it had been noon-ish on my last visit.

Ana was seated at the table, a glass of what I was going to pretend was red wine in one hand. The chair across from her had been pulled slightly away from that table, an unsubtle indicator as to where I should sit.

Up close, she smelled every bit as good as she looked. And with the sunset framing her, the sexy librarian image had transformed into something almost divine. ·

We sat there for a moment, my eyes drinking in the sight of her, while she studied me almost as intently, albeit with far less drool and blatant adoration.

"I'm sorry for passing out before we could finish our talk," I told her, finally. "Whatever is going on, it feels like healing still takes a lot out of me."

"But you are feeling better?" Her eyes were large and luminescent, and it was all I could do to pay attention to the words she was speaking.

"I am," I assured her. "And Zorana's handiwork is still fading. I'm as close to one-hundred percent as I'm going to get without another long night of sleep, I think."

"That is good to hear, as I must ask a favor."

That wasn't really the romantic sentiment I'd been hoping for. I wasn't usually a proponent of sitting around and talking about my feelings or anything, but… this would surely have been the proper time for it.

Then again, what the hell did I know about successful relationships? The only winning models I had to follow were my parents and D and Kayla, and neither couple's example was much help in this particular situation.

"Anything," I finally said.

Ana bowed her head, and I found myself wishing that her hair was down just so I could watch it cascade over her shoulders. But then it would have hidden the elegant lines of her graceful neck.

I really *was* feeling better… and I needed to get a grip.

"I need your aid," Ana told me, choosing her words carefully, "to heal Queen Lucia."

Well, shit.

○○○

"You want me to go back to the House that's full of People who probably want to kill me? So I can in some way help the femmepire who actually *did* try to kill me just a few days ago?"

"If she had wanted to kill you, you would be dead, Mr. Smith," Anastasia told me quietly. "It could have easily been achieved without entering your mind."

That was a fair point. It wasn't like Lucia was particularly lacking in the strength department. Not to mention that she had a Talent which lent itself to the creation of stabby things. Like icicles. And glaciers. "What was she doing then?"

"I do not know."

"You... what?" I couldn't remember *ever* having heard Ana utter that particular phrase.

"I am not all-knowing, despite your beliefs to the contrary."

"You're blowing my mind here, Ana." My muttered comment won a brief smile, but I hadn't meant it as a joke. Ana was a one-vampire equivalent of the NSA. She *always* knew everything. "Maybe she wasn't trying to kill me, or maybe she just wanted to do it in the least efficient way possible. Regardless, Her Majesty and I are *not* on good terms."

"I know."

"And I don't see how I could help heal her anyway."

"You are bonded," Anastasia said simply. "You carry a piece of her in your mind. My hope is that bringing you and that piece into her vicinity will provide her the strength to break free from whatever has trapped her."

"So, you don't know if this will work?"

"There are neither precedents nor sureties for this situation, Mr. Smith. As often seems to be the case with you."

I sat there for a long moment, wrestling with my thoughts. Whether Lucia had been actively trying to kill me or not, she had hurt me. Badly. And then had the nerve to languish in blissful unconsciousness while Zorana batted cleanup. All this after being a thorn in my side for much of the last year. To say nothing of the whole attempted slavery thing. Other than maybe Thales and the Blood Witch herself, I was hard pressed to think of a single person I liked less in the world.

None of which really mattered at all.

"I'm ready when you are."

Anastasia blinked, the closest thing the femmepire had to a surprised face.

"You are?"

"I did say *anything*." I'd intended to say the words lightly, but they came out thick with emotion. Or like I had a head cold. "But I have a request. Or a favor of my own to ask, if you'd prefer."

"The young man I hired last year would never have sought to bargain with me," she told me slowly, and in a tone I had no hope of deciphering.

"I'm not bargaining," I corrected her. "I'll do whatever I can to help, regardless. Besides, that guy you hired last year was a moron. I'm a whole year…" I considered adjectives, and in quick order, discarded *smarter*, *wiser*, and even *craftier*. "…older now."

That earned me another smile, something that felt very much like a tangible reward.

"What then is your request?"

"I need answers," I told her, hurrying to get the words out before I lost my nerve for the hundredth time, "about us."

Watching her face was like seeing curtains being pulled shut across an open window. "I thought we had already discussed the matter on Tuesday."

"Well, yeah…" I coughed, in a futile attempt to hide my dismay. "But that was before you rescued me from torture, hid me away in the house that you share with your oldest and most trusted human companions, and nursed me back to health—"

"Something that took far less effort than expected."

"And then there were the kisses."

"Ah." The femmepire glanced away and brought the glass to her lips. It *was* wine, I decided. Blood would be thicker, right? Unless it had been diluted with water to make it easier to drink from a glass.

Damn it, now I was back to guessing.

"Kissing you might have been…"

"If you say *a mistake*, I'm going to throw myself off that balcony and into the ocean and ruin all your work in keeping me alive."

"I was going to say unwise," she clarified.

"It didn't *feel* unwise."

"Mr. Smith," she began, a slight note of discordance disrupting the smooth tones of her chocolate-cheesecake voice, "the events of the past few days change nothing. You must look elsewhere for romance."

Through some miracle of self-restraint, I managed to *not* pull my hair out in frustration. Instead, I lurched to my feet, and stalked over to the sliding glass door that led out onto the balcony. Behind me, Anastasia stilled, as if she truly did expect me to jump to my death. Which was ridiculous. With my luck, I'd just cripple myself, giving the femmepire a second opportunity to nurse me back to health, kiss me some more, and then tell me that we had zero chance of a future together.

Or I'd fall on the rocks and *die*, which would also suck. Either way, jumping was stupid. I spent a few long moments gazing out at the wind-capped waves instead.

"I don't get it," I finally managed. "If you don't care for me, then why did you bother rescuing me?"

"When have I *ever* said that I did not care for you?"

"Tuesday?" I suggested. "And then again, like… a minute ago?"

"I have never said those words." Her voice was hard. Somehow, I'd managed to piss off the Stone Lady. Without her beauty clouding my brain, that cold voice made it shockingly easy to remember why everyone in the House was afraid of the femmepire. "I said I cannot pursue a relationship with you. Do not take that to mean that you are unimportant to me or that I will not fight to keep you safe."

I refrained from banging my head against the glass, but only because my steadily growing headache didn't need any further help.

"But you *kissed* me!"

"Yes." Her voice softened minutely. "But the world is what it is, John. And I cannot be who you need me to be."

"And who is that, exactly?"

"Someone to share your days and nights. Someone who will put you above all others. Someone who will grow old with you."

"Jesus, Ana," I retorted, "I'm not saying we should get married and have children or anything—" I turned from the balcony and cocked one eyebrow. "Is that even possible? Children between our species, I mean."

"It is not," she informed me, her face a mask.

"Damn." A horde of miniature Anastasias toddling about would have been awfully cute. I shrugged it off. "My point is, I'm twenty-six! Humans may have gotten married young back in your day, but my generation takes its time. Like… thirty, at least!"

Frankly, and with all due respect to the preternaturally cute miniature-Anas that my brain had conjured up, I wasn't sure I *ever* wanted kids.

"Anyway," I continued, "I *know* we're different people, I know what it is you do for the House, and I know your first loyalty is to Lucia, although I can't for the life of me see why she deserves it." I managed not to growl the blonde queen's name, but it was close. I also refrained from pointing out that Anastasia had spent the last few days taking care of me, while her so-called *first loyalty* had been stuck in a coma. "But we both do care for each other, right? Would seeing where that takes us be such a bad idea?"

She sat there, swirling the glass in her hand, and said nothing.

Which was kind of an answer in and of itself.

I sighed.

"Okay. Thanks for clarifying things. Again." I came back from the balcony. "Shall we go?"

"I beg your pardon?"

"To heal Lucia."

"You still—"

"I *told* you I'd help, and I will. You being madly in love with me wasn't a requirement." I nodded to her still half-full glass. "Finish your drink, Lady Dumenyova, and we'll go wake Sleeping Awful."

CHAPTER 31

I didn't see a lot of Anastasia's house on the way out, but my journey the length of the upstairs hallway, down a flight of stairs, and then through *another* hall was sufficient to confirm my earlier guess as to its size. It was also sufficient to leave me out-of-breath, seeing stars, and wondering exactly when my legs had been replaced with rubber.

"You are not ready for this," Anastasia finally said, the third or fourth time I stopped to rest. "We can wait another day for you to recover."

"I'm fine," I lied. "And at the rate I'm healing, I'll be as good as new by the time we make it to Scripps Ranch."

That was less of a lie. Probably. Regardless, I wasn't prepared to walk back *up* the stairs I had just descended. I was used to being out of shape, but it had been a long time since I'd felt this *weak*.

Anastasia eyed me carefully for a moment, but either I did a good job hiding my infirmity or she chose to overlook it. She slipped into a black suit coat that was a match for her skirt and ushered me into the garage.

Directly in front of us was…

"Seriously? A Prius?"

"It is Teresa's," came the reply. "She believes strongly in preserving the environment."

"You should buy her a Tesla then," I muttered to myself. My confidence in Anastasia's *car fu* had just been dealt a monstrous blow.

Thankfully, the other cars in the garage more than met my expectations. I'd already seen—and drooled over—Anastasia's convertible red Jaguar XKR-S, of course. But just past that, in a green so dark it bordered on black…

"Holy crap! How did you get the new F-type already? You've only been back in the country for like… a week!"

"I placed the order before I left, Mr. Smith," she explained. "Even for such as we, the waiting list was… substantial."

"Yeah, I can imagine." I followed her over to a car that made even the XKR look almost dowdy. "Please tell me this is what we'll be driving."

"Not this time, I'm afraid." We continued to a very nice, very sedate Mercedes SUV. She unlocked the doors and got in.

"Now I *know* you don't love me." I pulled open the passenger door and hoisted myself inside. The SUV's luxurious interior did little to lift my spirits.

As we pulled out of the garage, I looked back toward the ocean. Despite how it had seemed from the upstairs dining room, the water was a good fifty yards away from Anastasia's house. If I'd jumped, I would have cracked like an egg on the rocky shore.

This was why I left melodrama to the professionals.

ooo

The evening sun was at our backs as we turned off the 5 to drive inland to Scripps Ranch. The two-lane 56 was free of the cars that regularly brought it to a standstill in rush hour, and we breezed along in silence. I watched the cyclists and runners that paced the highway to the south and tried to think of anything but my impending return to the House.

That worked just as well as expected. Mental discipline had never been one of my strengths.

"Are you cold?" Anastasia stroked a button on the dashboard, and the air coming from the vents weakened dramatically.

"Yeah. Cold. Thanks." There was no way in hell I was going to admit I was freaking terrified. Especially not after I'd already cried like a baby. But the thought that I might run into Zorana again… I shivered a second time. Damn it. I wrapped my arms around myself and fumbled for something new to occupy my mind.

"The one thing I don't get," I told Anastasia, "is why."

"You will have to be slightly more specific, Mr. Smith."

"You're brilliant, you're lovely, and you're a badass."

"Is there a question in there?" I was back to being Mr. Smith instead of John, but it hadn't erased the tease from her voice.

"Yeah. You could do anything you wanted, and I'm sure you'd kick ass at it. So why spend your time following Lucia's orders and cleaning up her messes? What is it about her that makes her worthy of your service?"

Anastasia gave the question serious consideration before replying. "I admit that Queen Lucia is arrogant, quick tempered, short-sighted, occasionally vain, and all too often dismissive of races and perspectives other than her own, but she also has an inner strength that has seen her weather situations that would have crushed other individuals. She is also my oldest friend. One of the few friends left, in fact, and the closest thing to a family I have. When we were young, the flaws in her nature were balanced by the knowledge of her destiny and the responsibilities of the crown she would one day wear."

"And then?"

"Then that future was stolen from her. She was stripped of rank, disowned by her own family, and expelled from the Italian courts. Every principality in Europe closed their door to her. Even the few established Houses in your country rejected her." Anastasia glanced in my direction, a sad smile on her lovely face. "For the first few decades of our exile, she was fixated on the idea of reclaiming her throne. When that dream began to fade, she decided her destiny might instead be to create a new court in the Americas. When we lost half the House to the so-called Cedar fire, she began to despair that either goal would ever be attainable. Since then, her actions have been ill-considered and erratic."

Given that my enthrallment was the result of one of those ill-considered actions, I couldn't disagree. Nor could I find it within myself to muster up even a shred of sympathy for the femmepire queen.

"Even so," Ana continued, "she is still my queen, my friend, and the sister I never had by blood. If I can help her regain her sense of self, it is my duty to do so."

"You're a good friend," I said. "You deserve better."

○○○

Two exits later, I squeezed my eyes shut and groaned.

"What is it?"

I cracked open one eye to find Anastasia glancing worriedly over at me. "I was supposed to meet with some clients last night. For work, I mean."

"Is this the case you have been working on?"

"Yeah. I'm helping the White Ladies out with an investigation and was supposed to give them a weekly progress report." The ghosts were going to be pissed. Especially when they found out how much time I'd wasted getting tortured.

Maybe there was a reason my professional reputation sucked.

"Given your injuries, I suspect they will understand."

"I guess we'll find out."

"Could Lady Middleton have attended in your stead?"

"The only way I got to the meeting place the first time was Valentina whisking me away. I doubt she'd do the same for Juliette, even if the Duchess had thought to go to my house." I pinched the bridge of my nose, and sighed. "Oh well. One more thing to deal with after we wake up your queen. You do know that Juliette quit the House, right? You don't need to call her by title anymore."

"*What did you say?*"

The look on Anastasia's face was worrisome.

"That Juliette quit the House?" Jesus… was that *still* supposed to be a secret?

"Before that."

"Valentina doesn't know Juliette."

"The ghost haunting your home is *Valentina Zhukova?*"

"I guess so. Didn't I already tell you that?"

It was Anastasia's turn to sigh. "You did not."

"Do you know her?"

"Only by reputation." Anastasia shook her head as she accelerated past a particularly slow Accord in the fast lane. "You do attract a particular type."

I had no idea what *that* meant.

"As for Lady Middleton, she earned her title. While I do not agree with her decision to leave us, I will continue to accord her the respect she deserves."

Which said a lot about Anastasia, really… especially since Juliette had no issues whatsoever with flinging mud in the opposite direction.

"How did you convince her to come to Cardiff?"

"I asked her to," Ana said simply.

"And *after* she told you to shove it…?"

Anastasia's flawless profile remained composed, but I could hear the answering smile in her voice. "I explained that I needed someone to help protect you while you healed. Given your recent interactions with the House, Lady Middleton is one of the few I can trust in such matters." She glanced over at me. "She is rather protective of you."

I could think of a few words to describe the yellow-eyed femmepire, but protective wasn't one of them. "We *did* just become partners," I reasoned. "It would be bad form for her to let me die."

"Yes. Partners." Something in Ana's voice made me glance across the car at her.

"You disapprove?"

"Your life is yours to live as you see fit, Mr. Smith. And I cannot fault Lady Middleton's loyalty."

"But?" Why was there *always* a but?

"But you must realize that her continued presence in your life is a complication."

"How so? My time with the House is *done*, Ana. As far as I'm concerned, I'm no longer an ally or an employee, which means Lucia gets no say in who my friends or business partners are." Not that she ever had, even when I was on the payroll.

"After this," I continued, "I'm going back to my job. I'm going to finish the Ladies' case before it kills me, and then I'm going to let all of San Diego know that the city's number one mediator is free and clear of vampire politics, and once again a paragon of neutrality."

"So, you will be severing ties with the Pack as well?"

"Well… no." Especially since I still had to convince Carolyn to give her ex-husband Jason another shot.

"And the pixies? And the Temecula coven?"

"That's different—"

"And Lord Beel-Kasan and his human ward?"

"Okay, maybe *paragon of neutrality* is overstating things, but at least I won't be on retainer for one of San Diego's ruling powers anymore. The mediation cases should start flowing back in once word gets out."

I hoped. Especially because, without the stipend the House had been paying me, rent was going to be damn near impossible otherwise.

The femmepire was silent as we merged onto the 15 and headed south. We wove between a battered old Buick and an equally battered Camry before she spoke again.

"John…"

Finally! I had seriously been wondering if she was *ever* going to use my first name again.

"Yes, my Lady Anastasia Dumenyova?"

"Have you ever thought of simply allowing Mr. Van Stahl to take over as mediator?"

"I haven't been doing a whole lot to stop him," I pointed out, "but I wasn't planning on abandoning the position entirely. San Diego's a big place. If the past year is any indication, I'm sure there will be plenty of supernatural drama to keep us both busy. Why do you ask?"

"Since taking office, you have almost died on numerous occasions. While your bond with Queen Lucia makes it impossible for you to withdraw from our world completely, I suspect your chances of reaching thirty would rise dramatically if you were to remove yourself from the public eye."

"But didn't you say Van Stahl was a bad dude?" Not that I really believed it, but still...

"I said it was a possibility. Yet none of us are without blood on our souls, Mr. Smith."

"And?"

"And my soul is dark enough without your blood being added to it." Anastasia's words were soft but heartfelt. "Unusual abilities aside, your current pace will have you dead within the year."

"Ana, there's such a thing as being *too* honest."

"I only promised you the truth, Mr. Smith. I never said it would be easy."

"Did you... just quote The Matrix?" While Juliette was a television, film, *and* comics fiend, I had a hard time picturing Anastasia scarfing down buttered popcorn while watching sci-fi.

"I have no idea what you mean."

I eyed the femmepire from my car seat, but her face was impossible to read.

"Never mind. Anyway, I'm not too concerned with long-term career goals right now. I'd be happy just to survive the week."

CHAPTER 32

IN WHICH A HOUSE IS ONLY AS GOOD AS ITS
PEOPLE

A few minutes later, we pulled up to the iron gate that led
onto the House grounds. After a moment's hesitation, the black-clad
manpire on duty waved us through. I looked over my shoulder to find
him staring after us, speaking quietly into his headset.

"They know we're here."

"They would be a poor Watch otherwise."

"Yeah." I turned back around, stubbornly refusing to
acknowledge that the gate's black posts had looked an awful lot like
prison bars. I was already returning to a House full of People who
probably wanted me dead, to assist a Queen who *had* tried to kill
me…

Further negativity seemed like overkill.

"Remember," Anastasia cautioned me for at least the fifth
time, "I will endeavor to keep you safe, but you must do your own
part in the matter."

"I know… I know. I'll try to avoid pissing anyone off." I
didn't point out that such things tended to happen whether I wanted

them to or not. If the supernatural world were a little bit less hidden, I'd have been voted *Most likely to be eaten by a demonic hell beast* in high school.

"Perhaps," Ana said, as if in response to my unspoken thoughts, "you should simply remain silent for the entirety of our visit."

As we approached the main entrance, the double doors swung inward. A grim-faced Thales, in ludicrously form-fitting black, met us at the door.

"Lady Dumenyova." He drank in the sight of her, dark eyes sparkling with appreciation, before throwing a withering glance in my direction. "I see you have found our wayward monkey."

Per Ana's request, I held my tongue, but it was way harder than it should have been. I really, really hated that asshole, from his GQ-perfect hair to the golden tan that made my own recent efforts at the beach seem vaguely sad.

And the way he was looking at Ana wasn't helping.

"Duke Barros and the Council have asked to speak with you, my lady."

"I expected as much," said Anastasia. Which came as something of a surprise to me, since this was the first I'd heard of it. Even more surprising was the femmepire's demeanor. With her hair up in a bun, and the jacket and skirt combo, Anastasia looked almost… meek? It was not a word I would normally have used to describe a woman who had driven her fist all the way *through* her ex-lover. "Would you take us to them?"

"Must *he* attend as well?" I looked about to try to determine exactly who Thales could be referring to with such obvious scorn.

Oh. Right.

"It is my intention to keep Mr. Smith out of trouble. Which necessitates keeping him within arm's reach, I fear." Her words were so matter-of-fact that it took me a full five seconds to realize I'd been insulted.

Thales' laugh clawed at my already frayed self-control. "It is good that you have returned from abroad, my lady. I heard much of you, even in Brasilia, and look forward to getting to know the woman behind the legends."

"As is often the case," said Anastasia, "stories grow in the telling. I suspect you will find the truth considerably more mundane." She nodded toward the House's interior. "Shall we?"

The House felt… different, as we walked through the foyer, past the stairs, and to the elevator, but I couldn't quite put my finger on how exactly. Had it always been this quiet? It was the sort of silence that made me picture vengeful vampires lurking around every corner, secretly plotting my demise.

Our elevator opened onto the fourth floor, which meant we were again headed for one of the many conference rooms. Ana didn't seem concerned by the development. She allowed the other vampire to escort her down the hall, the manpire's hand resting comfortably against the small of her back.

I mentally painted a target between Thales' shoulder blades and wished, for the thousandth time, that I still had Bill's hell gun, a pistol that belched fire like a nuclear-powered flamethrower. If I hadn't lost that gun during my panic-filled escape from a burning building, the last few days would have gone differently.

Very differently.

We walked for what felt like a mile, and was probably closer to one hundred feet, before stopping outside the conference room where Lucia had read me the riot act a week earlier. Whereas Steve had knocked before ushering me inside, Thales simply opened the door and walked right in.

I followed the two vampires through.

Seated at the table, directly across from us, was Duke Barros himself. While he and Thales had sort of blended together into a blur of Brazilian superiority on my one previous meeting, I'd spent enough time around the new Captain to now easily tell the two apart. Both were obnoxiously handsome men in the perpetual prime of their lives, but the duke had a more severe, military-style haircut than his subordinate. His eyes were a pale grey and the casual cruelty that Thales could never quite mask was missing entirely, replaced by a cold light that made Lucia's own winter powers seem mild by comparison.

And on his left…

I froze, caught between the desire to run screaming back to the elevator and an equally strong urge to curl up into a ball on the carpeted floor.

"Hello, monkey." Zorana flashed a smile that might have been cute on an actual twelve-year-old. Her fangs were hidden and her eyes clear of blood. She wore a pale-yellow dress with multi-colored butterflies and had a matching ribbon in her dark hair.

It took all of my willpower and internet-purchased Jedi training just to keep from pissing myself.

ooo

Seemingly by accident, Anastasia stepped between the Blood Witch and me, offering a respectful nod to the still-seated Duke.

"Ah, Lady Dumenyova!" The manpire flashed brilliant white teeth in a smile. "We have missed you these past few days."

"Your pardon, Duke Barros. Upon receiving your call, I returned with all due haste to San Diego, whereupon I encountered this one." She motioned in my direction without even a glance. "Sadly, he had no insights to offer as to Queen Lucia's malady."

"Indeed." The smile faded from the manpire's face, replaced by what appeared to be genuine regret and concern. "Her condition is as tragic as it is perplexing. We few—" He motioned to those of us in the room, although I suspected my inclusion was purely incidental. "—are doing what we can to keep the House running until Lucia returns to us. Assuming she ever does."

"Do you think it possible that she might not?" I goggled at Anastasia's back. She sounded more like a young woman in search of reassurance than the ultra-competent femmepire I had grown accustomed to. Had Thales drugged her when I wasn't looking?

"In truth, I cannot say," Barros answered mournfully, rubbing his cleft chin in careful thought. "As you well know, our species is not prone to such weakness. I would never have thought one of us—let alone the queen, who would traditionally be the strongest of her House—might lapse into a coma."

"Despite our best efforts, Lucia will not drink," said Thales, taking a seat at the table, "and if she does not feed…"

We all stood about for a long moment, presumably envisioning a world where the exiled vampire queen starved to death. All the while, I was painfully aware of Zorana's steady gaze. I was once again trembling like a small animal.

Or a recently tortured fratman.

"It is my fervent hope that Lucia recovers," said the duke, "but until that time, we must take up the reins of authority. I believe she would have desired nothing less."

Which told me that the dude didn't know Lucia at all. The femmepire I knew would have gladly dropped a mountain on the House if she wasn't going to be around to rule it.

"While I am but a poor substitute and new to this land," the manpire continued, "I give you my oath that I will do my best to provide guidance in her absence. But this House needs its Secundus. Can I count upon you for aid, Lady Dumenyova?"

Duke Barros rose to his feet, and I was gratified to discover that I topped the dude by almost a head. It was one of the few good things about hanging with centuries-old individuals.

"Of course, Duke Barros," said Anastasia, unaware of my sudden superiority complex. "It will be my privilege to serve."

The other vampire's toothy grin returned, as if it had been lurking just out of sight. "That is most gratifying to hear. Please then, take a seat, and we will return this House to greatness."

Anastasia placed one hand upon the chair in front of her, and started to pull it away from the table, then paused. She turned a green-eyed gaze in my direction, as if remembering my presence for the first time.

"Actually, I should deal with Mr. Smith first, my Duke." Her voice was cold enough to make a penguin shiver.

"Why *did* you bring the human with you?"

"He is registered as an ally of our House, is he not?" the femmepire replied. "If we are to get any value out of our investment, we must keep him close to us and... properly motivated."

Duke Barros' laughter was a rich, golden waterfall of music. "Again, well said. I can have one of the Watch take John Smith to his quarters."

Anastasia hesitated, but Thales filled in the silence.

"The Lady Dumenyova is concerned that the monkey might get into trouble on his own, my duke."

"He does possess a talent for such things, as my queen no doubt informed you," admitted the auburn-haired femmepire. "I should see him secured."

"Very well then. After you have dealt with Mr. Smith, please return with all haste. We have plans to make."

"Yes, my Duke." With another short bow, Anastasia ushered me out into the hall.

We were in the elevator before she spoke again.

"You are taking this well, John."

"I'm not a complete moron, Ana," I replied, speaking for the first time since we had entered the House, "and unlike Duke Barros, I actually *know* you."

"Ah."

"So, it's another coup?"

"As I feared," she confirmed.

"And we're going to get Lucia out of here before the Brazilians decide a dead queen is even less threat to their authority than a comatose one?"

"Precisely. Can you sense her location?"

I fumbled about for Lucia's presence in the back of my head. With the queen in a coma, our bond felt a bit muted, but the direction remained clear. "Yeah. She's close by. A little below us, a little bit... *that* way." I shrugged. "It feels like she's still in her suite."

"Thank you." The smile she gave left me weak in the knees. I reminded myself yet again that the two of us had no romantic future whatsoever. "I have a separate task for you, if you are willing."

I gave her a questioning look.

"Barros is not so foolish as to leave the queen unguarded," Anastasia explained. "I will be unable to protect you and rescue my liege at the same time. And there is another individual we dare not leave behind."

"Who?"

"Summer," the femmepire answered, referring to the House's lone child. "If there is to be war, she must be taken somewhere safe." She handed me her car keys, before pressing the button for the third floor. "Will you see to it?"

"I'll do my best." Summer—Princess Tea Leaf to a select few of us—was an adorable little hellion who would no doubt grow up to break men's hearts and drown the world in an ocean of blood. And I couldn't bear the thought of her becoming a casualty. "But if the Watch really has flipped to serving Barros, they aren't going to let me just carry her out of here."

The elevator dinged open. As ever, two black-clad Watch members guarded the door to the Council suites. The two vampires turned unfriendly glances in my direction. I had a few friends on the Watch, but these two were clearly *not* card-carrying members of the John Smith Fan Club.

"Eric. Hidalgo." Anastasia greeted the manpires, as she strode to the door.

"Lady Dumenyova," said the one on the left. Both men offered short bows.

"I am sorry for this," she told them sincerely.

Before either could reply, the femmepire struck, her hands taking on the mottled grey of granite. The crunching of bones was barely audible above the impact the vampires made in the wall. The manpire who had spoken collapsed in a boneless heap. The other, made of slightly sterner stuff, stayed on his feet, and lunged at the femmepire.

Even I could have told him that was a stupid move.

The door didn't so much fall as explode inward, helped liberally by the vampire-sized missile hurled headfirst into it. Down the long hall, I saw another pair of guards, heavily armed and flanking Lucia's door. They drew their weapons and advanced, joined by additional figures that must have been within the queen's chambers.

"Remember, John," Anastasia told me, stripping off her suit jacket and handing it to me before she advanced toward what looked like a sea of black uniforms. "Get Summer to the car. I will join you as soon as I can."

There were a lot of things I wanted to say, but at vampire speed, she was already two dozen feet down the hall. So instead, I hurried in and to the second door on the left.

"Tea Leaf?" I called, stepping into the foyer of the little girl's suite. On the wall across from me, an animated fox blinked, and then scurried behind a bush. Cartoon birds flitted across the painted ceiling. "It's John, sweetie. I need you to come with me."

"John!" came the excited reply, but the little girl's voice was swiftly followed by another.

"Mr. John!"

And before I could even groan in recognition, Princess Tea Leaf and Jee Sun both came rocketing around the corner.

CHAPTER 33

"Jee Sun, what are you *doing* here?"

Even as I asked, I knew it was a dumb question. An unlikely friendship had blossomed between the vampire child and Lord Beel-Kasan's purely human ward. Summer rarely left the vampire House, and it was not at all unusual for Jee Sun to spend time with her whenever Bill was busy... doing whatever it was a demigod of nightmares, terror and vindication did.

"You are very silly, Mr. John!" said the little Korean girl.

"Yes, I am." I patted both girls on the heads. "I need you two to come with me, okay? There are bad things happening, and it's not safe to stay here." I tried to usher them both to the door, but Tea Leaf set her feet, pouting cutely up at me.

"You're supposed to say hello the *proper* way!" She stamped one foot irately, clutching her stuffed rabbit, Sir Floppy, by his ears.

"I will," I promised her, "but right now, we really need to hurry." The *proper way* involved almost ten minutes of courtly introductions between me, Sir Floppy, Mr. Arf, and all the rest of her stuffed animals.

Tea Leaf's pout only deepened. The little vampire was already every bit as strong as I was, which made moving her difficult. And if I tried to pick her up without permission, there was every chance I might get an accidental size two shoe in my groin. I turned to the slightly older Jee Sun for help.

"Jee Sun, we're in *danger.*"

She looked up at me through her thick glasses, smiling the slightly off-kilter smile that always worried me. "Boom?"

"Exactly."

"Will there be ice cream if we go?"

"Absolutely," I promised.

Before the word had finished leaving my mouth, Jee Sun was sprinting out the door and down the hall toward the elevator. God bless that child's sweet tooth.

I turned to the little vampire at my side, noting with relief that her pout had been replaced with a dazzling smile. She extended both arms in my direction, Sir Floppy still firmly in one hand.

"Pony ride?"

○○○

A year earlier, and that pony ride could have lasted for hours… or at least until the mercurial little vampire's attention had moved on to something new. But Tea Leaf had grown quite a bit, and I was a long way from full strength; I barely made it to the elevator before I had to set her down.

Jee Sun was rhythmically pushing the button to summon the elevator, even though it was already there, doors wide open. In contrast to her friend, the young Korean girl hadn't aged a day as far as I could tell. I'd asked Bill how old his ward was once, but the demigod's answer had involved an ever-shifting number of rotations on his Mickey Mouse clock, and that had been no help whatsoever.

The elevator swiftly deposited us back on the ground floor, and I exited with the two girls. Jee Sun seemed eager to head off to the promised ice cream, but Tea Leaf, like most of her species, paid me very little attention. I took her by the hand and did my best to cajole her into something faster than an easily distracted stroll.

We had almost reached the front doors when a shadow blocked our path. Shit.

Steve was in his Watch uniform. He'd trimmed his mohawk down at some point in the past few days, and the short red bristles looked even cooler than usual.

"John." His eyes moved from me to the girls by my side. "Where are you taking Summer?"

"Ice cream!" chirped Jee Sun helpfully.

"And boom!" added Tea Leaf, who might have been spending a bit *too* much time with Bill's ward.

"I'm really glad to see you, Steve. I thought Barros might have replaced the whole Watch with his stooges." I glanced around us at the still-silent House and lowered my voice. "The Duke and Zorana have made a move against Lucia, and the queen isn't awake to stop them. I'm trying to get Summer out of the line of fire."

Steve nodded and said nothing.

"But you already knew that," I realized, my tension ratcheting up by a few thousand percent. Even on my best day, with an army of robot ninjas at my back, I couldn't take Steve. If he decided to stop me, my brilliant escape plan was doomed. "Dude. I need to get these two to safety."

The tension continued to mount, but finally, the manpire shrugged and stepped aside. "If anyone asks, we never saw each other."

"I owe you one. Another one." Between Ana's suit jacket and the two little girls, I didn't have a hand free to bump fists with, but I gave Steve a nod of appreciation, dude to dude. "Why don't you come with us?"

"I'm sorry, John." He shook his head. "You and me… we're cool, but Queen Lucia…? After the last few decades of her leadership, after the way she's treated both you and Kayla … maybe the House is better off without her."

I didn't know what to say to that. Something told me the duke would be just as bad, but Steve's defection showed just how badly Lucia's power base had eroded over the past year. I wasn't sure what allies the queen had left.

Other than the woman I loved.

Who was busy fighting a dozen of Steve's fellow guards.

To rescue the femmepire I hated.

My life was such a disaster.

"Okay," I managed through a lump in my throat. "Take care of yourself then. And maybe we'll see each other at the Bitter End sometime?"

"Maybe once things have died down. In the meantime, you should get going. I can't vouch for your safety if anyone else shows up."

I hurried outside to Ana's SUV and buckled the girls into the backseat, Ana's blazer carefully draped between them. Then, I climbed into the driver's seat, inserted the key in the ignition, and started the car.

And waited.

"Booooooooring!" shouted Jee Sun at a decibel level reserved for rocket engines and stadium speakers.

"Use your inside voice, Tiny Flower," I said absently, eyes scanning the building. Ana's skills were legendary, but there had been an awful lot of Watch members between her and Lucia. What if she was unable to fight her way to the queen? Or back out? How long could I wait before someone decided to investigate what Lucia's human thrall was doing out front?

And why were the girls suddenly being so quiet?

Alarmed, I looked to the rearview mirror, but Jee Sun and Tea Leaf were still precisely where I expected them to be. Sir Floppy was sitting atop Ana's suit jacket, and the two girls were whispering back and forth, sharing silent giggles. I had a moment of panic that they were laughing at *me* before remembering I wasn't in elementary school anymore.

Whoever said time heals all scars clearly had enjoyed a significantly less humiliating childhood than me.

When I turned back to the House, a body was falling from the sky.

I couldn't discern many details before that body struck the ground, but whoever it was had been wearing black. I retraced the angle of their descent and found a gaping hole in a large bay window on the third floor. Moments later, Anastasia appeared, a white-clad body in her arms.

And then she jumped.

As the femmepire started to fall, something golden and angry lanced out of the suite behind her. Even in mid-air, Ana managed to twist away, shielding Lucia with her own body. Moments later, she reached the ground, landing on her feet like a cat. An impact like that should have broken every bone in her legs, but she seemed none the worse for wear.

Above her, Zorana appeared at the window, a glowing nimbus of blood floating beside her dark curls. Further tendrils streaked down, but Ana was safely out of range. With a scowl, the Blood Witch began to follow, only to stagger backwards, clutching her shoulder. Anastasia had shifted the queen's limp body to one shoulder, and her other arm was a blur of motion, sending sharp and shiny projectiles in Zorana's direction.

I pushed open the passenger door. As soon as Ana was inside, she turned to me, eyes glittering jade and gold.

"Go."

And I went. I'd never actually driven a car the size of the SUV… but its engine had to be three times the size of my new Corolla's. I pointed the beast downhill and jammed my foot to the floor. Our sudden acceleration prompted delighted cheers from Jee Sun and the vampire princess.

The gate was shut but proved far from an immovable object as the Mercedes' irresistible force slammed right through. Anastasia sent another three shards of shimmering metal into the gate house, and the guard was too busy diving for cover to even think of stopping us.

For the next ten minutes, I drove like a madman, charging down the back streets of Scripps Ranch at well over ninety miles an hour, one eye on my rearview mirror. It was only when we reached the 15 with no pursuit in sight that it became clear we'd gotten away.

I slowed to a more sedate—and far less attention-grabbing— eighty miles per hour and waited for my heart rate to similarly decelerate.

"What were you throwing at them?"

Ana's lap was overflowing with curvaceous, comatose, femmepire queen, but she showed me a handful of projectiles.

"Are those shuriken?" I recognized the bladed stars from a dozen terrible martial arts movies and my own childhood ambitions of becoming a ninja.

"They are."

"Where on earth were you keeping them?" I'd looked her over *very* carefully back in Cardiff—as only a trained private investigator or creepy stalker with delusions of romance could do—and she sure as hell hadn't been carrying an armory with her then.

Anastasia regarded me slyly for a long moment, as the gold slowly faded from her luminous eyes. I had just decided that she wasn't going to answer my question at all when she shifted Lucia's dead weight, resting the queen against the passenger-side window. She hiked up her own black skirt, pulling the hem just far enough to show off an even greater expanse of mouthwatering leg... and the very bottom edge of what looked to be a leather bandolier wrapping her thigh. What had appeared to be simple seams in the skirt's fabric were careful slits that allowed the femmepire access to the weapons strapped out of sight.

"Holy shit. You are *so* sexy right now," I breathed.

"Shit!" said Jee Sun supportively.

"Ice cream!" crowed Tea Leaf.

CHAPTER 34
IN WHICH SIR FLOPPY KEEPS WATCH

After the adrenaline rush of our escape from the House, the forty-minute trip back to Cardiff was a blur. I followed Anastasia's directions and we were soon pulling into the enormous garage of her equally enormous beach-front property. Parking was a little bit touch-and-go—I *really* wasn't used to driving anything that big—but I managed to avoid scraping against the side wall... or hitting the shelves that lined the far wall. All things considered, that was pretty miraculous.

"Now what?" I whispered. At some point in our drive, the two girls had dropped off to sleep, leaving the stuffed rabbit, Sir Floppy, as the closest thing to an alert and aware individual in the backseat.

"I will take Queen Lucia up to a room," Anastasia murmured back, "and have Gustavo and Teresa assist you with Summer and Lord Beel-Kasan's ward."

"And then?" As I slowly came down from the high of not being dead, I was finding it harder to ignore the recent developments at the House. Something told me my part in the whole thing was going to come back to haunt me, to say nothing of the possibility of open war among the vampires. Shit was most definitely getting real.

"We wait to see if my hypothesis was correct." Ana shook her head. "There is much to do, but little of it has any value unless Lucia can be awoken."

I decided not to point out that she had just omitted her queen's title, for perhaps the first time in recorded history. Instead, I went around to Anastasia's side to open the door.

The femmepire stepped down from the SUV, holding Lucia in her arms as if she were a feather pillow rather than a very solid, very voluptuous, and no doubt heavy, woman. Vampire strength really did have its advantages. I scooted out of her way, and headed to the rear doors where I could collect Summer and Jee Sun.

Before opening the door, I paused, and cocked my head. "I think your car has a leak," I finally decided. "I can hear it dripping oil from here."

"That's not oil, Mr. Smith." For the first time, Ana's voice was ragged, showing far more strain than Lucia's weight should have warranted. I turned and found the femmepire already halfway across the garage. But behind her, a small trail of golden liquid had stained the cement.

"Holy shit. You're wounded!" Ana's formerly pristine blouse bore all the hallmarks of a hard-fought battle, but it was her right sleeve that had my attention; the cloth was plastered to her arm and drenched in vampire blood.

I left the kids in the car and hurried over.

"Zorana arrived more quickly than I expected," Anastasia admitted through gritted teeth, "and struck when I was least able to defend myself. Barros may not be a total fool after all."

I took Lucia from the femmepire's arms, trying not to let my own knees buckle as I did so. The queen wasn't *that* heavy, but I was a long way from one hundred percent, myself, and my devotion to Kayla's suggested workout plan had been… less than inspiring. Still, of the two of us standing there, I was the one *not* dripping blood all over the pavement.

Her weight notwithstanding, Lucia felt surprisingly *right* in my arms. Golden flesh was warm and soft against my own bare skin, and her platinum blonde hair swept over one arm like a lover's caress. The queen's curvaceous form nestled into my embrace like we had been designed for each other.

That weirdness terrified me every bit as much as our desperate flight from the House. My feelings for Lucia hadn't changed even the tiniest bit. If anything, they had gotten worse. So, why the hell was I responding to her like this?

It had to be our bond, which was as unfair as it was unacceptable. As soon as I retrieved my phone, I was going to give Nepenthe a call. Maybe we could move up the date of her coven's ritual?

I shook off my worried thoughts and followed Anastasia inside, trying not to wince when I accidentally bounced Lucia's feet, and then head, against the wall. In my defense, I didn't have a whole lot of practice in carrying a woman across the threshold.

"How can I help with your injury?"

"I will be fine," Ana insisted, "although you might have to go without Gustavo's aid for a short while."

As if just speaking the name was enough to summon him, the old man appeared at the end of the hallway. He discerned the situation a lot faster than I had, and disappeared, returning almost instantly with a thick towel. He wrapped it tightly around Anastasia's arm, and then assisted her down the hall without a word.

I trailed along behind them, taking the corner a little bit too quickly… with predictable results. If I ever did get married, I decided, I would just let my wife cross the threshold under her own power. I was clearly not suited to this archaic form of transportation.

I really, really hoped all that scientific data about comatose patients being aware of their environments didn't hold true for vampires. Otherwise, Lucia was damn well going to kill me. Again.

○○○

Much later, I was sitting in the upstairs dining room with a mug of homemade hot chocolate in my hands. I had deposited Lucia into the appointed bedroom—just down the hall from mine—and made separate trips back to collect Jee Sun, Tea Leaf, and Sir Floppy. The two girls hadn't even stirred when I tucked them into a large king-sized bed in yet another room. I left Sir Floppy on a dresser by the door with strict orders to battle to his last bunny breath should any invaders get past the rest of us.

It's possible my exhaustion was starting to get to me.

I was staring into the murky depths of my cocoa, dimly aware that it had been several minutes since I'd taken a sip, when a sound roused me from my stupor. Anastasia stood in the doorway. She'd exchanged her tattered blouse and weapon-hiding skirt for a deep blue camisole and wide-legged pants of some fabric that looked unspeakably soft. Her bare right arm was wrapped in a bandage, but she otherwise looked fine.

"How are you doing?" I asked, since it was either that or babble incoherently about how pretty she looked for someone who had just been bleeding all over the garage.

"I am well, John," she replied, padding into the dining room on bare feet to take a seat across from me. "It was just a flesh wound, after all."

"And now you're quoting Monty Python," I muttered.

"I am certain that I have no idea what you mean." A smile flashed across her face, breathtaking and ephemeral. "While Zorana's magic made the wound worse than it would have otherwise been, the gift of Gustavo's blood has gone a long way to repairing the damage."

We sat there in silence. I remembered to take another sip of the rapidly cooling, but still delicious, hot chocolate.

"I was relieved to see that you did not encounter any difficulties in making it to the car," she finally continued.

"Me too. As action-movie-cool as your escape route was, mine seemed a lot less painful." I shrugged. "I did run into Steve though."

"Stephen Grant?"

"Uhm… maybe?"

"You did not know his surname? Are not the two of you drinking partners?"

"He's a black vampire with a mohawk," I grumbled. "Why would he need a last name?"

"A fair point. What did Mr. Grant have to say?"

"That our drinking days might be nearing an end." I sobered quickly as I remembered the conversation. "Even if Lucia does wake up, I'm not sure she has many supporters left at the House."

"That is a problem for another day, Mr. Smith."

"I guess so." I found my eyes drifting shut of their own accord. "I'm amazed we made it out of there, honestly. And I guess it was a good thing we *didn't* take the Jag." The idea of trying to fit Anastasia, myself, Lucia, *and* the two girls into the sporty two-seater was laughable.

"Indeed."

Something about Ana's reply made me glance across the table at her.

"You *knew* we were going to need the extra car space?"

"I knew it was a possibility," the femmepire replied. "Historically, the People have not reacted well to weakness. And there was little chance my queen's coma would be seen as anything else."

"Is that why you were so weirdly subservient when speaking to the manpires?"

"Indeed. While we are perhaps less prone to bias than your own species, there remains a casual chauvinism among some of the older males. Duke Barros is not a stupid man, but his beliefs are a weakness that can be exploited."

"Jesus. Remind me to never, ever play chess against you." It had never occurred to me that even clothing could be strategic. "Although I would have appreciated some sort of warning that we were walking into a trap."

"My apologies, John." Anastasia bowed her head briefly, but when her gaze rose again to meet my own, there was a glimmer of contrition in her glorious green eyes. "I was trained to examine all possibilities, and to plan for the worst, but I underestimated the danger. I did not truly believe that Barros would move so quickly, nor that Zorana would join him. I would never have taken you to the House otherwise."

I waved one hand dismissively. I was too tired to hold onto my irritation, especially when someone like her was looking at me like that. Maybe tomorrow I'd remember to be pissed off.

"It's fine. Like you said earlier, not even *you* can know everything all the time. And we all got out alive…" I sat up straight, as a brief surge of alarm burned through my tiredness. "Most of us anyway. What about Kayla? Or Darlene? Or Celeste and Akiko, for that matter?"

"The operators should be fine," replied Anastasia thoughtfully. "Their role in your retrieval, to the best of my knowledge, remains a secret. There is no reason for Barros to move against them, assuming they avoid open sedition."

"And Kayla?"

Anastasia's long silence spoke volumes. Finally, she spoke. "The Council has only just moved against my queen. Even if the majority of the House accepts the change in leadership, taking action against well-regarded individuals such as Kayla would likely weaken the Council's position."

"Or it might help them consolidate their authority by weeding out potential problems."

"Perhaps." Before I could say more, Anastasia handed me her cell. "There is only one way to know for sure."

I was too busy dialing Kayla's number to reply.

ooo

With every unanswered ring, my tension spiked higher. Why hadn't I thought to call them on the way home? Or at some point during the laborious process of taking Lucia and the girls to their respective rooms? Or ten minutes ago, when I'd started sipping my hot chocolate like an idiot without a care in the world? If anything had happened to my friends, I'd...

Kayla's voice interrupted my stream of recriminations.

"This is Kayla. Who am I speaking to?"

Oh, thank God. "Kayla, it's me."

"John! Where have you been? And whose phone is this? D and I left like half a dozen messages for you."

"It's a really, really long story," I hedged, "and not super important right now. Where are you?"

"If you'd actually listen to your messages, mate," she replied with a touch of good-natured sharpness, "you'd know Darlene decided to whisk me away to Zion for the week. I take it that you're not driving up to meet us? She thought you might want to get the hell out of San Diego too for a few days, on account of... well, things."

"Things? Oh... right. The whole Anastasia bit," I realized, conscious that the femmepire in question was seated across from the table from me.

"The *whole Anastasia*—" Kayla's voice cut off. When she spoke next, her voice was suspicious. "John, maybe you'd better tell me what is going on."

"Well, you picked a really good time to be gone," I explained, relief making my words light. "Lucia's in a coma, I was tortured for a few days, and my spectacular idea for getting you back your job as Captain was an equally spectacular failure. Oh, and Duke Barros and Zorana have taken over the House."

"What?!"

In the background, I could hear Darlene's voice, asking what the hell was going on, and Kayla repeating what I'd just told her. The next thing I knew, D herself was on the line. Given that Kayla would still be able to hear every word, the arrangement made sense.

"John, you're giving tall, sweet, and sexy over here heart palpitations. If this is some sort of weird joke..."

"It's not. I promise." I filled her in on the high (or low) points of what had happened over the past few days, including the fact that we were all currently hiding out at one of Anastasia's properties. "So, you might not want to return to the House just yet. I don't know how your and K's friendship with me might affect things. In fact, you guys might just want to extend your camping trip for a while. I hear Utah is lovely this time of year."

"Hmmm." I could almost hear Darlene's mind working over the phone. "We'll head back tomorrow."

"Didn't you hear what I just said?"

"Yeah. You've been tortured, Lucia made everything worse, as usual, yadda yadda."

"*And* the two of you might be in danger if you come back to San Diego!"

"We won't go back to the House," she assured me. "Not until we know which way the wind is blowing, at least. But you're a complete idiot if you think I'm going to leave you alone with the woman who broke your heart."

I very carefully avoided looking in Ana's direction. "But Juliette is here too... occasionally," I protested weakly.

"Like *she's* any better," shot back Darlene, with a scowl I could hear in her voice. "She kissed you, John! Even if she *was* just trying to work a sweetheart blood donor deal, you need someone with you who's looking out for *your* interests. We'll be there as soon as we can."

My protests fell upon deaf ears. Literally, it turned out, when Kayla picked up the phone and informed me that D had already left to pack. I gave the Aussie femmepire our address and hung up the phone.

"So, they seem to be okay," I said awkwardly, "Is it alright that they're coming here?"

Anastasia nodded, but said nothing.

"It's probably too much to hope that you *didn't* hear that?"

"Lady Middleton kissed you?"

"Twice," I found myself admitting. "But she was just looking for a convenient donor, since we're business partners now."

"Gustavo and Teresa have been my donors for almost six decades," she pointed out coolly, "yet I have never kissed either of them."

"Well, Juliette and you are very different people."

"Indeed." She tucked a strand of her hair behind a ridiculously perfect ear. "And it is no business of mine, regardless."

"True, I guess." I slid the phone back across the table to her. "But if it were, I'd tell you that there is nothing between Juliette and me. And that kissing her was a lot like kissing my non-existent sister. Totally the opposite of when you and I…"

I cut myself off and shrugged.

"And the rest of what young Darlene said?"

"I was kind of hoping you hadn't heard that bit," I admitted, "but you know how dramatic Darlene can get. Me and my heart are totally fine." I pulled myself to my feet. "Anyway, I should be getting to bed."

I made my way out of the dining room, and down the long hall, feeling the femmepire's eyes on me the whole way.

INTERLUDE

I wait for an explanation. I know better than to ask; that was one of Papa's first lessons, and it has stayed with me even if the bruises did not. I look at a spot somewhere above the two strangers and clench one fist behind my back to keep myself from fidgeting in a manner unbefitting my station.

Papa waits a long time. I cannot tell if he is testing me or the grey man and his wife. Finally, he claps his large hands together, the noise cracking like a horse whip. The grey woman flinches, and I bury my superior smile before it can be seen.

I am only a child, but I did not flinch.

The door opens again, and both the man and woman climb to their feet. They turn to face the entryway. For a moment, nothing can be seen through that door other than our tapestry on the far wall. Then, a girl appears. She is a few years older than me, and stone-faced, her eyes a green that glows from across the room.

"Lucia, mia figlia," Papa rumbles, taking the other girl by the hand, "le presento signorina Dumenyova."

CHAPTER 35

I woke slowly, troubled by my continued bizarre dreams. I didn't speak Italian, but I was pretty sure the big dude had said both the names Lucia and Dumenyova. What did it say about my subconscious that I was dreaming about Anastasia and Lucia as children? And who the hell were the other three people? I had an active imagination, but it tended more towards cartoon characters, song and dance numbers, and trips up an animated Mount Everest. This sort of dream was way outside my usual experience.

I shrugged and decided I'd ask Ana about it later.

As had become my habit over the last few days, I took inventory of my body, pleased to find that I was not only free of pain but full of an energy that had been sadly lacking earlier. God bless whatever bizarre circumstances had apparently kept the werewolf virus in my system while simultaneously protecting me from its furry aftermath!

Satisfied that all was well in Le Temple Smith, I opened my eyes.

An enormous brown eye stared back at me.

"Aghhhh!" I was overcome by a sense of déjà vu, even before that eye pulled back from me, and resolved into the smiling face of a little girl.

"We have *got* to teach you a better way to wake people up, Jee Sun."

"We're hungry," she said brightly.

"We?" I looked over and found Summer also on my bed, blue eyes wide as she nodded vigorously. "How did you two even find me?" I had a sudden mental image of them running down the hall, opening every door they found, and fought to suppress my grin.

"I followed Tea Leaf," Jee Sun said, leaping off the bed to pirouette like the world's least graceful ballerina.

"I used my nose!" said the vampire child.

"You can find me just by smell?" Every time I thought I was used to vampire powers, I discovered otherwise. Apparently, showering once a day didn't cut it.

"Of course, silly!" She joined Jee Sun on the carpeted floor and tugged at my hand. "You're my donor!"

"Oh. Right."

In our very first meeting, I had—sort of—agreed to be Summer's donor in the initial slaking of her Thirst, the vampire ritual that would herald her ascension into adulthood and define the age and appearance she would maintain for the rest of her life. With a few unfortunate exceptions, like Zorana, that first feeding happened in a vampire's late teens, and I had assumed that the little girl would find someone new to fixate on by then.

While we still had twelve years to go, I was no longer as confident as I had once been.

"Can that nose of yours," I tapped the organ in question with one finger, to riotous giggles from both girls, "help us find breakfast?"

The answer, once I had pulled on some clothes, was yes. But it didn't take a supernaturally potent sniffer to do so. As soon as we reached the hallway, even I was able to pick up the smell of what seemed to be...

"Mmm. Bacon."

Ten minutes later, we were downstairs in a far less formal dining room, working our way through enough scrambled eggs, bacon, toast, jam, and warm rolls to feed an army. The food was delivered to us by Ana's other donor, Teresa, a stocky, elderly Italian woman whose severe face had broken out into a delighted smile at the sight of the children.

Anastasia had been seated when we arrived, contenting herself with a cappuccino, while doing whatever it was she did at all hours on her tablet. She remained focused on her task, long hair pulled back into a loose ponytail. Several chairs down from her, in her own habitual uniform of skintight jeans and faded punk rock t-shirt, was...

"Close your mouth when you chew, little bird," sniped Juliette. "Or people will start to think you've been raised by wolves."

"Awooo!" cried Tea Leaf, as Jee Sun took the opportunity to show just how far she could keep her mouth open while chewing. Eggs were spilling everywhere.

Mindful of Teresa's accusatory glance in my direction, I carefully finished the mouthful of bacon before replying.

"You missed quite a day yesterday, Duchess."

"So I hear. But *someone* has to be keeping our agency afloat."

"You got us another job?" Holy crap. I was going to have to promote her.

"No, moron. We already have a job, remember? Ladies who can kill you with a touch?"

"Of course I remember. But we don't…" I paused, a smile slowly sneaking onto my face. "You found him? The zombie prince?"

"I did." Juliette smirked. "Simon will be spending the next few days hanging out at—"

"Mount Hope Cemetery," said Anastasia.

The smirk fell off Juliette's face. "You *knew* where he was?"

"Of course. Part of my job is to keep track of the individuals of note in our city."

"Why didn't you *tell me* that and save me the last few days of effort and annoyance?" The Duchess of Snark was working her way into a towering snit.

"You never asked," Anastasia pointed out, "and as has recently become apparent, I am not always privy to what passes between you and Mr. Smith."

I choked on a spoonful of eggs.

"Whatever." Missing the subtext entirely, Juliette turned back to me with a scowl. "Anyway, that's where he is. When do you want to go speak with him?"

"As soon as we can," I said, finishing my fifth piece of bacon. "Sometime after sundown, I guess?"

"You've got something better to do in the meantime?"

"No, I just… are you saying zombies actually shamble about during the day?"

"Well, duh. They're not chupacabras, you doofus."

"I didn't know. This is my first zombie, remember?"

"And you *always* remember your first!" Juliette smiled sweetly, batting her eyelashes in my direction.

"*So* inappropriate," I muttered through another mouthful of eggs. I hated it when Juliette used my own jokes against me. "Let's head out after breakfast. The sooner we find Simon, the sooner we find Graciela. And the sooner we find her, the sooner we get out of some serious…" I glanced over at the two little girls. "Doo doo."

"Shit!" said Jee Sun.

"Right."

It said something that the little girl had been raised by an insane demigod, yet I was the one who had taught her to swear.

My mom would be so proud.

○○○

It wasn't until we were outside that I remembered my Corolla was *still* parked at my parents' house in Chula Vista.

"Not to worry, little bird," said Juliette with a smirk. "We'll take my bike. You can ride bitch."

If she thought the affront to my masculinity would be too great to bear, she was gravely disappointed. She rode a freaking Ducati. I'd wear a pink helmet if I had to.

Which did beg the question…

"Where's my helmet?"

Juliette lacked both a jacket and a helmet, but she was a vampire. Some of us were made of more delicate stuff.

"Grow a pair, John." She ran one hand through her spiky hair and twisted about on the bike to scowl in my direction.

"It's not my pair I'm concerned about. I've seen how you drive *cars*… I'd rather not die on our way to the zombie prince."

"In case it slipped your mind—" The femmepire's voice was deeply sarcastic. "—it took you less than two days to go from a broken, blood-drained mess to *your version* of perfect health." Her yellow eyes darted up and down my body, lingering, I was sure, on my gut. "Whatever is going on with you, I say enjoy it! Screw helmets. Screw speed limits. Screw caution."

"Screw *that*. All the leftover werewolf virus in the world isn't going to help if I crack my skull open like an egg because you wipe out taking a corner at… what, ninety?"

"If I wanted to stick to ninety, I'd be driving a Prius like your girlfriend's housekeeper." Juliette rolled her eyes. "Now, I don't have a helmet, and I'm running dangerously low on patience. Are you going to suck it up and roll with the big boys, or should I call you a taxi?" Her scowl grew at whatever expression was crossing my face. "And I'm not calling you a taxi, damn it!"

"Then why offer?"

"I may have actually preferred you unconscious." She shook her head. "Here I thought you finally getting laid would actually mellow you out."

That wiped all expression from my face. Finally getting laid…? Wait, did she actually think…?

"What?!?" she asked impatiently, and I thanked whatever deities might call Cardiff home for the fact that Juliette lacked Anastasia's perceptiveness.

"Nothing," I climbed onto the bike behind her. "You're right; let's go."

○○○

Mount Hope Cemetery was only ten or so blocks northeast of my office in Logan Heights. I'd been there once before, on a pseudo-date with a girl from my English lit class. In retrospect, I think Hannah had just needed someone to help carry in her camera equipment. Which was too bad, as she'd been really cute, in a *my-fascination-with-death-makes-me-so-deep* sort of way.

Juliette pulled up on Market Street and turned the Ducati through an open gate and into the cemetery grounds. A few cars were parked along the various roads that crisscrossed the interior, but we left them behind as we headed deeper. It was just as I remembered; enormous and well-maintained; green fields dotted with rows of headstones in all shapes and sizes, from crosses to obelisks to the single pillar bearing the name Horton.

After crossing the trolley tracks into the older portion of the cemetery, Juliette pulled up at the base of a mid-sized oak tree. She flipped down the kickstand and wrapped a long bike chain around both the oak and the rear axle of the bike. It wasn't going anywhere without us.

She was two steps down the path before she realized I hadn't joined her.

"Are you coming?"

"I think I'll just sit here for a minute," I offered weakly, feeling the blood rush to my cheeks. What little blood hadn't already gone elsewhere, anyway. Being pressed up against Juliette for an entire bike ride had had an all-too-predictable effect on portions of my anatomy.

My mind remembered our complete lack of a spark, but my still undersexed body apparently didn't care.

Bodies are stupid that way.

The femmepire smirked and stalked back over in a liquid motion that did nothing at all to ease my discomfort. "Good gods, little bird. How are you *still* a walking hormone? It seems Anastasia's reputation is wildly overblown."

"Reputation? For…"

"You tell me," Juliette purred. "She's *your* girlfriend."

"Actually," I finally admitted, "she's not."

"What?!?"

"Whatever you think happened between us… didn't."

"Are you kidding me?" The smirk was replaced by a look of horror. "She slept in your room. And your bed! You've reeked of her for days!"

I mentally upped my requisite daily shower count from two to three. "Even so, nothing happened."

"Nothing?"

"There may have been a kiss or two," I acknowledged, feeling my body react again just at the memory. I was never going to be able to walk comfortably at this rate. "But afterward… we talked, and nothing has changed. Ana's still not interested."

"You are *such* a moron." Juliette paused. Peeking up at me through thick lashes, her voice took on a honeyed tone. "You know, if you wanted to go for another ride, I'm still looking for a blood donor."

That suggestion cooled my hormones considerably. "Nothing has changed there either."

"Like hell it hasn't! Lucia's lost her House, John. I find I'm not overly concerned anymore what she'll think of me drinking from her thrall."

"She would *still* kick your ass," I pointed out. "Assuming she ever wakes up again. But what I meant was nothing has changed in terms of it *hurting when you feed on me*." A fact the femmepire kept conveniently forgetting. "And telling me yet again to *suck it up* is not going to change my opinion on the matter."

"Fine." Juliette's growl told me I had correctly guessed what her response would have been. "But you're being a total shit about all of this."

"It's a gift," I agreed, finally dismounting from the Ducati. "Wait. Why am I a moron?"

"There aren't enough hours in the day to answer *that* question," she snarked. "Anyway, I'm your business partner, not a relationship counselor. Figure it out yourself."

"Fair enough. Let's go break bread with a zombie."

The path we were on forked in two separate directions, but neither had a sign proclaiming *Zombie Prince, 100 yards*, and Juliette wasn't taking either fork. Instead, she was eyeing me again.

Having great-tasting blood wasn't all it was cracked up to be. In fact, most of the time, it just made things weird.

"What?" I finally asked.

"Your mood seemed unreasonably sulky when I thought you and Anastasia were shagging like bunnies. But now that I know the truth, I have to wonder... why aren't you *more* upset? What happened to Sir Mopes-a-lot?"

"Maybe getting tortured, almost dying, and then risking my life to rescue a woman I loathe helped put things in perspective."

"Really?"

"Hell no."

"So then...?"

"She *kissed* me, Juliette." I couldn't restrain the smile that bubbled up from somewhere deep inside me. "Lady Anastasia Dumenyova kissed me. Twice! And..."

"Yeah?"

There was a warning in that monosyllable. Telling Juliette just how spectacular those kisses had been seemed less than diplomatic, given our own recent history.

"And she wouldn't have done so if she didn't at least feel something," I said instead. "I don't know what's going on between us, but I'm not giving up."

With a grin, I started off down the left-hand path.

"Maybe you're not such a moron after all," Juliette decided, falling in beside me.

"No?"

"No. Hopeless, obsessive stalker doomed to disappointment and an untimely death as a near-virgin? Sure. But less dumb than you look."

"I know," I said smugly, choosing to hear only the compliment in her words.

"There's just one problem."

"Yeah?"

The femmepire pointed back toward the right-hand path. "Simon's that way."

"Of course he is."

I calmly pivoted to walk back the way we had come, working hard to maintain my dignified air.

Juliette's snicker did nothing to aid the illusion.

○○○

We journeyed deeper into the cemetery, raising the question of why we had parked the Ducati so far away from our destination. I wasn't quite huffing and puffing yet, but this was way more exercise than I'd been looking for, especially after my near-death experience just a few days prior.

While the grounds were still tidy and well-kept, the headstones here were more weathered, the dead less likely to have living relatives who might visit. In fact, we were the only two people in sight, isolated in an ocean of graves. It might have been a little spooky at some other time of the day and in some other city.

San Diego did a lot of things well—festivals, concerts, beaches, and bars—but spooky was a stretch.

The noon sun passed behind one of the many clouds in the sky, and I shivered. Maybe it was a *little bit* spooky. There were enough dead people around us to fill Petco stadium, and we were, after all, only a few blocks from my work office. *That* neighborhood was enough to scare anyone.

In addition to the headstones, monuments, and often-gaudy statues, a few small mausoleums dotted the hill. It was to one of these that Juliette led me.

"This is it?" I finally ventured, after we had stood in front of said mausoleum for a solid twenty seconds without anything of importance occurring.

"No, little bird; we traveled all this way as part of some elaborate practical joke."

I checked to see if she was kidding. It *did* seem like the sort of thing the femmepire would do.

The mausoleum was a squat little stone structure, the peak of its roof spattered with bird droppings and barely reaching my own height. The exterior walls were bare of decoration, and the names chiseled into the door itself were almost entirely illegible.

I had nothing against cemeteries, but when I died, I was going to be cremated. And leave orders for NASA to fire my ashes into space, where aliens would eventually find them, reconstitute my body, and crown me as emperor.

"Now what? Do we click our heels or light a candle or...?" I stopped. "Wasn't the mausoleum door *closed* just a second ago?"

It must have been. After all, I'd made note of the illegibility of the names etched into its surface. But now, those faded markings were hidden entirely, the door's two halves split wide to reveal the darkness of the tomb's interior.

And from that darkness, noises began to echo. First, a slight scraping, like something being dragged along the concrete floor. And then, a hoarse moan that echoed and warbled, dry and phlegmy at the same time. A shape emerged from the depths of the tomb, and the moan resolved itself into a single, horrifying word.

"Braaaaaaaaaaaaaaaains."

CHAPTER 36

I found myself twenty feet away in an eye blink, two tombstones and a femmepire between the mausoleum and me. I scrabbled about for something that would work as a weapon: a shotgun, a chainsaw, a fire axe…

Well, shit. There was never a good zombie killing weapon around when you needed one. Just one more way that life paled in comparison to video games.

I tugged off one of my shoes instead and waved it about as an improvised weapon, aware that the odds of successfully decapitating the brain eating zombie with my almost-new Air Jordans were… to put it mildly… low.

It was only then that the zombie's low war cry came to a coughing halt. And the noises that followed sounded disturbingly like…

I glared up at the mausoleum from behind my shielding tombstone. "Are you laughing at me?"

He was. Having finally emerged entirely from the mausoleum, the zombie was bent over at the waist, laughing so hard he seemed to be having trouble maintaining his balance.

"Oh, man," he finally gasped out in that same asthmatic voice, "that was *hilarious!*"

"It was almost impressive, little bird," said Juliette. "If I'd known you could move that fast, I wouldn't have gone so easy on you the one time we sparred."

I gathered what was left of my dignity, slipped my shoe back on, and rejoined the duo. "I take it you're Simon?"

"Last time I checked," he said cheerfully. Up close, he looked a bit like my homeless doorman Dale, from the layers of unwashed clothing to the wild, bedraggled hair that hadn't seen a comb—or a bottle of shampoo—in years.

But at least *Dale* still had his whole face. A loose flap of skin dangled from Simon's right cheek, exposing the bone beneath, and it looked like someone—a dog maybe—had chewed on a lower lip that now drooped like an unlit cigarette from the yawning chasm of his mouth. That face was the only portion of the man exposed to the elements, and it was bloated, the flesh a sallow grey.

Which probably explained the miasma of stench that had finally reached my nose.

I fought really, really hard not to gag.

"Take a picture, asshole," he barked, torn lip wagging like a dog's tail. "It'll last longer."

"Sorry. It's just… well, you're my first zombie," I admitted.

"Yeah, no kidding." One gloved hand reached up to rub the Mercedes hood ornament hanging around his thick neck, while the other adjusted a shapeless piece of fabric that must have once been a hat. "Least you didn't piss yourself, I guess. As thrilled as I am to have a vampire and her boy toy show up on my door, I'm in the middle of some truly epic shit. State your business, and then go away."

"We were hoping to—" I began.

"Not interested." Simon turned to head back into the mausoleum.

"—hire you," I concluded weakly.

He stopped in his tracks, having managed roughly half a step in the slow shamble that I recognized from every zombie movie ever.

"Are we talking barter or...?"

"I was thinking actual money."

"Well then!" A wide smile split his face—not literally, although that did seem within the realm of possibility—and he flashed a surprisingly full set of unsurprisingly yellow teeth. "Why don't you step into my office?"

I had to duck entering the mausoleum, but a series of stone steps led down into the earth. Three strides later, the ceiling was close enough to touch, but no longer a potential hazard. The tomb's interior was... well, not very tomb-like, to be honest. Several plaques in the far wall announced the names of those interred within, but the open space was dominated by an oversized, moth-eaten couch. In front of that couch was an equally shabby coffee table, and on that table...

"Is that an iPad?" I peeked past Simon to look at the tablet's shiny screen. "Netflix? *This* is your *epic shit?*"

"Gotta finish watching Orange is the New Black before the new season releases." Simon shuffled around the table, and dropped heavily into the couch, resulting in a cloud of dust and... aroma. He directed his attention to Juliette. "What can I do for ya?"

The femmepire nodded in my direction. "It's his show. I'm just the—"

"Peanut gallery?" I offered innocently.

"Thuggish muscle?" countered Simon.

"—facilitator," finished Juliette with an icy glare for both of us. "*And* transportation."

I decided it would be best to not piss off Juliette until after I'd recovered the Corolla.

"Alrighty then," said Simon, turning rheumy, flat grey eyes in my direction. "Go."

"I'm sorry?"

"Time's money, kid. And I mean that literally. So, tell me what you want to hire me for, and we'll talk fees. And just so you know," he added ominously, "I don't do parties cheap."

"Parties?" I was already *so* confused.

"Birthdays. Weddings. Bar mitzvahs. You know; that whole *hire a zombie to liven up the festivities* deal."

"I'm not sure that's a thing."

"Huh." He chewed on that for a moment, and then shrugged. "Give it time. Zombies are huge right now."

"If you say so. We're not looking for an undead party favor. Lord Kala thought you might be able to assist us."

If I'd expected Simon to be dazzled by my connections to the old and mighty—and I had, which was why I'd dropped Kala's name in the first place—I was disappointed. The zombie didn't react at all to my mention of the demigod. I gave it a few more seconds, on the off chance that his reaction speed was just *that* slow, and then gave up.

Apparently, zombie princes did not impress easily.

"Anyway, there's a missing persons case I'm currently dealing with, and…"

"Oh, right." He huffed in displeasure, accompanied by a sound not unlike ribs cracking. "Someone disappears and it must have been the brain-eating zombie's fault." Simon rose to his feet and thrust one heavy arm in my direction. "Sorry to burst your bubble, junior, but the last time I ate brain was in '72."

"*Nineteen*-seventy-two? What have you been living on since then?" We were heading way off track, but—as Simon had said—zombies were the current *in* thing, and I had a ton of questions.

"Hennessy, mostly." He pulled a bottle of the stuff from under the coffee table. "I had a small disagreement with a forklift in '72. Shredded my intestines, which makes solid food a total bitch, as you can imagine."

I *couldn't* really imagine, but I didn't let that stop me from nodding sympathetically. On the other hand… "That was forty years ago." Give or take a few years; I didn't sweat the minor mathematical details. "That must have been some disagreement."

"Zombies don't heal, little bird." Juliette had taken up a position along the wall to our right, carefully positioned to be as far away from the zombie as possible without making it look like that had been her intention.

"At all?"

"At all," confirmed Simon after another long swig of cognac. Alcohol dribbled off his chin, where it was quickly absorbed by his clothes. "We take a licking and keep on ticking, but eventually we reach a point where the body's too messed up to continue."

"And then?"

"Then we head off to Valhalla to French-kiss angels and shit. How the hell would I know?"

The heady scent of spilled cognac was mixing with the less appealing stench of unwashed, dead flesh, and my nausea was returning with reinforcements. Further zombie-related questions would have to wait.

"We didn't come to accuse you of anything. In fact, the missing person isn't even alive." I hurriedly explained the particulars of Graciela's disappearance, taking care to breathe through my mouth while doing so. "Kala was able to verify that Graciela is still… around, but thought you'd have a better shot at actually locating her."

"Well duh." Simon wiped a sleeve across his face, heedless of what the motion did to his mangled lip. "Ghosts ain't dead. Old Dusty has no dominion over the Ladies."

"But you do?"

"Nah. Those birds won't have shit to do with me."

"I… see." I traded confused looks with Juliette.

"But," he continued, after another swig of cognac, "you're not hiring me to sweet talk 'em… you just want me to find their leader. Right?"

"Right."

"That I can do." He tossed the now-empty bottle aside. By some minor miracle, it didn't shatter, but instead bounced off the near wall, and then rolled along the floor to disappear under the couch. "Rank has its privileges, y'know."

Rather than ask a leading question for the tenth time in as many minutes, I waited for Simon to explain himself. Eventually, he did so, but his scowl told me he'd been enjoying my curiosity.

"See, the unliving—and that's the correct term for us, junior; none of this undead shit, if you please—come in many forms and shapes and sizes, from the ghostly to the skeletal to the—" He motioned at his own form. "—paragon of masculinity you see before you."

He paused, anticipating a rebuttal, or perhaps a disbelieving laugh or two, but I was mostly amazed to hear the phrase *paragon of masculinity* come out of a zombie's mouth.

"But what we've all got in common," he continued finally, "is that we exist on the same general wavelength. And I'm the guy that can surf those waves."

"Wait… what?" I shot another look at Juliette, but she seemed equally lost. "Can you explain that in some way that doesn't involve ocean metaphors?"

He rolled his eyes—all the more disturbing because one of them took longer to complete the motion than the other—and thumped a gloved fist against his temple.

"Me gots radar. Me detects ghosties. You pay moneys."

"Nobody likes a wiseass, dude," I muttered under my breath. "So, you can tell me where Graciela is right now?"

"Sure," he replied easily, "assuming you've got the cash." He named a sum that would have seemed exorbitant if my professional reputation hadn't been on the line.

"Deal." I motioned to Juliette. "Pay the man."

"Excuse me?"

"It's not like *I* have any money on me, on account of that whole kidnapping, torture, and imprisonment thing. Think of this as your partnership buy-in."

"Little bird." There really *were* a thousand different ways the femmepire could say my nickname. Right now, it sounded an awful lot like a curse. "I am a smoking hot, ridiculously awesome, and titled Lady of the People." Yellow eyes glowed in the dim light. "Why the hell would I ever need to carry cash?"

Well, shit.

CHAPTER 37
IN WHICH PAPER BEATS PLASTIC

I turned back to Simon and pasted on my most winning smile, the patent-pending Dealmaker™. "I don't suppose you take plastic?"

I held my hand out to Juliette, but the femmepire was already shaking her head.

"Oh, come on! You don't have credit cards either?"

"As you may recall from our conversation last week—the one where you offered me a partnership that has so far involved *me doing your job for you*—there are outside factors that prevent me from presently accessing my funds." She sounded uncannily like Anastasia at that moment, although the other femmepire had never achieved that level of nasty inflection. "Besides, you're the human. Where are *your* credit cards?"

"In my wallet, back at my parents' house," I shot back. "I didn't have a chance to grab my stuff before Thales freaking kidnapped me!"

"Then maybe we should have gone there first?"

"Well maybe *you…*" I trailed off, realizing that I didn't really have a rejoinder.

Juliette's smirk was depressingly victorious.

"As adorable as this is—and really, it's like watching kittens wrestle—I only work for cold, hard cash," said Simon.

"How about an IOU?" I offered with near-manic desperation. "I promise I'm good for it."

"Sure you are. Because if you can't trust some random human off the streets, who *can* you trust?" He gestured rudely in my direction. "For Pete's sake, kid… you're doing business in a *cemetery*. You're clearly not right in the head."

"I'm not just some random human!" I drew myself up to full height, sucked in my gut, and solemnly declared, "I'm John Smith."

"Just go."

"Wait… what?"

"It's bad enough that you came without the cash to actually hire me… but now you think I'm dumb enough to accept the world's most obvious pseudonym? I'm unliving, asshole. I'm not stu—"

He stopped talking in mid-conversation, and thoughtfully hawked a glob of phlegm into the corner. "Wait. John Smith… knows a spicy little slip of a vampire… spoke with Old Dusty."

He banged one hand onto the arm of the couch and crowed. "You're the mediator! The one who keeps getting everyone killed!"

My still-forming smile swiftly withered away. Why did everyone have such a skewed view of my cases?

"You're *awesome!* Funniest damn thing to happen to this city of nimrods since that one time an immortal had the seagulls shitting like they were elephants."

That was not an image I'd ever expected to have in my brain.

"To be honest, I thought you'd be fatter. Can't believe everything people say, I guess."

"Does this mean we're in business?" I chose to ignore the latest round of career *and* personal defamation. Saving Graciela would go a long way to proving my competence… and that I wasn't a stooge of the vampires. And fat was better than dead. "I'll write that IOU right now. Assuming you have a pen?"

"Are you telling me that *wasn't* a pen I felt in your pocket on the ride over, little bird?"

I gritted my teeth and avoided answering.

Simon was already shaking his head. "Sorry, Smith. From what I hear, you don't have two nickels to rub together."

Which was true… but kind of irrelevant. I mean, who carried nickels these days anyway, and why exactly would they rub them together?

"If I'm going to find Graciela for you, I'm going to need cash." Rheumy eyes slowly focused on my face. "Or a favor."

"I don't know." I frowned. "I read that I'm not supposed to agree to favors. Or eat or drink anything in your home." I glanced around the dusty tomb, but even the empty bottle had disappeared from sight. "Which won't be much of a problem…"

"That's faeries, you moron."

"Oh, right." I nodded my thanks to Juliette. "In that case, what would I be agreeing to?"

"The usual. At some point in the future, I'll need your help. And you'll give it, no questions asked."

"I'm kind of lousy at the 'no questions asked' bit."

"He really is," agreed my traitorous junior partner.

"Fine," sighed Simon. "You can ask questions, but you'll still do what I ask. Good?"

"Better." I mentally reviewed what few historical documents I'd found regarding djinn contracts. This wasn't the same thing at all, but *some* of the legalese had to translate, right? "But you can't ask that I kill someone, and this favor can't bring harm to my friends or family."

"If I wanted to hire a killer, you'd be way the hell down the list. As for the harm clause… let's say *direct* harm. It's impossible to predict who or what an action might impact indirectly."

"Deal."

"Sweet." Simon hawked up another glob of phlegm, spat it into his gloved hand, and extended that hand to me.

I eyed it warily, as if it were some form of venomous snake. But deals were deals, and I really, really needed to close this case.

I gritted my teeth and shook his hand.

It was wet and squishy. I was going to need a bottle of Purell after this. Hell, maybe I'd just bathe in the stuff. I held the now infected hand awkwardly away from the rest of my body and smiled brightly. It wasn't the Dealmaker™, but it was the best I could manage.

"It's a pleasure doing business with you, Smith," Simon told me, wiping his own hand surreptitiously on the dusty fabric of the rotting couch, "and you'll be hearing from me on that favor."

"Sounds good," I cheerfully lied. "In the meantime, feel free to point us to Graciela."

"Yeah yeah. And then I can get back to my show."

Simon went silent, all animation leaving his body. In moments, he was a clothes-wearing tree stump that just happened to be growing out of an orange couch. Remembering Lord Kala's own admonitions when the demigod had searched for Graciela, I forced myself to stay quiet and still as I waited.

And waited.

And waited.

"Huh," Simon finally said, sounding like someone coming out of a deep sleep.

"Where is she?"

"You know… I have no idea," the zombie admitted.

I wanted to scream. But the Smith men are made of stronger stuff than that, my recent weeping histrionics notwithstanding. Instead, I asked a careful question, designed to efficiently clarify the situation we now found ourselves in.

"Huh?"

It wasn't one of my finer moments.

"This has never happened before," the zombie growled, scratching at his scalp.

"Men *always* say that," said Juliette.

"You can't sense Graciela?"

"Oh, I can sense her. But she's muted. Like she's a long, long way away."

"Like Los Angeles?"

"More like Turkey."

"I can't afford to fly to Turkey."

"I didn't say she was *in* Turkey. It could be Nigeria. Or Antarctica. Or the moon."

"I'm pretty sure it's not the moon." I hoped not, anyway. "And how would she have gotten to any of those other places?" Valentina and I had traveled quickly when visiting Ghost Hill, but I was reasonably sure the Pacific Ocean would present more of an obstacle.

"No clue. Spirits are pretty tightly chained to the place of their death or an object they had on them at the time."

"Then is it possible that something other than distance is muting her presence?"

"Maybe. I could have sworn I felt an energy surge with her signature just a few days ago." Simon shrugged heavy shoulders, momentarily sounding like a physics nerd rather than a mound of decaying flesh. "But if she were still local, she'd have showed up to her little club's meetings."

"Unless the same thing that's muting her signal prevented her from doing so," I pointed out.

"Ghosts are souls, kid. And souls are just energy. Ain't been the fiend yet who can keep pure energy from going where it wills. It's like trying to throw a net around an electron. Nah…" he shook his head again, dust, leaves and other detritus sprinkling onto the couch. "…she's got to be in Turkey. Or Nigeria."

And people said *I* sucked at my job.

"I'll keep looking. If she's nearby, I'll find her. If not…" Simon grimaced, chewing on the dangling piece of his lip like it was tobacco. "…I guess that whole favor thing can be waived."

Damn straight it would be waived. "Should we meet back up here in a few days?" Marge was going to freaking *kill* me. Unless her evil Spanish-speaking compadre, Begoña, got to me first.

"Can't. This is my last night at Mt. Hope for a while." Simon nudged his iPad to the side and picked up the phone that had been hiding beneath it. "I'll drop you a line when I have something."

There didn't seem to be much else for me to say—and the fumes were starting to make my lungs ache in unpleasant and unexpected ways—so we exchanged numbers and I made a dash for the door. Juliette was right on my heels, although I'm sure she somehow made the panicked quest for fresh air look good.

Behind us, just before the mausoleum's doors boomed shut, the theme music to Orange is the New Black started to play.

ooo

"What's the plan now?"

"Duchess, I'll let you know as soon as I have one." I shrugged, feeling a soreness in my calves as we walked down the hill. "At least this wasn't a total loss. Simon has a better shot of finding Graciela than we do. And in the meantime…"

"Yeah?"

"We can swing by my parents' house. Pick up my wallet, phone, and car. Verify that Mom and Dad are still alive and persuade them to flee the state for the hundredth time. You know, the usual."

"And how do you plan to get there?" There was very little that was sweet in the smile Juliette was giving me.

"I was hoping my valued not-so-junior partner would consent to take me there?"

"Fine."

One more victory for the Dealmaker™.

"But then you're on your own," she continued. "It's almost two, and I'm getting hungry."

"You're always hungry. Still making do with donors off the street, I guess?"

"Yeah." She sighed, in a very non-Juliette bit of melancholy. "Brenna and her pets are back at the House, thanks to all this nonsense with the Brazilians. Not that she and I ever shared the same tastes anyway."

I'd last seen Brenna slow-dancing with a two-headed, purple skinned behemoth, so that was actually a strike in Juliette's favor.

"How does she feel about the whole coup thing?"

"Cautiously optimistic. Lucia may be a queen by birth, but she really stinks at running a House. After the last few years of chaos and death, people are ready for a change."

"It's hard to argue with that." Not that Anastasia—or Lucia herself—would be happy to hear it. "What about you? Are you going to rejoin now?"

"*Hell* no! I'm permanently back on lone wolf status. Hungry, homeless, lone wolf status."

"I'll talk to Ana about getting your assets unfrozen," I promised.

"By all means," Juliette purred, her mood shifting on a dime, "I'm sure Lady Dumenyova would love to hear you talking about my... assets."

I didn't dignify that comment with a reply.

A short time later, the Ducati came into view. Juliette unlocked the chain and packed it back into a small saddle bag. Then, she swung one leg over the bike, and flashed me another brilliant grin.

"Hop on, little bird. And don't worry... while you always remember your first... the second time is usually *way* better."

Thinking impure thoughts, I climbed on behind her.

And soon realized that she was right.

About riding a Ducati, anyway.

CHAPTER 38

IN WHICH YOU *CAN* GO HOME AGAIN, BUT IT WILL TAKE A WHILE

On a good day, it takes about fifteen minutes to reach my parents' home from my office. The cemetery was a few blocks closer, and we were riding Juliette's nuclear-powered street bike, so I figured we might make it in something closer to ten.

I was wrong.

We *did* reach Chula Vista in under ten minutes—a feat that should have terrified me but instead left me exhilarated—but our pace slowed once we exited the 5. Soon after, it stopped entirely. We'd just crossed under the 805, at the point where L street became Telegraph Canyon, when Juliette veered across all three lanes of traffic and braked to a halt at the curb.

"What the hell, Duchess?"

She didn't seem to hear my question. The femmepire's attention was focused on the shopping center on the far side of the road.

I didn't see anything out of the ordinary.

"What is it?" I asked again, voice now hushed. "Did you spot Thales? Or are we encroaching on some other species' native turf?" I'd lived in Chula Vista for almost my entire life, but it had never occurred to me that something sinister might claim the town as their own. Maybe my cranky old neighbor Mr. Brown really *was* a hell beast.

"What? No. Don't be an idiot." Juliette flipped down her kickstand, and twisted about to face me, in a movement that only a vampire or gymnast could have managed without spinal injury. "Your house isn't too far from here, is it?"

There was a trap there. I could sense it but had no idea how to avoid it.

"Not really? Maybe a dozen blocks or so." Or roughly fourteen seconds, by Ducati.

"How do you feel about walking the rest of the way?"

"I'd rather n—"

"Let me rephrase," she interrupted. "You're *going* to walk the rest of the way. There's someone I need to introduce myself to."

"I'm confused."

"I'm hungry. And since you won't be my blood donor, it's time I made other, more permanent, arrangements."

I looked again—having finally deduced that she was watching a person and not a building, shrub, or cloud formation—but there still wasn't much to see. An Indian couple was making its way up the street, the mom pushing a stroller, but it seemed unlikely that Juliette would take one of them as her donor. Slightly further down the road, several people stood at the intersection, waiting for the signal to cross. I focused on the individual in front; a heavyset white man somewhere between twenty-five and forty, wearing a Batman t-shirt, long khaki shorts, and aviator sunglasses.

Jesus. I really *was* Juliette's type.

"I know you're a DC fangirl, but… *that* dude?"

"If we weren't pressed for time, I would kick your ass for even suggesting it," growled the femmepire. "Not him. *Her.*"

In this case, *her* was standing just behind Batman, clothed in tattered jeans, a sleeveless grey tank, and at least two cows' worth of leather bracelets on her skinny wrists.

"Oh." The woman gave off a bit of a barista-from-hell sort of vibe. "I forgot you swing both ways."

"Blood is blood, little bird. And I'm guessing hers tastes fantastic." Juliette slowly licked her lips, and I found myself slightly nauseated. And maybe even a little bit jealous, which made absolutely no sense.

"You've had a week to find a donor. Why now? Why her?"

"It takes a particular type. Someone who can keep my interest, but also stay out of my way. Someone with sweet-tasting blood who will be able to handle exposure to the real world. That sort of person is rarer than you think."

I smiled, oddly flattered.

"I'm not including you in that description, idiot. You would've just been convenient."

The warm, fuzzy feeling faded.

Still, I reminded myself, it would be a *good* thing for Juliette to find someone new to snack on. And not just because I was otherwise her go-to option. As her friend, I wanted her to be happy.

And maybe she'd be less of a pain in my ass if she was getting blood regularly.

"Cool. So, how do we play this?" At the intersection, the light had finally turned red, and Juliette's target was crossing the street.

"We? There is no *we.*"

"I'm an awesome wingman, Juliette. You can ask Mike… if the two of you ever meet." Hell, I had been at least partly responsible for his last two girlfriends. For all the good *that* bit of selflessness had done me.

"The day I require help to find a donor *or* seduce a human is the day I drown myself in a puddle." Her golden eyes met mine again, and even I could read the hunger in them. "Now, get off."

"You were *serious* about me walking? It's like… a mile to my house! Maybe two!"

"Exercise is good for the soul, little bird. And for your muffin top."

That wasn't *technically* below the belt—just the opposite in fact—but it still hurt.

"Maybe I can just wait here while you chat her up? Once you've laid the femmepire hoodoo on your barista, you can take me to my parents' house."

She shook her head. For the first time all day, I realized she was wearing small platinum hoops in each ear. Further proof that my mind fixated on inconsequential details in moments of extreme crisis.

"If things go as expected," Juliette explained, "my future donor and I are going to be way too busy for that. Now, are you going to get off my bike or am I going to have to throw you off?"

"You wouldn't really—"

Before I could finish my sentence, the femmepire had proven me wrong. I scraped asphalt off my ass and watched Juliette pull away down the block. At the light, she took a right, trailing potential blood donor number one.

"She'll be back," I told myself. "First, she'll strike out with the goth barista… then she'll drive over to pick me up."

I was wrong on both counts.

○○○

Much, much later, I rounded the corner past Ms. Givens' house. I was so tired that not even the sight of my brand-new Corolla, safely parked in front of my parents' house, could lift my spirits. I muttered nonsensical curses at my femmepire partner under my breath as I shuffled past the Corolla and up the driveway.

It was Tuesday, which meant my dad should have been at work, but the family Rav-4 was parked out front. I peered through the driver-side window, finding only the usual immaculate interior. Even so, this was troubling. If Lucia's former House had done anything new to my parents, I was going to kick some ass.

And by *kick some ass*, I of course meant *seek vengeance and probably die*.

I let myself inside, once again regretting my lack of weaponry.

"John!" My dad was in the hallway, shoving a pile of clothing into his suitcase, a blue, battered monstrosity almost as old as I was. "I didn't think you'd be home until the weekend!"

"You didn't?"

"Not with that case you're on." He misunderstood my confused look and elaborated. "Your girlfriend told us all about it. You could have just called, you know. Not that seeing Anastasia again wasn't lovely." My dad waggled his eyebrows.

"Oh yeah." I nodded. "Ana. And my case."

"Are you already done with your work for Borghesi International? I don't want to tell you how to do your job, son, but when you're on a big company's payroll, there's such a thing as being *too* efficient."

"I'm still working on the… uh… case, but I'll be back in town for at least a day or two. Although I'm planning to spend it at Ana's. I just needed to pick up a fresh change of clothes… and my car."

"Staying with your lady friend, eh?" My dad's grin was enormous. "The Smith charm strikes again! Your mom was worried you might be a little bit out of your league with that one, but I knew better! After all, the same could have been said about your mom and I, twenty-eight years ago, and yet here we are!"

"Yeah, here we are." I bumped my dad's hanging fist—doing otherwise would just hurt his feelings—and changed the subject. "Are you going somewhere?"

"Yup. The office is sending me to Austin for the week. Only this time, I'm bringing your mother with me. Gonna show her the sights!"

"Austin? Weren't you just there like… a month ago?"

"Almost two, but yeah. A lot of our business has moved out of California lately."

"Oh." What I knew about Austin could fit on the head of a pin, but Austin meant Texas, and Texas meant way the hell away from the shitstorm brewing in San Diego. I wasn't going to look a gift horse in the mouth. "I hope you have fun."

"Oh we will, Johnny boy… we will." Yet again, he waggled his eyebrows.

I loved my father, but I dearly hoped I wasn't going to turn into him as I aged. Otherwise, I might have to join Juliette in drowning myself in a puddle.

I made myself a sandwich, added a bag of chips and a vitamin water for good measure, and loafed around the house as the two of them packed. An hour or so later, I helped my dad carry out the luggage—and God only knew why they needed *four* suitcases for a single week—and hugged my parents goodbye.

Then I went back inside and ate a second sandwich. Because that was just how I rolled.

When I was done, I took the stairs down to my basement bedroom. After a quick shower, I gathered up several changes of clothing, and grabbed my wallet and phone from the dresser. The latter was entirely dead, so I added a charger to the pile. Then, I swept everything into a duffel bag and started back up the stairs.

I reset the alarm, locked the door, and stepped out onto the porch, where I came face-to-face with Valentina.

A very unhappy Valentina.

CHAPTER 39

IN WHICH SILENCE ISN'T ALWAYS GOLDEN

It wasn't just Valentina's expression that tipped me off to her mood, though the wide black eyes and tremendous scowl were—as indicators went—fairly conclusive. Dark curly hair radiated out in all directions, and the bony hands extending from the frayed sleeves of her full-length nightgown were clenched into fists. To say nothing of the cold wind that had arisen out of nowhere. Or the fact that she was standing there, in broad daylight, something I had previously assumed to be impossible.

I wasn't what anyone would consider an expert on ghosts—let alone female ghosts—but I recognized *pissed off* when I saw it. Probably because I saw it more often than most.

So, when Valentina moved toward me in a blur, the last thing I expected was a hug.

As always, Valentina's touch was bone-chillingly cold, but it had none of the dangerous, life-sucking energy that I'd experienced in the arms of crazy Jennifer on Ghost Hill. The physical contact itself was slight, at best, and Valentina's body swayed in and out of mine, bringing fresh waves of cold each time. As hugs go, it was a bit lacking—mostly because her intangibility left me unable to hug her back—but I sure as hell appreciated the sentiment.

As soon as it had started, it was over. Valentina stepped back, brushed the hair out of her face, and wagged a finger, scowling yet again. In the direct sunlight, she was almost entirely translucent, but I was able to read her expression with ease.

"I know. I'm sorry I disappeared like that. Vampire trouble."

She bared her black-gummed teeth in a respectable approximation of a particularly fiendish bloodsucker.

"Exactly. And I doubt it's over yet. But what else is new, right?" I shrugged. "I hope the other White Ladies aren't too pissed at me for missing the meeting. Although Marge has no grounds for complaints after no-showing on Monday. Anyway, I'm making some progress on the search for Graciela." Honesty—and good old Catholic guilt—forced me to amend that last sentence. "Sort of. I hope."

Valentina was gesticulating wildly, contorting her features in what I recognized was a futile attempt at speech. What small sound escaped was, as might be expected, entirely unintelligible.

"They *are* pissed off?" I asked.

She shook her head, then shrugged, then waved one of her hands in a gesture that was clearly supposed to mean something to me. Unfortunately, even after six months of these one-sided conversations, my charades skills remained woefully underdeveloped.

I offered a few other guesses, but each was met by the same series of gestures, and a growing sense of frustration from my ghost companion.

"This would be so much easier if you could just tell me or send me a postcard or—" I stopped in mid-sentence. "I am *such* an idiot."

I spun to re-enter the house, and then turned back to Valentina. "I'm going to get a notepad and a pen. Would you like to come in?"

She casually walked right through the front door before I could open it. Within the relative darkness of the house, her appearance solidified. I led her into the living room, where I snagged the pen and pad from the dresser next to my parents' landline and presented them with a flourish.

"I don't know why I didn't think of this earlier." I set the pad down on the coffee table with the uncapped pen next to it. Then, another thought occurred to me. "Crap. I should have asked; do you know how to write?" I wasn't entirely sure when Valentina had died, but even today, literacy wasn't universal.

Valentina nodded and took a seat on—and in—our couch. She narrowed her eyes and reached out to the pen, a look of concentration on her face.

It took three tries for the ghost to successfully pick up the pen, and another two before she was able to keep it in her grasp long enough to use it, but eventually, she got the hang of things, and started to write.

Five minutes later, Valentina had finished her message. Rather than handing the pen back, she simply let it drop through a suddenly insubstantial hand to fall onto the coffee table with a clatter. Her expression was fierce but satisfied.

I leaned past her to read what she had written.

Or tried to anyway.

"Is this… Russian?" I thought I recognized the backwards R from a bar in Las Vegas, but everything else was complete gobbledygook.

Valentina nodded happily, her mouth spread in a wide and black-gummed grin.

Well, shit.

○○○

I thanked Valentina profusely for the note, while also explaining that I couldn't read anything other than English. Unfortunately, while she clearly understood *my* native—and only—tongue, she was unable to read or write it. If the note had been in Spanish, I could have taken it to Mike. But I didn't have any Russian-speaking friends.

"Maybe Ana can help." Italy wasn't all that close to Russia, but… she'd just recently been vacationing in Romania, right? What language did they speak over there?

Oh, right; Romanian.

I shrugged. If the lovely femmepire couldn't help, she would know somebody who could. Her circle of influence was significantly larger than my own, despite my snazzy website and *two* service-oriented careers.

Explaining this to Valentina took some time. Eventually, I think she understood, although the look I received when I asked her to set up another meeting with Marge was a slightly terrifying mix of exasperation and irritation. However, as I started to leave, she stepped into my path. She carried out a complicated pantomime that involved pointing at herself, pointing at me, pointing at the door, and then waving one hand about while toying with the hair in front of her face with the other.

"You think we should go to the zoo?"

My interpretation provoked a silent laugh from the ghost. She shook her head and repeated the movements.

"You want to come with me?" This time, I got a happy nod. "Of course you can! My parents will be away for the next week, and you know I always appreciate your company. But how does that work? Do you have to fill out some sort of relocation form or something?"

That provoked another laugh. After a vigorous shake of her head that sent dark hair flying in every direction, the ghost phased through the living room wall. I hurried into the foyer, and then out the front door to find her standing on the porch, once again almost entirely translucent.

Eyes on my face, she slowly floated backwards and into the front yard. An extended finger indicated where I was supposed to stand, and then she waved her other hand. With that motion, topsoil and earth slid aside.

My immediate thought was that she'd buried another body in our front yard. After all, the last time I'd seen Valentina move the earth, it was to show me the corpses of the werewolf and vampires who'd come to my house for vengeance.

My second thought was concern that she was doing this in mid-afternoon on a Tuesday. But Valentina was hard to see from even a few feet away; she'd be entirely invisible from across the street… even if she *wasn't* expending energy to remain hidden from eyes other than my own.

As for the crevasse magically appearing in my front yard? Well… California *was* the land of earthquakes.

Thankfully, the hole Valentina opened was only a foot wide, and two to three feet deep, which reduced the odds of corpse burial dramatically. Unless that one pixie in Kristin's congregation had been serious about the blood feud. I took a careful step to the lip of that hole and looked down.

At the bottom of the small pit was a dirt-covered wooden box the width of my hand. It looked like a primitive attempt at a jewelry box, complete with hinges on one side.

I opened it roughly half a second before remembering the story of Pandora's box. If I'd just released unspeakable evils on San Diego… well, it wasn't going to help my reputation very much.

For once, luck was on my side. No screaming demons. No bursts of light or darkness. The interior was slightly nicer than the exterior, with a soft cushioned base in pink satin. And on that cushion was a very small, very delicate ring with a minuscule diamond solitaire in its setting.

It was a wedding ring, albeit one that made my mom's look modern—and *that* heirloom had been passed down through three generations of Smiths.

"Is this yours?" I asked Valentina, as earth slowly refilled the hole. "From when you were alive?"

She nodded solemnly.

I managed to avoid my usual stupid assumptions. There was no way she was proposing to me.

"Is it tied to your haunting? Like a tether or something?" I received another nod in confirmation, once I explained what a tether was. "So, if I bring this with me to Ana's house, you won't have to worry about eventually being pulled back here?"

She smiled and whirled about me in a circle.

I'd been *way* too hard on myself earlier; I kicked absolute ass at charades.

"Okay then." I added the ring box to my duffle bag and bowed deeply, extending one hand in invitation. "If you'll follow me, my Lady, your chariot awaits."

The trip to Cardiff was... interesting. It was fantastic to be back in my new car, where I got to learn all over again how much smoother a ride it was than the now-retired penis-mobile. It wasn't a Ducati, but the presence of a windshield significantly reduced the chances of bugs flying into my open mouth. And while riding with Juliette had been almost obnoxiously enjoyable, my current companion brought delights all her own.

Valentina rode shotgun. Her window was rolled all the way down, but the air blew right through her without stirring hair or fabric. Grass-stained feet were up on the dashboard, exposing skinny, bare legs, and she howled wordlessly in apparent delight to the accompaniment of FM 94.9. And if those feet occasionally phased *into* the dashboard, and her body and the seat only rarely maintained contact with one another... well, she was a freaking ghost. What else was new?

I was just pleased to see her having so much fun.

The sun was plummeting toward the ocean by the time I finally parked outside Anastasia's home. There was no sign of Juliette or her bike. Apparently, blood donor negotiations were still ongoing. I grabbed my bag from the backseat and Valentina trailed me through Anastasia's front door.

We were in the hallway when the screams began.

CHAPTER 40
IN WHICH A DAUGHTER DOES HER DUTY

I barely had time to lament the fact that I was *still* weaponless before I burst into the downstairs dining room… and discovered I had nothing to worry about. Tea Leaf and Jee Sun were screaming and running in circles around the central table, chased by a lumbering Gustavo who was making low growling noises and pretending to be the world's oldest and smallest white-haired bear. Teresa was primly seated, holding on to her water glass like it might otherwise flee the table, but not even she was able to keep from laughing at the antics of her husband and the girls. And as for Anastasia…

The femmepire had a fond smile on her face as she watched the mayhem. I took it as a personal victory when that smile didn't fade at all as she turned her gaze from the girls to me.

"Is something wrong, Mr. Smith?"

"I heard screams."

"And then rushed into the room with neither a plan nor a weapon?" That lovely smile turned wry. "Haven't we talked about this sort of thing?"

"This once, I actually did have a plan."

"And what did that plan entail?"

I nodded past her, to where Valentina was phasing through the rear wall.

"I was serving as the distraction."

All expression vanished from Anastasia's face as she pivoted to regard my ghost.

"Valentina Zhukova." Her cool greeting cut through the mania in the room in a way that a bullhorn and air raid siren couldn't have managed. "Be welcome in my house."

Beneath a curtain of tangled curls, Valentina's dark-eyed gaze was trained upon the two girls. And Jee Sun and Tea Leaf were staring right back.

"White!" Jee Sun yelled at the top of her lungs.

"That color actually makes sense." Bill's ward had the uncanny ability to discern supernatural creatures at a glance, her brain assigning each species a distinct color. Vampires were yellow. Werewolves were red. And ghosts were apparently white.

Gustavo straightened from his pseudo-bear stance, and spoke quizzically to Anastasia, his eyes scanning the room. At her seat, Teresa looked similarly confused.

Anastasia replied in kind, and then explained to me, in English. "Humans cannot see ghosts, Mr. Smith, unless the spirit expends energy to make themselves visible."

"But Jee Sun and I see her just fine," I pointed out.

"Lord Beel-Kasan's ward is a special case, in many ways. And I suspect it is your bond to my queen which allows you to bridge the gap between worlds."

"Ah." That sort of made sense. "Is that why I'd never seen any ghosts before last year?"

"Precisely." She took in my new clothes and the bag over one shoulder. "I assume you have her node with you?"

So that's what it was called. "How did you know?"

"We are a long way from Chula Vista, and the sun is still in the sky, restricting Ms. Zhukova's movement. She would not have been able to come this far without it, and no spirit can touch, let alone transport, their own node."

That made a lot of sense. And would have been a good thing to know months prior. "This is why people think you know everything, Lady Dumenyova."

"Ignorance has a cost. I try to avoid paying it."

I grinned. "Spoken like a true foreigner. In this country, we don't worry about how much things cost. That's why God invented credit cards."

"This explains so much." Her eyes twinkled.

Teresa had returned to sipping her water, while Gustavo cleared the table of what must have been dinner, but the girls were still staring up at Valentina with rapt expressions. Tea Leaf, I noticed, was accidentally flashing fang; two of the smallest, cutest, flesh-ripping canines the world would ever see. And Valentina…

I stepped past Anastasia to approach my ghost.

"Is everything okay, V?"

With a visible effort, Valentina tore her gaze from the two children. I flinched back from the pain and grief in her black eyes, but she just shook her head sadly, spared another forlorn glance for the two girls, and drifted through the floor and out of view.

There was a moment of silence, and then Jee Sun and Tea Leaf returned to their play.

"Do you know what that was about?" I asked Ana.

"I do," said the femmepire, "but it is her story to tell. And the tale is not a happy one."

"Oh." I glanced again at the children. "Are Jee Sun and Summer… in danger?"

"Always." The femmepire caught my look and shrugged strong shoulders. "Danger is an unavoidable fact in our world. There is a reason I would prefer you return to your human life. But I am confident Ms. Zhukova would never harm either child. Quite the opposite."

That was good to hear, but the whole meeting had kind of bummed me out. The last thing I'd wanted to do was upset Valentina, especially given that she was already displeased with the whole Marge situation.

Which reminded me…

"Ana, I need your help."

ooo

With a dozen rooms *and* a staircase between us and the girls, my borrowed bedroom was an oasis of peace and quiet. I followed Anastasia inside and shut the door. Tea Leaf and Jee Sun were each cute as buttons, in their own disparate and slightly terrifying ways, but the concept of *inside voices* had yet to make an impression on either of them.

The bedroom was much as I'd left it, with a few notable exceptions. First, the bed had been made—prompting a flash of remorse over the state I'd left it in. Second, my water glass had been removed from the bedside table, replaced by…

"Is that a knife?" I set down my bag and crossed over to the table for a closer look. It sure *seemed* to be one, though of a style I'd never seen before. It was about the length of my forearm, its wide, double-edged blade a metal other than steel and tarnished by age.

Whatever had been used to wrap the hilt had long since decayed, but the weapon was surprisingly clean for something that looked to come from the Paleolithic era.

"It is."

"Something tells me this blade comes with a story?"

When she didn't reply immediately, I grinned. "As an insanely beautiful, ridiculously competent femmepire once told me, *ignorance has a cost.*"

"Sometimes, knowledge costs even more." Anastasia took a seat on the edge of the bed and said nothing further.

I wasn't the sharpest of knives—much like the strange weapon on my dresser—but even I could sense that the time for teasing had passed. I took a seat next to her.

"Does it have to do with your trip to Romania?"

"It does," she affirmed. With both hands in her lap, she gazed off into the distance, as if there were no walls to obstruct her view of the horizon.

"If you don't want to talk about it, you don't have to."

"Of that, I am aware."

We sat in silence for a long moment, Valentina's note still tucked away in my bag and awaiting translation. *Maybe,* I decided, *it would be better to focus on that note, rather than what was feeling like a deeply personal—or deeply painful—story.* But before I could make that concession, Anastasia spoke.

"Last year, on the twelfth of December, I slew the heir to the New Mexico Pack," Ana began, "along with two lieutenants, four of his closest friends, and the she-wolf who was his intended bride."

Holy shit. I'd known she was a badass, but eight werewolves in one day was kind of insane, even by her standards.

"They were each complicit in the plan to invade our territory," the femmepire explained, her voice composed, "and my order was to remove the entirety of that threat, not just the head."

"How did you do it?"

She studied my face. "Do you really wish to know?"

Part of me did. I'd seen enough action movies over the years to find the idea of a black-clad Anastasia mowing down werewolves ridiculously hot. But what little combat I'd experienced in real life had been anything but pleasant. So, I shook my head no, and was rewarded by a nod of approval from the femmepire.

"Thank you. Bloodshed is sometimes necessary, but it is my duty, not my passion."

Which raised the question of what her passion was. Once again, I somehow restrained myself from asking.

"With the New Mexico job completed," she continued, "I laid low for several weeks, rather than making my way directly back to San Diego."

"Because if the wolves could prove that you were the assassin, there would have been war?"

"No. The New Mexico Pack broke the tenets of the Toulon Concordat. Our retaliation was justified and fully sanctioned."

"Aren't the people who made the Concordat supposed to be responsible for enforcing it?" I still didn't know much about the ancient set of rules, other than that they were the reason mediators like me were hired, and that the penalties for transgression ranged from merely bad to scorched-and-salted-earth destruction.

"In the past few centuries, overt action from the ancients has become a rarity. It is believed they are passing that responsibility on to the rest of us as a test of our growth."

"So, the god of vengeful smiting was on a break, but you acted in his stead."

"Her stead, but yes. By the laws of the Concordat, our response was entirely justified. However, among the People, it is considered bad form to not at least make a token effort to disguise our actions."

"Kayla said something about that. That's the whole reason for your position, right?"

"It is. In politics, appearance is everything. For a member of the peerage to act on their own behalf suggests a certain—" She paused, hunting for the words. "—clumsiness of character. Me leaving a clear trail from and to San Diego would similarly have reflected poorly on my liege."

"So even though the werewolves couldn't retaliate, you had to disguise who was responsible, in order to avoid hurting Lucia's reputation among the other vampires?"

"Precisely."

"That's annoying." And not just because Lucia was one of the least subtle individuals I'd ever met. Being Secundus sounded an awful lot like work.

"Politics frequently are. Yet we have strayed again from the subject of this discussion."

"Romania."

"Yes." Despite her words, Anastasia seemed reluctant to continue. After a few minutes of silence, she sighed and spoke again. "I was in Phoenix when I received a phone call. It was my father."

"Your father?" For some reason, I'd never really thought about Anastasia's parents. It was one thing to know that the creature seated within arm's reach was several centuries old. It was another entirely to realize that the generation that preceded hers was still walking the earth.

I felt very, very young.

"Yes. We had not spoken since I followed my queen into exile, but he sought me out nonetheless." Her voice was soft, her eyes opaque. "He wanted me to know that his time was near."

"You mean…" I couldn't bring myself to say the words. There was only one time an aged vampire would reference, and that was the time of their passing.

"Indeed." She bowed her head.

"I'm so sorry, Ana." I shook my head. I wasn't sure what was harder to imagine; not speaking to my own dad for a century or having him contact me just to let me know that he was dying. "You went to Romania to say goodbye?"

"Not quite."

I waited and said nothing.

Eventually, she found her voice.

"As you may recall, our energy strengthens over time. It is how the People develop our Talents, and why age has an impact on our respective power. However, there comes a time when that energy has grown beyond the ability of our mortal shells to contain. Madness is the initial warning sign. At a certain point, that energy twists us into something else, a creature that is nothing but power, endless Thirst, and rage."

This was all new to me. And horrible.

"Much like the Infected, we become a danger to those around us. And like the wolves, we believe in meeting death on our own terms. By tradition, it is the duty of that individual's loved ones to help take the necessary steps."

"Steps?" What could another vampire possibly do to help with what was apparently an unavoidable ending? Other than…

I felt the blood drain from my face.

Anastasia's eyes were on me. She nodded.

"Yes. We honor our elders by helping them die, Mr. Smith. Better that they be sent into the void by those who love them than to become the enemy of all life."

"So you went to Romania…"

"To kill my father." She nodded to the ugly dagger on my nightstand. "With his own blade."

Holy shit.

ooo

I moved toward the femmepire, hesitated, and then threw caution to the wind, taking her hand in mine. "I'm sorry. That must have been awful."

"A woman tells you that she slew her own father, and that is your response?" She was stiff and immobile under my touch, but I could feel a sort of energy coming off her in waves. "I know how your species feels about such things."

"Murder is one thing," I replied, choosing my words slowly and with great care. "Mercy is something entirely different. Assisted suicide is something we humans are still struggling with, but I don't see the morality in forcing someone to live in pain."

And *we* didn't have to worry about evolving into serial killers.

She was silent for so long that I was convinced I had bungled the sentiment. But when she finally spoke, some of the tension had left her voice.

"I did not expect you to understand. As it was, I almost arrived too late. Exile makes travel through Europe… difficult. It took me two months to reach my father's village in Romania. By then, he was deep in the throes of madness and did not recognize me."

"You didn't get to say goodbye."

"He was in no condition to hear the words. Or return them."

We sat in silence again, the centuries-old femmepire and the twenty-six-year-old human, joined by clasped hands and the sadness of her tale.

"I wish I'd known. Maybe I could have helped somehow, even if just by giving you someone to talk to."

"Perhaps you could have, but it was a deeply personal matter. From the moment I received my father's call, I was focused on the task at hand. My journey through Europe was accomplished in fits and starts and on burner phones. I did not even receive your messages until I had returned to this country."

"I can't imagine how hard that trip was on you. Your father was lucky to have a daughter like you, Anastasia."

"My parents led a simple life," she said softly. "I don't believe either ever understood exactly what I do or why."

"Did they need to understand it?" I asked. "From what I've seen, even your enemies respect you. And those of us who do know you—" My voice broke embarrassingly, but I soldiered on. "—think you're ridiculously awesome. Your parents must have known that. They'd have been proud."

For the first time, Anastasia's hand squeezed mine.

"I don't know why I brought you his blade. I only know that I could not bear to keep it myself... and my queen, for all her strengths, has little room for sentiment." She looked down at our clasped hands. "You were the one person I could think of who might appreciate it for what it represents."

A wiser man would have known what to say to that, but all I had were lame jokes and a dagger older than modern civilization. I freed my hand from hers, scooted closer on the bed, and wrapped an arm about her in a loose hug. After a moment, she turned into me, burying her head in the space between my neck and shoulder.

I breathed in that scent that was unique to Anastasia, fully prepared to hold her for hours, as my arms fell asleep, as her sweet-smelling hair tickled my nose, and as the muscles in my back slowly tightened into knots. She had infiltrated a continent to find, mercy-kill, and bury her father. Nobody could begrudge her the need for a little bit of human comfort.

No one except the lady herself, it turned out.

It was less than a minute before I felt the femmepire stiffen in my arms. When I released her, she withdrew—as I had feared she would—but her face was open, her grief still visible, her eyes large and dark with sentiment.

"Thank you," she said simply.

"Always."

I watched her iron discipline reassert itself, locking emotion and weakness away behind the familiar mask of classical perfection.

It was as impressive as it was sad.

"Now," she continued briskly, "tell me of your meeting with the zombie prince and why it is you have brought Valentina Zhukova to my home."

CHAPTER 41

By the time I'd finished my retelling, Anastasia was firmly back in control.

Sort of.

"Are you telling me," she asked, voice hard like iron, "that Lady Middleton abandoned you in the middle of town, leaving you without protection of any kind?"

"It's Chula Vista, not North Korea. Having to walk home sucked, but it's not like I was in any danger."

"Of course not. As you are a friend to all, and entirely without enemies who might wish you dead."

I was pretty sure that was sarcasm but didn't rise to the bait. I was still alive, right? This was a clear case of *no harm, no foul.*

"John," Anastasia continued, in an exasperated tone that should have irritated me, but for some reason warmed me to my toes, "does everyone in your family have an impulse to suicide, or is it just you?"

"I think it's just me."

My joke was met with stony silence.

"What did you want me to do? I didn't have a phone or any money, and I wasn't going to get between Juliette and her snack-of-the-day." Not if I wanted to live, anyway. "Walking home was my only option. And look! I'm still breathing! I didn't even have to call on my sweet regenerative superpowers!"

Anastasia didn't seem to hear me. She had risen from her seat and was pacing back and forth. Finally, the femmepire stopped, pinning me to the bed with flashing green eyes.

"If I have to shackle you to my side to keep you safe, Mr. Smith, I *will* do so."

Enforced proximity? *That* sounded kind of like paradise. Although it would make bathroom visits problematic. And might cut into my late-night In-n-Out runs. And the subsequent, even later-night, Star Wars marathons.

Not to mention… you know… dude stuff.

"You can't always keep me safe, Ana. Like you said, it's a dangerous world. But I have to live in it, and I can't solve cases from my couch." Which was probably for the best, or I'd be whale-sized within a month.

"I know," she admitted, begrudgingly. "Lady Middleton and I will have words on the matter, even so."

As much as I loved cool, efficient Anastasia, and equally adored her rare moments of vulnerability, this new, overprotective Anastasia was really doing it for me too.

"But that is a matter for another time," the femmepire of my affections continued. "You said something about a note that needed translation?"

"Yeah." I grabbed the folded paper from my duffel bag and handed it over. "I think it's Russian."

"It is," she confirmed with a glance. "Ms. Zhukova wrote this herself? Are you certain?"

"I watched her do it. Why?"

"It is difficult for a spirit to manifest physically, and unheard of for one to have such fine motor control while doing so. Your ghost deserves her reputation."

Hell yeah, she did.

"Do you know anyone that can read it?"

"Several," the femmepire answered absently, "including myself."

"You speak and read English, Italian, Romanian, *and* Russian?" I was feeling undereducated. Again.

"As well as French, Spanish, German, Farsi, Swahili, Cantonese, and Mandarin."

She looked up from the note to find me staring at her.

"What is it?"

"God loves a smart woman, Anastasia."

"From what I know of human religion, I am not at all certain that is true."

"Then He's a moron. Or She is. What does it say?"

"It says that Valentina went to meet with someone named Margaret in your absence, but the other woman never showed. And that a third woman, Begoña, likewise failed to appear at assembly. Those are also White Ladies, are they not?"

"Yeah," I said, feeling like the rug had just been pulled out from under me. "They're the ghosts that hired me. In Graciela's absence, they're the nominal leaders of the group."

"Which suggests that the latter spirit's absence is not, after all, accidental."

I shivered. "Someone is hunting the Ladies."

"This is deeply troubling."

"Tell me about it." I'd made limited progress in locating Graciela over the past ten days, and now I had *three* ghosts to find? "I am so screwed."

"Not just you, Mr. Smith."

I flushed. "You're right. Three women are missing; I shouldn't be griping about my workload. Or reputation."

"You misunderstand me." Anastasia tapped her fingers against the dresser's surface in thought. "The White Ladies are a power in San Diego, one third of the triumvirate that maintains order."

"I know. The Ladies, the House, and..." I struggled to remember the last group.

"The Mer."

"Right. Them." Since I did my best to avoid the ocean—although not the beach—I'd never actually met one of the Mer, making them all too easy to forget.

"Yes. And if you remove one leg from a tripod, what occurs?"

"It becomes a bipod?" Before she could respond, I hurried on. "And falls over. You think this is political?"

"I do not know," she admitted, pulling her hair back into some sort of complicated knot that required neither a pin nor a tie. "It is possible that this person's motivation is something altogether more primitive. But the effect will be the same."

"Jesus," I complained. "Can't we go six months without the looming threat of city-wide devastation?"

"It *is* starting to approach absurdity."

My mind raced down all the avenues I'd already taken with this case, searching for something I might have missed, something that I could have done differently. I came up with an awful lot of answers on the latter question... but few of them were pertinent to the case.

Which was pretty much par for the course.

"Graciela was missing for at least a month before the White Ladies hired me. And I'm sure they would have told me if there had been any other disappearances in that time." I cocked an eye in Anastasia's direction. "But within a few days of my hiring, two more ghosts disappear?"

"What does that tell you?"

"Not much," I admitted. "If this were a crime novel, it might suggest that the attacker was growing more confident. Or that they were worried I was closing in on them. Or that the voices in their head were louder this time of year." I shook my head. "All I know for sure is that both Kala and Simon believed Graciela was still alive. Or… whatever the hell the term is. Unlive."

"Perhaps that holds true for the others," Anastasia reasoned, "and we still have time to find them."

"I hope so," I muttered, feeling a warm glow at her use of *we*. "I gave them my word."

"Though I must stay here to protect my queen, John, I will help however I can. But such talk can wait until tomorrow. Now, you should rest."

I glanced at the clock on the wall and was startled to find it was already almost ten. Where the hell had the evening gone?

"I'm alright."

"It has been only a few days since your ordeal. Sleep, Mr. Smith. Tomorrow, we will renew your search."

I'd have argued further, but seeing the time had made me realize how tired I was, so instead, I surrendered to the inevitable. We said our goodnights, and she vanished into the hallway, closing the bedroom door behind her. I plugged my phone in to charge it and slipped into bed.

ooo

An hour or so later, I was awake again. And my stomach was reminding me that I'd last eaten in mid-afternoon. The fact that I'd had *two* sandwiches at my house didn't seem to matter.

Grumbling, I rolled to my feet, pulled on the jeans I'd left by my bedside, and headed down to the kitchen. Hopefully, Anastasia's donors weren't the sort to be annoyed by a little bit of late-night foraging.

One cold Italian sausage and a slab of tasty homemade bread later, the gaping pit in my stomach had been reduced to a mere pothole. I headed upstairs, slipped back into my bedroom, and brushed my teeth.

Now, I was ready for bed.

Except… my wonderphone had regained enough juice to turn back on and it had multiple notifications. I moved both phone and charger to my bedside table, stepped back out of my jeans and into bed, and began reviewing my messages.

I had thirty-seven emails, but all of them were spam… a depressing number having something to do with impotence and/or penis enlargement. The spammers of the world were collectively trying to tell me something.

There were a handful of texts from Darlene, telling me about their now days-old camping plans, and a metric shit ton of voicemails. Three of those were from Kayla or Darlene, and I listened to several additional variations of their invitation to go camping. Kayla had described it as a chance to get out and enjoy nature, while Darlene had suggested it was a chance to meet *hot outdoorsy chicks*. Both had mentioned alcohol. Repeatedly.

That probably said bad things about my drinking habits, but I couldn't muster the energy to be concerned. I had awesome friends.

There was also a voicemail from Mike, who had escaped from his girlfriend just long enough to remember that I existed, word from Kristin that the ghost migration report she'd promised would be ready any day now—something even I could recognize as marketing-doublespeak for *it's going to be a while*—and a polite query from Nepenthe as to whether I'd been able to speak with Lucia about the merits of a representative democracy.

That last voicemail made me groan. The witch was enough of a realist to know the odds were against us, but I wasn't looking forward to explaining just how badly I'd mucked everything up.

Mostly because I knew how much delight Tommy would take in my failure.

But that, I decided, was yet another task for tomorrow. My belly was full, my body was tired, and the sooner I got to bed, the sooner Anastasia, Juliette, Valentina, and I could figure out our next step.

Between one breath and the next, I was asleep.

INTERLUDE

"Do you think the necklace is too much?" I eye myself in the mirror one final time, even though the view hasn't changed in the past hour. A string of flashing rubies dips pleasingly into my cleavage, the gift of some minor dignitary whose name I forgot that same night. "It is imperative that I draw the eye without being ostentatious."

"It is perfect, your highness." Anastasia's words are approving, but her tone is distant.

I turn to find my trusted servant on the balcony, gazing out over the expanse of Rome. To anyone who does not know her, she would seem at ease, but we grew up together, and I note the way one hand has tightened upon the banister. If she had already come into her power, that delicate wooden barrier would be crumbling under the pressure.

Which is, of course, the root of the problem.

"Asya."

She makes her way back over to me obediently, but I can read the tension in her brilliant green eyes. For the hundredth time, I wish there were something I could do about it. But Papa's word is, quite literally, law. And a small part of me—the part training to be queen—recognizes the merits of his strategy.

I do not have to like it though.

"Asya," I say again, "I wish this wasn't so hard on you."

"The world is what it is, my queen." She has spent the past decade undergoing her own manner of training, from combat to subterfuge, and I no longer find it so easy to read the truth in her expression. But then, she was always a quiet girl, even when her parents first sold her into my family's service.

"Be that as it may, I recognize this is difficult," I say, patting her arm soothingly. "I wish that you could end your Thirst with me tonight. Or that you had been able to do so on your own name-day."

I've had a hard time fighting off the Thirst this long, but Anastasia is my elder. The thought that she will have to delay her ascension for years yet seems unimaginable.

As her friend, I pity her.

As her future queen, I appreciate the sacrifice.

"It is the correct choice, your highness," she insists, as if I couldn't read the hunger in her eyes. "The longer I withstand the Thirst, the more assistance I will be able to provide when I do partake. And what are a few years to those such as we?"

"As you say," I agree, though I have my doubts. From all accounts, Papa fed on the evening of his eighteenth name-day, as I am about to do, and his terrible power does not seem at all diminished by that fact.

"Hold on for as long as you can," I bid her, "but if the need becomes too great, you must tell me. I will not let you destroy yourself on my account."

"No?" She quirks one eyebrow, an expression I am still endeavoring to master, and smiles.

"No. You are my Secundus, and one day, the two of us will turn this Empire on its ear, bringing the dried-up old sticks of the Court screaming into the seventeenth century!"

"In that case," says Anastasia, eyeing my white gown—a dress which exposes far more skin than what is currently considered fashionable, "I think the necklace will do just fine."

CHAPTER 42

IN WHICH THINGS GO BUMP IN THE NIGHT

I stirred briefly, long enough to remember that I was, in fact, a full-grown, slightly out-of-shape man, and *not* an eighteen-year-old vampire princess. Either my imagination was running amok or something was really, really wrong with the bond I shared with Lucia. Either way, there wasn't a hell of a lot I could do about it until morning.

I rolled over and went back to sleep.

○○○

Now, *this* was clearly one of *my* dreams. I could tell that just from the presence of cartoon characters and the unmistakable silhouette of Mt. Everest, smoking a pipe in the background.

The show tunes were a bit of a giveaway too.

I patted the six-legged bunny to my right on the top of his chair-sized, furry head, and eyed Everest with delighted anticipation.

"Well, Sir Floppy, we're not going to reach the summit by just standing here."

I hoisted a pack onto my shoulders, drained the ice-cold bottle of Pete's Wicked Ale that had materialized in my hand, and made my way out of base camp, as cartoons joined together in a riotous rendition of One More Day, from *Les Miserables.*

"John?" The voice rang out in the sudden silence.

I spun to find the camp had disappeared. In its place was a tepee. A purple buffalo had been painted on the wrapped hide above the tepee's entrance, but my attention was reserved for the woman who stood in front.

"Anastasia." I doffed my sombrero and bowed low. Next to me, Sir Floppy copied my movements with considerably more grace.

"What are you doing?" Ana's hair was loose and down, cascading across strong shoulders. She had wrapped a woven blanket around her body, and held it shut with one pale hand, but lusciously bare legs peeked out from underneath. In the moonlight, her skin glowed like pale fire.

"We're headed to climb Mt. Everest."

"We who?"

I glanced down and saw that Sir Floppy had disappeared. In fact… one glance over my shoulder showed that Mt. Everest was likewise gone. Away on another walkabout, no doubt.

"That's weird."

"Come back to bed, love." The smooth richness of her voice was flavored with humor and a dash of wickedness.

I blinked and was next to her. Blinked again and her arms were around my neck, pulling me closer. We were inside the tepee, on a bed the size of a football field. Flat on my back, I looked up at Anastasia as her mouth met mine. Her lips were even more lush than I remembered, her body curved against my own, bare skin like hot silk against my overmuscled chest.

I pushed my hips up, irritated at the obstruction of our clothing, and she ground down on me with a throaty laugh. Her entire body undulated, and those soft lips left mine to trail kisses along my jawbone and down to my neck.

I groaned with the knowledge of what was coming. Sure enough, fangs sliced into my flesh, bringing with them a wave of all-consuming pleasure.

○○○

As a child, I never woke easily or quickly, to the point where my mother despaired of ever getting me up in time for school. Between my love of beer and my lack of a steady nine-to-five, matters had only worsened with adulthood. It typically took me a half hour or more—not to mention a long, hot shower—before I was even marginally useful.

This once, I moved from dreaming into wakefulness so swiftly that I initially didn't even realize the transition had occurred. The crisp bedding beneath me was nothing like the satin sheets from my dream, but everything else was the same, from the warm, curvaceous body grinding against my own, to the ripples of pleasure from Anastasia's bite.

Wait a minute.

Only one vampire's bite had ever been pleasurable for me.

As that thought was forming in my mind, I became aware of other, equally telling, discrepancies, from the absence of Anastasia's scent to the fact that the naked flesh pressed against my body was both substantially curvier than the femmepire Secundus' and scorching hot to the touch.

I opened my eyes and looked down.

Even in the darkness, the shimmer of platinum blonde hair was apparent.

Half a year ago, the pleasure of Lucia's bite had left me a quivering wreck in front of half the House. My body now seemed intent on a vigorous repetition of that experience. The queen was undeniably gorgeous, with proportions more closely resembling something from a comic book than reality. Even without the pleasure of her bite, she was the sort of goddess any twenty-five-year-old fratman would be delighted to worship.

So, it was a damn good thing I'd recently turned twenty-six.

I put my palms against the femmepire's shoulders, dangerously close to what my own bare chest informed me were large, very soft breasts, and pushed. Hard.

If Lucia had been ready for my reaction, I would never have been able to move her. If her arms had been wrapped about me, like Ana's in my dream, she might not have even noticed the effort. But I was both monkey and prey, and the thought that I might resist clearly hadn't occurred to her. Plus, I outweighed her by at least seventy pounds. So, I wasn't altogether surprised when I was able to push her off me.

Tossing her several feet into the air like she'd been bounced from a trampoline though? *That* was shocking. I was still gaping when the dark silhouette of her body came back down and to the right, limbs flailing gracelessly. She impacted the carpeted floor next to the bed with a resounding thud.

It didn't take a genius to guess how the volatile femmepire would react to *that*. I scrambled to the opposite side of the bed, one hand clasped over the bite marks that continued to throb pleasantly.

Lucia rose to her feet with a hiss of rage.

"Wait just a second…" I trailed off. What was I supposed to say? *Sorry about the whole coma thing; please don't bite me anymore?* Or maybe *As San Diego's mediator, I doth forbid thy continued snacking upon mine blood?* Or even *Cool it, doll face; I'm not interested?*

That last one was the sort of thing the John Smith of my daydreams might have said… you know, the tough-as-nails master detective who traded his left eye for a carton of cigarettes and bottle of Scotch. The man who had fought the werewolf virus in his bloodstream to a standstill, was legendary for his investigative prowess, and never went anywhere without his two best friends, Smith and Wesson.

That guy was way too cool for base desire.

I, on the other hand, was almost painfully aroused, which is a horrible state to be in when you're arguing for your life. I inched backwards, and held my hands up defensively, fumbling for the words that might save my life.

Given an hour, or maybe three, I would have come up with something eloquent and properly mediator-like, but Lucia didn't seem inclined to wait. She hissed a second time and blurred into action.

And that was when all hell *really* broke loose.

○○○

I didn't have time to do anything but flinch as the vampire queen hurtled through the air. I didn't even manage to shut my eyes or squeak, both of which ranked high on my list of instinctive reactions. As a result, I knew to the millisecond when Lucia should have impacted me… and when she instead flew right *through* me to smack into the wall next to the bathroom door. At the same time, an icy wind swept through my body.

I turned and found a softly glowing Valentina next to me, standing in what was my otherwise solid bed. One hand was on my bare shoulder, and it was that hand—and the fact that the ghost had used it to phase my body—that had just saved my life.

The spirit's face was turned toward Lucia, and the cold wind I had felt like a shiver through my system was taking physical form, causing Valentina's dark curls to stream back from her face like a mass of whirling tentacles. Her black eyes, now fully visible, were decidedly angry, and the howl she directed at my attacker drowned out the femmepire's own angry hisses.

In the spirit's glow, I noticed a few things.

First, Lucia was not—despite what I'd felt in my dream—naked, but clad in a loose white nightgown. Second, naked or not, there was an awful lot of flesh on display. Seriously. The nightgown might as well have been a silk handkerchief, for all the good it was doing.

Third—and this last observation was by far the most important of the three—the femmepire's bloody fangs were fully extended, and there was no sanity in her wide, staring eyes.

Queen Crazy Pants was living up to her name.

Even without pants.

"You need to calm down, Lucia," I told her, words coming easily now that I was safe from reprisal. "We all saw how much good attacking me did you at the House."

She paused, and for one shining moment, I thought I'd yet again managed to mediate my way out of an impossible situation. Instead, the queen extended a hand in my direction. A wind that made Valentina's seem warm and balmy swept toward us on a wave of frost and snow.

"All the blizzards in the world aren't going to help you" is what I *would* have said, if I hadn't found myself suddenly gasping for breath while the air in my otherwise insubstantial lungs went ice-cold. What I managed instead was something between "Ack" and "Gah", and neither of those arguments seemed likely to be persuasive.

A glance at Valentina showed her unaffected, but also painfully aware that the same didn't hold true for me. She glanced between the femmepire and me in a moment of indecision. If she allowed Lucia to continue her assault, I would asphyxiate. If she left me to attack the queen, I would freeze to death.

Neither option seemed like a winner to me.

Maybe I should have just let Lucia drink me dry.

Valentina's hand tightened on my shoulder until it was almost painful, and then she flew at the queen, dragging me behind her like a man-sized purse. This time, I had ample opportunity to squeeze my eyes shut, but the burst of light that followed was blinding, even through closed eyelids.

Had we just gone super nova? Had Lucia summoned the northern lights. Or had…

"That is enough!" Anastasia's voice cracked like a whip, cutting through Valentina's howls, Lucia's hisses, and my own labored breath.

I cracked one eye open to find the femmepire by the door, one hand near the light switch she had just flicked on. In her other hand was a long-bladed knife, the sight of which reminded me that I had my own—significantly less sleek—weapon within reach on the bedside table.

"Lady Zhukova," Anastasia addressed my ghost in that hard-as-nails voice, "you are a guest in my house. I will not stand by as you assault my liege."

"She was just—" The air in my lungs had warmed sufficiently for words, but my voice cut off instantly, when Ana turned her cold-eyed glare in my direction. I did my best to look meek and harmless.

The femmepire turned to Lucia, her gaze taking in the other woman's state, from the nightgown that was—still—barely covering anything at all to the blood that looked like badly smeared lipstick around her mouth. "As for you, my queen, what are you doing in Mr. Smith's room?"

"Hungry." Lucia's voice was rough from disuse, and in the room's light, I was able to see that her glacial blue eyes were almost entirely dominated by gold. Someone's inner vampire was in control.

"Of course you are." Ana's voice had regained its unflappable coolness. "And now that you have returned to consciousness, I will find you a fitting meal."

The gold was rapidly draining from Lucia's eyes, and I watched her spine stiffen as her natural haughtiness reasserted itself. However, her fangs were still partly extended when she spoke.

"Mr. Smith is my thrall, Lady Dumenyova. Who better than he to slake my thirst?"

For one crazy moment, I heard *stake* instead of *slake*. The sentence wouldn't have made even the tiniest bit of sense, but it was dangerously close to the thoughts currently running through my head.

"Mr. Smith has already seen sufficient injury because of you, my queen," replied Anastasia in those same measured tones, "and I have taken him under my protection. I will not let him come to harm."

Lucia drew herself up to her full—not particularly impressive—height. "I am your monarch!" She even sounded regal, despite being mostly naked and still covered in blood.

"You are." Anastasia said nothing more, but something in her expression took the wind right out of Lucia's sails. The femmepire queen broke gazes with her Secundus and turned a black look in my direction.

"I will see you banished from this House, human. Your name will be stricken from our records, your visage forgotten, and—" She took in the unfamiliar bedroom for the first time. "Where are we?"

"We reside in one of my properties," said Anastasia, "due to circumstances of which you are yet unaware. If you come with me, I will see to your feeding, and we may discuss such matters further in private."

Lucia wasn't listening, gaze distant as if staring into the past. "Mr. Smith and I quarreled," she remembered, "and then—"

"You tried to kill me."

"If I had wanted you dead, human, you would be so. Not even your pet ghost would stop me."

Valentina drifted closer to the femmepire queen, small hands clenched into fists.

"Lady Zhukova, please." Anastasia's voice was gentle this time. "Would you excuse us? I give you my word as a titled woman of the People that your ward will not be harmed."

The ghost turned to me. Her hair was once again a curtain in front of her face, but the question was clear.

"Go ahead, V," I told her softly. "I'll be fine. And thank you, again, for saving my life."

With a nod and a black-gummed smile, the ghost slipped down and through the bed, and was swiftly out of sight.

Anastasia turned to Lucia.

"Remember your father's lessons, my queen. Royalty must remain above petty conflicts. This spat with Mr. Smith diminishes you."

"What did he have to say about crawling half-naked into someone's bed to drink from them in the middle of the night?"

"You are not helping matters, John."

"He is John now, is he?" Lucia's tone was cold and reproachful. "Tell me, Secundus… when did you start taking a human's side over my own?"

"Probably when yours became recognizably insane."

"John." Ana's voice cracked again.

"Sorry, Asya," I mumbled.

Silence fell like it had been dropped off a cliff. I looked up to find two absurdly gorgeous faces locked on my own.

"What did you call her?" whispered Lucia, her eyes bleeding back to gold.

"Ana," I repeated. That was what I'd said, wasn't it?

"You said Asya," she argued. "Where did you hear that name?"

Well, shit.

CHAPTER 43

I was reasonably sure that two days of torture hadn't improved my ability to lie, so I didn't even try.

"I've been having weird dreams. You two seem to be in most of them."

"We are not interested in your banal fantasies," sniped Lucia, but Anastasia was regarding me with narrowed eyes.

"What sort of dreams, Mr. Smith?"

"Dull ones, mostly." I shrugged. "Rome. Spiteful little brothers. Uncomfortable chairs. That sort of thing." The evening's dream came back to me, and I pointed at Lucia. "Tonight, I was you, and we were wearing rubies and some handkerchief of a dress, getting ready for our first feeding, while she—" I nodded in Anastasia's direction. "—was doing that noble, suffering-in-silence thing because *someone* had decided it would best for her to wait a few more years for her own feeding."

Shocked silence met my announcement.

"How did—" began Lucia, after a long moment.

"To be honest," I added, overriding her startled words with a savage sort of glee, "I *do* think the necklace was a bit much. And given what little I know of seventeenth century fashion, I can't imagine people were delighted with your outfit."

"They were not," confirmed Anastasia.

"My sartorial decisions of four centuries ago are not up for debate, Mr. Smith," snapped the femmepire queen. "I am far more concerned with matters of relevance, like how it is that you came by this information. Who have you been speaking to?"

I raised an eyebrow and took a seat on the edge of my bed. "Lots of people. I'm a busy man. Occasionally. But you and your teenage rebellions have never come up as subjects for discussion."

"Then how—?"

"I just *told* you; I've been having dreams. Pretty much from the moment you tried to kill me." She opened her mouth to protest, but I waved off her objection. "Fine; from the moment you tried so hard to *not kill* me that I lost consciousness and woke up in a dungeon."

The femmepire's gaze hardened. She turned to Anastasia. "What is going on?"

"It would appear," suggested her Secundus slowly, "that your bond is dangerously flawed."

"I see."

"That would be a first," I muttered, none too quietly.

"Anastasia." Lucia looked to her companion, as if I was no longer even present in the room. "Are you absolutely certain that we cannot kill the human?"

"I must insist upon it, my queen."

Anastasia's reply brought a victorious grin to my face.

"Given the peculiarity of your bond," the femmepire continued, "and the results of your last confrontation, I cannot dismiss the possibility that such an attempt would bring harm upon you as well."

That qualifier wiped the grin right back off, as Asya had no doubt intended.

Ana. Not *Asya.* Shit, I was even doing it in my head.

"I see." Lucia speared me with a glare. "Stay out of my memories."

"As long as you stay out of my dreams. And my bedroom!"

Our glaring contest was interrupted when Gustavo appeared in the doorway. Over one arm, he carried a plush white robe for the vampire queen.

"If you and Mr. Smith are done testing each other's patience," said Anastasia, "Gustavo will take you to your meal."

"Will you join me? We have much to discuss."

"Always. I will be along shortly."

The door shut behind Lucia and Gustavo, leaving Anastasia and me alone once again. I was starting to become accustomed to the long silences between us. Either we were communicating on a deeper, emotional level, or we didn't know what to say. I watched Ana, and she watched me, and somewhere on the floor beneath us, I could *feel* Lucia getting her drink on. It was disturbing and foul and kicked every one of my pleasure centers into high gear.

"John, I would appreciate it if you would speak to Lady Zhukova. As guests in my house, you are accorded certain rights and privileges, but I will not allow her to assault Queen Lucia."

"She was just protecting me," I reminded her.

"I know." A small smile appeared on her lovely face. "As I said, you do attract a particular brand of defender."

"Thanks to my youthful charm and innocence."

"No doubt."

"Do you really think this dream thing is because of our bond?"

Anastasia took a seat on the end of the bed next to me. "You described the morning of Queen Lucia's first feeding precisely. Only two of us were present on that day… and only one has a direct link into your brain. How long have you been having these dreams? And why didn't you tell me about them?"

"They only started happening recently. It wasn't until last night that I even recognized who was involved."

"Have we changed so much in the centuries since?" The small smile had yet to leave Anastasia's face, and it illuminated the small room every bit as well as the overhead lighting.

"Most of the dreams were of you as children."

"Really? What did you see?"

"Nothing embarrassing, if that's what you're worrying about."

"It is not. This was centuries ago, John. The idea that you might be experiencing those events for the first time… makes the past seem almost tangible. If you would indulge me?"

Given that I'd already followed her into the House to rescue a woman I loathed, there was little chance that I was going to refuse a simple trip down memory lane. Especially with her sitting so close that I could feel her breath upon my skin.

"Most of the dream memories faded as soon as I woke, but I think I saw your initial encounter with Lucia."

Ana was silent, but her eyes were intense.

"There was an older manpire and his wife," I began, remembering their shabby dress, and Lucia's disdain for both that fact and their rustic mannerisms, "who met with Lucia and a vampire she called Papa." I described the participants in as much detail as possible.

"My parents and the late King Borghesi."

"I figured. Then, you came in from the hallway and were introduced."

"I was terrified, waiting alone in the hall by a tapestry that cost more than our village," admitted the femmepire, without a trace of self-consciousness. "I had never been to a city before then. As big and noisy as Roma herself was, the Borghesi summer palace was even more frightening."

"What was that meeting about, anyway? My dreams didn't provide much context."

"Ah." She shrugged, but the smile left her face. "My parents were there to sell me into service."

"They were *what*?!?" I remembered Lucia thinking something like that from my most recent dream, but hearing it said aloud...

"Even the People experience difficult times, Mr. Smith. In many ways, life is easier now. My family was very poor, and the winters had been some of the harshest in memory. While my parents never treated me as anything but a blessing, I was a drain on the village's scarce resources. News that the king was seeking to hire a companion for his daughter reached us in Romania, and my parents seized the opportunity."

"Jesus." She'd been what... eight at the time? Ten? I shook my head. The more I learned about vampire history, the less glamorous it seemed. "There must have been a lot of competition for the position."

Among those who had never *met* Lucia, anyway.

"Less than you might imagine. Remember, children are a rarity. Only a dozen or so in Europe were of the appropriate age, gender, and political affiliation, and most of those belonged to noble families. They were understandably disinclined to exchange peerage for servitude. It came down to myself and two others." Her smile turned inward. "In the end, Lucia chose me, and in doing so, lifted my family out of poverty."

I repressed a frown with great difficulty. I loathed the vampire queen, but I was starting to get a glimmer of an idea why Ana was so unshakably loyal.

A very, very faint glimmer.

"I should be with her now, in fact, instead of keeping you awake." Anastasia rose gracefully to her feet.

I tried to assure her that I was fine, but my yawn gave away the lie. "Sorry. It's been a long… year."

"I understand." Before I could react, soft lips brushed my cheek. "Sleep well. And for one night, at least, I hope that sleep is dreamless."

"From your lips to God's ears," I murmured back sleepily. "Thank you, Ana. Or do you prefer Asya?"

She paused by the door to consider my question. "Few people refer to me by anything but title these days, Mr. Smith, and only you have ever called me Ana. I find myself liking the way it sounds."

She was down the hall before I could remind her, for the ten billionth time, to call me John.

As tired as I was, sleep was hard to come by. I tossed and turned on the previously comfortable bed. Finally, I opened my eyes and stared up at the ceiling.

"Valentina? Are you there?"

I felt her appear in the darkness of the room.

"Oh good." I fumbled for my phone on the dresser and brought up my latest playlist. Soft music filled the room through the phone's tinny speakers. "It's not as nice as the stereo back home, but I thought you might enjoy some music anyway."

She said nothing in reply—of course—but I felt her happiness wash over me like it was a tangible thing. Soon after, she began to dance.

After that, I slept like a baby.

CHAPTER 44

IN WHICH TOMORROW IS ANOTHER DAY

Wednesday dawned warm and blessedly free of any eyeballs looking me dead in the face. *Dawned* being a figurative term, of course; a glance at my phone showed me it was already noon. Twenty minutes of near-scalding water restored some measure of wakefulness. I ran a razor across my face, gargled some mouthwash, and got dressed for the day. Then, I followed the sound of familiar voices to the downstairs dining room, voices that sounded suspiciously like…

"Kayla! Darlene! When did you two get in?"

Darlene put down one of her skyscraper-sized sandwiches to wrap me in a tight hug. Her short red hair was damp. Apparently, I wasn't the only one who had just showered.

"Just a bit ago. We got started early."

Behind her, Kayla flashed a brilliant smile. "You're looking well, John. Better than I would have expected."

"Yeah, pretty close to one hundred percent. Lycanthropy is a powerful thing." I glanced to the side. "No hug, Duchess?"

"Not even if your life depended on it." Juliette's hair seemed even spikier than usual, as if in competition with both her mood *and* the studded leather wrist guard that graced one arm. She sent a fang-filled scowl in my direction.

"Someone struck out with Starbucks employee number seven," I told the other two women.

"Her name is Angel," Juliette growled, "she works at a Coffee Bean, not a Starbucks, and I did *not* strike out."

"I don't know," I parroted. "You seem awfully irritable for someone who got some action last night."

"Maybe because I left her *and* a warm bed to come meet with my partner, only to have that partner sleep half the day away?"

"People who abandon their partners in the middle of Chula Vista without money or phones don't get to bitch about reliability." For the first time, I really looked at the other femmepire. While she was still dressed in her usual outfit of skintight jeans and vintage t-shirt, the boots she was wearing were clearly new. As was the open vest over her tee. "Juliette… did you let Angel dress you this morning?"

The femmepire actually blushed, which had to be worth at least a billion points in our endless competition.

"I figured I'd give it a try," she muttered.

"Add a tiny hat, and you'd be the world's oldest hipster."

"Which beats being the world's oldest virgin," she hissed back.

The fact that it was untrue in no way lessened the burn.

"Juliette found herself a girlfriend, John's living with Anastasia, and Lucia's getting a much-needed timeout… We really did miss a lot this week, didn't we?" D didn't even try to hide her smile.

"It's been pretty hectic," I swiped a piece of bread from Juliette's plate. "Where is everyone else?"

"Summer and Jee Sun are playing on the beach," said Kayla, "being watched by Lady Dumenyova and one of her donors."

A lovely spring day on the beach? Smart kids. I went into the kitchen to pour myself a glass of orange juice. When I came back, the remnants of my stolen piece of bread were nowhere to be found. I eyed Juliette suspiciously.

"He seems awfully domestic, doesn't he, K?" Darlene's mischievous grin had returned now that she was well and truly convinced I was uninjured.

"He does. Making yourself at home, John?"

"I was. Until last night, anyway."

"Oh ho ho," chortled Darlene. "What happened last night?"

"I did, young woman," came Lucia's icy reply, as the femmepire queen stepped into the room. She was dressed in what had to be Anastasia's clothes, given that the top was beyond snug, and the pants had received an emergency hemming to avoid dragging on the floor. They were also in the other woman's preferred ocean colors. It was the only time I'd seen Lucia in anything but white.

She floated past us to pour a glass of juice, as if unaware that Darlene and Kayla were both frozen in shock. Juliette, to my right, was staring daggers in my direction.

"What?" I asked innocently. "I was going to tell you."

"When did—"

"Last night," I answered.

"And does she know—"

"That, thanks to Mr. Smith, I have been ousted from my own House, Lady Middleton? I am all too aware."

"Thanks to me? *You* attacked *me!* If anyone is at fault here…"

"Do you truly think *now* is the appropriate time for assigning blame?" Lucia shook her head. "Recriminations should come only once the matter has been rectified."

Orange juice sloshed over the rim of my glass and onto the table, but I managed to refrain from saying anything that might incite another attempt on my life.

"Rectified, your Majesty?" asked Kayla carefully.

"Indeed. Our first concern must be regaining control of the House." She glanced around the table. "I would have hoped for at least one other Council member, but we must work with the tools we have. I will instruct Lady Dumenyova to assemble a tactical plan, and the means to coordinate with our remaining allies within the House. Shall we reconvene on the hour to discuss it?"

"Let's not." Juliette didn't even flinch when the vampire queen's heat-seeking laser eye beams turned in her direction.

"I do not think I heard you correctly, Lady Middleton."

"I think you did." She met Lucia's gaze with her own flat-eyed expression. "I don't work for you anymore, remember?"

"She quit the House, you froze her assets, and good times were had by all," I clarified.

"I was in a coma, Mr. Smith, not lobotomized." The queen's eyes never left Juliette. "This is our opportunity to put such trifles behind us, Lady Middleton. I believe in rewarding those who remain loyal through adversity."

"Unless they're human," I said. "Then, you enslave them."

"Believe me, my thrall," snapped the queen, "there is *no one* less pleased with our current arrangement than I."

"I kind of doubt that."

Lucia dismissed me with a wave of her hand, and extended that same hand, palm downward to Juliette. "So then, Lady Middleton. Can I count on your support?"

The other femmepire chewed on that, thrumming her fingers on the wooden surface of the table. "Nah," she finally said. "I already have a job."

I had to hand it to the queen; instead of losing her shit like usual, she nodded and turned to Kayla instead.

"Sorry, your Majesty," said the former Captain of the Watch, before Lucia could even speak, "but Darlene and I are leaving the House too. That was one of the things we talked about on our trip. The past few months have been hell, and I refuse to put this one through any more of it." She wrapped a long, muscular arm around Darlene, who snuggled into her appreciatively.

"You would abandon your House in favor of…" Lucia's mouth worked silently, as she realized her normal, pejorative terms for my species probably weren't going to fly this time.

"The woman I love? Damn skippy."

"I see." Again, Lucia swallowed her anger—I was starting to think Anastasia had dosed the queen with elephant tranquilizers—and again, she rotated, this time to regard the last person in the room.

"Oh *hell* no!" I didn't bother to sugar-coat it.

Head high, shoulders back, and spine ramrod-stiff, Lucia turned and exited the room, carrying her orange juice and the tattered remnants of her pride.

"That went surprisingly well," said Juliette.

Darlene nodded. "She didn't even seem particularly angry."

"Not as much as I'd have expected anyway," I added, just to be part of the conversation.

"So, do you all think she's—" began Kayla.

"Plotting to kill us?" finished Juliette. "Probably."

"Not probably," I said. "Definitely."

CHAPTER 45

"You're dreaming Lucia's memories now?" Kayla's eyes were the widest of the three women, but only by a narrow margin. The latest twist in my already bizarre life story had taken them all by surprise.

"I guess so." I shrugged. "At first, I just figured she or Zorana had given me some sort of weirdly specific brain damage, but… Anastasia actually remembers some of the events I've dreamed."

A wicked smile spread across Darlene's face. "And exactly what *kind* of memories are we talking about, John? How naughty do they get on a scale of one to steamtastic?"

"*Please* don't go there, D." I wasn't going to mention the *other* dreams I'd had. "The last thing I want is some sort of a voyeuristic back-stage pass to what sex is like as a woman."

"It could be educational," she suggested with a grin.

"I dropped out of community college. Clearly, education isn't a priority."

"Clearly." Juliette smirked.

"Have I mentioned how happy I am that you're all here today?" My attempt at an angry glare was spoiled by the grin I couldn't quite hide. "In fact, maybe we should take this party outside to the beach—"

My phone flickered to life, moments before the now-familiar ring tone started to play. I waved an apology to the others and wandered to the far side of the room.

"What's up, Jason?"

"Dude… where have you been? I called you like… thirty times over the past few days!"

I double-checked my recent calls. "I see one missed call, and it was Thursday. At one in the morning."

"Well, it *felt* like more than that."

Juliette snickered in the background.

"Anyway," the young wolf continued, "where've you been?"

"Busy," I admitted. "Vampire stuff, unfortunately."

I received two sets of rude gestures from the vampires in the room, before they remembered what that *stuff* had entailed. Kayla at least had the grace to look apologetic.

"Say no more, dude. Unless…" Excitement leaked into his voice. "Are we talking fang-babe orgy here? Because I could totally stand to hear more on that subject!"

"Hearing about it is all you'll ever do, furball," called Juliette.

"You're only saying that because I'm a taken man, oh sexy one," he called back. "Or will be, whenever Mr. Mediator gets off his ass and patches things up for me with the ex."

I groaned inwardly. Another thing I'd forgotten about. I needed to start keeping a list. Preferably in digital form. On a brand-new tablet. Which I could then write off as a tax expense…

I put that totally brilliant plan aside for a moment and focused on the conversation. "Sorry, Jason, I haven't had a chance to chat with Carolyn yet."

"No sweat, bro. As long as things are settled by this weekend, we're cool."

"You want me to undo your divorce in the next…" I glanced at my phone to verify that it was, in fact, Wednesday. "…*three days?!?*"

"At this point, it's more like two and a half," opined Juliette.

"Who said anything about undoing the divorce, dude? I just want you to hook the two of us back up."

"That's not a lot of time, Jason, even for someone with my skills." None of the women in the room even bothered to mask their laughter. Jerks. "What's the rush?"

"It's personal."

"Okay," I started to say, but he just steamrolled right over me.

"But you're a bro, so it's cool. Ever since I realized Cara and I belonged together…" His voice lowered to a whisper. "I've been going without."

"Without what?"

"He means no sex, John," said Juliette. "As in, *your* normal day-to-day existence."

"Bingo. I've got mad respect for you, dude… the last week has been *brutal.* I've got no idea how you manage."

"I'm kind of a rock star that way," I said dryly.

"No shit! But I'm not like you, man… sex is *totally* important to me, you know?"

I banged my head against the wall… softly, to avoid damaging anything. In my head, I mean; I wasn't particularly concerned about the wall's well-being.

"I'll talk to her," I finally promised.

"Sweet." And then, after a slight pause. "Today?"

"Not today…. I'm on a case that just went pear-shaped."

From her seat at the table, Juliette perked up. I waved off the silent question.

"Tomorrow then?" Jason was simply not going to give up. "You owe me for all that awesome surveillance I did."

"Right. The *awesome* surveillance." I was going to hurry him off the phone, when an idea popped into my head… a result, no doubt, of the blunt force trauma I'd just inflicted on it. "Actually, why don't you invite Carolyn out to dinner this weekend?"

"On a date? Come on, bro… if it was going to be that easy, why would I need you?"

"It doesn't matter how she responds," I told him. "You just need to get the idea that you're interested—again—out there, so she can think about it. Tomorrow, I'll swing by and chat with her." Out of the corner of my eye, I could see Kayla just shaking her head, holding a whispered conversation with Darlene.

"Sweet! That'll totally work!" At least someone thought it was a good idea. "I guess I'll send you the rest of the pics I took after all. Real talk though; I still think this chick's too old for you to be obsessing over."

"Different strokes for different folks, Jason." I didn't even bother correcting him this time, either about Nepenthe's age, or why I had wanted the surveillance.

"I hear that."

The call ended, and I made my way back over to the table.

"Do you seriously think that's going to work, John?" asked Darlene.

"Were you eavesdropping, D?"

"Nah…" She nudged Kayla with an elbow. "*She* was eavesdropping. I got all my information second-hand."

"I'm not sure that's any less dodgy, morally speaking." I grinned. "As to your question… not really. But Carolyn *did* see something in him at one point, or they wouldn't have agreed to the marriage to begin with. Maybe that spark is still there? Regardless, I promised to try."

"Forget the furball," growled Juliette, "and let's focus on doing our freaking job. What were you saying to that moron about our case? Did Simon call?"

We all turned to stare at Juliette. Since when was *she* the responsible one?

"What?" she protested. "My assets are frozen, remember? I've got expenses. And a donor to keep wooing. The sooner Smith & Middleton starts turning a profit, the better."

"Good point." I paused to organize my thoughts. "Simon hasn't called yet. I was thinking of phoning him instead."

"He would have told us if he had located Graciela, John." Juliette waved a hand dismissively. "No point in micromanaging the help."

"Actually, I need him to *broaden* the search." I explained Valentina's note, and that two more ghosts had gone missing.

"Wait… isn't Marge the ghost who hired you? And by you, I mean us?"

"Yeah. And she and Begoña are number two and three in the White Ladies' hierarchy. Or number three and two… I'm not entirely sure who outranks who. Anyway, we're now missing the top three ghosts in San Diego. The shit is definitely hitting the fan."

"And who exactly is planning to pay us if Marge turns up dead?"

"Dead? Is that really the correct term?" I asked carefully.

"Re-dead. Or ultimately dead. Or… whatever the hell it's called." Her yellow eyes flashed. "Now you've got *me* doing it!"

"Ana and I talked about that last night. Both Simon and Lord Kala say Graciela is still with us. I'm guessing whoever or whatever is doing this will keep Marge and Begoña around too, which means we're not totally screwed yet. But the sooner we find them, the better; rent on our office is due next week."

"And the company reserves can't cover it?"

"You mean the shoebox of cash under my bed?"

"A shoebox, John? Isn't your dad an *accountant?*" asked Darlene.

"Worst. Partner. Ever." growled Juliette.

"It was a joke! The agency totally has a bank account." I took another sip of orange juice and shook my head. "But there's nowhere near enough in it to cover rent."

"Maybe Coffee Bean is hiring," mused the Duchess of Snark.

"Speaking of rent…" Kayla rose to her feet. "Unless either of you needs us, D and I are going to do some apartment-shopping today. Now that I'm leaving the House, we need to find a new place to sleep."

"Don't you have any other properties in the city, K?"

"If I did, I'd have loaned you one as a bachelor's pad, mate." The Aussie shook her head sadly. "You living with your parents has made it *really* difficult for us to get you laid."

"That's why you're a *true* friend." I shot Juliette a look of significance. My partner rolled her eyes and said nothing. My ongoing plan to guilt her into loaning me one of her properties was failing spectacularly. "Anyway, I'll walk you guys out."

Outside, the weather was every bit as nice as I'd anticipated. If it hadn't been for the whole ghost thing, I might very well have spent it at the beach. But some things had to be sacrificed in the pursuit of responsibility.

Sometimes, I was so damn mature it scared me.

Kayla's Jeep was parked just behind my Corolla.

"Are you sure you're okay, John?" Darlene looked up at me, one small arm around my waist.

"Yep." I thought about busting out some jumping jacks to prove it, but sanity reared its head in the nick of time. "Even the scars are starting to fade. This werewolf virus is an amazing thing."

"I'm pretty sure lycanthropy has a limited window of potency, John." Kayla leaned back against the passenger-side door and grinned. "Since you're not furry, your body should have—"

"—driven the infection out of my system. So I've been told. Given last night's craziness, I'm pretty sure my healing is just another side effect of the bond going berserk."

"So why pretend differently?"

"Because otherwise," I answered cheerfully, "I might have to accept that there's a *positive* aspect to having Lucia in my brain. There is no way in hell I'm going to do that."

"That... makes no sense whatsoever."

"That's our John," agreed Darlene fondly.

"Willful ignorance is what I do best."

"Anyway, I wasn't asking about your health, you dork," persisted the pint-sized coed. "It's pretty obvious that you're healed. You even lost a bit of weight."

On cue, I attempted to suck in my gut. Hmm. There did seem to be less of it than I was used to. Apparently, a day or two without food made a difference.

"Then what *did* you want to talk about?"

"How are *you* doing?"

"Oh." I shrugged, my smile dimming. "Okay, more or less. I guess. Kind of had a panic attack when I saw Zorana, but I've been kidnapped quite a few times, and partially eaten once." I swallowed. "This was worse, but I'll get over it."

"And now you're staying with Anastasia… but not, you know, *with her?*"

"She's still not interested." I sighed. "At least I don't think so. Now that my parents are out of town, Valentina and I might head back to Chula Vista anyway. Lucia's sudden and miraculous recovery kind of puts a damper on things."

Darlene studied me for another long moment.

"I'm fine, Auntie D!" I grinned. "And even if I wasn't, I'm too busy to curl up in a ball and cry about it. When this case is over… we'll go get some beer and see how I feel. Deal?"

"Deal."

"Good luck with the apartment hunting. If you guys need help putting together a raid to retrieve your belongings from the House, just let me know. I'm practically a part-time commando at this point."

"You're nowhere near butch enough to be a commando in my army," chuckled Kayla. "But from what Steve tells me, there shouldn't be any problems."

"No?"

"Nope. Duke Barros has offered amnesty to anyone in the House who wishes to leave."

"Seriously? That's… actually, that's kind of brilliant. He's demonstrating just how different he is from Lucia. How many of the People have taken him up on the offer?"

"So far, only a few. I think a lot of us had become disillusioned with Lucia's rule. People are willing to give the new regime a chance."

"But you're still leaving?"

"Yeah. Houses are focused on the long game, John." She stepped closer and dropped a kiss on Darlene's forehead. "I've got to start focusing on my present."

"She's talking about *me*," whispered D.

"You know it, love."

Darlene squeezed me once, and then skipped into Kayla's arms. "Then let's go find ourselves a new home. This *present* can't wait to be unwrapped."

I waved to them both, and watched the Jeep pull away. And if I was just a bit jealous of what they had... well, who wouldn't be?

CHAPTER 46

Once their Jeep had turned the corner, I went back inside. While I reached out to Simon, I'd have Juliette go retrieve my laptop from the office. It was time for us to start detecting the shit out of this case.

Unfortunately, Juliette wasn't in the dining room when I got there. Presumably because of who *was* there.

"How is it that, in a house twice the size of my entire office building, we keep tripping over each other?"

Lucia gave a half-shrug. "There are two dining rooms, but only this one borders a kitchen. And we each require food."

I *hated* it when she used logic.

"Have you seen Juliette?"

"The former Lady Middleton made her way upstairs some time ago, after I informed her that I had removed the lien on her assets."

"You gave her everything back?"

"I never took anything in the first place, Mr. Smith, so a physical transaction such as you are suggesting would be impossible… but yes. You are surprised?"

That the most spiteful non-Blood Witch I knew hadn't tried to punish someone for leaving her? Was this a trick question?

"Yes."

"I believed she would return to my Council when her momentary temper had passed. I was incorrect." She shrugged again. "So, I let her go."

"And Kayla?"

"Nothing I do to her could be worse than the fate she has willingly consigned herself to."

"That sounds an awful lot like…" *A threat*, I was going to say. Except it didn't when I replayed her words in my mind. "Actually, I don't know what it sounds like. Or what you're talking about."

"In as few as two decades, Kayla's human lover will be middle-aged. In four, she will be an old woman, and in six, she will be on death's door, assuming one of the numerous maladies your species suffers from hasn't managed to kill her long before that point. And there will be nothing my former Captain can do other than watch it happen. I do not envy her that experience."

"Maybe all the years between now and then make it worth it," I challenged. Hell, she'd just basically described every successful human relationship ever.

"They do not." There was no malice in Lucia's voice. Seated at the table, she still looked wan and exhausted, like the illness she had caught before her coma was lingering.

I almost felt bad for her.

"Your kind make excellent house pets, my thrall," she said in that same tone of voice, immediately squashing any sort of sympathy that might have started to form, "but that is all. You are tiresome, you are short-lived, and you break far too easily."

"Well, this tiresome and short-lived human will do his best to not break anything on his way out of here. Have fun storming the castle, Lucia."

There was no question that Juliette would have gotten the reference. I liked to think Ana would have also. But Lucia...?

"I *own* the castle, Mr. Smith. When the time comes, I will simply walk in and reclaim it."

Yeeeeeeah... okay.

ooo

I found Juliette in the second of the house's two dining rooms. The spectacular view more than made up for the room's distance from the kitchen. The femmepire had her boots up on Anastasia's antique—and no doubt expensive—table, eyes closed and hands folded in her lap as she balanced on a single leg of the chair.

"Ana will kill you if you scuff up her table," I pointed out, taking a seat across from her.

"It is... possible." She didn't seem perturbed by the possibility. In fact, she was positively laconic. I recognized a food coma when I saw one.

"Well, maybe you should avoid that. We have work to do."

"Do we?" For the first time, she cracked an eye.

"Yup. We need to let Simon know about the other two missing ghosts, so that—"

"Done." She waved one hand dismissively, the chair remaining perfectly balanced despite her motion.

"Done?"

"Yes. I called the number he gave us. No answer, but I left a message."

"Well, cool. Hopefully, he'll have a location for us."

"Yep." The partially open eye slid back shut again.

"While you become one with your chair, I'm going to head to the office to pick up my laptop. I might as well use the downtime to go through Jason's stalkerazzi shots."

"Also done."

"Really? You downloaded and reviewed his pictures?"

"Gods, no. I still have *some* sense of self-worth. But I grabbed your laptop this morning. And left it on the dresser when I arrived." She nodded in the direction of my temporary bedroom.

"My *bedroom* dresser?"

"Duh."

"This morning? Before I woke up?"

She didn't even bother replying this time.

"Are you sure it was my room?" After Lucia's attempted feeding, my senses had been on high alert. There was no way Juliette could have come into the room without waking me.

For the first time, the femmepire opened both eyes, if only to give me an annoyed glare. "Of course I'm sure, you moron. You were spooning a pillow and drooling like a senile Great Dane." She shook her head, but again, the chair didn't even wobble. "Aren't detectives supposed to be masters of observation? Are you telling me you didn't see the laptop bag on the dresser *right next to the door?*"

"It was a rough night."

"So you keep saying."

I struggled for an appropriately biting reply, but nothing came to mind. I headed back out of the dining room and down to the bedroom.

The laptop was exactly where the femmepire had said it would be. As the only item on that dresser, it was also virtually impossible to miss, and would have been directly in my line of sight when I left the room that morning.

Damn it, I was starting to think I *sucked* at my job.

I stalked back to the dining room.

"And?"

"It was on the dresser."

"Moron," she said again.

"I'm kind of starting to wonder. What are you doing up here anyway? Hiding from Lucia?"

"Hiding? Please. She knows where to find me if she wants to throw down."

I failed to stifle a laugh. Juliette was many things, but badass was not one of them. Not compared to a vampire elder anyway.

"Seriously," I persisted, "what *are* you doing up here?"

"I'm waiting."

"For what?"

She swung her feet off the table, bringing the chair back down onto all four legs, and leaned forward to look me dead in the eye.

"For you to figure out what the *hell* we do next."

"Isn't that the *junior* partner's job?" I grinned.

"I'm already the brains, the brawn, and the beauty of this agency, little bird. The sad truth is that you have only one thing I don't."

I inadvertently glanced down.

"Okay… *two* things," she allowed, with a roll of her eyes. "Although, strictly speaking, it's more like one-and-a-half. And nobody even knows for sure if that half works anymore."

"That's not what your mom said last night," I shot back lamely, before remembering that her mother was presumably both still alive and—if the daughter was anything to go by—terrifying as all hell.

"I'm sure she was too busy laughing to bother with words." The femmepire held up one hand, the index finger and thumb an infinitesimally small distance from each other. "She did send along some visual aids though."

My ego was in full retreat. I decided there was no shame in quitting the field. "So, what was the other thing?"

"I'm sorry?"

"You said I had something *else* that you lacked," I reminded her.

"Oh." She sobered. Marginally. "Experience."

"I *have* had a handful of girlfriends," I admitted, "although most of them were back in high school or college. But you're like a hundred years old… and just slept with someone you met *yesterday*. I'm guessing you are way, way ahead of me on the experience front."

"That's not what I—" Juliette swallowed her words, and her golden eyes glittered dangerously. "Are you calling me *easy*, John?"

"You're the one who brought up experience."

"I meant job experience!"

"Oh. Right." I cleared my throat and returned to the table. "Well, there's a reason I'm the senior partner."

"I'm starting to doubt that," she sniped, "but this once, I'm happy to lean on your experience."

"Great. So… what now?"

"First, I'm going to beat you to death with your shoe. Then, I'm going to go find Angel and try to forget this conversation ever happened." She fixed me with a mildly scary glare. "Or the so-called senior partner could get off his overfed ass and decide what our next step is in closing the case!"

"Let's not threaten the dude who was just tortured, okay?" I
held up my hands defensively. "Don't you think I *want* to solve the
case? I promised Valentina I would help!"

"Which one is Valentina again?"

"Dark hair, white nightgown, bloody chest wound, haunts my
house? Seriously, Juliette; you were with me that very first night we
saw her!"

"Oh… right. *Excuse me* if I don't bother keeping track of
your loser friends. I have a life, remember?"

"Yes, a life spent in fruitful pursuit of baristas." I rolled my
eyes. "Until Simon gets back to us, I don't know what we can do."

"And so, we wait."

I finished booting up my laptop. "If you're bored, you could
always help me review the pictures Jason took of Nepenthe over the
past week."

"I don't think I could *ever* be that bored."

ooo

"Yet another picture of a butt." Juliette scowled.

"He's nothing if not consistent."

"That one might be a guy, actually."

"Really?" I took a closer look. "Huh."

It had taken a grand total of sixteen minutes for Juliette to get
bored enough to join me in looking at Jason's photos.

"This Nepenthe woman may be the least interesting person
alive," said Juliette. From what little we'd been able to glean between
gratuitous ass shots, Nepenthe had spent her time in San Diego doing
terribly mundane things; shopping at a hardware store; eating at
Panera; meditating on the piers at Seaport Village. She was equal parts
yogini and tourist. "I can't believe you're into her."

"I'm not into her!" I protested. "I wanted to make sure that she and her coven were on the level, so I didn't end up getting kidnapped *again.*"

"Right."

"And yes, I'm aware that I ended up getting kidnapped anyway… but *not by witches*! It's hardly *my* fault that your species blows!"

"Even so, I'm pretty sure this literal witch hunt of yours is a massive waste of time." She rose out of her chair to address a non-existent audience. "Ladies and gentlemen… come one, come all… Watch as a mostly mundane woman buys yoga supplies! Witness her meeting another sad sack human for lunch! Marvel as she devours the entirety of her pita sandwich! And a bag of potato chips!"

I rolled my eyes. "Like I said, I was just trying to cover my bases—" I paused in mid-sentence, and eyed one of the photos that Juliette had just mocked. "Wait. I know that guy."

"Friend from the local bowling alley?"

"Don't badmouth bowling," I warned. Where *had* I seen that dude? He had slightly greying hair that made him look distinguished, open and unguarded brown eyes, and a face that practically screamed honesty…

Oh.

"I guess Nepenthe wanted to cover *her* bases too."

"Say what?"

"This guy," I said, tapping my screen, "is Caleb Van Stahl. San Diego's other mediator."

"He's not terrible looking for an old guy."

"If you say so." Jason had barely managed to catch both Nepenthe and Caleb in the frame, but I looked down at the witch's profile with a sense of betrayal.

Truthfully, Caleb probably *was* a better liaison between the coven and many of the other groups in San Diego but still... Nepenthe had made it sound like *I* was the linchpin to her democratic ambitions. Maybe Caleb and I could *both* be linchpins? Two good dudes doing their best in a difficult job for troublesome clients?

Yeah, that sounded pretty accurate.

"You never did tell me what Nepenthe met with you about."

"She wanted me to float the idea of an elected council to Lucia. Sort of a supernatural, San Diego-based version of the United Nations."

Juliette snickered. "She wanted *you* to suggest *that* to *Lucia?*"

It sounded even more ridiculous in hindsight.

"Coven leadership must be an inherited position," decided the femmepire. "There's no way someone that stupid could rise to power on their own."

CHAPTER 47

IN WHICH PICTURES TELL A THOUSAND WORDS,
BUT FEW OF THEM BEAR REPEATING

The number of pictures Jason had taken would have been impressive if their quality had been even close to mediocre. As it was, I was starting to think the werewolf had gotten the better end of our deal. I wasn't the world's best mediator, but I wasn't worthless either… and that was more than could be said of the werewolf's photography skills.

"This is a waste of time," I finally decided.

"You think?" Juliette wasn't looking at the screen anymore. Her boots were back up on the table, and she was gazing out at the Pacific.

I rubbed my eyes and wandered over to the balcony, feeling frustrated. Had any of the great detectives in literature ever wasted a day doing nothing but waiting for a phone call? I suspected the answer to that was a resounding no.

What would Holmes have done in my shoes? I was pretty sure he would have disproven the existence of ghosts entirely and then delivered conclusive evidence that the supposed kidnapping was instead a cover for an underground opium smuggling ring… all without ever leaving his flat.

Which didn't help me at all, to be honest.

But it did get me thinking.

"I've been letting this whole ghost thing screw with my process."

"You have a process? Does it involve beer?"

"Obviously." I eyed the femmepire momentarily, to see if she had an actual point. "Anyway, why should I treat this any differently than a normal case, just because the people involved happen to be non-corporeal?"

"I think you just answered your own question."

"Nonsense." I paced in a circuit around the table, trying to think. "Whatever else holds true, the central questions remain the same. As always."

"If this is where you tell me about your one and only journalism class for the nine hundredth time, I'm going to throw you off the balcony."

"I wouldn't dream of it," I lied. "But if we *do* approach this as a regular case, what are the facts?"

"Multiple women are missing, and our only hope of finding them is a prince of the undead whose pinkies fell off five decades ago?"

"Not super helpful, but accurate. Three women are missing. That's the *what*. And we know the *when* too; Graciela disappeared at least a month ago, and Marge and Begoña went missing in the past week. So, all we're lacking are the where, the why, and the who."

"And the how."

I stopped in my tracks and favored Juliette with a proud look. "You *have* been listening!"

"Any other day, I would knock that expression off of your face with a tire iron," she warned me with a smirk.

"Then I'm glad you're feeling more merciful than usual." I grinned. "I'll send Angel a thank you card."

The femmepire's laughter was a delicate thing, entirely at odds with both her persona and appearance. "So, we know the what and the when, but not the how or any of the remaining W's of journalism. What does that do for us?"

"It gives us a starting point." I dropped back into my chair, thinking furiously. "And raises some other questions, too. Like why there was such a big gap between when Graciela was taken and the others this week."

"Maybe whoever is doing it was out of town a while?"

"Could be. Or maybe they wanted to lie low after the first kidnapping. Or were taking time to improve their technique."

"Or had to mine uranium for their nuclear-powered ghost trapping device." Juliette shook her head. "Or were waiting for the moon to tell them to strike again. Or any of a billion other things. We don't know what the pattern means. We don't even know if there *is* a pattern!"

"Yeah, that's pretty much what I said to Ana last night. The *when* is suspicious, but we don't have enough information to put it in context. So let's talk motive instead. When it was just Graciela missing, I thought this might be a personal vendetta. You know, like maybe someone she wronged in her mortal life became a ghost themselves and came looking for revenge?"

"I think I saw that movie."

"But with *three* victims, that angle seems less likely."

"Unless the vendetta was against all three women, rather than just Graciela."

"Or against the White Ladies as a group." I pondered that for a bit. "But this doesn't really *feel* personal. Personal is messy, right? And emotional? It leaves a trail, which is the one thing we don't have. This feels… organized. And stealthy."

"So, we're looking for a band of ghost-nabbing ninjas with a dispassionate ambivalence toward spirits. Got it." Juliette pretended to search the room for the aforementioned ninjas.

"Hilarious. Remind me to double the salary I'm currently not paying you."

"That would hurt, if I weren't about to be rich again." Juliette flashed a superior smile in my direction. "If it's not personal, what is it?"

The obvious answer was *impersonal*, but Juliette's eyes were already narrowing before I could say it.

"Well, it's probably not about money either, given the lack of a ransom note and the nature of the victims. Which only leaves one thing."

"So, you *do* suspect political motivations now?"

Both Juliette and I looked to where Anastasia had, for all intents and purposes, materialized in the doorway. Juliette's boots dropped from the table to the floor in a blur. I'd have to remember to give her a hard time about that later.

"What are you doing here, Anastasia?" asked the spiky-haired femmepire.

"It is my home," the other pointed out calmly. "And I have always enjoyed watching Mr. Smith's mind work."

"Sucks for you that it happens so rarely then."

"Worst. Partner. Ever." I mimicked under my breath, earning a smirk from Juliette. I turned back to Anastasia. "And yeah. I've been thinking about what you said. Especially since all three spirits are way up there in the Ladies' command structure."

"It's not *another* freaking coup, is it?" Juliette had joined me by the balcony, a destination that just happened to put the dining room table between her and the other femmepire. "I think the city's filled its quota on coups for the year."

"They seem like a vampire specialty, anyway. Besides," I added, remembering the scene on Ghost Hill, "the other ladies were genuinely upset at Graciela's disappearance. I can't see any of them wanting this."

"Which leaves one of the other species of the city seeking to displace the White Ladies in San Diego's hierarchy."

"Like we were talking about last night." I nodded to Anastasia. "But who stands to gain? Who is currently number four in the so-called rankings?"

"It's not quite so linear as that, Mr. Smith," said the femmepire, "but I can draft a list of groups positioned to ascend in the event of the White Ladies' dissolution."

"That would be fantastic. It's hard solving a case when the suspect pool is *everyone*. Maybe we could also filter out the people on that list who are incapable of managing something like this?"

"Incapable of kidnapping ghosts?" asked Juliette. "Isn't that everyone? Spirits phase through walls and people and whatever the hell else gets in their way, little bird. Ghost kidnapping just isn't a thing. It's impossible."

I sighed. "That's what I keep getting stuck on. It's impossible... and yet it clearly isn't, because someone has done just that, and not just once, but three times! But how? Lord Kala and Simon both said it themselves; ghosts are pure energy. How do you trap energy?"

"Did I mention my nuclear-powered ghost-trapping device?"

"You did. Which would have been helpful if such a thing actually existed." I could feel some memory nibbling away at my brain. But what *was* it?

"You have something, Mr. Smith?"

"One sec."

I realized, after a long pause, that I had just casually dismissed a woman who was both the deadliest assassin I would ever meet and the femmepire that made my insides mush.

"Sorry…"

"Don't be." Ana's voice was quiet but warm. "Focus on the matter at hand."

That's exactly what I was doing. Something in what I had said to Juliette had partially triggered that other memory. But what? Someone doing the impossible? Kala? Simon? What?

Wait.

It was like a light switch had been flipped in my brain. The memory I'd been seeking was right there, waiting like a personally engraved invitation or a plate of fine Italian dessert.

"Oh shit." I turned back to the computer and clicked through Jason's photos.

"Are you going to fill us in on your little revelation or should we just stand around looking gorgeous?" asked Juliette.

"A little bit of both would be awesome, really. Something Kala and Simon said reminded me of a conversation from last weekend. I mean… ghosts are just energy, right?"

"You've said that already. Like twenty million times." Juliette was getting impatient.

"Well, I have it on good authority," I continued, "that if you want to manipulate energy, there's only one group in town worth talking to."

Silence fell as the others pondered my words. I clicked to another photo.

"You don't mean the witches, do you? *Witches*, John?"

"On this, I must side with Lady Middleton."

"Don't do me any favors."

"Despite what you've seen in television shows and movies," Anastasia continued, "there has never been a Merlin or a Gandalf in our world. Human magic is fragile and unsuitable for more than the occasional illusion."

"One of the witches I met last weekend transformed a door handle into a snake. Venomous bite and all. The thing trapped me in the bathroom for like half an hour."

"Which part of *illusion* did you *not* understand, little bird?"

Instead of replying, I tapped my temple, and gave Ana a significant look. She nodded, her expression pensive.

"Mr. Smith's gift shields him from illusion and any magic that affects his perceptions or mind. The past year has proven this conclusively. If he saw a snake, then it *was* a snake. And that suggests the coven's power is greater than reported. Well-reasoned."

"I'm not saying they *did* kidnap the ghosts. They're just the only group I can think of who might be capable." Which sucked, because Nepenthe had seemed like a genuinely nice person. And had promised to help remove my freaking bond in less than a month.

For free!

I really, really hoped Simon came up with another viable suspect, because accusing the coven of ghostnapping was going to ruin my only shot at evicting Lucia from my brain.

I clicked to another photo.

"What exactly are you looking for, Mr. Smith?" Anastasia wandered over to stand behind me, close enough that both her scent and presence were distracting as hell.

"I've had Jason, from the Pack, following Nepenthe around. She has yet to return to Temecula. So, if she *is* our mysterious kidnapper…"

"Then the spirits' prison might be somewhere in these photos."

"Exactly."

Unfortunately, the pictures were, as previously mentioned, out of focus, poorly framed, and—all too often—of someone other than Nepenthe. A solid twenty-five minutes later, we were no closer to finding anything of value.

Luckily, that was when my phone finally rang.

CHAPTER 48

"Hello?"

"What's up, kid? Got your message."

"Simon! Thanks for calling back."

Both Anastasia and Juliette perked up.

"At Zombies-R-Us, service is our middle name."

"Shouldn't it be *R*?" asked Juliette rhetorically.

I shushed her, but it appeared that—unlike werewolves and vampires—zombies didn't have super hearing.

"Still no luck on Graciela," Simon continued, "but those other two chickadees… *them* I can help you with."

Thank God *one* of us was competent. "What do you have?"

"Remember how I told you I caught a whiff of energy earlier this week that could have been Graciela? Well, sometime around three this morning, I *definitely* sensed your two other ghosts. Same general area even, I think."

"Why would you be able to positively identify Marge and Begoña by their energy, but not Graciela?"

"Probably because the energy pulse was a shitload stronger. That first one was so weak I couldn't get any sort of bead on it. Beats the hell out of me why though. Unlife didn't come with an instruction manual."

It wasn't the home run I'd been hoping for, but it was something, at least. "You said you thought it might be in the same general area? Any chance you could point me in a direction?"

"I can do better than that, kid. I can give you an address."

"You can pinpoint a location from a single, momentary energy signature?" That was so freaking cool.

"Well... no. That *would* be pretty killer though." Simon fell quiet for a moment, as if pondering the idea. "I sent some of my friends to check things out."

"Friends?"

"I *do* have friends, asshole."

"I just wanted to thank them for their assistance. Besides, any friend of yours is a potential client of mine."

"Ha! You and me... we're businessmen," said Simon, all traces of irritation gone from his phlegmy voice. "If you want to say thanks, just tip over your garbage can the next time you take it to the curb."

"Uhm... what?"

"They're rats."

I let my silence speak for itself.

"The city's crawling with them, y'know, although it's nothing like back on the East Coast."

"And you make friends with them?" I hadn't—really—been bothered by Simon's own slowly degrading form, but... this was disgusting.

"Not the live ones, of course."

"Zombie rats?" Just like that, it was kind of cool again.

"You betcha. Anyway, as I was saying, I sent them out as rangefinders."

I must have looked confused, as Anastasia clarified quietly. "He checked the location of their respective energy signatures and compared them against that of the Ladies."

"So, you were able to determine the origin of the energy spikes from this morning by measuring it against the position of your vermin hordes?" I gave Anastasia a thumbs up and smile of gratitude for the save.

"Vermin hordes. Huh. You've got a way with words, kid. And yeah. Looks like the signal came from up in Sorrento Valley. Any further and I doubt I'd have sensed it at all."

Sorrento Valley…. Sorrento Valley… why did that seem familiar? I scrolled back through Jason's photos.

"The place you're looking for is an office building. My vermin hordes couldn't get inside, which means it ain't no normal tower. Near as I can tell from Google, the place you're looking for used to be—"

And there it was.

"Qualcomm's old headquarters on Morehouse," I finished for him. The tech giant had gone bankrupt several years earlier, and many of their buildings in the area remained vacant.

"How the hell did you know that?" Simon's voice was distinctly unamused.

"I've been working the case from a different angle," I told him, looking at the crystal-clear photo of Nepenthe entering the tower in question, "but your evidence was what brought it all together."

"Well… good," he offered, slightly mollified. "I'd hate to think you were trying to back out of our deal."

"Smith men keep their words, dude. I'll probably be a bit busy in the short term, but you can reach me at this number when you want to call in that favor."

"Will do. Say hi to your vampire squeeze when you see her."

"She's not—" I started to say, but the zombie had already ended our call. On my laptop, I brought up the address for the tower in question. Google Maps helpfully informed me that the trip would take slightly under half an hour in current traffic conditions.

Juliette was the first to break the silence. "I don't know what's more surprising… that Simon actually came through, or that Jason's so-called surveillance ended up being marginally useful."

"I never doubted either one of them."

"Sure you didn't. So, what now? Send a kill squad to hit the warehouse?"

Anastasia and I both looked at her.

"Duchess, where are we going to find a kill squad?"

"Well, the House—damn it, I forgot." She shot me a yellow-eyed glare. "You picked a hell of a time to cost Lucia her powerbase, little bird."

"Why is everyone blaming *me* for the coup? Need I remind you that I was chained up and being tortured at the time?"

Juliette rolled her eyes. "Are you going to use that as an excuse for *everything*?"

I looked at her, my mouth moving without any coherent sounds coming out, before I noticed her grin.

"Maybe. Do you think the IRS would accept it as a valid reason to not pay taxes?"

"You should try," said the femmepire sweetly. "What's the worst they could do to you?"

Anastasia glanced between the two of us, and shook her head slowly, but none of the exasperation she was clearly feeling made its way to her face.

"Despite the situation at the House, you do have other allies to call upon. Aid from the Pack and Lord Beel-Kasan might prove invaluable."

"Good point. I need to call Carolyn anyway about Jason. Also, I'm not entirely sure if the Pack has voted yet on helping us."

"*Voted.*" Juliette spoke the word like it had four letters. "Once again, one of your mediations comes back to bite us in the ass."

"You prefer a different form of government? A monarchy, perhaps?" I asked sweetly.

The only response was a swiftly raised middle finger.

"If one of you could speak with Jee Sun about Bill, I'll try to get us some furry muscle for tonight."

Juliette looked to Anastasia, but the older femmepire showed no sign of rising from her seat any time soon. "I guess I'll do it," my junior partner muttered, sweeping out of the dining room with a vaguely injured air.

"Do you think we're on the right track?" I asked the lady of the house.

"I do, but there are a great many questions that remain unanswered."

"Like where the witches got the power to kidnap ghosts, and why they're doing it?"

"Precisely."

"I might know the answer to that second question, actually." I rehashed the conversation I'd had with Nepenthe over dinner at Bencotto. "Maybe she thinks the best way to create a new government is by toppling the current one?"

Where had I heard something similar?

Oh, right; from Lucia, when she turned down Nepenthe's proposal.

Well, shit.

"It stands to reason." Anastasia's words were light, her tone distracted. "Bencotto, you say? How was it?"

"The food was good. The company was decent—which just proves that I'm the worst judge of character *ever*—but I'd rather have been there with you."

Ana bowed her head, momentarily hiding her features behind a curtain of auburn silk. The urge to reach out and touch that hair was almost overpowering.

"Next weekend then?" she at last suggested, the glint of jade the only sign that she had raised her eyes to mine.

"Huh?" My eloquence continued to amaze even me.

"Unless you would prefer not to …?"

"There is no eventuality, world, or dimension where that would be the case," I assured her, unable to restrain the smile that was bubbling up inside of me. "But I'm really confused. Again."

Cool fingers caressed my cheek in a lightning-quick move that I couldn't even see, yet alone react to. "It is a surprisingly good look on you, Mr. Smith."

CHAPTER 49

I sat in the dining room after Anastasia left, trying to figure out what had just happened. In the span of a week, the elegant femmepire had returned from a six-month-long father-killing odyssey and, in sequential order, shut down any possibility of a romantic relationship between us, rescued me from torture, made out with me in one of her bedrooms, reiterated that we would never be a couple, and then, without further prompting, suggested we go out on a date.

Confused didn't even begin to cover it.

My mother had always said that if something seemed too good to be true, it probably was. But she had also warned me not to look a gift horse in the mouth.

As far as pithy pieces of advice went, those seemed diametrically opposed.

I shook my head. The mysteries of my increasingly perplexing relationship would have to wait. For now, I had three ghosts that needed rescuing. I fished my wonderphone back out, and scrolled through my call history, when one of those calls caught my eye.

What did the pixies have to do with all of this? Was Kristin a willing accomplice or a dupe like I had been? And was there any way to find out without revealing that I was on to Nepenthe's plan?

Sort of on to her plan.

Okay… on to the fact that there *was* a plan, even if the particulars of that plan were escaping me at the moment.

I shook my head again. I couldn't afford to risk tipping off the enemy, and I had zero faith in my own ability to construct a believable means of fishing for the truth.

With a sigh, I dialed Carolyn instead.

"John? I was just about to call you!"

"You were?" I hadn't spent enough time around Carolyn to be able to read her moods over the phone, but something in her tone worried me.

"Yeah. Did you have something to do with my idiot ex asking me out for dinner?"

I hesitated. My inability to lie well was notorious, but part of that was my complete and utter lack of a poker face, something that wasn't an issue on the phone. Which meant I could for once take the easy way out and—

"Yeah," I heard myself admitting. "Sort of."

Damn it. This was my parents' fault. If they hadn't provided me with a stable home and quality upbringing…

"What in the goddess' name were you thinking?" Carolyn could growl with the best of her species.

I sighed. "It was his idea, really, so I'm not entirely sure how much thought was involved."

"Is this some sort of bizarre practical joke…"

"It's not," I assured her.

"But why would he ask me out? We *just* got divorced!"

"Tell me about it. And that divorce nearly got us all killed." It occurred to me, as my mouth continued replying on autopilot, that I was not being a particularly good wingman for my dudebro quasi-friend.

"Exactly. Is he insane? Is it possible his bloodline succumbs earlier than the rest of us?"

I hadn't considered that possibility, but Jason hadn't seemed insane. Just... Jason.

"I think he just misses you."

"Oh." It was her turn to sigh. "Well, I know the feeling. But we've already been through this once. I'm not getting married again. Ever."

"Nobody's saying you have to." And just like that, I had figured out a plan of attack. Conversationally speaking, anyway. Whatever anyone else might think, I knew in that moment that I was a born mediator.

Kind of.

"What do you mean?"

"Let me ask you this; do you still love him, even a bit?"

"Love might be a little strong..."

I waited.

"Maybe. But we already saw that love wasn't enough the first time around, John."

"Of course not," I agreed, from my position of absolute inexperience. "It takes commitment and compromise and lots of other words starting with c."

"Right. And if we'd had any of that, we wouldn't have almost gotten the Pack destroyed."

I winced and changed tacks. "You know I interviewed you both as part of the mediation process, right?"

"Given that I was part of that process? Duh."

"Sarcasm does not become you, Carolyn. Anyway, I learned that both of you were pretty happy with your first few months of marriage."

"Obviously. We spent most of the time with our clothes off."

Not an image I needed in my head. "And it was only later that things became untenable."

Untenable was an awesome word. *Very* mediator-like.

"I lived through all of this, John. Is there a point?"

"Yeah. Things only seemed to go to hell once Jason's so-called friends from New Mexico arrived. And we know now that they were sent to San Diego for just that purpose."

"Oh."

"I'm not saying you and Jason would work any better the second time," I admitted, "or that you aren't perfectly justified in rejecting the whole idea, but he seems serious about starting a family, and he seems serious about wanting it to be with you."

"How can you be sure?"

"I can't. Not really. But it's the impression I got."

"Huh." Carolyn packed a lot of emotion into that one syllable. "Well, that's something to ponder, I guess. Thanks for talking to me about it."

"No problem. It's not actually why I called though."

"It isn't?"

"I wanted to see where the Pack was on the whole *help John Smith search for a missing ghost* proposition."

"Oh, that. Sorry, John. We didn't make it that far down our agenda at last week's meeting. My motion to ban motorcycles in favor of environmentally friendly electric bicycles caused some controversy."

"Seriously?"

"The Earth is all we have, John." Having delivered her environmentally friendly rebuke, Carolyn's voice softened. "But I promise we'll take a vote tomorrow. In the meantime, a few of us *have* been keeping our noses out, at least. I'm just not in the position to make it a Pack-wide mandate anymore."

I swallowed a curse. Juliette was right. Even my positive actions were doomed to haunt me for all eternity.

"I take it you haven't made any progress in your missing person case?"

"Actually, I think we have. We think the Temecula coven was responsible and have an address to check out."

"The witches? Are you sure? Nepenthe seemed pretty cool."

"You've spoken with her?"

"Sure. She stopped by to see our own democracy in action. Said she wanted to implement that sort of government on a wider scale, with us as a model. The warlock was a bit of a dick, but it's not like we don't have a fair number of those in the Pack too."

"Thomas is a witch, actually."

"But he's a guy!"

"I don't get it either. Anyway, Nepenthe said the same thing to me, but I've found evidence that suggests she was lying."

"That's a bummer." Carolyn sighed. "I guess it was too much to hope for. So, you're going to send some of Lucia's killers to wipe out the coven?"

There may have been a hint of reproach there. The vampires had come within a hair's breadth of doing the same to the Pack.

"I wish. There's been a change of leadership at the House. Lucia, Ana, and I are currently persona non grata."

"*Another* coup? What is the deal with vampires, anyway?"

"Too much iron in their blood," I opined.

"Must be. But wait…" Carolyn's voice grew suspicious. "Why are you calling me then?"

"Well, first to let you know what happened." This time at least, the white lie came out smoothly, proper upbringing be damned. "Given that the Pack has an alliance with the House, I thought you should know."

"Our alliance was with Queen Lucia's House," Carolyn pointed out. "If she's no longer in charge, then I'm pretty sure that alliance is null and void."

"Take it as a warning from a friend then." Given that the Pack had been forced into that alliance, I wasn't shocked to hear her jumping at a reason to vacate it.

"What are you going to do about the witches?"

"That's the second reason I called."

∘∘∘

"The Pack is in," I announced to Juliette.

"Seriously? How did you pull that off?" For once, the femmepire looked impressed. My ego swelled to three or four times its usual size before I remembered all the qualifications that had come with Carolyn's agreement.

"Technically it's not the *whole* Pack," I admitted. "Volunteers only, but Carolyn said we'd get at least a few willing participants. It's that time of the month again, and some of the dudes are looking to blow off steam."

Carolyn herself had *not* volunteered, but just convincing her to ask around for help had been a monumental achievement.

"Given how tough a single Infected can be," Juliette mused, "a few of them should be plenty for taking out one little coven."

"Especially with Bill batting clean-up," I agreed.

"Yeah, about that..." The femmepire ran a hand irritably through her short, spiky hair.

"Seriously?" I shook my head. "You had *one job*, Duchess."

"It's not my fault that San Diego's insane demigod of nightmares is—yet again—nowhere to be found!"

I frowned. "That seems to be happening a lot lately."

"Tell me about it. His creepy Korean ward didn't seem concerned, but she also didn't know where he was. All she had to say was—"

"Gehenna go boom?"

"Exactly."

"That's been happening a lot too. Whatever the hell it means." I sighed. "It was anyone's guess whether Bill would have gotten involved anyway. You, me, and a bunch of wolves will have to do."

"You're forgetting someone."

"Who?"

"Anastasia? You know, the cyborg sent from the future to slaughter Lucia's enemies while rejecting your weak sauce attempts at romance?"

"Sadly," came Anastasia's cool voice, in another moment of perfect timing, "I will be unable to accompany you."

"Seriously?" If Juliette was troubled by Anastasia's appearance, she didn't let it show. "How come?"

"Because she has to protect Lucia," I reasoned through the sinking pit in my stomach. While Juliette's description had been as unflattering as it was untrue, Anastasia *was* the most capable individual I knew. Not having her along, even just as a sort of safety blanket, worried me.

"Precisely." Anastasia met my gaze from the doorway, dismissing the other femmepire as if she did not even exist. "Her

Majesty is not recovering as quickly as I would have expected. Should Barros discover our location, I am not convinced that she would be able to defend herself."

"As far as I can tell, his coup was a smashing success. Maybe he's satisfied with having claimed the House?"

"It is possible."

"But you can't take the risk."

"I cannot."

"I get it."

"You do?" Juliette looked from me to Anastasia. "What-freaking-ever! For someone who chewed my ass out for leaving John in the middle of the oh-so-deadly territory of Chula-freaking-Vista, you have a lot of nerve, Anastasia."

"It's fine, Juliette," I assured the fuming femmepire. "I really do get it. Even better…"

"Yes?"

"I have a plan."

CHAPTER 50
IN WHICH THE PLAN GOES SIDEWAYS

For most of my life, Qualcomm had been the biggest name in San Diego's tech industry, a corporate behemoth that grew to occupy at least a floor of almost every office building in Sorrento Valley. When the company went under, the void left behind had been every bit as big. Two years later, very little of that suddenly plentiful office space had been filled.

The campus on Morehouse, one of the oldest of the former Qualcomm buildings, had actually been scheduled for partial demolition, but our local government's usual blend of incompetence and corruption meant none of that work had begun yet. The specter of the company-that-was loomed above us like a five-story monument to corporate hubris.

"What a dump," Juliette decided.

Yeah. Or that.

We'd parked my Corolla down the hill to keep its still-pristine paint job well out of the potential combat zone. Now, the two of us crouched across the street from the empty office tower, awaiting our werewolf backup.

Some of us waited more patiently than others.

"What the hell is taking so long? Tell Carolyn to get her puppies here before we all die of old age."

"It was a miracle that she agreed to ask for volunteers at all; I'm not pushing my luck. Besides, you've got centuries before you have to worry about dying of old age." I wrapped my jacket more tightly around me to ward off the surprisingly cool afternoon air.

"Boredom, then. I should have known—" She cut off as three shadows crept up the hill toward us. I didn't recognize the two in the back, although each was the size of a small Volkswagen, but leading the way, mustache and all, was Emilio, one of Carolyn and Jason's most trusted wolves.

The pot-bellied werewolf grunted in our direction before turning his mustache to regard our destination in grim silence.

"Sorry we're late, everyone," offered one of Emilio's companions—long-haired, unshaven, with a jaw like a pit bull. "Traffic on the 805 was a bitch."

"When isn't it?" asked the third wolf. "Where do we think the witches will be?"

"No clue," I admitted. "I'm hoping to use your noses for that."

"Probably at the top," Longhair decided morosely. "I shouldn't have done legs yesterday."

"Legs?"

"At the gym. You lift?" He took a closer look at me. "Never mind."

"Once the adrenaline hits, yesterday won't matter," said the other wolf with a wide smile. "This is going to be just like the Raid. I can't wait to kick ass."

"We're here to find the White Ladies, figure out what is holding them, and get them out," I reminded them. "If we can do so without bloodshed, so much the better."

Emilio's grunt did a masterful job of expressing how unlikely that eventuality seemed to him.

"No problem," said Longhair. "We know how to seek and destroy."

"Definitely," said the third werewolf.

"Great," said Juliette. "You guys go first."

○○○

With the electricity long since cut to the building, not even the emergency exit signs were lit, but I was relieved to find my eyes adapting quickly to the darkness. Whatever the hell was going on with my body—left-over lycanthropy virus, hyperactive vampire bond, or something else—I had to admit it came with perks.

The downside of night vision reared its head when the three wolves shrugged out of their clothes, revealing way too much in the way of dude-parts for my comfort. Behind me, Juliette hummed appreciatively, but before she could make her usual inappropriate comment, one of the weres was shifting.

Less than a minute later, an enormous shaggy wolf was standing where the man had been. I glanced over at the other two men.

"You guys staying human?"

"Nah," said Longhair. "Matt went full wolf because that's where our senses are sharpest. But Emilio and I... we'll be ready for mayhem."

With those words, he and Emilio both shifted into the hybrid form I'd seen only a few times before. Familiarity, I decided, did not make that form any less terrifying.

Or any less naked, really.

Emilio cracked his neck loudly, and yawned, revealing a mouthful of very sharp teeth.

"Alright." My words were hushed. "Let's do this."

Matt picked up a scent almost immediately, which was a bit of a relief. If the building had been empty, after all the drama and buildup… well, my reputation was already lousy enough as it was.

We followed him away from the lobby and down a long hall to the stairwell. Emilio nudged the door open, and Matt padded in and up the first flight of stairs.

"Looks like you were right," I told Longhair.

Five stories made for a lot of stairs. Even if I'd been in shape, I was pretty sure the combination of tension and adrenaline would have left me exhausted by the time we reached the top.

Since I *wasn't* in shape, I expected to be wiped out by the second floor. Instead, I made it almost to the fourth. This super-soldier serum didn't suck.

On each floor, Matt stuck his snout out of the stairwell, checking for scent traces, but the path that we were following hadn't forked even once. Lobby to stairs. Stairs to top floor. The coven was almost making this easy.

Finally, we made it to the top. Matt paused for a moment, as if confused, and then slunk down the hall to our left, gliding from shadow to shadow so that even my unexpectedly passable night vision had difficulty spotting him.

The rest of us crept after, with varying amounts of stealth, down the hall and into a double-doored conference room. I reached one hand into my jacket pocket and gripped the hilt of Ana's lumpy knife. This was feeling less like the Raid and more like one of the way-too-many Amityville Horror remakes.

"That's close enough, I think."

I recognized Thomas' nasal whine even as lights flared to life, temporarily blinding me.

"I'd say it's nice to see you again, John," the witch continued, "but it's really not."

"The feeling is mutual, Tommy," I replied through gritted teeth. Around me, I could hear the others moving to encircle the witch I still couldn't see. "But if you release Graciela and the others now, I may be able to convince them not to kill your pathetic poser ass for this."

The room was slowly starting to swim into view. The hulking dark shapes of Emilio and Longhair had flanked the diminutive form of what could only be Thomas, while Matt was creeping up on all fours behind the witch.

"That's *one* option," Thomas agreed. "Except the ghosts clearly aren't here. Aren't you supposed to be a detective? Now, if you—"

Whatever Thomas had been planning to say—and I was betting it would have been both obnoxious and self-aggrandizing—cut off as an office chair flew through the air and struck the little witch like an ergonomic bullet.

"Little bird, you really need to stop letting the bad guy make speeches. It's just bad form." Juliette came up beside me, her features indistinct as my eyes continued adjusting to the light.

"It's a character flaw," I admitted, motioning one of the wolves to recover Thomas' body.

"Do you think the—"

"As I was saying," Thomas continued, rising to his feet like nothing had happened, "before I was so RUDELY interrupted—"

Matt leapt at Thomas in a blur of red fur, enormous jaws wide…

…and somehow missed, landing ten feet past his intended target with a thud and pained whine.

"Really, John," continued the witch. "Are you going to let *everyone* fight your battles for you?"

But I wasn't listening, because my eyes had finally fully adjusted. Instead, I waved frantically to Emilio.

"Emilio! Nos vamos!" It was one of the few phrases of Spanish I knew, and I'm sure I bungled the pronunciation, conjugation, *and* accent, but it got Emilio's attention. The wolf-man's massive head spun my way.

"Time to go, Duchess." I grabbed Juliette by an arm and pulled her to the door.

"What are you doing?" the femmepire started to ask.

"Where do you think you're going?" cried Thomas, almost at the same time, but I was through the double doors, and sprinting down the hall, first dragging Juliette, then running with her, then chasing after her, as she decided I knew what I was doing.

Emilio made it around the corner as well, Matt and Longhair hot on his heels. And then everything behind us exploded in fire.

○○○

"How did you know?" Juliette asked.

We were huddled together back down the hill, far enough away to be ignored by the fire engines and police cars streaming toward the still-burning Qualcomm building. Next to us, Emilio was in human form and soot covered, smoke wafting up from his rapidly healing skin. I'd already pulled a piece of shrapnel the size of my fist from the burly werewolf's back.

Longhair and Matt were in worse shape. I wasn't sure how Emilio had gotten the other two wolves out, but there wasn't an inch of them that wasn't blackened and bleeding. Longhair had at least opened his eyes briefly, but the only sign Matt was even alive was the occasional twitch of now-human limbs.

"Seriously, how?" the femmepire asked again.

I shook my head slowly. "I couldn't figure out why Thomas would be there alone, why he would taunt us instead of fleeing, or how he could have survived your chair attack for that matter. It didn't make any sense."

"And that's all it took to realize that it was a trap and they'd somehow primed the room to explode?" Juliette's eyes, glowing golden in the darkness, were wide and genuinely impressed. "Maybe you *are* a detective."

"Actually, I figured Nepenthe just left him behind for us to kill," I admitted. "But when I could finally see again, I realized something."

"What's that?"

"I could see *through* Thomas."

Juliette cursed softly. "We almost lost two wolves to a witch who wasn't even there?"

I nodded.

"Please tell me that *this* wasn't what you meant when you said you had a plan."

"My *plan* was for dealing with a hostile coven. I wasn't expecting an illusory Tommy-bomb."

"Wait; if he was just an illusion, why could you see or hear him at all? I thought you were immune to that sort of thing."

"Yeah." I hugged my knees, listening to the sirens. "So did I."

CHAPTER 51

IN WHICH PAST MISTAKES ARE NO GUARANTEE OF FUTURE RESULTS

Telling Carolyn that I'd almost gotten three of her wolves killed went just as well as I had expected. I didn't even want to imagine the shitstorm that would have started if one of them had *died*. As it was, Juliette and I were a dispirited pair when we finally made our way back to Cardiff.

Anastasia met us at the door, took one look at my face, and ushered us into the downstairs dining room and kitchen. On the table, a first aid kit was open and waiting.

"What happened?"

"We may have burned down part of Sorrento Valley."

Anastasia raised one elegant eyebrow.

"It was a trap. The coven left an illusion behind to draw us in and then tried to blow us up."

"Perhaps you should start at the beginning?"

With the events still fresh in my mind, rehashing the night wasn't high on my list of things to do, but I nodded anyway. My first try at playing general had been a spectacular failure. It was time to give the floor to someone with actual experience and a talent for this sort of thing.

When I was through, Anastasia drummed her fingers lightly on the wooden table, eyes distant. "How did they know you were coming?"

"I don't know. All I can think is they somehow found out we'd hired Simon and used that to lure us into a trap."

"At least you won't owe him a favor anymore," said Juliette.

"You think *he'll* agree to that? He did help us figure out who was responsible."

"We have larger problems," said Anastasia. "I have never heard of an illusion that could fool the nose as well as the eyes and ears. Couple that with the actual explosion, and this coven's power is unprecedented."

"They even fooled little bird," added Juliette. "Mostly anyway."

"If anything, that is even more disturbing." The gaze that pinned me to the chair was anything but distant. "Do you have any idea as to how they managed it, Mr. Smith?"

"No. Especially since they tried some sort of illusion on me when we met at the restaurant, and I didn't even notice it." I grimaced. "Either they were just pretending at the time or something has—"

I stopped in mid-sentence with a groan.

"Something has?" Juliette prompted.

"Changed." I looked down at my hands, not wanting to meet either femmepires' eyes. "Like me giving them a vial of my blood."

For a moment, silence reigned.

"You did *what?*" That was from Juliette.

"Oh, John." That was from Anastasia.

"It made sense at the time," I muttered defensively.

"Sure," sniped Juliette. "What's a vial of blood between complete strangers? I'm starting to think your mother did *more* than just drop you on your head as a child!"

"Juliette," warned Anastasia, but the other femmepire was having none of it.

"Why would you even *consider* giving someone your blood?"

"They said they could use it to break the bond."

"Oh." Juliette sagged in her chair.

"If your bond could be broken, Queen Lucia would have most assuredly already done so, Mr. Smith."

"They seemed to think otherwise." I shook my head. "The whole point of the meeting was to get me to talk to Lucia about democracy. We only got onto the topic of the bond by accident."

"Are you certain?"

"Knowing what I do now? I guess not."

"Your thorny relationship with her Majesty is not widely known, but it is not a closely guarded secret either," Ana pointed out. "If Nepenthe truly has been conferring with the other species of San Diego, she might easily have learned of it."

"I don't see why they'd even bother. I haven't had a mediation case in months. Why is it so important for them to find a way past my gift?"

"Maybe," said an icy voice, "this was never about you at all."

If anything, Lucia looked even more tired than she had earlier. I was the one who'd nearly been Tommy-bombed to death, but I felt almost fresh by comparison.

"What do you mean?"

"I mean that you are entirely unremarkable," the queen told me, glacial blue eyes hard, "save for three things. Two of these you have already noted—your position, which you have stupidly allowed Mr. Van Stahl to erode, and your gift, which evidently has its limits."

"And the third thing?" I was irritated enough with my own idiocy that I didn't contest her earlier points.

"The bond itself, and your relationship with me."

"What a shock," murmured Juliette. "It's all about her."

"In this instance, I believe she may be right."

I looked at Anastasia in confusion. "What do you mean?"

The femmepire's face was a mask, but green eyes flickered from Lucia to me and back again.

"We know," she finally said, "that the bond you two share is unlike any in the history of the People in that its channel is bi-directional."

"That means it goes both ways, little bird," said Juliette.

"Something you'd know all about."

"Once the bond settled," Ana continued, ignoring our bickering, "it reached equilibrium. You were aware of each other's locations, and had some dim sense of mood or emotion, but the usual abilities a master has over their thrall never manifested. That you react pleasurably to her Majesty's bite, suggests the bond has weakened your gift's ability to defend against her, yet she remains unable to impose her will upon you."

Thank God for small favors. The idea of Lucia looking out my eyes or sucking down my life from a mile away was freaking horrifying.

"And now?"

"I think the coven may have used your blood to disrupt that equilibrium." She gestured from the wan queen to me. "The flow would appear to be reversed."

"What?" Juliette, Lucia, and I all spoke in unison, but Ana remained unruffled.

"Her Majesty is suffering from an illness when no member of our species has *ever* been sick. Mr. Smith spent mere days recovering from the sort of damage that could and perhaps should have killed him."

"He's faster too," added Juliette thoughtfully. She looked over at me. "Remember the cemetery? I told you I'd never seen a human move that fast before."

"I thought you were just busting my balls."

"That too."

"This is *intolerable*," grated Lucia.

"But if I'm pulling on Lucia's power—" Which was both kind of cool and totally justified by the rules of karma. "—shouldn't I be more of a badass than this?"

"You should," Anastasia agreed. "Your gains have not in any way been commensurate with her losses."

I had to puzzle that sentence out in my head—I'd gone to community college, damn it!—and frowned.

"So where is the rest of that power going?"

We all reached the obvious conclusion at the same time.

"The witches are sucking Lucia's power? That's not good." Juliette was back to balancing on one chair leg, yellow eyes glittering thoughtfully.

A thought came to me unprompted. "If the energy is flowing somewhere…"

"Then the two of you might be able to track it. Well done, Mr. Smith."

ooo

Shockingly, it really was that easy. Not that I was much help. Even though I was the conduit through which Lucia's power was being leeched, I couldn't sense where that power was going at all. Lucia, on the other hand, didn't have that problem. With my presence close at hand to avoid muddying the results, she had identified a likely location in under twenty minutes.

Given that she'd used those same skills to stalk me half a year prior, I wasn't as enthusiastic about the demonstration as I might otherwise have been.

"This must be the place." Juliette spun the laptop around so we could see another of Jason's photos.

"C&H Transportation?"

"Yeah. It's a warehouse in Vista in the area Lucia pinpointed. And it's further north," Juliette pointed out, "which might explain why Simon was unable to sense it. So, what now? More furry muscle?"

"Good luck getting the Pack to agree to that." I shook my head. "And even if they did, can we be sure this isn't another trap? We still don't know how they knew we were coming last time."

"Assuming they did so at all," Lucia interjected unexpectedly. "If their magic is as powerful as you claim, they could have set the trap days ago."

"And we triggered it when we rushed in like Rambo." I shook my head. "No… assuming the pulse Simon felt was them arming the trap, they only set it last night."

"Then it seems they knew you were hunting them even before you did. The newest missing ghosts, perhaps?"

That seemed possible.

"Perhaps this time, reconnaissance would be advisable before the assault?"

I nodded and glanced over to Juliette.

"The things I do to get my name on the letterhead." Juliette sighed. "Fine. I'll reschedule my date. But you owe me."

Lucia's gaze narrowed at the word *agency*, but before she could speak, Anastasia was on her feet.

"This time, I will accompany you both."

"No, Lady Dumenyova. You will not."

"My queen?"

"I need you here. Not traipsing about the city."

"This matter involves us as well."

"It does, and if my thrall and the former Lady Middleton find anything of note, I will send you back with them to mete out justice." Her voice dropped to something cold and dry as an arctic desert. "But tonight, you will do as I say."

Ana stiffened, jade eyes blazing.

"It has been a long time since you first swore to serve me, Asya." The queen's voice softened without losing any of its edge. "I understand if your oath has begun to chafe. If you wish to be released…"

"I do not." The auburn-haired femmepire's face was a mask, but her eyes were hard, like the precious stone they so often resembled.

"Very well." Lucia nodded regally, and I was pretty sure I'd never hated her more than at that moment. "Speak to Gustavo. We will have dinner in my room."

Anastasia bowed stiffly and was gone.

"Ana's help could be invaluable tonight, Lucia." I was amazed how even I'd kept my voice.

"Surely a simple scouting mission is within your abilities."

"One hour," I pressed. "Ninety minutes, tops. Why not let her accompany us?"

"Because I have ruled otherwise." Lucia's blue eyes were angry in the landscape of her sickly face. "You have taken too much from me already, human. You will not have her as well."

○○○

While Juliette called Angel to reschedule their evening plans, I headed upstairs to get my game face on… which mostly entailed splashing water on my face, brushing my teeth, and throwing on my leather jacket. Before we left, I went in search of Jee Sun and Princess Tea Leaf.

Tea Leaf was in the den, sprawled on a pile of blankets and pillows and gazing up at the enormous LED television that was hanging on the far wall. On the screen, Anna was on her way to find her sister, Elsa.

The little vampire's sharp ears had her turning and waving as soon as I had entered. I knelt to speak to her.

"Tea Leaf, have you seen Jee Sun?"

"Nope!" The adorable little girl grinned impishly up at me. "We're playing hide and seek!"

"You are?" I looked to the tv and then back to Tea Leaf.

"Yep! She has until Olaf to find a spot to hide."

Of course she did.

"Juliette and I are going out again. We probably won't be back until late tonight."

"Okay. Bye!" Tea Leaf's eyes returned to the flickering screen.

I was clearly no match for Disney's marketing genius.

CHAPTER 52

By the time we arrived in Vista, the sun was diving into the ocean, the incoming night sky almost visible through the glare of city streetlights. We'd left late enough to avoid the typically horrible rush hour traffic on the 5, and the trip to our destination took under twenty minutes.

"We could have been here in fifteen on my bike," Juliette grumbled, as I pulled the Corolla into a parking lot across the street and out of sight from the warehouse.

"Because nothing says stealthy reconnaissance like a Ducati," I fired back. It was the fourth time we'd had this argument. "When we're done with our snooping, I'll take you back to Ana's and you can rattle every window in Cardiff."

"Like I need your permission for that. What's the plan this time? Do we knock?"

"I thought we could find a side door and take a look around," I answered quietly, crossing the empty street. "We need to find out if the ghosts are still here, and what it is we might be up against before we come back with Ana and Kayla to start kicking ass."

"Well, shoot," complained Juliette. At my questioning look, she smirked. "Makes me wonder why I bothered wearing these boots at all."

"Because your barista donor dressed you in them." I snickered. That was *never* going to get old.

We crept up to the warehouse in question. It looked nothing like the den of evil and twisted black magic I'd been expecting. In fact, other than the name and logo of the company, there was little to distinguish it from the many other warehouses in the area. A series of oversized garage doors were shut and locked, hiding the bays where trucks could be loaded.

Past those bays was another door, this one roughly human-sized, but it was also locked, and entirely too exposed for my tastes. We continued around the side. On the far corner, there was another door.

"Here we go." I pulled out the trusty set of lock picks I'd purchased on eBay for the unimaginably low price of $19.95. I selected a torsion wrench with the hook pick that looked best suited to the job and bent over the lock.

"Seriously, John? We don't have time for you to play with your toys." Juliette leaned past me, placed a hand flat against the door just above the lock itself, and shoved.

A crack echoed through the still night air like a gunshot, and the door swung open. I froze, waiting for someone to come looking.

Miraculously, nobody did.

"That's exactly what I was trying to avoid, Duchess. What part of stealth do you *not* understand?"

"It's open now, isn't it?"

"This is going on your performance review," I swore. The door *was* open. Unfortunately, it was also now broken. "What are we going to do when the witches notice someone broke down their back door? What if they move Graciela to a different location?"

Juliette winced.

I shook my head. *This* was why I was the senior partner. "Let's see what we can find. This recon may have just become a full-blown rescue attempt."

I tucked the lock picks back into my pocket and motioned to the broken door.

"Ladies first."

The interior of the warehouse was dark and… well, mostly it was just dark. We crept through a maze of shelves, each of them three times my height and loaded with what appeared to be automotive equipment.

As far as I could tell, we were totally alone.

"We're not alone," Juliette murmured in my ear, causing the hairs on the back of my neck to stand straight up. When had she crept so close?

"Have I mentioned how much it sucks not having super senses?" I whispered back. "What is it you're seeing?" For the second time in a day, my night vision was better than it should have been, but I was a long way from being a vampire.

"About twenty feet in that direction and around the corner, there's some sort of faint light source. And I think I hear a heartbeat."

"Just one? This might be easier than I thought."

"It's not like I'm trained to pick out individual heart beats at thirty paces, little bird."

"Which is a shame," I murmured back, "as that skill would be pretty damn useful right about now."

I could hear the irritation in her own whisper. "Wait here if you want, but I'm going to go break someone's neck, free your ghosts, collect our paycheck, and take Angel out for a drink."

"I thought Angel *was* the drink?"

Beyond the warehouse shelves, an open space had been cleared. I crouched low to the ground and turned the corner.

In the center of the room, the floor was glowing.

No, not the floor, I realized. Runes that had been chiseled *into* the floor. A soft white glow surrounded each sigil, illuminating what appeared to be a series of concentric circles.

As wild as that sight was, however, my attention was reserved for the twenty-odd women—and one man—who stood outside the ritual area.

Every one of them was facing in our direction.

"Shit."

The warehouse's overhead lights flickered on with a loud hum.

"John. Vampire. Be welcome." Nepenthe's voice was exactly as I remembered it, warm and sincere, the voice of a respected older friend, or an unreasonably attractive soccer mom.

I was starting to think I sucked at judging people.

"You were expecting us?" I finally managed.

"Not at all. I didn't expect to ever see you again after our trap triggered earlier today," she admitted. "But your entrance wasn't exactly quiet, was it?"

I gave Juliette a pointed look.

Behind Nepenthe, the rest of the coven was silent. The witches came in all shapes, sizes, and outfits, but each of them was staring at us with the same intense expression.

Except for Thomas, the dude-witch. *He* stood next to Nepenthe with a mocking smile on his face. In the runes' dim glow, the middle-aged goth looked almost scary.

"There's that one guy again," Juliette pointed out. "Please tell me he's not another bomb."

"Nope. This time, that's the real Thomas."

"He dies first."

"There *will* be death," said Nepenthe, still sounding entirely reasonable.

Thomas' smile widened.

"I don't get it, Nepenthe. You *seemed* like a normal, rational person with normal, rational goals."

"That I am, Mr. Smith."

I peered past the coven. At the center of the multitude of circles, were three pinpricks of light in an entirely different spectrum, like candle flames under a fluorescent spotlight. Two of those flames burned steadily, but the third was weak and flickering.

"Rational people don't kidnap ghosts."

"Or assemble in warehouses for rituals," agreed Juliette.

"What happened to your vision of some sort of super council, where every supernatural body gets a voice?"

"Why do you think I'm doing this?" Nepenthe spread her slender arms wide, and the look she sent my way was almost pitying. "Look to our own nation's history, John. For democracy to take root, the old authority must first be vanquished."

"By which you mean *killed*."

"Do I?" She gestured at the flames within her ritual circle. "These unnatural things are already dead, John. We will merely be sending them on their way."

"Those *things* are the souls of mortal women who were betrayed and killed," I growled back, "and whose wills were strong enough to keep them here even after death."

"As I said, unnatural. I take no pleasure in our actions, but the city's current establishment stands in the way of progress."

"What about the Toulon Concordat?" I asked, stalling for time. "You're committing an open assault on another supernatural power. That's just asking to get wiped off the map."

"Open your eyes, mediator," sneered Thomas. "When is the last time a primordial being showed up to enforce the rules? We're all alone down here. To the victor go the spoils."

That was a slightly different take on what Anastasia had said and I really hoped it wasn't true. If the Concordat *was* toothless these days, humans were in serious trouble. And so was my position as a mediator.

"How did you capture Graciela anyway?" I risked a glance at my watch. It was five to eight, which meant the sun almost had to be down. Still, it paid to be certain. "I didn't think human magic had that sort of kick."

"Magic is everything," answered Nepenthe. "Its *kick* is determined by the will of the wielder and the power of their words. I have always had the will. Dear Thomas found us the words."

"A book?"

"A *grimoire*. Hidden by this country's first inhabitants, it contains spells that no witch of our age has ever seen."

"Including spells to trap ghosts."

"Not just trap, Mr. Smith. *Use.*" Nepenthe's smile widened, and I finally, finally got a whiff of crazy from her. If I somehow survived this experience, I was damn well going back to my online detective classes. My powers of observation had been failing miserably all month.

"Use them how?" I fumbled with a small object in my pocket.

"It was serendipity," Nepenthe continued, as if I hadn't spoken, "that one of my coven stumbled upon the location of Graciela's node. Do you know what a node is, John?"

"Doesn't everyone?"

"We transported it here, into the circle we had already prepared, and when the sun rose, and the spirit was summoned back to her node—"

"She was trapped within your magical cage." I glanced at Juliette, telling her with my eyes that her priority was to somehow disrupt that cage.

She nodded back, which would have been reassuring if our previous attempts at nonverbal communication hadn't all been disasters.

"And then you interrogated Graciela for the location of Margaret and Begoña's nodes, I'm guessing," I said, trying to keep all attention off Juliette.

"Not at all." The witch shook her head. Behind her, several of her coven mirrored the motion exactly. It was creepy as hell. Kind of like being trapped in a warehouse with a bunch of insane magic users. "This is not just a cage, John. It's a siphon. Between Graciela's energy, and that of your queen's, we have been able to amplify the original ritual many times over. When these two stumbled upon our warehouse, it was child's play to capture them."

"I must admit," she continued, "that the question of how to deal with the vampire monarch cost me more than a few nights of sleep. Luckily, the foolish woman took a thrall, and that thrall provided us with the means to flip the current on their bond."

"Thanks for your help, loser." Thomas slicked back his hair with a black-nailed hand.

"Now, if the two of you will excuse me, I have work to do tonight, and a yoga class first thing in the morning." Nepenthe turned to a blonde-haired slip of a witch. "Kill them."

Juliette blurred into motion… or started to, anyway. She managed a single stride before she stopped dead, frozen like an insect in amber.

She wasn't the only one either. From the waist down, the air around me had thickened like swiftly drying cement. Breathing wasn't a problem but there was no way in hell I was going to be able to move.

Thankfully, my plan didn't rely upon me moving.

"Nepenthe," I said, "there are two things your insane plan failed to take into account."

The witch favored me with an expression of polite disinterest. "And what would those things be, John?"

"First, it's nighttime. And second," I said, clutching the slim ring in my pocket, "we didn't come alone."

And with those words, Valentina and the White Ladies appeared around us. The enraged spirits took to the air, streaking towards the shocked witches like arrows of vengeance.

CHAPTER 53
IN WHICH THE BEST DEFENSE
IS OVERWHELMING POWER

I had one glorious moment to enjoy the look of panic and surprise on Nepenthe's face, before the first ghosts reached her—

—and were pulled right through the coven and into the ritual circle behind. Where once there had been three flames in the cage, there were now well over twenty.

"Oh shit."

When Nepenthe's smile returned, it was undeniably smug. "If you had tried that even two days ago, it might have worked. Instead, with a single action, you have delivered us all the energy we could ever need. We sought only the power to enforce our will, but you… you have made us into gods. On behalf of the free San Diego, I thank you."

"On behalf of the actual San Diego, go to hell," I said back.

To my side, Juliette had yet to manage a second step, though her yellow eyes had gone completely golden, strain evident in every line of her face.

"I believe you were preparing a spell?" Nepenthe said to the blonde witch who had been appointed as our executioner.

"I won't let you cast that," I told the unnamed witch.

"You can't stop me," she said, sneering. Between her and Thomas, I was starting to think Nepenthe had focused on traits *other* than intelligence in assembling her coven.

"Actually," I countered, "I bet I can." I stretched one hand toward her and made a pretend gun with my thumb and index finger.

Next to me, Juliette sighed. "Worst. Partner. Ever."

I ignored the femmepire. The blonde witch had already started her chant. I dropped my thumb like it was the hammer of the gun. "Boom."

The crack of the rifle was loud in the confines of the warehouse. The blonde witch toppled backward, a neat hole in the center of her forehead, and a messy crater in the back. The bullet had traveled right through her and struck a second witch. The resulting screams almost drowned out the sound of the next shot.

As quickly as that second shot came, Nepenthe was even faster. The air around the coven shimmered like molten glass, and a bullet ricocheted away with an angry whine. The witch glanced at something above and behind us, and a wave of throbbing force lashed out.

A single figure tumbled from a catwalk that had suddenly ceased to exist, her controlled dive and roll bringing her to a spot only twenty or so feet to my right. There was no sign of the rifle she had been using, but I watched as her long fingers and muscled arms slowly took on the appearance of granite. Auburn hair and jade eyes completed the picture.

"How did you know?" asked Juliette.

"I didn't," I admitted, "but I was really hoping."

"You'd have looked damn stupid if she wasn't here."

"We'd both be dead, so what would it matter?"

"Style *always* matters, little bird."

Anastasia made her way over to us, keeping one eye on the coven's shield. "Your ability to attract trouble remains unparalleled, Mr. Smith."

"It's a gift," I agreed. "Does Lucia know you came?"

"By now, she must." Ana shrugged. "She will have words for me later, should we survive."

"No doubt." I grinned. "No warrior goddess costume tonight?" The femmepire was dressed in matte black leggings and a compression shirt of similar material. Her long hair had been pulled back and braided and a blade was sheathed at her waist.

"Have you ever tried to move swiftly or silently in leather? I do not advise it." Her eyes darted to my own leather jacket and then back to the coven. As she spoke, she hurled the occasional shuriken in the witches' direction, but nothing was penetrating Nepenthe's shield. "How do you suggest we proceed?"

I tested my feet and verified that I was no longer stuck. "Judging by the fact that we're all still alive, I'm guessing they'll have to drop their force field thingy to attack us again. Get to the cage when they do. That thing can't have been designed to hold so many ghosts at one time. If we can disrupt the patterns—"

"—we will free the ghosts and deprive the coven of their power source. Very well. Please remain at a distance, Mr. Smith. Lady Middleton and I will attack from opposing sides." She drew her sword, handed it to Juliette, and began to circle the room.

"Ana," I called to her. "Thank you for coming."

She nodded. "I told you I would not allow you to be harmed again."

As the words left her mouth, the witches' shield dropped. Both vampires blurred into motion.

Unfortunately, our enemies had not been idle.

Two massive figures, eight feet tall if they were an inch, pushed their way past the gathered witches. Charred black skin had split and cracked in spots across the creatures' bodies, exposing what looked like burning magma underneath. Powerful arms ended in vicious looking talons, and each figure sported two curving horns. Their mouths were almost comically full of teeth.

"Seriously?" I complained to the world at large. "Nobody said there would be demons!"

ooo

The femmepires had the unquestioned edge in speed, but that advantage was insufficient to get them past the hulking forms of their opponents. And when it came to raw power… well, the demons were twice their size and formed from lava.

I looked between the two women in a moment of indecision. It was a given that I was going to get involved, but… who should I try to help?

It *should* have been an easy choice. Juliette, God bless her, was a friend… and a good one… but Anastasia was more than that. However, Ana was also exponentially more skilled than my junior partner…

As if to prove the point, Juliette mistimed her dodge. The femmepire flew in one direction, and her borrowed weapon skidded almost to my feet.

I scooped up the sword and charged in to help.

By the time I arrived, Juliette was back on her feet, but she was limping and struggling to avoid the demon's furious assault. My short sprint had me wheezing, but I didn't even slow. The sword went back, and then the sword went forward, swinging at the creature's leg.

If this had been Little League, I'd have crushed that pitch. The opposing team would have spent years waiting for the ball to come back down to earth. My baseball team might have won a game, for the first time all season. Even a pizza party would not have been outside the realm of possibility.

But this was the real world, and I'd never used a sword in my life. So, I was utterly shocked when the blade sank into the demon's muscular thigh. A wave of heat sent me staggering backward, robbing me of my vision.

When my sight returned, I saw that Ana's blade was only a foot long now, its twisted metal remains scorched like they had been dipped in fire. And my hand… I could *see* that my hand was still tightly clutching the smoldering hilt, but I sure as hell couldn't feel it.

Not yet, anyway.

Still, the demon I had hit was down on its hands and one knee, and that was making all the difference for Juliette. Even keeping the weight off her own injured leg, the femmepire was a blur, tearing at the fallen demon with supernatural strength. I made my way over to her, waited for the demon to ineffectually swipe at Juliette, and drove the remnants of Ana's sword into his skull.

This time, I was ready for the resulting blast of heat and fire. As magma consumed the sword, I forced my unresponsive fingers to open. I tore my hand away from the hilt, leaving a fair bit of skin behind.

That was really going to suck whenever my body decided to start feeling it.

I helped Juliette up with my other hand and looked to Anastasia in time to see the House Secundus step into and past her opponent's blow. I remembered a similar move from her battle with Xavier and cheered the hammer-like strikes that drove all the way through the demon's body.

The fallen demons smoldered and faded away, returning to whatever hell dimension the witches had summoned them from. Across the room, Anastasia had begun to close in on the circle once more.

"You know," I said, "I kind of thought demons would be tougher."

A roar split the air, like the sound an avalanche might make. The creature that appeared dwarfed the two we had just slain, its head nearly brushing the warehouse's ceiling. An ebon carapace armored its body, enormous batlike wings sprouted from its back, and a long, scaled tail ended in a vicious stinger. It also had four arms, six eyes, and two… yes two… mouths.

I swallowed a curse. With the power I'd given them, the witches could conceivably just keep summoning things until we wore down. And since Ana had no choice but to fight the big dude, and Juliette was barely standing… it was up to me to break the circle.

As I started to move towards the witches, the air congealed around me again.

"Oh, come on!" I shouted up at whatever gods were watching and—no doubt—laughing.

"Stay put, Mr. Smith," Nepenthe told me, her voice amplified to be heard even over the battle. "The Hound of Tartarus will deal with you soon enough."

With my ace cards already played, I had little choice but to watch.

"Your plans *suck*, little bird." Juliette wheezed.
"Noted."

ooo

Anastasia was brilliant. I'd seen a Battle Lord fight, but even though such vampires were supposed to be the greatest warriors of the species, the femmepire was at another level entirely. Her entire body now stone, she still remained a step ahead of her opponent, always just out of reach of its many-armed strikes. Every motion she made was carefully controlled and impossibly precise.

Which made it that much scarier that she was losing.

As the battle proceeded, the demon only grew in power, its attacks accelerating, its armor thickening even further. Anastasia landed blow after blow, but nothing was penetrating the demon's carapace. She had just dodged one riposte when a vicious swipe from the demon's tail sent her flying.

The femmepire skidded across the concrete surface, and rose to her feet in a single motion, but her pace was clearly slowing. She took a long breath, eyes glittering like golden pennies. When she exhaled, her stone form shifted again. Hardened granite gave way to shimmering black rock, its surface laced with veins of golden ore.

"That's—"

"—the same stone used for the walls and stairs of the Bitter End," Juliette confirmed.

"Did *you* know she could do that?"

"Little bird, I didn't know *anyone* could do that."

As we spoke, the Hound reached Anastasia, but this time the femmepire stepped forward to meet it, an ebon engine of destruction. Her movements were less fluid, but every strike of her own rang like a bell against the demon's carapace. I watched two of the creature's eyes wince in pain.

"God damn, I love that woman."

"She's starting to grow on me too."

Anastasia's blows were taking a toll on the demon. She drove it back… first one step, then two, and the Hound's many eyes cast about as if looking for an escape.

Then its wings unfurled, and the demon blew Anastasia back into the air.

Again, the femmepire turned her backwards fall into a roll, but in this form, her movement was just the tiniest bit too slow. The Hound was there to meet her, one of its massive claws dropping in a blow that could have split an aircraft carrier in half.

Without the time or space to dodge, Anastasia dropped to one knee and desperately threw her own arm up to block the demon's attack.

The taloned hand crashed down upon the femmepire's slim arm—

—and stopped, its momentum impossibly arrested by Ana's seemingly fragile defense.

Next to me, Juliette began to curse.

"What's—?" Before I could complete my question, the answer become apparent. Cracks had appeared in Anastasia's raised arm, spiraling out from the epicenter of the blow. As I watched, those schisms widened, and the arm itself began to crumble.

The Hound threw back its head and roared in triumph.

I strained to pull myself free, but even though my blood pounded with the effort, the witches' spell had my legs trapped. I reached out to the femmepire, but she was thirty feet away, and there wasn't a damn thing I could do to save her.

Ana struggled to her feet, but her right arm was gone from just below the shoulder, and she seemed stunned and unaware of her surroundings.

Two of the demon's arms whipped down, talons angled to drive straight through the femmepire's body.

"No!" I screamed, my heart feeling like it was going to burst. A wave of heat washed through me. Sweat drenched my t-shirt like I'd just jogged twenty miles in a sauna, and from my outstretched hand, a spear of shimmering blue ice, seven feet long and as thick as my Corolla, rocketed across the chamber to impale the Hound.

If it weren't for the witches' spell, I would have fallen over. As it was, I found myself gasping for breath. Vision blurry, I heard the Hound collapse, an impact that sent shelves tumbling in a cacophony of noise that drowned out the demon's own anguished death.

For a moment, there was only silence.

"That was unexpected," admitted Nepenthe. "I guess if you want something done right…"

Behind her, the members of her coven began to chant in unison. I looked from Anastasia, who was barely upright, to Juliette, who was only standing at all because of my support, and shook my head.

"Shit."

"Shit!" agreed another voice cheerfully.

Jee Sun stepped her way through the wreckage of shelves, cape blowing behind her. In her small hands, she held a Capri-Sun.

"Hi, Mr. John!" She waved the Capri-Sun about, sending flavored juice everywhere.

The witches seemed as stunned as I was. For the third time, their chant dwindled to silence.

"Jee Sun… how did you get here?"

"I came with you, silly!" she replied, skipping her way around the scorched cement that marked a minor demon's passage.

I shared a confused look with Juliette. "The trunk?"

"It must have been," she agreed.

I needed to have a talk with the little girl about appropriate hiding spaces.

"Tiny Flower," I said, "You need to get out of here. This is not a safe place."

"Nobody's going anywhere." Thomas waved his hand in a flourish, and whatever enchantment was holding me expanded to include Jee Sun. "There can be no witnesses."

"Nepenthe, she's just a little girl. There's no reason to kill her!"

"That you don't want it to happen sounds like reason enough," Thomas replied with a sneer. "Although maybe a few tears and some begging will change my mind."

"Thomas." Nepenthe's voice thrummed with power. "Escort the child out of the building and let her go."

"But—"

"We are not monsters. We will not behave as they do."

I didn't point out that draining energy from the dead and using it to summon demons was about as monstrous as it got. If accepting the witch's hypocrisy was the price for Jee Sun's survival… then so be it.

"Fine." Thomas scowled and released Jee Sun with another incantation. "Come here, you brat."

The little girl stepped past his outstretched hand and drove a tiny fist directly into his groin.

"I am not a brat," she told the witch as he collapsed to the floor. "I AM JEE SUN!"

Thomas was on his hands and knees, but the look in his kohl-ringed eyes would have made a mass murderer shiver. One hand disappeared into his coat. When it re-emerged, it was holding a gun.

The witch fired.

Jee Sun jerked upright, eyes wide behind her thick-framed glasses, and slowly toppled over.

CHAPTER 54

Jee Sun hit the floor, and every light in the warehouse exploded.

The glowing sigils of the ghost cage continued to illuminate the center of the room, but everything else—the wreckage of shelves, the truck bays, and the body of the little girl who had just been shot—was swallowed by darkness.

Something unseen scraped against the floor, like a Buick-sized centipede or the Midgard serpent. Two crimson orbs flared to life in the heart of the darkest corner, ten or fifteen feet off the ground. Directly in front of me, I saw for the first time the tendril of blackest night that had encircled Jee Sun's huddled form.

From the darkness came a voice.

"WHO WOULD HURT TINY FLOWER?"

The extended tendril unspooled from around the child, to become a hand, and from that hand dropped a bullet that had been flattened like a pancake. Jee Sun rubbed her stomach gingerly and glared over at the man who had tried to shoot her.

Thomas looked from the crushed bullet to the unharmed little girl, and for the first time, his sneer disappeared entirely. He turned to the crimson orbs and stammered. "It was an accident… I didn't mean…"

"THEY WILL BE PAID IN BLOOD AND FIRE!"

Darkness flickered and *something* took a bite out of the witch's arm. The floor split open. For only the third time ever, I caught a glimpse of Gehenna, from the magenta thunderclouds to the scarlet plains. As ever, the hell world's most prominent features were the fields of twenty-foot-high candelabras, upon which figures of every species and gender had been crucified.

And then the portal slammed shut, nothing left of Thomas but the gun that had brought about his own destruction.

Those crimson orbs turned to the remaining witches.

"BLOOD AND FIRE," thundered Lord Beel-Kasan.

∘∘∘

Within moments, the interior of the warehouse was chaos. Tendrils and unseen beasts struck at the coven from the shadows, repelled by shimmering shields of light. The demigod roared with fury, redoubling his efforts, but the witches were holding their own, and even mounting counterassaults.

Nepenthe had told me I'd given her coven the power of gods. I was starting to think she might be right.

The only good news was that, with the witches focused on Bill, the spells holding us vanished. I staggered as I again became responsible for bearing all of Juliette's weight. I glanced from the femmepire's pain-wracked face to the battle being waged thirty feet away.

"Duchess… will you watch over Jee Sun and Ana?"

"I can't even stand, little bird," came the tired reply. "How am I supposed to protect them?"

"With your usual blend of sarcasm and sex appeal," I suggested. One glance at her mangled leg had me looking away. Vomiting in the middle of a fight seemed like a poor tactic for victory.

"And what are *you* going to do?"

I scooped up Thomas' fallen pistol with my uninjured left hand and nodded towards the coven and their ghost cage. "Whatever I can."

Boom. Badass hero achievement unlocked.

"John, wait." When I looked back over my shoulder, the femmepire grinned. "If you die, I get the agency."

I rolled my eyes. "You're about to be rich. Again. Why would you want a failing P.I. agency?"

"It's—" she coughed, and something bloody splattered onto the floor. "It's just the principle of the thing."

I left her behind with a smile on my face and a gun in my hand.

I'd been involved in a depressing number of dangerous situations over the past six months, but this was the first time I'd found myself in a battle between an enraged demigod and an empowered coven of ghost-draining witches.

It sucked.

Things were flashing and flying and slithering in every direction, and the chaos only worsened with every step I took toward the ghost cage. With all the power being hurled about, I don't know how I made it as far as I did. Maybe Bill was looking out for me or the witches assumed I was one of their own. Maybe everyone had just dismissed me as any sort of threat. Whatever the reason, I found myself standing outside the first circle of runes.

Now what?

The runes had been etched into the stone floor, which meant my original plan of simply erasing them with my foot was a non-starter. I placed a hand against the hardened air above the nearest sigil and pushed. No good. Whatever the spell was doing to keep the ghosts in was also working to keep me out.

"What do you think you're doing, Mr. Smith?"

A hand on my shoulder spun me about. Nepenthe's hair had come loose from its ponytail to float in a cloud about her head, charged with electricity from all the power in the air, but her eyes were calm and peaceful.

Which was a good indicator of just how crazy she was.

"I'm freeing the Ladies, Nepenthe," I shouted back, even as I raised the gun. "Please don't make me hurt you."

"Hurt me?" Nepenthe shook her head sadly. "Your compassion does you credit. We could have done great things together once the old world was wiped away." A wave of her hand tore the gun from my grasp, sending it skittering across the floor.

I tried to stagger backwards, but my feet were fixed to the floor yet again. Whatever power I'd summoned to kill the Hound of Tartarus was gone, slipping like smoke through my fingers. I reached into my coat pocket instead, with the insane idea of calling 911 on my wonderphone, when my fingers found something cold and lumpy.

Nepenthe stepped closer, brown eyes shining with genuine compassion. "I will make this quick, John." She threw her arms into the air, and her eyes rolled back in their sockets as she began to chant.

The knife Ana had given me slid easily into the witch's stomach. Hot blood gushed over my hand. Nepenthe staggered but stayed upright through pure force of will. Her chant continued and a glowing nimbus began to form.

I pulled the blade left to right through the witch's mid-section, and then angled it upwards, and pushed as far as I could go.

More blood. More sickening noises that would haunt me in my sleep. And finally, Nepenthe's voice broke, mid-chant. The witch slid to the floor and lay still.

I looked about, but the battle around me continued unabated, the ghost cage still glowing and impermeable.

Shit. That sort of thing *totally* worked in movies.

Past the melee, I could just see the forms of Juliette, Anastasia and Jee Sun. Of the three, only Jee Sun was mobile. Juliette sat awkwardly where I had left her, and Ana… If she lost her focus and reverted to flesh and blood…

Wait. Blood.

I looked at my left hand, slick with Nepenthe's life blood. To the witches, blood had been a marker, a way of locating me, and draining Lucia's power through me. But if *my* blood had granted access to Lucia's power, might Nepenthe's—?

With bloody fingers, I reached out to the nearest rune.

My hand passed through the barrier like it didn't even exist, but the rune's glow continued, unabated.

Damn it.

I thought for a moment, then shrugged. Using those same bloody fingers, I drew a scarlet X through the rune's body.

The effect was instantaneous. The rune's glow guttered out, setting off a cascade of failures, like dominoes toppling. Within the cage's center, dozens of tiny flames transformed back into spectral women. At their forefront was a woman I had never seen—small and Mexican, with hair that had likely been glorious in her mortal life. Her form flickered weakly but the eyes that met my own were full of steely determination.

Graciela gave me a nod and then she and her ghosts joined Bill in his assault.

○○○

With Nepenthe's death and the White Ladies' release, the balance of power shifted in a hurry. The flurry of bright, destructive lights and hurried incantations dwindled from a hurricane to a spring shower. Tentacles of darkness, once stymied by glowing nimbuses of protection, began to strike without impediment, and the Ladies…

I turned away from the sight of the mad teenage ghost, Jennifer, riding the decayed remains of a black-robed witch to the floor. Jee Sun's small hand found mine, and I shielded her from the carnage unfolding behind us.

"Little bird, are you crying?" Juliette had made it to her feet but was leaning heavily on the black stone form of Anastasia.

"No." I brushed my cheeks with my free hand and was surprised to find them wet. "Maybe."

"Is this a human thing?" Juliette's eyes wandered to whatever was happening past me, unmoved. "They were going to kill us all."

"I know. Still. It's such a waste."

"Shit," murmured Jee Sun agreeably.

Even Anastasia's eyes had changed to stone, but I could feel the femmepire's gaze upon me as she staggered closer. The shattered remnants of her right arm extended only inches from its shoulder, ending in a jagged protrusion of sharp, gold-laced obsidian. She raised the other arm and brushed wet, sticky hair out of my face with cold stone fingers.

"False alarm," announced Juliette. "It was just blood."

I let go of Jee-Sun's hand, took a few quick steps to the side, and lost what was left of my lunch.

The slaughter ended before I had finished throwing up. Bill strode out of the darkness, shrinking down to the seven-foot-tall asparagus form I was used to. An arm extended from the stalk of his body to grasp Jee-Sun's hand even as charcoal eyes rotated around that same stalk to regard me.

"John-o-rama! When did YOU get here?"

"I was here all along, Bill," I reminded him.

The magic-marker outline that passed as his mouth formed a small 'o'. "You were?"

"I was."

"They tried to hurt Tiny Flower," he told me, body shuddering slightly. "And we could NOT let that HAPPEN."

"No, we couldn't." I dredged up a smile. "You saved her, Bill. Again."

"It's what I do, Johnny Quest," he told me proudly.

"That and the whole nightmares and terror bit," Juliette added from the peanut gallery.

"Yes!" Bill agreed. "The nightmares and the terror!"

"Mr. Bill?" asked Jee-Sun in a small voice, her wide eyes looking up at the demigod next to her.

"Yes, Tiny Flower?"

"Can we have ice cream now? And Pooh?"

"I think that's our cue to leave," said Juliette.

I looked from one femmepire to the other and shook my head. "Not quite yet."

○○○

"God, I hope this works."

"This is the seventh time you have said so," came Lucia's icy reply. "Unless your God is as idiotic as his prized species, he has surely already heard your prayer."

I glared daggers at the deposed queen. It had been a long eighteen hours since my return from the warehouse, and we were only now finally nearing the moment of truth.

Between us, on a layer of plastic that Gustavo had hastily thrown over one of Anastasia's beds, was the lady of the house herself. She was *still* in her stone form, for fear of the massive blood loss that would ensue when she transformed back to flesh.

Unless all the work that Juliette and I had put in actually paid off.

It hadn't been easy gathering up the stone fragments of Anastasia's shattered arm, but that effort had been a cakewalk compared to actually reconstructing the arm. It had been like assembling a three-dimensional puzzle with seven hundred, nearly identical pieces. The threads of gold had helped, slightly, but what we had spackled together with rubber cement and super glue bore only minimal resemblance to the femmepire's usual limb.

Gustavo stood to Lucia's left and at Anastasia's head, one sleeve rolled back from an arm that was all wiry muscle and sun-spotted skin. Teresa stood to my right, in a similar position. Each was quietly murmuring in Italian, but Lucia didn't seem bothered by *their* prayers.

"Lady Dumenyova," Lucia finally said, her voice ringing with an authority that belied the concern seeping across our bond, "it is time."

Ana shuddered. Stone cracked and split open, giving way to flesh and auburn hair, the tattered remnants of her clothing shockingly black against the marble coolness of her skin. And her arm…

What formed looked only slightly more like an arm than it had in stone form, although the torrent of golden blood made it difficult to see. Gustavo extended his wrist and Anastasia bit deeply. Next to me, Teresa awaited her turn.

Neither she nor I paid the slightest bit of attention to her husband's orgasmic shudders. There were more important things at stake.

When Gustavo fell away, Teresa stepped up and took his place. The fountain of blood from Ana's mangled arm became a stream, then a trickle. Finally, it stopped altogether, leaving a long, glistening lump of exposed muscle and bone.

"Did it work?" I asked Lucia finally.

"I am not a doctor, Mr. Smith. And yet look."

I followed her gaze down to what could only charitably be described as Anastasia's hand. "What am I looking at?" Then, I saw it. Skin was slowly reforming over new nerve endings and tissue. More importantly, her fingers were moving.

"Thank God."

Across the bond, Lucia's relief was as tangible as mine. For a brief moment, we were just two people, sharing in the joy and relief of our mutual friend's recovery.

Just as quickly, the moment passed. Pale blue eyes slowly hardened, and Lucia looked from me to Anastasia with a scowl. Finally, she turned to a hollow-eyed Gustavo.

"When your mistress is ambulatory, inform her that I wish to see her."

Gustavo nodded hesitantly and the queen swept out of the room, her borrowed clothes spattered with Anastasia's blood.

"If she needs more blood to heal," I told Gustavo, as Ana continued to drink from his wife, "I can help."

"That will not be necessary." Even reedy and weak, that voice made me think of chocolate and cheesecake. I looked down to find that Ana had released Teresa's arm. Her jade eyes were open and looking in my direction. "There is a limit to how much any healing can be accelerated."

"But you'll be okay? Eventually?"

"I will. And when I am fully healed…" the femmepire continued, the strain of speaking evident upon her usually expressionless face.

"Yes?"

"I believe we had agreed upon… a dinner date?"

My smile was so wide that it felt like my face might break.

EPILOGUE

"So, Juliette and I are back to one hundred percent," I told the attentive ghost at my side, "and Anastasia is slowly getting there."

Valentina nodded, flashing her black-gummed smile. The White Ladies had disappeared shortly after the melee, but V had returned to her tether the next morning. And if my sometimes-invisible house guest had at one point killed four witches in the blink of an eye… well, who was I to judge?

The blood on my own hands was starting to add up.

Figuratively, anyway. One of the first things I'd done after Ana's healing—at the insistence of… well, everyone around me—was take a long, steaming hot shower, washing off the blood, vomit, and gore of the past day. Just watching that cocktail stream down the drain had been enough to set my stomach off again.

"Any thoughts on what music we should listen to tonight?"

Valentina shrugged happily, swinging her feet through the porch bench. I had moved back to my parents' otherwise empty house as soon as Ana was upright. Lucia was less than pleased by Anastasia's decision to come rescue me, and that displeasure had grown to outright fury when she heard exactly *how* I had killed the Hound of Tartarus.

I swirled the bottle of beer in my hands and focused my concentration. A thin layer of frost formed on the outside of the bottle. The next sip was ice cold and incredibly refreshing.

"Yeah," I said to Valentina, who was clapping spectral hands in silent appreciation, "I still have access to Lucia's Talent. With the coven gone, she's not being drained anymore, but our bond is all kinds of screwed up. She's busy plotting to regain her House, but I'm told she is *not* happy with me."

Valentina made a rude gesture.

"I'm not losing sleep over it either. But that's enough about me. How are the rest of the White Ladies? Have you heard anything from Graciela? Is she recovering?" I frowned. "It was never my intention to put any of you in danger. I hope you know that."

Valentina cocked her head, and brushed the dark, stringy hair out of her face. She then leaned closer and planted a bone-chilling kiss on my cheek.

I touched my cheek. "What was that for?"

She shrugged and floated up from the bench to perform an honest-to-God curtsy in my direction.

"Are you saying thanks?"

She rolled her eyes and nodded.

"You're very welcome, V. But I think I still owe you one."

The dark-haired ghost waggled her hand in the air and grinned.

○○○

An hour later, my parents' car turned the corner and rolled up our driveway. I met my mom and dad with hugs before helping to carry their luggage inside.

"How was the trip, Dad?"

He was quiet for a long time. "It was good."

"If you had to think *that* hard about it, it couldn't have been great." So much for Texan exceptionalism.

"John, honey?" My mom stood in the open doorway, her expression serious. "We need to talk."

"Can't it wait until tomorrow, Maria?" asked my dad.

"No, dear, it can't." There was no give in my mom's voice.

I was starting to get concerned.

"Fine." My dad sighed. "I may have… fibbed about the reason I've been traveling to Austin so much lately."

"Holy crap. Do you have another family in Texas? Do you love them more than us?" I widened my eyes theatrically. "Did you buy your *other* son a pony?"

"He gets his sense of humor from *you*, love," said my mom.

"Unfortunately," replied my dad, his voice still serious, "with the economy the way it is, my company has decided to relocate its headquarters to Texas."

"Oh. That sucks." I frowned. "Business still isn't great at the agency, but I can pitch in a little bit more with the mortgage until you find another job."

"Actually, we've decided to relocate with the company."

"You're leaving California?" My mind went blank. Why would *anyone* want to leave California? Sure, we had fires and earthquakes, a multi-year drought, depressed economy and some of the highest taxes in the country, but…

"We are," confirmed my mom, "and we're selling the house."

Well, shit.

AUTHOR'S NOTE

Thank you so much for reading!

Ghost of a Chance represents a little bit of a shift in the series. Humor will always play a sizable role, but the stakes are getting more serious, the cases more involved, and the cast… well, as you can tell, it keeps growing. As Anastasia said, John does seem to attract a certain breed of protector.

San Diego natives will note that I once again took some liberties with the city, chief among them Qualcomm's closure. In the real world, Qualcomm is still very much around, Eclipse's service is nowhere near as bad as I made it out to be (and the food is even better), and there aren't any zombie princes hanging out in mausoleums in Mount Hope Cemetery. That I know of, anyway.

The next book, *The Italian Screwjob,* will really kick certain plot points into high gear, as circumstances take John out of his beloved San Diego for the first time. Hopefully, you'll enjoy the ride as much as I'm enjoying writing it! *The Italian Screwjob* will be out in 2022.

In the meantime, if you're looking for something a little darker to read, please check out *See These Bones*, the first book in my post-apocalyptic superhero trilogy, *The Murder of Crows.* It and its sequel, *Red Right Hand,* are already available, and I've been delighted with their reception. I'll be finishing that trilogy with *One Tin Soldier,* later this year.

Finally, if you enjoyed *Ghost of a Chance,* please consider leaving a review. As an indie author, I depend heavily on word of mouth and the feedback and support of readers like you.

Thank you!

ABOUT THE AUTHOR

Chris began life as a gleam in someone's eye, but birth and childhood were quick to follow. He's been fortunate enough to live in Spain, Germany, and all over the United States of America, and is busy planning a tour of the distilleries of Scotland.

A graduate of the Johns Hopkins University's Writing Seminars program, he put that degree to ill use for twenty years as a software engineer but has finally circled back around to the idea of writing for a living.

Chris currently lives in Nevada with his angelic wife and ever-expanding whisky collection and occasionally ventures outside to peer upwards, mutter to himself about 'day stars', and then scurry back into the house.

Ghost of a Chance is his fifth novel and the third book in *The Many Travails of John Smith*. Chris frequently shares updates and new content on his author website at https://christullbane.com.

www.ingramcontent.com/pod-product-compliance
Lightning Source LLC
Chambersburg PA
CBHW060724190726

48285CB00001B/66